FIC
OLM
Olmstead, Robert

A trail of heart's
blood wherever we
go

$19.45

co/90

NF

ALSO BY ROBERT OLMSTEAD

River Dogs
Soft Water

A TRAIL OF HEART'S BLOOD

WHEREVER WE GO

A TRAIL OF HEART'S BLOOD WHEREVER WE GO

ROBERT OLMSTEAD

RANDOM HOUSE
NEW YORK

The author wishes to thank Amanda Urban and David Rosenthal for their constant support, and to acknowledge the generous help given to him by the John Simon Guggenheim Memorial Foundation.

Copyright © 1990 by Robert Olmstead

All rights reserved under International and Pan-American Copyright Conventions. Published in the United States by Random House, Inc., New York, and simultaneously in Canada by Random House of Canada Limited, Toronto.

Grateful acknowledgment is made to the following for permission to reprint previously published material:
BUG MUSIC, INC.: Excerpt from "Love at the Five and Dime," words and music by Nanci Griffith. Copyright © 1986 by Wing and Wheel Music (BMI). Administered by Bug. All rights reserved. Used by permission.
FESTIVAL ATTRACTIONS, INC.: Excerpt from the lyrics "The People in Your Neighborhood," words and music by Jeff Moss. Copyright © 1969 by Festival Attractions, Inc. Reprinted by permission of Festival Attractions, Inc.

Library of Congress Cataloging-in-Publication Data
10190 BuT 11.14
Olmstead, Robert.
    A trail of heart's blood wherever we go / Robert Olmstead.
        p.   cm.
    ISBN 0-394-57539-3
    I. Title.
    PS3565.L67T7   1990
    813'.54—dc20   89-43414

Manufactured in the United States of America
98765432
First Edition

Book design by Debbie Glasserman

TO MOLLY AND EMILY

PROLOGUE

I thought I saw a zebra today but it was a horse of a different color.
I think about Cody's Cougar at the bottom of Spofford Lake, lati-
tude 42°52′47″ N, longitude 72°26′40″ W, or if you will, UTM Zone
18 07365394.

He sends me postcards from across the country, around the
world. He never writes anything on them. When I was in school,
a friend of mine split with his wife. She took off in the night with
the checkbook and the credit cards. Every month he'd get a statement and with it he could track her whereabouts. When I asked him
why he didn't just close them out, he said it was because he wanted
to know where she was all the time, even if he was a few days
behind, even if he might not still love her the way he used to.

Years ago there was a family I knew. The father tried to kill them
all, and then I'll be damned if there wasn't a story on the tube just
like that. Then there was a man and a woman who lived around
here, and they were in love with each other. He tried to kill the both
of them by driving off the road and into the river. She was married

to someone else at the time, and people can only speculate that she wanted to go back to her husband. How do you account for the unaccountable, for the things we do to each other?

Mary graduates college this year, something she's always wanted but kept getting put off so she could have the children. She's going to be a teacher. She just turned thirty-two and worries she's oversexed.

Last week I had to bury a couple who died while they were out parking. There was a hole in the exhaust system and it poisoned them. When they were found, nobody wanted to disturb them, they looked so peaceful.

The girl's mother said to me, "They were so much in love, even you won't be able to keep them under."

It happens this way in Inverawe. Minds work backward and forward. The young dream about God knows what and the old carry on as if it were another time, a time before reason got so damn important.

I am constantly trying to bury the dead, but so often they won't cooperate, and I have long since given up being adamant about such things. We take them wherever we go as life expends its velocity on us.

About Cody's Cougar. There's been talk that a salvage company is going down after it. It was the first thing he lost to water and should be left alone.

PART ONE

1

Eddie Ryan is reading up on heat. He considers drilling deep wells, two hundred feet or better, into the ground and pumping water and glycol through them, installing a heat exchanger and using a small electric unit for backup. It's called a ground-coupled heat-pump closed-loop water system. Bob Vila did one on *This Old House,* on the educational channel. It's a near perfect system, something akin to a perpetual-motion machine.

He gets up from his chair and puts another log in the stove. Outside he can hear the windchill factor breaking records, a weatherman's delight. Could be worse, he figures. Could be a thousand feet up on the mountain behind the house. Could be on Mount Washington, where the temperature is minus 20 and the windchill 30 below. In that weather the icicles run parallel to the ground, and hot water freezes so fast the ice is warm.

When he sits down he looks up *wood* in his Department of Agriculture Bulletin No. 180. He learns a cord of wood weighs two tons and has the same value as a ton of coal. It makes him wonder how the Poissant boys, who delivered his last cord, did it in a half-ton Chevy pickup.

He looks up *coal*. He finds the words *anthracite, bituminous, stoker* and *fly ash*. He's a big fan of words, always appreciative of what they can and can't do, and for that reason he wanted to be a poet, but became a mortician instead. In a way, he thinks, they are the same kind of work, although how, he isn't quite sure.

Eileen comes down the stairs on her bottom, making soft thumping noises as she lets herself take one tread after another. She loves words too, words like *morose, nauseous, disgusting, superb, tasty* and *wonderful*. She's six and, as her teacher says, sometimes a little too big for her britches.

"Mother, Father," she calls from the third step. "Little Eddie said the 'f' word. He said it twice."

Eddie Ryan looks up from his heat books. He sees his daughter, her face pressed into the space between two balusters.

"Little Eddie said the 'f' word. Little Eddie said the 'f' word," she chants.

"That's nice," Eddie Ryan says. "Go tell your brother we don't say the 'f' word in this house, though it does have its time and place. Make up something about Santa Claus not liking it, not bringing him weapons for Christmas if he keeps it up. Now you both get back to bed."

Mary looks up from the ledger books. It's her job to collect the bills the dead people run up. She doesn't always have the best of luck, but they get by. In fact, there's an outside chance they'll be able to barter with a retired heating man for a new furnace. His idea, not theirs. Eddie considers it unseemly, while Mary thinks it's good business.

"Good God, Eddie. Go easy on her. Everything you say she takes to heart."

Eddie feels his neck and face surge with warmth. He knows she's right and of a sudden it makes being a father and thirty-eight years old more burdensome than he thought, not that he'd underestimated it. He thinks he's held up pretty well. But lately, it's been the small things, like watching your every word.

He goes back to his heat books without saying anything. He decides the deep-well system is too exotic, having to do with squeezing heat out of water, heat that's picked up deep in the earth. He knows he'll settle for a new oil-fired boiler. It's simple—hot air blown through ducts and then returned to get heated and blown again.

He flips to the chapter on oil, and learns it has numbers and that oil burners are of two types, atomizing and vaporizing. He thinks it to be like a little science-fiction saga played out nightly in a few square inches while the wind howls and the snow blows.

The atomizing type appeals to him. A gun burner forces the oil through a special atomizing nozzle, a fan blows air into an oil fog and a spark ignites the mixture, which burns in a refractory-lined firepot. Eddie's now excited. It sounds like a combustion engine, or better yet, a heart. He'll have to explain all this to Eileen because he knows she'll get a big kick out of it, just like she does having naked dead people in the basement and fully dressed dead people in the living room. The oil-fired boiler will be the Christmas present he and Mary will give each other. They decided this weeks ago and now must pick one out to install this summer.

The lights flicker as the power lines take a beating from the weather. Eddie looks up, fixes on the Christmas tree. Its colors seem to pulse in the soft light of the room.

This is where the dead lie in state, somewhere between modest and extravagant in death. In the afternoon and evening, friends and relatives come for their leave-taking, come to be assured of death. But in the morning, Eileen and Little Eddie sit on the floor at the foot of the shroud and eat their cereal while on *Sesame Street* they sing, *"Who are the people in your neighborhood, in your neighborhood, in your neighborhood?"*

They are still children and pretty good about things like death.

"Eddie," Mary says, her voice sounding as if it's coming from inside a drum, "you'd better turn on the scanner. I just had a premonition of fire."

He looks across the room at her. She's sitting on a stool at the rolltop desk that was his father's. Her waist is as high as the ledger book, and as she leans over to work on it, trying to catch up on the bookkeeping she's let slide these past few weeks, she looks to be inside the tambour.

He feels cold again because sometimes she means it when she says she's had a premonition and sometimes she doesn't. When it comes to pass, she meant it, and when it doesn't, she didn't mean it.

"It makes sense," he says. "Furnaces working too hard and wood stoves igniting creosote. Sometimes people open their presents on Christmas Eve and then stuff all of the wrapping paper into the fireplace. *Voilà*—chimney fire. It's in the book here."

Eddie knows this stuff because he's a volunteer fireman. He has bunker pants, a coat, a helmet and his own Scott air pack. He has a sixteen-channel Bearcat scanner with search, lockout, delay and squelch.

"Damn," she says, slapping her red pen down. "In this fiscal year we did almost as many freebies as we did paid-in-full. I have enough accounts receivable to wallpaper this room. These veterans are breaking our backs. The VA and their measly four hundred and fifty dollars if you're getting benefits and one hundred and fifty if you're not. I'm telling you, they can shove it."

"You can't be a good businessman and a good mortician at the same time."

She crosses her arms on the desk and puts her head down, her back along the line of the floor, only higher. Eddie gets up from his chair and goes to her, reaching under her curls and stroking the back of her neck and shoulders, feeling the warmth and smoothness of her skin. She's had a perm recently and the smell of it is still in her hair. It's like the smell of something burned, handfuls of it. She said it would go away. It's just one of those things you have to live through.

Eddie Ryan does what he can for vets. He was in charge of graves registry at Khe Sanh after attending the Simmons School of Mortuary Science. He still has the *Life* magazine, the one about the job they were doing over there, the special G.I. edition that didn't get sold back in the States. Doing vets at a discount is a small way for him to keep doing his part.

He takes her by her upper arm and gently tugs, letting her know he wants her to stand. When she does, he moves the stool aside, then wraps his arms around her and holds her back to his chest, her head against his sternum, her hands up and holding his forearms.

"Did you pick us out a nice furnace?"

He laughs and lets his chin go down, resting it on the top of her head. He then kisses her, his lips in the tangle of hair. He breathes deeply, filling his head with her smell, remembering and yet still wondering how they got to be where they are.

"Yes, as a matter of fact I did," he says. "It has something for all of us, a gun for Little Eddie, an atomizer like in perfume for you and electric sparks for Eileen. Snap, crackle and pop."

He jolts against her backside when he says "pop," and she laughs, letting her weight go heavy in his arms. She sambas her hips, working her body into his.

"What about you?" she says softly, but he doesn't answer, not knowing whether to say oil fog or firepot, and he's caught like that with cheer in his heart, but a bad choice between two ugly images.

Mary stops and leans back into him, turning her head under his chin, knowing how he can get sometimes, but not knowing why.

"And what do you want?" she says suddenly in a stern voice.

Eddie looks up and sees Eileen bent over and looking at them from between the balusters again, the hem of her flannel nightgown held up in her hand, her girl legs bone and skin inside her knee socks, the material straight and ribbed like two bundles of matchsticks.

"What are you doing, Mom—getting a little excitement while I'm up there sleeping?"

"I asked you a question."

Eileen looks up the stairs and then about the room. She works hard at making her eyes go huge.

"Mother, Father," she whispers. "The night is nothing but a shadow and it goes all the way around the earth."

■

For just a moment, Cody stops what he's doing and looks up into the night sky. Through the swirling snow banner cuffing off the clear-cut mountaintop and the flood of light measured at two hundred thousand candlepower flowing from the Brinkman Q-Beam jacked into the pickup lighter, he finds the planets Venus, Mars and Mercury orbiting on their mindless paths through space.

Infusing their silent revolutions with the roar of the D-7H Cat dozer idled up to his right, he thinks of the Stellite-faced valves, hard-alloy steel seats, cam-ground and tapered aluminum three-ring-design pistons, steel-backed bearings, through-hardened crankshaft, full-flow filtered and cooled pressure lubrication system and No. 2 fuel oil jetting through its thrumming 638 cubic inches.

"The engine knows no cold," he yells. "The engine knows no cold."

He thinks of torque loads resting quietly inside the planetary power-shift transmission, clutch pack, ring gears, sun gear, continuously oil-cooled for long life, and of the turbocharger waiting to pack more air into the cylinders to make more combustion, more power, more work, and the night becomes huge with noise, so huge he thinks for a second it will knock him off the friggin' earth, flat on his ass in space.

He expands his chest inside his overalls, feeling the straps bind at his shoulders, and is proud that he knows the difference between cosmetology and cosmology. Something a wife he had long ago, before he took up this renegade life, learned in beauty school and passed on to him. As he understands it, both have to do with beauty, one with how it's created and the other with how it's made, and right now he doesn't give a good goddamn which is which, but it's a fine distinction nevertheless, one worth knowing.

His chest expands again and he's proud because a man named Archimedes had the balls to say, Give me a long enough stick of wood and a place to stand and I'll move the Christly planets. What glorious work, he thinks, to rearrange the stars, put all the young blue ones together, where they can play like bumper cars, and all the old red ones off to the side, where they can shoot the shit until they expire, go out like candles or maybe slip into a black hole for the ride of their lives. He and Archimedes, landscaping the cosmos.

Stars begin to fall around him, and with a mittened hand he pretends to hang them up where they belong. He tries to outroar the Cat's 215 horsepower, making his lungs swell and his throat ache, but he's feeling old and tired right now, and besides it's work for other men, men younger than him and old Archimedes.

He decides he'll do this one last job, get off this mountain and then take life easy. He'll find a hobby, read a book, catch up on his diddling and watch nature shows on public television until he dies.

Cody settles down and smiles, feeling the cold air come at his teeth and gums. He dares them to crack, and when they don't he smirks, knowing full well they don't have it in them, just old enamel, like they wrap around bathtubs, sinks and toilets. The snap of a wrist, the fall of a hammer and what have you got? Just old shattered enamel. He takes off his mittens and quickly lights a cigarette, cupping the flame close to his face, so close he almost torches his beard.

He decides that when he gets down off the mountain, he'll spend his winters on the Yucatán at the Rancho San Carlos, hunting blue-winged teal in the morning and lying drunk in the hot afternoon with a girl named Rosalita under one arm and a girl named Juanita under the other. He'll become a sailor and learn to navigate by the stars, becoming intimate with them, loverly, a man among stars. He'll sail to the Southern Cross, see the Magellanic Clouds, galaxies as neighbors. He'll figure out just what in hell the big bang theory is and if in fact it has to do with sex, like his partner, G. R. Trimble, told him.

"Fuck public television," he yells. "Fuck public television and the horse it rode in on."

Filled with strength and the conviction of a future with ducks, stars and Mexican women, Cody goes back to work, closing down the landing and hitching together the caravan of equipment he'll haul out behind him. He goes about his business, feeling the snow crunch under his boots, and everything he touches clanks and clangs, resounding in the stiff cold air, the noises coming sharp and distinct over the roaring diesel, through the black slashing wind.

He works quickly, pinning a clevis through the steel tongue welded to the mainframe of the cable skidder, running a length of chain through its yoke to the Cat's drawbar. He then chains the lowboy behind the skidder and drifts back through the snow, reefing the binders that secure the pickup and horse trailer riding on the flatbed of the lowboy.

When he's done, he cuts the power to the spotlight, and the whole world goes dark. He holds out as long as he can, waiting for his eyes to adjust, but they don't do it fast enough, and he's afraid he might never see again. He shuts his eyes and, reaching his arms out in front of him, walks toward the sound of the Cat. As he gets close, its noise fills his head to the point where he thinks it will burst, and then he thinks he'll be sucked into the vortex of roar, to become a machine part forever melded with other machine parts. Then, a moment later, his hands are on the cold steel track running over the tops of the cleated shoes, and he can't say he isn't a little disappointed that it doesn't happen.

It's then he opens his eyes, and he can see again as, one by one, the stars reveal themselves, and he wants to cry with relief and with the pain he carries in his heart, but he knows it will weaken him.

He knows that letting it all out ain't what it's cracked up to be. It isn't like good feelings pour in to replace the bad ones. He wonders why so many rush to blow off steam when if you get enough of a head built up, you can run a big-assed turbine, one that can light up whole cities, make machines go in factories, send the rides at amusement parks to the edge of centrifugal force and bring them back again.

So he holds his tears, and before long he has another cigarette lit and is sitting inside the cab atop fifty-seven thousand pounds of bulldozer, right hand on the throttle, left hand on the steering levers. It's knowing what he does that brings him pleasure, knowing this machine will pull more than its weight, knowing the chain speed of a saw, the line pull of a winch and that love can be known too, held like a fact of life. These are the things to live for. These are the things to die for.

■

It's late Christmas Eve. A powerful light fills the room where Eddie is reading and Mary is running tallies through November. A low deep rumbling follows the light, building intensity as it does until the house begins to shake.

Eileen comes bouncing down the stairs on her hind end, scared, but hopeful it's Santa Claus and she's finally nabbed him on his appointed rounds.

"It's him," she says. "I watched him come down the mountain from the bedroom. It was a little light and now it's a big one. He doesn't ride a sleigh. He drives a bulldozer and he brought me a horse in a trailer. Son of a gun."

"It's coming right through," Eddie yells, snatching Eileen off her feet and handing her to Mary. "I'll get Little Eddie. You get out of the house."

Then the sound and light stop coming at them. It rests with all its noise and luminosity just outside the back door. Little Eddie is at the top of the stairs, rubbing his eyes with his fists. Eddie goes up to him, lifting his son into his arms and telling him it's all right. The boy wraps his arms around his father's neck and Eddie holds him up with a forearm under his butt.

"Get blankets," Mary yells, and Eddie does, pulling them off the kids' beds. In Eileen's room he stops and looks out her window. On the back lawn is a caravan: bulldozer, log skidder, pickup truck and horse trailer. Behind them, a wide path trails up the mountain and disappears in the darkness. It's like the wake of a landship or giant fish pulled out of water, hauled across the wet sand and over dry dunes, its sashaying tail leveling them as it goes, sweeping them to naught.

He comes down the stairs with blankets under his arm and they wrap them around the children. Mary looks at him, and he shrugs, nodding toward Eileen and raising his brow as if to say she just might be right.

Eddie takes Eileen because she's heavier and Mary takes Little Eddie, who still isn't awake enough to figure out what's happening. They go through the house slowly to the kitchen, passing in and out of the white light that makes the windows blind and fills the downstairs. They pick their way like deer in a forest, cats in high grass.

"It'll be all right," Eileen says softly. "It's only him."

Eddie unlatches the door and swings it open. Noise and light pour in through the windows of the storm door. Wind and snow buffet it. It quickly fogs over, then Eddie opens that door too, and the fullness of it gets them right where they stand. They step out into the four elements that seem to work so well together: wind, snow, noise and light. It's all Eddie can do to stop from turning and getting his family back into the house, but he holds his ground.

In front of him are headlights, cab lights and running lights. Just off the porch is twelve feet of dozer blade, its concavity a bullnose of snow packed from thumping into drifts and buffing them flat. Behind the blade is the huge diesel, sucking air through its folded-core radiator, and the lift cylinders to either side, rising ten feet above his head.

Taking a step closer, Eddie sees the machine is white with ice and snow, its yellow paint only a shadow, only visible at the sharpest corners. The tracks and sprockets are packed with snow, and a man is astride the machine sitting upright, stiff in the roll-over cage, one mittened hand on the throttle, the other on the steering levers, the black end of a cigarette butt plugged into a corner of his mouth.

He too is white, with trails of ice starting at the corners of his eyes and running down into his beard.

"I hope it's a palomino," Eileen whispers, but no one can hear her, and she's pleased, because after she says it she thinks it may not be the right thing to say.

The man stands and claps his arms to his chest. Snow bursts forth from his body and flies away in the wind. He touches his beard and face tenderly, then takes off his mittens and does it again. He rubs his cheeks and slaps at them until he seems satisfied he hasn't been frostbitten. After killing the engine, he jumps to the ground, but his legs can't hold him, so he takes the fall, his body dropping through the air that still carries the ghost of noise. Tumbling into the snowpack, he rolls and then comes to a rest on his side.

Still holding Eileen, Eddie walks down the steps and, with his free arm, helps the man to his feet. He brushes him off, the smell of hemlock and diesel fuel stirring from the man's overalls with each clap of his hand.

The man laughs and Eddie joins in. Mary and the children are smiling too.

"Ho, ho, ho," he says, "and Merry Christmas. Aren't you kids supposed to be in bed? I've gone and come too early, I guess."

"Do not fret," Eileen says. "The stockings are hung by the chimney and there's graham crackers and milk for you. Let me down, Father."

Eddie sets her standing on the porch in her knee socks. She rearranges her blanket and motions for Mary to set Little Eddie down.

"Come along," she says. "It's off to bed."

She takes her brother's hand and leads him into the house, where they both go up the stairs, one step at a time. They go into her room, where they can peek out through the ferns and leaves sketched on her windows with spines of frost, where they can watch just what's happening on the ground below.

"Please make coffee," Eddie says, and Mary goes inside too. The man waits for her to close the door before he speaks.

"Mr. Ryan," he says. "I have something for you."

He goes to the dozer blade and starts slabbing off the packed snow, thrusting his arm into it and muscling his way through.

Eddie steps up beside him. As the snow falls away to the ground with a thump, he can see strapped to the steel face the two halves of Cody's partner, G. R. Trimble, his black belt cinching shut the waist of his trousers and his shirttails ragged and frayed as if they've been dynamited. He's been cut clean across the middle by a chain saw high on gas at full throttle and now he's wearing the frozen blue face of death.

2

Mary stands with her back to the sink, her hands behind her, palms flat where the stainless steel meets the Formica. Eddie and Cody come in from the cold, stamping their feet and clapping their arms to their chests to warm their bodies. It's a strange act because no sound comes with it, only the movement of men, as if they were great flightless birds. Once the bulldozer was shut down, its noise was replaced in their heads with a kind of deafness, and so now their movements have become the pantomime of movement.

"The coffee will be ready in a minute."

She says it again, pointing at the pot and holding up a finger. They nod.

Eddie pulls chairs out from the table for him and Cody and they both sit down. They fold their hands and stare into those folds, waiting for their coffee, waiting for their hearing to return.

In the hallway can be seen the wash of reds, blues, greens and yellows from the Christmas-tree lights, and in the windows are plastic candles with white bulbs. Mary looks at the men, her husband and the stranger, and just now she feels more tired than she has in a long while, the energy flushed from her body.

There is no downtime in life, she thinks, no moment without prospect, no act without consequence. Eddie's father died four years ago, and lately he's been distant and drinking a little bit, and now on Christmas Eve this man has shown up. Though even a brief respite hasn't come to them, she's content it's out there, waiting for them. Her hearing begins to come back and she thinks she's never been able to hear so well in her life.

"So what happened to your friend?" Eddie is saying.

"He wasn't really a friend," Cody says, and then he stops speaking. He looks at Mary and she smiles at him. "He was more like a wife or a husband," Cody says.

Eddie looks to Mary. Her face draws tight over this one. She crosses her arms over her chest as if she's cold.

"I was up on the landing," Cody says. "Buck was twitching logs out and up to me, and G.R. was down in the hollow."

"Buck?"

"Why, Buck's a horse," Cody says as if it's news to him too. "Anyways, he'd run his saw a little and shut it down, run it a little and shut it down. It was a regular tangled-up mess and we only had a few more sticks to get out. And then one time Buck didn't come so I waited. Smoked a cigarette. I knew in my heart what'd happened. I knew in my heart there was nothing to do. So finally I went down the switchback and found him laid 'cross the bar, his hand just a-grippin' the throttle."

Cody stops talking. He looks down into his hands for a time. He unfolds them and looks at one palm and then the other. He looks to Mary and they both smile, only they keep their mouths in tight lines, Cody's so tight his lips disappear in his beard and mustache, which are now shiny and wet with melted ice.

"It took his backbone to stall it out," he tells her. "He had the strongest back of any man I ever knew. He always did like to run them saws hot. A hot saw runs near eight thousand RPMs. Miles and miles, just like that," Cody says, snapping his fingers. "I always told him he'd burn out a piston, running a saw hot, but he never listened. He was an old man. You couldn't tell him nothing. It was cold too. His blood was cold. He was cold. By the time I got there, and it wasn't long, I could've collected his blood like it was tiny little rubies strewn in the snow."

Cody looks at the floor and Eddie and Mary look too, half expecting to see it littered with blood rubies.

"He was just getting blue and there was a bit of a smile on his face. There still is. I can see it when I look at him. Buck was standing over him, nuzzling him under the arm and at his neck, around his ears. When I come down on them, Buck just looked at me, his eyes wet from the wind and where he'd been lashed by high branches.

"He looked at me as if to say, He's really gone and done it this time. So I said, 'G.R., what in hell kind of mess have you gone and gotten yourself into?' But he didn't say nothing, being as he was by then, long dead, dead as a doornail."

Cody looks back into the palms of his hands, and then after a while he raises his head, his eyes bright with an idea.

"Listen, Mr. Ryan, what would be the chance of stuffing him and sewing him back up? Fix him to be upright with his arms cocked such that we could wire a chain saw into his hands?"

"Oh, Cody, we can't do that—it's against the law. There must be a death certificate and a burial permit. There could be a postmortem medical examination. Listen, you're tired right now and you've been through a lot. We'll talk about it in the morning."

Eddie knows he should be more diplomatic, more adroit. It's the kind of strange thing he's always anticipated being asked, and he's devised a set answer, but on this night, he's been taken by surprise.

"I figured as much," Cody says. "It was just something me and G.R. talked about. It was a thought he had and he made me promise I'd ask when the time came."

"He talked about his death?"

"People get that way when they feel it coming on them. I knew it was going to happen. He did too. It was his time. He was a big believer in time. Time for this; time for that."

"Cody, it was an accident. He must have tripped and fallen."

"No, I'd say it was more like he threw himself down on it."

The coffee maker hisses, pumping the last of the water out through the pipe and sprinkling it into the basket. Mary gets cups and saucers and sets them on the table. She gets sugar and a pitcher of milk in case they're something Cody likes in his coffee, but he doesn't. They all sit at the table, drinking it black.

"If we can't stuff him," Cody says then, "we'd better at least put his guts back inside him. They were pretty well chewed up, but I collected what I could and stuffed them in his pockets. They're all there. All the meat and everything."

"Cody," Eddie says, "you try to relax. What you're experiencing is a great loss. You are bereaved over the loss of your friend. You're experiencing a kind of grief, a condition called shock. It's the kind of thing that can hit you now, or years later."

"You know, ma'am," Cody says to Mary, "I was going to leave him up there sitting astride the horse. It's what he wanted, but I just couldn't bring myself to shoot old Buck.

"Now this shock thing," he says, turning back to Eddie, "I've heard of it, but I'm not sure what my opinion is. It seems to me that if it's a condition people go through, then what's to stop you from slicing off other pieces of life and saying that's only a condition too. I don't think I like this idea of shock being something to get through. If I'm in shock then that's what I am and I damn well plan on enjoying it. I'd rather you didn't mention it again. In fact if alls you've got is warmed-over shit like that, I'd rather you didn't even talk to me."

"I'm sorry," Eddie says. "I didn't mean to upset you."

"No. I'm sorry," Cody says. "It's just that I get so weary, I go off like that. It happens more and more lately. Let's talk about something else. How about the Celtics? How are they doing?"

Eddie wants to say how weariness is another symptom of grief, but thinks better of it. He wants to say something about the Celtics, but he hasn't been following them. He decides to just let the man talk himself out.

"With him gone, Mrs. Ryan, it feels as if a great burden has been lifted off my shoulders. It's as if I'm a free man. He had it pretty hard in the last few years. He was having a little softening of the brain. The slightest things would provoke him to fits of anger. Toward the end he wouldn't go to town. During his last year, I was the only human being he ever saw."

"What will you do now, Cody?"

"He took to reading Revelations aloud. Alls he could talk about was children being struck dead, women being swallowed up whole. Oceans to blood. Much light going out all over the place. Chapter Eight, verse seven. There will be a great loss of prime timber. Shit like that. It's such a shame.

"G.R. kept his life in order after that—no blaspheming, no idolatry, no fornication, no smoking and no littering."

Eddie taps Mary on the wrist. When she looks at him, he smiles, letting her know she should continue. She knows this. She thinks that maybe she can draw him out a little. She's happy to do it. Many times she's watched Eddie counsel the bereaved and always admired his graceful and elegant manner, his way of getting them to talk a little if they can't and to shut up if they won't.

She looks at Cody, who's staring into his hands again. She decides he's not so old as he looks and that in fact he's young. She thinks how strange it is he's brought death to them in this manner, on this night, strange in that she doesn't feel the instant throb of dull compassion; she feels light in her tiredness, almost joyful he's brought G. R. Trimble to them, blue with death.

Her stomach makes noises that sound like words. Cody looks up at her and then Eddie does too, and both of them smile. She smiles back, remembering for some reason the words to a song that go something like *"can't live without my man,"* and then she's not sure if the words are from a song or if they're ones delivered up to her by her most womanly mind. She's overwhelmed with the need to tell Eddie she loves him, but knows it wouldn't be right for the moment, so she saves it like a letter in her pocket not to be opened until it can't be held off any longer.

"Cody," she whispers, "what will you do now?"

"I don't know," he whispers back. "I have a number of options. I could sell off the equipment and get out of this racket. I do have quite a bit of money. I never had any reason to spend it. But you know, the entrepreneurial spirit is in my blood."

Mary listens to him. The voice is Cody's, but sometimes the words seem to be another man's. She thinks it must be his partner, G. R. Trimble.

"I've been self-employed as long as I can remember. I don't really know to be honest with you. I like to keep my options open. It comes down to the fact that I can't stomach the thought of working for someone other than myself."

"Do you or G.R. have any family besides each other?"

"G.R. had the horse and I have a wife and a boy. Last I knew, they lived in Winchester. She and I never did get a divorce. I put money in the bank for her and every time I do the slips show the money gets taken out. I guess you could say we're all right. Two thirds, you know. Two thirds of what I make goes in there. I figure there's three of us: me, her and the boy. That's a third for each. But the equip-

ment's all paid for and now it becomes mine. Dozer's worth quite
a bit, skidder, pickup. Buck, though. It'd surprise you how much
he's worth. But I think he'd be the last one I'd part with. You can't
really sell a friend, now can you? I'm told you can't buy them
either."

"No," Mary says. "No, you can't. Friends can't be bought and
sold."

"I'll tell you one thing," Cody says, letting himself smile and then
looking into his cup. "Tonight on the mountain, I felt like a king.
King of the mountain. In a way, G.R.'s dying was the grandest thing
I've ever witnessed. It will take me awhile to figure that one out. I
know there are cheap reasons, but it wasn't any of them. I'm in no
rush either to figure it out. I'm still enjoying the feeling. You
wouldn't think that somebody dying could have that effect on you,
now would you?"

Mary and Eddie shake their heads. Eddie can see strength and
compassion in her eyes. He covers her hand with his own and feels
her grip to be so strong it makes his fingers ache.

"You two go in by the wood stove, where it's warm," Mary says.
"You still look chilled and Eddie, you keep him company, and what
I'll do is fix something for us to eat. You go in there and stay. And
another thing, you're welcome to spend the night and to spend
Christmas with us. I think that would be best."

Cody looks to Mary and then at Eddie.

"Yes," Eddie says. "Tomorrow we're having turkey, dressing,
cranberry sauce, squash and mashed potatoes, and we'd just love
it if you could stay and eat with us."

"I know why you're saying all this, but I'll stay anyways," Cody
says.

"It sounds like you've had a hard life," Eddie says, a little
ashamed that his invitation had not been as sincere as Mary's, but
it had struck him as an unprofessional thing to do.

"You could say that, but some have it harder. Coal miners have
it harder. I can't imagine going down underneath the earth to make
money. A man dies every day under the ground. Couldn't do it.
Every day I thank God I'm not a coal miner."

Cody stands and stretches inside his brown duck-cloth overalls.

Eddie thinks him to look squat and rolled-shouldered, like some
white basketball players do, but he knows it's the way men and

women get who work with tools every day. Eddie stands too, then leads the way down the hall.

Mary watches them leave the kitchen, Cody shuffling along in his stocking feet, moving quickly as if he's trying to get away from himself. She can see the red heels of another pair coming through. He'd insisted on leaving his boots at the door. It was something he and G.R. always did, he said. It won her good feelings to see a man who was concerned about tracking on a clean floor.

"I see, Mr. Ryan, that you have been reading up on heat," Cody says, sitting down in Eddie's chair.

"Yes, I have. The furnace is an old coal burner that's been converted to oil. It's quite inefficient. It's about on its last leg. This summer we're going to pay the shot and get a whole new system put in."

"I see, I see. Can't imagine seeking a livelihood under the earth," Cody says, thumbing through a magazine on heat. "Mr. Ryan, you can sew him back together, can't you?"

"Yes, Cody. I will."

"That's good, because in a way G.R. wouldn't want to go down as half a man. He always talked about that. You can't go through life as half a man, he'd say. He said that's what a lot of us had become, half men.

"He said he went to a grocery store once in Keene, and you know now they have big decks of salad makings? Well, anyway, G.R. said he saw a grown man with tongs, plucking at sliced beets as thin as wafers and heaping them up on greens in a little plastic container. Right there in public. He said it was the damnedest thing he ever saw."

"Well, Cody, salads are good for people. It's become the thing now to eat a lot of salad to take care of your body."

"I can tell you I was born in the wrong time," Cody says.

"What do you mean? You should've been born a mountain man or maybe sometime around the Revolutionary War?"

"No. Nothing like that. In the future, after they've dropped the big one. It's the only solution I can think of. A little radioactivity would be just the thing to separate the men from the boys. Get rid of the crybabies."

"That's a terrible wish," Eddie says. He'd had a taste of war to the tune of preparing a hundred bodies a month, some marked for viewing, most not.

"I know," Cody says, "but it sounds pretty good, doesn't it? I'd be lying, though, if I didn't say there was a grain of truth in it. That's not the point. You can't go through life as half a man and you sure as hell can't take the trip he's got as half a man.

"Listen," Cody adds, holding a finger to the side of his nose, "I've got an idea. I'll be your heat. I'll do it in return for your handling G.R., sewing him up, dressing him out and laying him down. I'll be your heat. I'll keep you in cordwood, more cordwood than you can use."

"I don't know. Mary was just going over the books and right now we're having a little cash-flow problem. Things are a little tight for us."

"Then I'll give you enough to sell. Pick up a little folding money. Say you'll do it."

Eddie's been down this road before. If it works out he'll be much better off. It will get them through the winter. If it doesn't, he's on the short end of the stick, a place he's been more often than he cares to remember. Mary's reminded him many times.

"You let me winter in your backyard and I'll pay you tenfold."

Mary comes in carrying a tray laden with coffee, and brownies and Christmas cookies.

"I'll tell you what," Eddie says, figuring to get himself off the hook. "Put it by her and if she goes for it, it's all right with me too."

"I've already heard. I think it's a great idea."

"Good. Then that's what we'll do," Cody says, reaching out to take their hands.

3

Mary is in bed when Eddie comes up the stairs. He puts on flannel pajamas and socks and then checks on the kids. Eileen sleeps like an ostrich, with her knees tucked up under her belly. Her cheek rests on the pillow, its folds against her lips. She once told him she was learning to be a good kisser by practicing with her pillow. Eddie touches her head and gets all the way to her door before he goes back and kisses her cheek. She turns her face into the pillow, and he thinks for a moment that's where the kiss for him goes.

Little Eddie's in his crib, tangled in his covers, sprawled out like a drunk on holiday. Eddie covers him and gives him a kiss too, but must have tickled him in the process because the boy rubs his nose as if he's trying to take his face off.

They're good children, he thinks, loving children, who've learned to eat breakfast and watch *Sesame Street* in the presence of dead people. Eileen thinks it great fun to include whoever was in the casket in the sing-alongs, the number counting and the dashes through the alphabet.

Mary is on her side, her back to him, so he crawls in behind her, curving his body to fit hers. They lie there like that, their breathing a match for a while and then not.

"Is he settled in for the night?" she whispers.

At first he thinks she means Little Eddie, but then he realizes she's talking about Cody. Before he replies, he takes time to think about how he's confused his son with the stranger who rode in on the night.

"He insisted on sleeping in the trailer. He said it was his home."

"He's a strange one. I'll say that. But nice enough, I guess."

"Yes," Eddie says. "Yes, he is."

"Well, I don't know about you, but I've had enough for one night. I'm going to sleep."

Eddie slings an arm around her body. He reaches inside her nightgown and holds her breast where it's against the bed. It's something he likes to do, hold her like that, because after a while his hand goes hot, sending its heat up his arm and to his shoulder, where it then pours into his body.

"Mary," he whispers. "Donahue says that a lot of women fake orgasm. How can a man tell if she is or not?"

"If the woman acts like she enjoys it."

Mary says this even though she's half asleep. It's a joke they heard once and they like to tell it to each other. It's become a way of knowing things are okay between them, okay enough to go to sleep, especially after nights like the one they just had.

"My God," Mary says suddenly, lifting her head off the pillow. "Did you get that man in the cooler?"

"No. Cody said he'd throw a tarp over him. We'll do it in the morning when the kids are busy. They're used to it. I didn't want to upset him any more than he was."

Mary leans back into him and sighs and then for the final time that night, she settles into sleep, and he isn't far behind.

After what seems to be only seconds, Eddie wakes up, hearing his son cry out in the night. And then there's silence. He looks at the clock on the nightstand and sees he's been asleep for at least an hour.

Why a child would do that, he can't understand. Even as an infant, a baby with nothing to fear, his son would cry out like that and then there'd be silence. The first months he was home were living hell. He was colicky, and the only reprieve was a long ride in the station wagon or the powder-blue limousine. A nurse who'd attended his delivery gave them the tape of a heartbeat, and that helped too. It'd go for ninety minutes, ninety minutes of a woman's heart pumping sound through the slats of his crib and into his ears.

Now he's better, but he still cries out sometimes in the night for no reason at all.

Eddie lies in bed worrying he'll become a sleepwalker. He read a story about an eleven-year-old boy who hopped a freight in his sleep. He had the need to roam, even in his sleep. They found him wandering in the woods a hundred miles from home, his pajama legs wet with dew. Some people eat in their sleep, some people fall, some people clean their houses. Eddie's mother used to do laundry in her sleep. She'd stuff it in the washer and when it was done she'd go outside in her bare feet and hang it up on the clothesline. His father could never understand why she didn't use the dryer. Both of them are dead now.

Eddie falls asleep again and has the same dream he had the night before. It's about a girl he doesn't know. When it's over he gets out of bed and takes his notebook from his bureau drawer, from under the socks, where he keeps it. He writes in the moonlight, *"Dream Simile,"* and in parentheses he makes a note to himself, *"as real as real can be."* He keeps writing:

> Last night I dreamt that I was living in your house and you came knocking on the kitchen door. The glass being the medium where hot air meets cold air, where they do their fog dance, hot air and cold making love until they become fog. I had a handful of palms, leftovers from Palm Sunday. I reached around and swiped the glass with them and you jumped back laughing.
>
> I looked out and saw you. Your hair was long and you wore a beret and a navy pea coat, wool, double-breasted, four big blue buttons. We stood there like that, both of us laughing, you holding a package, me holding a bouquet of dried palms.

When he's done he puts his pen down and reads what he's written. He likes it. He flips back a page and reads more.

> Two hearts laughing. Two souls entwined. What sound do they make? Can you hear them if you're not there, if they fall in the woods? Yes, yes.

They sound like a freestone creek, the ducks skimming the marsh, the
steam ghosts quavering into the cold morning air. They make the sound
the sunlight makes when it breaks the dark. They sound like a lone bird
crying like a baby as it crosses the sky east to west.

He likes this too. It's something he wrote a few nights ago. Mary moves in her sleep, and he feels sad because he'd like them to be for Mary, but they're not; these words were written for no one in particular. The dream girl wore the face of Susan, his first true love from when he was a boy in the seventh grade, but it really wasn't her. It was her face, but it was someone else. He thinks maybe it's just the idea of someone else. Some other. Maybe the woman inside of me, he says to himself. He thinks about stuff like that.

He wishes again the words could be for Mary and he could show them to her, but they aren't and he can't. They're just words and they're written down in a notebook. They're notions he has, and he feels compelled to keep a record of them. It's a case where things seem to come together, a momentary state where it's all clear and uncomplicated, a filling up to the brim and just a little over.

It would be wondrous, he thinks, to infuse his life with these moments so that they could be joined into a long seamless series, like the little windows in a blank filmstrip ready to be colored in. Where one left off, another would begin. Even the bad would be okay, as long as it was pure in its evilness, shiny black and shaped at the edge. He longs for the day when his notion will ascend to vision. What a life he'll have then. A life for all of them.

Eddie closes his notebook and lies back down with his wife. Since he has been out of bed, his feet have gotten cold. Rolling onto his side, he bends his knees and puts his soles against Mary's warm calves. She puts up with it for just so long and then she pulls away, but he doesn't mind because she's left him a warm spot in the bedding.

While he lies there waiting for sleep, it's revealed to him that the dream girl was Mary and it was a house by a lake where she used to live. This doesn't jibe with what he first thought so he begins to try to figure out what happened. He has a moment when it's clear how it goes together, and in that moment he's certain it's the key to it all, but then it slips away and he curses himself, feeling as if a trick has been played on him.

Mary moves back into him, somehow knowing his feet aren't cold anymore. She kisses his shoulder and he turns her way. Liking the feel of her body gone soft with sleep inside her nightgown, he moves his left hand from her thigh to her belly and then to her breasts, which are now almost flat on her chest as their weight settles them. He raises his hand up along her ribs, and gathers one where it's rounded. He lifts it to where it'd be if she were standing and then gently lets it go back to where it wants to.

"We'll figure it out in the morning," she says, but he knows she's only talking in her sleep.

■

Across the hall, Eileen moves her lips on the cotton pillowcase. She likes to think it's her mother's belly. She's happy she's now in school and learning stuff, though she doesn't quite get how it works. She thinks about the skeleton inside her body. It's made up of bones, and those bones are made of calcium. And there are four food groups, green, white, red and brown. That's a good one, she thinks, kissing her pillow and going to sleep again after never really waking up.

Now she dreams of the horses she paints. She uses watercolors and feathers from her pillow for brushes, a feather for every color. She used to be a unicorn, so all the horses she paints wear single horns on their foreheads, horns that spiral from the locks of hair growing between their ears.

Her best friends are Abbin and Delia. They're unicorns too. They're the last unicorns. That was in 1861, before there was time, when there was only black-and-white television.

There's a breath of wind and her mattress sags a little. She knows it's Max, the cat. He comes to sleep with her every night when he's finished mousing. He sleeps curled up at her feet. She's convinced he's a prince, but he's not a prince; he's a hunter cat, all black with white whiskers, chin and feet. He's a monster of a tom, part coon cat, mostly bastard. He belonged to Eddie's father and when he died, he was Eddie's inheritance. Now they get along like young brothers, affording wide berths and picking fights with each other for something to do. Eileen knows he's in love with her.

She knows this because Max brings trophies to the door, the heads of rabbits and squirrels. He positions them so they're cocked back and looking up, so it's the first thing you see when you come out in the morning.

He likes birds too. He likes to bring them onto the porch and eat their tasty parts on the steps. One time he brought a mole into the house. He let it run wild and then he snarfed it. When he isn't killing and eating animals, he's of a generally whorish nature, populating the countryside with more of his ilk.

■

Little Eddie sleeps on his stomach and back at the same time, a kind of Möbius strip of the body. His toes point down and out, but he has one palm face up and the other arm slung back behind him. It's a reckless way to sleep, but he couldn't be happier, ignorant as he is to the laws of comfort.

In his baby mind, he thinks, I want to know the world through my mouth. I want to eat it and everything in it. Only when I get older will I spit out the bad parts, but for now, I want the whole enchilada.

This is lint, this is a fur ball, this is a button. Take and eat, for it is pretty good. This is a singular Cheerio I left between the rug and wall when I scuttled by in my walker, a small cache of fiber. This is a toenail. I'd better be fast because she'll give him hell for leaving it on the floor if she sees me with it.

And just for the hell of it, I am the destroyer of block worlds, the ripper of blue books, green books, *Redbook, Field and Stream, The Director, The Law of Cadavers, Cosmopolitan.* I see it all from six inches off the floor. It's a world to climb.

Little Eddie moves in his sleep. He's like bread rising, or an angel food cake, light as air, gone giddy on egg whites.

Clothes are good, he thinks, especially when they're warm, just from the dryer. To me a basket of laundry is better than a breast full of milk. It's something to bury your small face in, roll off of and maybe knock your head so your brain sloshes around inside and you begin to cry.

I climb right back up, though, because even better than knowing no fear, I'm incapable of learning. I've yet to learn a goddamn thing, and for that I'm thankful.

So I seek out cups of hot soup, and wall sockets. I want to get inside them and eat my way out.

His little-boy brain thrums inside his head, caught in the thrall of test-driving future thoughts, trying them on for size.

God comes to me at night. He tells me of my fate and then he makes me forget. That's why sometimes I cry out in the night. He says he does it for all sentient beings. Or did he say penitent? Screw that. He does it for geese, bears, rabbits, chipmunks, bobwhites, walleyes and possum. He does it for all his critters here and abroad. It's a service he provides so the moment the need comes to get off the dime, you'll know what to do. You won't have to think about it.

And when the *big* moment comes, you'll remember what he told you and it won't be such a kick in the teeth. It's why the monarchs migrate to the Transvaal volcanic range and why it takes an armadillo a half hour to die.

I tell him, Thanks, and then he hangs out awhile. He talks about life, mostly his own, but he also tells me things. He tells me all that I will learn and all that I won't learn. He tells me I'll learn to walk and to not shit my pants, which, to be honest, I'll miss doing. Besides fitting everything into my mouth, shitting my pants is the next best pleasure. It's my way of giving a little back for all that I take.

He tells me I'll learn to ride a trike, a tyke on a trike, and throw a ball, both of which I'll be very good at. Eileen will teach me to play crazy eights, go fish and slapjack. Then a day will come when I try to get in the tub with her and she won't go for it and that will be the last time for a long while I ever see a woman without a stitch of clothes on. He sighed and shook his head when he told me that one. It was as if he carried all the weight of heaven on his shoulders, full of its losers, believers, victims, children, grandparents, roadkills and stillborns. All of this, bearing down around his white august head.

So I ask him what's up and he says I'll know how to change a tire, run power tools, snap on jumper cables. I'll shoot rats at the dump and drive like hell in a pickup truck over dirt roads on summer nights. He says I'll learn that hell is just an expression some people use.

Then he tells me I'll never know the love of a woman as good as my mother. I say, What the hell—I can't imagine wanting to anyways, and he says, Good, because it's not all it's cracked up to be.

And he tells me not to worry, because women can be a pain in the ass and that's why he never married. He messed up once and it gave cause for him to add twenty-seven new chapters to his book until he finally got fed up and wrote one that'd scare the daylights out of anyone. Once is enough for God.

He did the right thing by the woman, though. He claimed his son. He claimed to be the boy's father. There'd be no paternity suit against him.

It saddens him to talk about his son. He sighs, and when he does, he draws in so much air the curtains stand out on their rods—not a quaver, not a ripple, but pointing straight at him like arrows.

My heart goes out to the man Joseph, he says. My heart goes out to all the fathers. I'll tell you a story.

God's story: When Moses came up the mountain, there was much hoopla, many distractions. What I told him and what he wrote down were two different things, but I'll tell you, down at the bottom they were sleeping with their sisters. Things had really gotten out of hand, so it isn't a wonder. Anyways, I told him to write, *Thou shalt honor thy mother and love thy father.* But he wrote, *Thou shalt honor thy mother and thy father,* or something like that.

I didn't think much of it at the time. Down below they had the golden calf done and a batch of unaged bourbon. I'm telling you, it was coming apart at the seams. So I let it stand. Besides, I thought it had more of a ring to it.

Then this Joseph and Mary thing came along and I knew at that very moment why I'd said it the way I did. Honor your mother and love your father because God knows the poor guy has a rough row to hoe. Most ways, they're only good for the drippings. That's why I've inspired the writing I have since then.

He stops talking and sighs again. The windowpanes bulge out into the night. The New Testament, I think, trying to help him out a little.

No, he says, looking at me. Country-and-western music.

It gets quiet in my room. I watch him through the slats of my crib. He's standing next to me with his arms folded and one hip cocked. He's wearing a down vest over his heavenly white robes. They look to be snowy soft and every so often the gold piping launches sparks of light that verge on becoming beacons.

I look at him standing there, and I wonder who's on the inside and who's on the outside. He laughs and cries at the same time because he knows I've just had an original thought, one tinged with angst and pathos. I have empathized with God.

How do you do the laughing and crying thing at the same time?

Oh, that's a neat one, he says. The first time it happened to me was after I loved the woman Mary. It just comes over me in the oddest of moments since then, the Spartans at Thermopylae, Shays' rebellion, the little Dutch boy, the movie *Zulu* and when I handed Hitler the gun.

He pauses and then he says, No, the last one I take back. That was sheer joy to watch that bastard off himself. I've had other thrills, the battle of Clontarf, Little Big Horn, Buddha in diapers, Columbus . . . and pain too, pain to and through the bone: the children's crusade, the Easter Rebellion, Pol Pot, Oppenheimer, the '86 Red Sox. And regrets. That boy of mine, trading him in for all of this.

God sweeps his hand through the air and brings forth the pageant of time. All things that were and will be, rocks, plants and animals, lava flows and disposable razors, pemmican and tapioca, the popularity of baldness.

He could do all of those neat things with bread and fish and water, God says.

Then he looks around my room. His eyes turn into pretty lights, like the dashboard in my father's car late at night. He makes the stuffed animals dance and the airplanes go round and round. He shoots plumes of cool sparkles from his mouth and nostrils. The sound of his heart pumping builds in the room like drumbeats on a hollow log. The sparkles turn to surf, then to fire. It begins to snow. He's having a grand time.

And with it all going off in my room, swirling and dashing, he puts words in my head: It's time to forget.

I know, I say.

It's time you started forgetting, he says. It will happen with a *floof*, like the sound a skirt makes when it's thrown up over a woman's hips, but before that, let me ask you—have you ever eaten fried bread? Do you know the joke to the punch line "Wrecked 'em, hell, it killed him"? Have you tried the one where you take two pot lids and bang them together or bang one of them on the linoleum? Oh, what a glorious sound, he says, singing the words into my head as if he alone were all the choirs that ever lived or ever would.

And with that we go about the business of putting off my memory for as long as we need.

■

The house wakes up at first light on Christmas morning, groaning and creaking as all its components contract and expand in the exchange of air. A nail pops here; a spike is clenched tighter there. It's dead load, static and fixed, its structure, skin and equipment, all that tonnage tucked nicely on compact gravel, capable of bearing twelve thousand pounds per square foot and yet, when the mantle shrugs, when the frost heaves, when the earth hits a bump in the ecliptic road, this house of Eddie Ryan's squeaks a little. It becomes a seismic gramophone in the clench of gravity.

Eileen and Little Eddie go into their mother and father's bedroom. Eddie is already awake and standing at the window facing east. He can see to the town common, its monument, maples and flagpole. Roads run off its hub in the directions of the compass points, north, south, east and west. He has a map of Inverawe in his head, where he sees from three thousand feet up the belt of land around the town, the roads lacing through the mountains and down to the Connecticut River, crossroads forming delicate webs and brooks as brooks will go.

He knows the common is the center of town. Close by is the village store, the town hall, the red-brick church, the post office, the elementary school, the fire station and Ryan's Funeral Home.

Mrs. Huguenot, the matriarch of Inverawe, knows this about the common too. She wants to put a fountain smack dab in the middle of it. She wants to tap the groundwater they all drink from and let it plume through the air in geysers, thin as the veins in a leaf. She wants the fountain built as a kind of shrine, where people can come to get in touch with the source of their water supply. The place around it should invite contemplation. She told Eddie on the sly that she thinks the texture of water induces water dreams, brings people close to their unconscious. Mrs. Huguenot is getting very old and is dying.

The children climb in under the covers on both sides of Mary. Eddie gets in next to Eileen and tickles her in the ribs.

"Walk and talk, walk and talk. That's all you do," he says.

"You're a regular walkie-talkie." He winks at Mary, and she smiles. They bought the kids a set of walkie-talkies at Radio Shack. It will be the one big surprise. The room gets quiet again.

"So what do you anticipate?" Eddie whispers.

"Stickers, and some My Little Ponies and books. I always get books."

"What about you, sport?"

"Toy men," Little Eddie says in a language only Eileen can understand.

"He said, 'Toy men,' " she says.

"Yes, and then your father can show you how he used to have fun melting his down with gasoline and matches."

"Jesus Christ, Mary. That was a morbid thing to say," Eddie tells her, the hurt showing in his eyes.

"Well, you told me that's what you used to do."

"Jesus Christ, Mary. Not on Christmas Day," Eileen says.

Mary grabs her and pinches her belly until she laughs and then they all laugh.

"Come on," Eileen says. "Time to get up and open presents."

Eddie picks up Eileen and Mary picks up Little Eddie. They go down the stairs in their nightclothes, padding silently in their stocking feet toward the rising glow of the tree lights.

"How'd those get on?" Eddie asks; he'd been conscientiously pulling the plug every night.

At the foot of the stairs they set the children down and then the four of them stand and stare off into the living room. New presents have arrived in the night while they slept. The wood box is full and there's a microwave oven in the armchair, its window facing them. There are twelve-inch McCullough chain saws hanging from spikes in the mantel, nose down in the children's stockings. And warmth comes from the wood stove, which by now usually holds only embers, waiting to be raked and stirred. There is no sound from the converted boiler in the basement, only dry radiant heat rising off the shell of the stove and heading for all corners of the house, heat that quakes and wavers in the colored air.

Eddie goes to the kitchen and looks out the back door. The caravan of machinery is gone.

"He left in the night," Eileen says, her voice so near it startles him. "I watched him go."

4

Eddie stands inside the sandbox, surrounded by the track left from Cody's machine train when it circled, picked up its trail and headed back up the mountain. He holds his coffee cup to his chest, wondering how he missed the noise and the lights this time. It could've been a moment with deep sleep, shut-down lights and the engine at low throttle. All at once.

The coffee cup steams in the cold air, sending up a column of white vapor that tails off to wisps and feathers a foot from the brim. Those mountains Cody disappeared into are locked tight with snow and frost, the cold that can make tree trunks explode.

Inside the house, Mary is basting the turkey and having a conversation with Eileen, who's upstairs in her bedroom buried under the covers. They're using the new set of walkie-talkies. Mary is the mother ship and Eileen is Ponce de León. She thinks she's discovered some dinosaur eggs.

Little Eddie is transferring wrapping paper from one room to another, clutching it to his sides and belly with his fat forearms. He chugs along with a rolling bowlegged gait, his overalls festooned with bows. He takes the lids off empty boxes and tries to get inside. He considers going after the wood stove again, wondering what's the big deal about touching it. He wants to know better and doesn't understand why touching isn't the way. The low balls on the tree come into view. Maybe he'll mosey on over there and take hold of one, maybe eat it.

In a few days there will be dyings, one or two or perhaps six. They come in a burst after Christmas and then again at the end of January, sad deaths, old deaths, unexplainable deaths. Eddie decides he'll leave tomorrow morning to go find Cody while he still has a little time off. He doesn't know whether to hike in or borrow a snowmobile. The hike could be miles; the snowmobile could raise questions. He looks past the crushed hedge where the two tracks get closer, almost converging before they disappear in the still unlit forest, the brow of low branches knocked clean of their winter load. He looks intently, trying to understand what he sees, but can't. It bothers him, but the cold is just too much and he's come out here without an overcoat. He turns and goes back to the house.

■

"Look," he says. "I've got to go up there and see what's going on. There are laws involved here, the status of human remains, disposal of those remains. He could get in a lot of trouble."

"I know," she says. "It's your way of doing things, but it's Christmas. Couldn't you turn this one over to the state police? It is their job."

But she knows he won't. Too many of the wrong things got said. He hadn't sufficiently calmed the man, and meeting the needs of the bereaved was something he took pride in. And deep in her gut, she knows it had to do with his father dying. It was some years ago, but since then, he's been walking around like a man who was carrying something and looking for a place to put it down.

"How 'bout if I hike in tomorrow and leave myself enough time to get back, or if I find him, to come back the next day?"

"Mother ship, mother ship. This is Ponce de León. I got another dinosaur egg. I'm going to sit on it for a while and try to hatch it."

"You do that, Ponce, and when you get tired let me know and I'll send your father up to take over."

"Roger. Over and out."

"That's it," Eddie says. "I can take one of the radios. They're good for five miles."

"That's it."

Eddie goes into the living room. The glass balls have been removed from the bottom of the tree and put in a box. Little Eddie is standing under the mantel next to the wood stove, where it sits on the hearth. Over his head are the four stockings, yellow engines sticking out of two, their bars and chains sheathed inside.

He holds a red glass ball in his hand. It's flecked with white and has a satiny finish. Its hook is missing. Before Eddie can say anything, the boy heaves it and it goes *pop* on the hot black steel. One half turns to flickering shards that cascade and then disappear, while the other half falls to the rug, and that's the piece they both look at as if expecting something to emerge.

Mary comes running in to find them both bent at the waist, their heads almost touching, the jagged half on the floor between them.

"That's it," she says. "You two find something to occupy yourselves until dinner."

▪

The day is done and the children are now alone in their beds. Little Eddie gets dumb with sleep while Eileen anticipates another Christmas on the weekend, when they will drive to Rhode Island to her grandmother's house. There she'll make another pretty good haul.

Her grandmother is her mother's mom. She lives alone. She has a house that looks over Narragansett Bay, and sometimes huge ships pass by, filling the picture window. Her mother is different when she's in Rhode Island. She takes long baths and they fool around with their hair. They spend most all of their time at the beach; even in winter they'll go to hike. Sometimes her father goes, but mostly he sits downstairs reading stacks of newspapers and eating cheese and crackers.

Gram takes Little Eddie and they go on what she calls *jaunts.* Sounds like part of your body. Eileen never met her dad's mom. She died. She thinks she remembers her dad's dad. She keeps saying Dad's Dad, and finally it puts her to sleep.

Eddie and Mary lie in their bed talking about the turkey. Mary says it was too dry. Eddie says it was just right. When it's morning he'll hike the trail left by the machinery. The extra clothes he'll need are already laid out and on the chair.

"You know," Mary says, "I never received a furnace for Christmas. It's the one thing I've always wanted."

"Next year we'll be selfish."

"Next year."

"Yes, next year, but until then," he says, reaching under the bed and coming up with a box, "until then, here's a little something for my lady's boudoir."

"Eddie, we agreed not to," she says, opening the box and taking out a white flannel nightshirt with plaid trim at the collar, cuffs and elbows. "It's the one in the Spiegel catalog," she says. "It's not fair. I didn't get you anything."

"It's all right. It's no big deal."

She knows he's telling the truth. He doesn't like to receive presents. It's the way he's always been, and still, there's so much she'd like to give him. She gets out of bed to change into her new nightshirt, but first she reads the labels, then holds it up in front of her.

"Mary, did you know there's an old road behind the hedge? You can't really see it, because there are so many bushes back there."

"No, I didn't. Where does it go?"

"Up into the mountains, I guess. I wonder if Eileen knows about it."

Eddie gets out of bed and goes down the hall. His daughter is lying on top of her pillow, her hind end in the air and the covers pulled tight to her jaw. He gets close to her face and asks her if she knows about the road.

"Of course I do, silly. It goes to Florida and dinosaurs lay their eggs in nests along the way. Me and Eddie sneak up it a little bit more every time. Now go to sleep."

When Eddie gets back in bed, Mary gives him a kiss, telling him that's for everything. He lies there beside her, wondering about the world his children inhabit, and he's afraid because he never fully realized it existed side by side with his own.

■

Eddie hasn't hiked in a long time. He's done a lot of walking, but this is a hike, and it's in winter along a frozen path made by steel track and rubber tires. To his left is an identical parallel path.

In his head he counts cadence to Mary's words, "Now tell him the presents are nice. Don't make an issue out of it. If it bothers you, we'll find a way to repay him."

It isn't long before he's out of sight of the house and climbing with every step, the road running to higher ground at each switch-back. It's an old logging road, newly opened by Cody's descent two days ago and improved with his ascent only a few hours later, both done at night in a blind snow, both done on a road hewn out for horses or oxen.

To the mountain side of the longer runs are rotted skidways, cribs of logs built up for the handloading of the sledge. At every turn he expects to see where Cody might've miscalculated and lost the lowboy or maybe the whole train and him inside the roll-over cage, crushed to death by the tonnage that followed him.

Eddie climbs higher until it's as if he's in the crowns of trees. Old hemlock still spires a hundred feet into the air, left behind when the prime eastern forests were cut over. A good timber tree, its wood is coarse, its bark rich in tannin, which dyes red.

He stops to strip a twig, palming the short flat needles in his hand. They're dark on the tops and silver-lined below. He thinks of trees as living things. He doesn't know it's the sheath that lives, the heartwood that dies, a trick nature plays on the fancies of men.

By noon Eddie's near the summit. Here the forest gives way to high meadows, juniper and poplar growing in tufts and bent thickets, serving as bones for the body of snow. There are abandoned apple orchards and at times stone culverts laid in to let streams sluice under the road. The remnants of stone walls line the now wider road and at one point he gains a view of the town hall, the church steeple, his own house. At another point he has a clean shot down the valley to the farthest southern boundary of town and sees the big diesels like specks across the Connecticut River or Route 91 in Vermont.

It's here he stops and tries to raise Mary on the radio, but he can't, something he warned her might happen. He pushes on, following the tracks higher and higher as they sweep along what used to be the lanes of commerce, of a community, land now owned by people wealthy enough to just have and hold while they live in Boston or New York and vacation in the islands.

Eddie reaches the summit, a land of drumlins. No view inside here, only the steep roll of hills like the middle of the distant sea, the road a storm passage made along the tapered ends of water canyons. He turns to see where he's been, but the track bends and disappears. He looks ahead and it does the same. He begins to like it that way.

The first sign of Cody is the smell of smoke, and that worries Eddie until the second sign comes, the ripping sound of a hot, well-tuned chain saw when it's in the possession of a sawyer capable of holding it at full throttle with one hand and yanking the pull cord with the other. It comes from Eddie's left, from the other side of a ridge. Ahead he can see where the road tails off and curves left, so he climbs up through the hardwoods, and from the top of the ridge he has a view of Cody's logging camp, but the saw has been shut down and he can't tell where the sound came from. He sits on a stump and waits, watching the camp below.

In the clearing stands a community of equipment. The hum of a generator becomes apparent. It's the Homelite, powering the heater inside the horse trailer, steam rising from its blue hull. Parked beside it is the bulldozer, the skidder and the pickup truck. They sit on the black frozen ground, the snow scraped clear and packed into a wall at one edge.

The source of smoke is a pit covered with slash at the far perimeter, the blackened snow sloped and melted around its edges and already turning back to ice.

Everything else in the world is silent, white with frost and snow, the hemlock and pine, their green colors closer to midnight, no other way in and only one way out.

Cody sits on a log a hundred yards from where the fire smolders. On the level ground below him is the lowboy, which holds half a jag of cordwood. It's stacked four feet high and the butts are in eight-foot lengths. He sits quietly, smoking a cigarette, his legs crossed and his hat pushed back on his head. He wonders how long it will take before Eddie Ryan spots him. It was only by chance he stopped and sat down and in the next moment saw Eddie emerge from the woods and take a seat on a stump.

He waits, making no effort to either conceal or reveal his whereabouts. He lights another smoke, and it becomes the flash off the end of the stick match that draws Eddie's attention.

The men stare at each other, but neither moves. Finally Cody smiles and waves and Eddie does the same. Then they get up and walk toward each other, meeting on the frozen ground.

"Good day, Mr. Ryan. Good day to you. You had a good Christmas?"

"Yes, Cody. Yes, we did, and I thank you for the presents. They were nice."

"Good. Good. Now before you even ask, just let me say I stepped out of line back there a day ago. You might say I crossed the border. Well, I'm back now and I hope we can go on as we did before."

The words sting Eddie, but then he realizes he's thinking with his mind, not Cody's. He realizes it's just something for Cody to say, a longing to return to what was before he even met Eddie.

"I wish we could do that," Eddie says quietly, "but I have an obligation, you see."

"I see that you want to get right down to business."

"No, that's okay. How about a cup of coffee?"

"You see, Mr. Ryan, I was coming out for good. It was one of those dramatic moves in life we all like to make."

"Cody, you're up to a different sort of business than I am. You must understand that this death of your friend does things to both of us. And the sad fact is, there are laws that must be obeyed."

"There are laws and there are laws."

Cody's words are bitter. Inside, Eddie can feel things breaking up, life's refusal to go by the book, ice floes on a river.

Becoming a mortician for him had more to do with life than death, or so he's always thought, essentially an optimistic move, one where ritual works like a good drug. At Khe Sanh, ritual became the way to live, a way to obscure living. He wants to say, Commit to me, and I will make it better for you. I will provide redemption. Like a poet I will bring you closer to what it means to be human. Eddie smiles at his own foolish thoughts.

"It's all taken care of," Cody says, nodding toward the hastily covered hole. "I cremated him. Ashes to ashes. Dust to dust. All that good shit. It's how he wanted it."

"That's not what you told me last night."

"He changed his mind."

■

The living quarters inside the trailer are small enough for two men to eat and sleep and store their provisions and gear. It's warm too.

Buck, the big Percheron, snuffles into his feed bag. His body gives off enough BTUs to keep the heater from overworking. Round balls of shit collect on the floor behind him, steaming pungently and slowly going cold.

"The early Semites believed in an underground community of departed spirits," Eddie says. "Inhumation was important to them. The cremated were destined to wander the world, forever disgraced."

"Wonder of the world," Cody says, spooning instant into a pair of mugs.

"Yes. In fact during the reign of Constantine the Great, cremation was actually outlawed. Christianity as a rule has never really taken a stance, although the more secularized groups, such as the Unitarians, actually favor it. Was G.R. a Unitarian by any chance?"

"No. He weren't a Unitarian nor a Rotarian. He was a logger, among other less desirable things."

"It's the Germans and Scandinavians who went in big for fire burial. They were afraid of the dead and at the same time they wanted to free the spirit from the body. There's a story about two brothers, Aran and Asmunder. They agreed that whoever died first would be attended by the other for three nights. So Aran drops dead one day."

"Jesus, that's a shame," Cody says. "I was beginning to like those boys. My kind of people."

"So listen, Aran's in the mound with his sword, his hound and his hawk and he has a horse too. The first night he kills the hawk and the hound and eats them. The second night he kills the horse and eats that too, offering some to Asmunder. On the third night he rises up again and tries to eat his brother, but Asmunder fights him off and escapes with only the loss of his ears."

"What?" Cody says, smiling.

"His ears. He lost his ears. Oh, I get it. You did hear me. You're making a joke."

"He lost his fucking ears? Is that a joke or something? I don't get it."

"It's not important," Eddie says. "They believed the spirit continued to live in the grave mound, and those spirits were in constant battle. The Valkyries were women who helped the heroes during life and bore them away to Valhalla after death."

"Knowing G.R., he has a whole harem of those women at his beck and call even as we sit here and talk. It was his way."

Eddie drinks from his mug. It's getting warm in the trailer, warm to the point of being uncomfortable. He shucks off his jacket and opens his shirt at the collar. He can't tell what belongs to Cody and what belonged to G.R. He sees where the microwave oven was. It's easy to tell because it's the only space where something doesn't sit or rest or hang. It's the only space where things aren't stacked, where work doesn't seem to happen.

"This is very nice, Cody."

"It's just a place to live."

"No, it's very nice."

"Could use a machine shop," Cody says. "Now *that'd* be nice. A shop to work on machines. You probably have a body shop, being in the business you're in."

"Yes, the basement, and then we use the living room for viewing. We're usually at it day and night. Now there's a man in the South with drive-through viewing. The bodies sit in windows and you can drive by."

"I've always wanted a job that never slept. Much like farmers or the men who plow snow. You can always be doing a little more. My wife could never understand that. I met her at the driving range just over the summit. She worked the takeout window. She wasn't awfully big in the chest, but every time she bent over to hand out a cone she'd come up wearing the popular flavors."

"You and your wife never see each other?"

"Do you see her around?" Cody says, sweeping his arm through the air as if to make a grand gesture. "It's the machines, Mr. Ryan. As a little boy, you spend your first few years with women and then you're turned over to the machines. It tends to warp what your sense of a good time is. Women have no feeling for machines. It's something men are born with. Do you know anything about ultralights, Mr. Ryan?"

"No, I don't. I haven't really read much about them."

"You read a lot, don't you? I don't trust the written word. It's always meant trouble—subpoenas, warrants, eviction. The law gets written down, and when it does, it's only the law whores who read it."

"Yes. Lawyers," Eddie says.

"Jesus, Mr. Ryan, how the hell do I know? The bottom line is, it's you on the shit end of the stick. Listen, am I in hot water for what I did or not?"

"I don't know, Cody. I just can't say right now."

Cody gets up and goes to the horse. The animal's face is either calm or dumb. Right now he can't decide.

"Cremation is on the upswing," Eddie says, his voice soft and distinct, far away. "From 1960 to 1980 it went from three and a half percent to ten percent." He likes Cody; he isn't afraid of death. He doesn't seem to be afraid of anything. "The greatest percent of those occur in the Pacific states."

"It makes sense they'd want to burn their dead."

"Why do you say that?"

"I don't know. Maybe because most of them are from somewhere else. G.R. was from everywhere. You ask him, he'll tell you."

"If you are from somewhere else, it's expensive to ship bodies around. From Switzerland it'd cost you more than five thousand dollars. Moscow's a little cheaper, about three thousand. Most people who die away from home never get back."

"Jesus, that's sad," Cody says. "Well, I guess I did okay then. I'll go down in that hole and collect up a bucket of ashes and then everywhere I go for the rest of my new life, I'll leave a pinch of G.R. in the wind."

"Where are you going to go, Cody?"

Cody comes back to the table. He's smiling. He takes a deep breath and then he begins to speak in a voice not his own:

"Doves in Kenya, blue-winged teal on the Yucatán, tarpon in Costa Rica, partridge in Argentina, turkey in Alabama, quail in Florida, sockeye in Alaska, salmon in Nova Scotia, geese in New Zealand, barracuda in the Bahamas, grouse in Scotland, whitetail in Pennsylvania and wild boar in Georgia."

And to Eddie the words are beautiful, filled with high intent, wonderment, imagination, thought and heart. They are only the names of places and the names of birds, fish and animals that inhabit those places, but it's as if it's a recitation of how lovely the world can be. The words bring forth rock paintings, men wearing skins, whole geographics, arrangements and apportionments. The horse trailer is a holograph and he's inside. Blossoms of words. Something to see.

"Don't worry," Cody whispers. "I burned him. And that will be our little secret."

Eddie and Cody sit at the kitchen table drinking Budweiser, a bottle of Jim Beam between them. They move it back and forth, keeping each other's glass at two fingers.

They started talking about building a small barn for Buck, maybe twenty by twenty. Eddie will provide a tiny square of land on the far corner, and Cody the lumber and labor. It'll be Buck's barn until he dies, then ownership will revert back to Eddie and Mary. Now it's late and dark and they're off on other matters.

"This table is the earth," Cody says, "as they thought it to be in 1492 when Columbus sailed the ocean blue."

"That's a poem, Cody. That's a poem. I wanted to be a poet, you know. It's what I grew up wanting to be and now I come up with rhymes and reason. You stab 'em; I'll slab 'em. Shit like that."

Mary orbits the table. After two weeks she knows how they get late at night, but she tries not to mind. She thinks this is how it will be when Little Eddie grows up and has a friend over for lunch. They'll sit at the same table, eating peanut butter and jelly sand-

wiches, drinking milk. She's happy for Eddie that Cody came back
to spend out the winter before he travels.

"I wrote a poem for my father," Eddie says. "It's a poem for
drunks. I call it 'The Drunk Poem, for My Father.' It's as far as I've
gotten. You know, in fact, I think that's all there is to it. I think that's
the whole poem."

"Well, I'll tell you, Eddie. My father was quite a man. Here's a
story for you."

Cody crooks his finger, indicating that Eddie should lean forward. When he does, Cody whispers out the words, but they come
loud enough for Mary to hear.

"We had a draft horse," he says, "one as big as 'ol Buck, and I
had a Shetland pony I'd ride through the woods, going like hell.
Well, when that pony come into her first season, the draft horse
fucked her to death. Please excuse my French, but that's what he
did. It's a sad story. I don't mind telling you we were all a little
hurt."

Cody and Eddie sit back, shaking their heads over the death of
the pony. Mary turns on the faucet, thankful for the bang in the
pipes from the built-up water hammer. She knows they cringe every
time they hear it. She knows it sobers them.

"My old man gave me two pieces of advice that I've clung to in
my travels through life. Drink your liquor straight and buy the
women stockings with seams up the back."

Eddie and Mary laugh at this.

"Cody," she says, tapping him on top of his head, "women don't
wear those kinds of stockings anymore. They wear pantyhose."

"Pantyhose," Cody says disgustedly. "The only thing pantyhose
are good for is in the winter. You put on three pairs and, let me
tell you, it's better than all the long johns made put together."

"You wear pantyhose?" Eddie says.

Cody looks back and forth from Eddie to Mary.

"I'm not telling," he says. "Besides, I don't get cold in the winter—only on summer nights. Drink your liquor straight and buy the
women stockings with seams in them. It's something to hold on to.
Something to take through life with you, and when your boy gets
old enough, I'll tell him the same thing. He's quite the lamb, you
know. When he gets old enough, old Cody'll show him the ropes."

Cody empties his glass and takes a pull from his beer. Eddie tips out some more Beam.

"This table's the world," Cody says. "The whole goddamn world right here in this room. Kitchens without tables are awful places. A table should be placed such that a man can reach behind him, open the fridge and take out a beer. That's the good life, you know."

Cody points a finger at Eddie and says, "Being as lame as you are you've struck on it without even knowing. About the only thing you lack in life is cable T.V."

Mary goes to the refrigerator for more beer.

"My father was something too," Eddie says. "He was a drinker. I don't know why he did it, but it killed him. He didn't drink for the reason the world thinks."

"*This* world," Cody says, rapping his knuckles on the table, "this flat world that hasn't existed in five hundred years."

"That's right. It's a reason best put in maybe a Latin or Greek word or maybe in a language spoken by people who live in a deep valley and who've yet to be discovered. Maybe they have a word for it in their language. The truth is all the reasons are the same. I'm not so quick to judge anymore. At one time I was, but not anymore."

Eddie stares off like a man who's just seen life scrape by, his own life, and what he saw wasn't too pleasant. Cody looks at him and then to Mary. She's intent on her husband. She's hearing things he doesn't often speak about and wants to go to him, put her arms around him, but just now he seems to be in a place where he can't be reached, a place where he's been for months.

"One New Year's Eve," Eddie says, "my father came home drunk. We were sitting at the table talking. I was a young boy, but I could tell. He was handing me dollar bills and telling me I could have them for keeps. A car pulled in the driveway and the dog started barking. His name was Bullet. He was a German shepherd. My father went out to see who it was. I looked on from the front steps. I could see him put hands on the door and lean in. Then all of a sudden his head snapped back and the man came out punching him. He got him down in the driveway and started beating on him.

"Bullet got the man by the pant leg. He tore into him. He was a good dog. He used to sit in the chair and watch T.V. with me. When Kennedy was shot in 1963, me and that dog sat in the chair all weekend, watching it over and over again. There used to be a snapshot of me and the dog sitting in that chair.

"My mother pushed past me and grabbed the man by the other leg and tried to drag him off. I didn't know what to do. Then my brother came out the door with his rifle. He's older than me, four years. It's like we came from different places, though. He shot that gun in the air and then held it to the man's head, right behind his ear.

"I remember thinking, Shoot him, shoot him. I wanted him to shoot that man in the worst way. That's when I knew I'd always love my brother, and I will. I'll always love my brother for what he did. That was the moment."

Eddie takes too big a sip of the Beam and retches as it burns at the back of his throat. His eyes go hot and tear up. Both Cody and Mary make a move toward him, but they don't go very far because Eddie holds his hands up, stopping them, waving them off. He starts to speak again, his voice sounding as if someone has his hands around his throat.

"My father's nose was pushed over to one side of his face and his eyes were already black holes in his head. It's the first time I ever saw so much human blood. It wasn't red—it was more like crimson, slick and shiny, and it ran. Trails of it down his face.

"My mother helped him down the hallway. When he saw me, he asked if I'd ever been in a fight. I didn't say anything and he punched me in the stomach. He punched me hard. He said, 'That's what it's like. That's what it's like to be in a fight.'"

Mary stands at the sink crying. The tears well up in her eyes and come down her face, huge tears coming slowly down her cheeks as if at their leisure, as if they are trying to sneak past her. She makes no move to brush them away. She's never heard this story before.

"I think that's why I've come to like you, Cody. It's because I know you would have shot the man. There aren't many people alive today who would. They all want some moral guidance. They all want direction, a conclusion before the facts. A truth before the lies. But when you give it to them, they don't like it. They don't like you. You're not like that, Cody. You would have shot the man, wouldn't you?"

"I don't know," Cody says. "Right now I just don't know. You've pushed me to the bone of things and here and now I can't say."

Eddie reaches across the table, knocking the bottle onto one of its corners, where it totters and then settles. He clenches on to Cody's hand.

"Tell me you would have shot the man. Please tell me you would have."

Cody looks to Mary. She nods her head.

"I would've shot him, Eddie. I would've shot him dead."

"Oh, that's good, Cody. That's good you've said that."

Eddie lets go of Cody's hand and sits back. They drink their beer. He pours more bourbon into the glasses and makes a move for the refrigerator, but Mary is quicker. She takes out more beer, opening one for each man and one for herself.

"Years later," Eddie says, "my father took a pistol into the woods in a brown paper bag. He was going to kill himself. He used to sing 'The Streets of Laredo' all the time. He'd sing, *'When I was a-walkin' the streets of Laredo, I spied a young cowboy all wrapped in white linen, cool clear water.'*"

Eddie's been gripping the edge of the table, and now his hand slips and he almost topples over. Mary and Cody both move to help him but he waves them off. He keeps speaking, only now he speaks softly.

"My grandfather had a room in the basement he moved into the last years of his life. He stayed in that room and never came out until he died.

"I'm sitting tonight thinking about the both of them. It seems that fathers, the fathers, all kill themselves. I'm sitting here tonight thinking about him and I can't remember when he died. I can't remember when he died. I can't remember the month or the day or the year. Mary. Mary, do you remember when it was?"

"February, Eddie. February eleventh, 1984," Mary says.

"Even now there are things I want to tell him. I think to remember them so when I see him I can tell him, so I write them down, but then I realize he's gone. On Sundays I stayed home with him when the rest went to church. He'd cook me fried potatoes, eggs and a piece of steak. We'd sit at the table and I'd eat it and it always tasted so good. He had a barrel next to his workbench where he used to smash his bottles when they were empty.

"I'd sit there eating breakfast while he had a Schaefer. Later on in life he got into the hard stuff. He always crossed his legs the way a woman does, one leg over the other, his calf tight to his shin, no space left in between."

"Eddie always notices little things like that," Mary says.

"What my father did was lay in secret stuff that goes off years later, long removed. I guess you could say they are time bombs that go off in my head and in my heart and only days later am I able to track them back to him."

"Time bombs. Time for bed. Let it rest for tonight," Mary says.

"You don't like to hear this?" Eddie says.

"It scares me when you go off like this because I don't know if you're coming back."

"Mary, it's in the life of men. They begin loving their mother and being afraid of their father, that terrible kind of fear that draws you in and makes you want, and from there you go to running with boys, and from there you go to loving women, especially one more than any other. Then she becomes your mother again and once that happens it's different, so you go back to loving men again."

"Drinking too," Cody says. "Men love to drink."

"You see, Cody, I witnessed the birth of both my children. I saw them coming out of my wife's body. I saw the life she was living in that moment, the pain and then the joy."

Eddie looks up to Mary. It's as if he wants to make sure she's listening and at the same time as if he didn't realize she was.

"It changed me," he says. "It changed my life. It's been a while now and I'm still changed, but I don't know how."

"Well, Mr. Ryan, given all the death you've had to live with, it seems to make sense to me."

"Do you think that's it? I tell you, I look at this woman and I think how beautiful she is and I know what a lucky man I am, but other times, all I see is those babies coming out of her, one after another, and I realize in that moment I've lost her to someone else. Instantly there was someone she loved more than me, and it's not that I'd have the loving part any different. God knows it is the children, but just now these thoughts are going off in my head like explosions. Given that and the pain I now sense my father went through, I'm terribly confused by it all. Day by day I make a case for love in my head. What makes her more of a woman makes me less the man. I think these thoughts, and as soon as I've gotten down and hit some bone, my head snaps back with the whiplash of self-pity. So I go back down again and it snaps back again and it gets so bad, I think, You can't even touch bone without feeling sorry for your-self. I can't seem to get over that one. That self-pity is a barbwire fence that'll rip hell out of you, and tonight I've been going across so many times I'm about stripped bare—my clothes are gone, my flesh is gone and now it's bone. But I figure if I keep going I'll make it and there'll be at least a little piece of me left on the other side."

"Windmills, Mr. Ryan. You're chasing windmills."

"I suppose so, but I tell you, if I can get over there and make it back, then I'll have something to pass along to my son. I'd settle for something in code, a sign, because there'd be no other way to sneak it all back through.

"I'm glad you're here, Cody. I've never been able to tell Mary these things. I'm glad you're here so I can tell them to her through you."

"What I don't get," Cody says, "is why you ever went into mortician work if this is how it goes."

"I guess it's because I like people, but I can only take them in a certain way."

6

Cody disappears again for three days at the end of January. Keene's finest has him in the drunk tank. He spends the time puking up his guts and sitting on the toilet with the dribbling shits. He concludes it was a kind of viral drunk, one of those seventy-two-hour bouts with the devil of delirium.

"Halloo, Eddie. I'm down to Keene in the drunk tank and they're finally ready to spring me. I need you to come get me."

Eddie hangs up the phone. He tells Mary it's Cody and he was picked up for drunk driving.

Mary shakes her head. She knows how Eddie's father used to drink. She's read too how it's a genetic thing. Like father, like son—that message courses through her brain. The articles spooked her. In her less fine moments she thinks he may someday go off like that, head down the road to rack and ruin. She thinks about her son and how sometimes genes leapfrog generations. Maybe he'll be the one to lust for the sauce.

She's a young mother with a young family, a young business to keep up. In that moment she makes her decision.

"Don't bring him back here," she says quietly.

"What?"

"I said, don't bring him back here."

"Mary, he needs some help. What are we going to do? Abandon him? We've become friends."

"I know."

■

Cody tells Eddie he woke up in his truck and thought it was years ago and Christmas Eve. It was cold as hell, and if he hadn't been so drunk he'd have frozen to death. All around him blue lights were flashing, sweeping the night, strobing in the darkness. For a moment he thought he was six years old, asleep in his mother's trailer under the Christmas tree. But then he realized he was about to be arrested. He'd stopped to sleep it off and now he was headed for the crowbar hotel. He was just being a safety-minded citizen, but that's not how it goes. They yanked his license and now he has to go to drunk school to get it back.

"If this keeps up," he says, "it's getting so nobody will know how to drive drunk."

"We'll come back for your pickup tomorrow. Mary can drive in and we'll get it then."

"Stop!"

"What is it?"

"I need some smokes. I haven't had a cigarette in three days."

Eddie knows what he wants, but he pulls in anyway. Cody gets out and comes back a few minutes later with a six-pack tucked under his arm. He hands one over to Eddie, then takes one for himself, draining half of it before they're moving again. He only stops when he chokes and it burns back up through his nose.

"Damn," he says, staring ahead. "If God invented anything better than riding around in a pickup and drinking beer with your best friend, he's keeping it to himself."

Eddie pulls out and drives slowly through the back streets, making for the back roads that will get them home. Cody is quiet until they get out of Keene and onto Hurricane Road.

"Seems like this whole country is shutting down. Everywhere you turn, there's another turn. It used to be that a man lived by the sweat of his brow, and now it's the moneylenders and the law pimps that run the show."

"Cody, it's against the law to drive drunk and there aren't two ways about it."

"By Jesus, it's not only against the law to drink and drive, it's become immoral, and that's the name of that tune."

Cody rolls down the window and flings his empty bottle into a stone wall running beside the road. It catches in the snow, withholding from him its delightful crash. He throws another, a full one, and it pops on the rocks, then goes silent.

"Jesus, don't do that," Eddie says.

"Arrest me."

Mary is waiting up for them when they come in the house. It's cold out, almost too cold for it to even get dark. The cold is like steel, ignorant of the dark, leaving the dark to, at best, be an ill fit on the world.

Cody shivers. He's caught a chill.

Being gone drunk these few days, these few weeks, has left him a cold hollow place. Eddie knows he needs a drink and will give him one, a small one, and then an even smaller one.

As a boy Eddie learned to drive at twelve. He had to learn because his father made him. His father'd either be drunk or drinking, and later on, when he'd call from the bar, Eddie's mother would send him out with airplane bottles, small shots to keep off the fits.

Mary has coffee and English muffins laden with peanut butter. Eddie laces Cody's coffee with whiskey, enough to calm him. Bad medicine that works. Eddie shakes his head. He thinks about how firemen fight fire with fire. They start backfires to burn out swaths of brush, which destroys the fuel for the flames raging on the wind. Firewater.

"You need a shower," Mary says.

Cody looks into his cup. He's come round enough to be ashamed of himself. He takes a bite of muffin, then has to work a finger alongside his gums. He drinks some coffee and burns his mouth but doesn't say anything.

"It's decaf," Mary says. "You won't have any trouble sleeping. You'll shower, then spend the night on the couch."

"Now, Mary," Cody says, "that's something I could never understand."

"What's that?"

"Decaffeinated coffee. Why does anyone drink the stuff except for the caffeine?"

"Because some people like the taste, I guess."

"Cody," Eddie says. "What now?"

This is a question Mary put him up to. She wants to know there's a plan of action. She wants it negotiated, made clear and agreed upon.

"My wings are clipped. They yanked my license on the spot and it will probably be for months. A fine. Probably somewhere in the neighborhood of three hundred and fifty dollars, and I have to go to drunk school. There's one forming up in Keene next month. The cop said I was lucky to get nabbed when I did. What I'm going to do is shoot down to Florida and pick up a license. Change my middle initial. I know a guy who did that."

"No, you won't," Mary says, needing to make the best of this, knowing he's back. "You're going to do this by the book. You've got your trailer here. You owe us cordwood and you have a barn half finished. We made a deal. You're going to do it right or you're going to get out and never come back. You leave again, the way you have, don't you ever, ever come back here. I won't have it."

Mary wants to cry, but she'll be damned if she lets herself do it in front of Eddie and Cody, so she smiles and sips her coffee. When she's done with it, she gets up and rinses out her cup and heads for the stairs.

After she goes up to bed, Cody and Eddie step out onto the porch for a smoke. It's cold, but there's no wind. The moon is huge in the sky. The land is blue.

"Cold as a witch's tit," Cody says.

A woman's voice can be heard in the night, high and quavering, singing an aria of sorts, and then it's gone. Overhead is a jet outstripping its noise, leaving it miles behind as it trails through the night.

"Why didn't you call sooner?" Eddie asks.

Cody takes a long time before answering, and when he does, Eddie isn't at first sure of what he says, but then he hears the words in his head, and they're clear as the ringing of a bell.

"The children."

They go back in the house for down vests and overcoats. For both men, being outdoors is always the place to be.

"She's right, you know," Eddie says.

Cody's blood is thin with liquor. He shivers inside his clothes. He shivers until he gets warm and then has to take off his hat and open the collar of his shirt.

"Women grow us up," he says. "They grow us up until we're old enough to be with the men and from then on we spend our lives with machines. That's been the way, the right way."

"You've said that, but some say it's not like that. Some say women are the victims in this society."

"Well, who the fuck are they to talk?"

"Victims, I guess," Eddie says.

"Those are only words. Take them away and what have you got? Words are a piss-poor thing to build a life on."

They don't say any more to each other. They hunker down in chairs and smoke. They'll stay out here long after it makes sense, long after they are too cold to move. They'll stay just outside the front door as if they're guarding it or waiting for a baby to be born. It's something men have done for a long time and some still do long after there's any reason for doing it.

■

"I'm Mr. Hurley and this is Mr. Nims. I'm a guidance counselor at the high school and Mr. Nims is the school psychologist. From the outset we want you to know we don't take sides, but we do think the DA's office is a bit overzealous. This course will run for six weeks, one night a week for three hours. Now remember, you can't miss a single class and you have to be good to avoid counseling at the end."

Mr. Hurley and Mr. Nims laugh at that last bit. They laugh like men do when they are overly familiar with each other's bodies even if they aren't.

"Plus," Mr. Nims says, "you get back one half of your fine upon successful completion of the course. For each of you, that's at least a hundred and seventy-five dollars. It's like you're paying yourselves to come. Now the first thing I'd like for us to do is make a circle so we all can have a chat."

At first the students of the class don't move, but then they have to because Mr. Nims has a way of grabbing their chairs while at the same time asking them to grab someone else's chair. The circle ends up being kidney-shaped. Mr. Nims has everyone sit down and then get back up again to try for a better circle. This one gets closer to a heart shape, so they do it again and get it right. The first hour has passed.

"Now. Good," Mr. Nims says. "Let's start off by telling our stories."

Mr. Nims and Mr. Hurley have been through this before. They have the routine down pretty good, from the making of the circle to these words by Mr. Nims.

"It will go randomly," he says. "I'll pick names from a hat. Let's begin."

Johnny MacDuffie is first. He looks like Hoot Gibson. He drinks to fill the emptiness left by his lost son. The Blond Bomber is next. She drinks for insight. Loretta Pelletier never drinks. Milt Tease has been drinking ever since he was a little boy. Torvalt and Wayne drink because they like the taste. Larry Fish only drinks Seagram's five-star rye. Valentine Gordon drinks because she has PMS. Stanley Garneau drinks because he's a war vet. Reggie Bodinka drinks because he's bankrupt. Freddy Clough has been here before and Leo Comeau drinks because drinking is the thing he does best. When it's Cody's turn, he doesn't say anything. He only shakes his head. Mr. Nims decides to let it go for now.

"Mr. Hurley, that leaves you."

Mr. Hurley is the ace up Mr. Nims's sleeve. He's the ace up his own sleeve. He belongs to AA while Mr. Nims belongs to Ph.D.

"My name is Joe and I'm an alcoholic. I haven't had a drink in twenty years. From my first drink I knew I was a goner. A pint of whiskey would put me in the hole for a week. Finally I got caught. I hit a deer on the highway and went off the road. I woke up in the hospital while they were drawing for the blood test. I'd get drunk again, though. I'd get so drunk I'd shit the bed. I couldn't fart without soiling myself. I forgot what it was like to strain to take a shit.

"Every morning the sweats would kick in at six and I'd have the need for a drink. Did you ever talk to yourself when both of you were drunk? Well, I have. I was a desperate person. I was soul-sick. I was powerless.

"Then I found twelve steps to a new life. I gave myself over to a power greater than me. I took stock of myself and admitted my wrongs. There's more, and over these next few weeks I hope we have a chance to talk some more about it."

"Thank you, Joe," Mr. Nims says. "Now we'd like for you to see a movie on alcohol, alcoholism and driving while intoxicated, and then we'll be done for the evening. Next week perhaps we can really begin this, really begin to tell our stories so we can know each other and know ourselves. Roll 'em."

Eddie is parked outside, waiting to give Cody a ride home.

"How'd it go?"

"Fine. Nothing really to talk about."

"Want a beer?"

"No, not now. I'm really already tired of the whole thing. I'd rather just sleep for a year. Either that or spend my time with your dead people. I see why you do what you do. Dead people and trees have a lot in common."

"Silence."

■

The Blond Bomber is a local celebrity. She used to work for the hippie radio station but now it's all computerized. Her show started at one o'clock in the morning and went through to five. All the farmers tuned in when they went to milking. She'd give the ag report and interview county agents, conservation agents, game wardens and 4-H leaders. Legend has it she gave a blow job on the air one morning, but then found God. It was a way for the farmers to keep from falling asleep under the cows.

"Hey, motherfucker," she says, "scar tissue is forever."

She tells her story to the class. She wants to self-actualize. She's tired of it all—pyramids, stone beads, minerals, yoga, metaphysics, holistic psychotherapy and crystals, to name just a few. And drugs. All of them. But nothing gets her off like a bottle of Johnnie Walker Red.

She tells them that's when she hit the power pole, blacking out West Keene. The lines came down and snapped out an image of Christ in electricity.

"He said, 'Hey, you stupid cunt, scar tissue is forever,' and I knew he was talking about my heart."

Valentine Gordon looks at the twinings she's made of her fingers.

"I wish you wouldn't speak that way," she says.

"What? What? What?" the Blond Bomber says.

"That word."

"Hey, baby. In the beginning was the word and the word was with God and the word was God and the word was freakin' good. The Gospel according to John. I am on a train to Christ."

Torvalt and Wayne are looking at Reggie Bodinka. They're smiling. They used to work for him on his farm. Every morning they'd listen to the Bomber. They made him listen too, and he did, but he'd always call her a slut.

Torvalt and Wayne tell their story. Torvalt's mom has loads of money. She has a locked room in the house where she keeps it in barrels. She is a psychiatrist. For the winter, Torvalt and Wayne were to keep an eye on her lake house, but it burned down. Wayne is Torvalt's new best friend. They met at a Dead concert in Hartford and have been inseparable these four weeks. The tickets to the concert were a present from Torvalt's mother.

"So one weekend, me and Wayne left for Stratton to go skiing. The weekend turned into a week, and that's when the house burned down. She's suing the company that made the microwave. Her lawyer claims the remote phone kicked it on and after four days of running it had a meltdown and torched the house. My mother says it's my fault and I can't come home until there's a settlement."

Wayne stares at Torvalt. He makes the others uneasy because he looks exactly like Charles Manson.

"So me and Wayne got jobs with Mr. Bodinka. We got jobs cutting cordwood. He let us live in a tent on his property. One night we were asleep and the kerosene heater went out and by morning we were covered with frost. I thought Wayne was dead. He was blue and his breathing was real low. I beat him till he woke up. We went running down the road in our felt liners to Mr. Bodinka's barn. It was the cows that saved our lives. We got in with them and their warmth saved us. We went back later and somebody had stole all our gear, our saws and tent and sleeping bags. Even the shells of our pac boots."

Torvalt looks as if he might begin to cry. Wayne turns to the class and looks at each one of them, giving each the eye until they look away. The last one he looks at is Cody, who doesn't blink. It's him that Wayne talks to.

"At night we go up to Bellows Falls. We go up to the Derry Café and get drunk as shit. It tastes good. We don't hurt anybody—only ourselves, and we ain't nobody special."

Mr. Hurley shuffles some papers. "It says here you two got caught driving a tractor down the interstate."

"Details."

■

"I shouldn't have been driving," Loretta Pelletier whispers. "I've had walking pneumonia for a month. I'm on NyQuil and aspirin. I went to the store for groceries. The road was slippery, black ice. I'm not from around here so I'm not used to driving in bad weather. I went around a turn and the car went off the road. The hatch popped open and all my groceries flew out the back. When the police came I was looking for my vegetables in the snow. Alls I could find was a head of cabbage.

"I asked the policeman to please help me find my vegetables. I said, 'My husband will be mad if I don't come home with the groceries.' They wouldn't help, though. They told me to put down the cabbage, but I wouldn't. They made me take a Breathalyzer and then they said I was arrested for drunk driving. I don't drink. I never drink. My lawyer says I'll get off but that I should go to these classes just in case."

Mr. Nims doesn't know what to say. He's heard this story before. Sometimes it's true and sometimes it isn't.

"I think he gave you good advice, Loretta. What say we take a little break for coffee? Refill our cups?"

When they settle back down, it's Johnny MacDuffie's turn.

"My boy was a Little Leaguer. It was a Saturday. He and the other boys were down to the dump soliciting money for new uniforms. In the town we came from in Connecticut it was the place to go for fund raising because everyone went there on Saturday morning. People were always gone during the week, into the city to work. There was a shack for a book exchange. When people ran for office they stood at the gate handing out candy bars, doughnuts and coffee, but now there's just a pickup station and everything goes to the incinerator.

"My office went fishing that morning. We took a party boat and were out all morning from before the crack of dawn. When I got home I started a chowder with the fish I'd caught, halibut with cream and milk, potatoes, celery and onions. I went down to the basement and forgot about it. When my son came home it boiled over onto him and the burns killed him. That was fifteen years ago."

Wayne leans over to Torvalt.

"That's a fine kettle of fish," he whispers in a voice loud enough for all to hear.

Johnny MacDuffie looks at them. His face is like that of a man who's just been stabbed and is about to die, a man who hasn't the slightest notion why it's happened to him. He starts to cry. The Blond Bomber goes to him and puts her arms around him. She holds his head to her stomach and strokes his neck.

Cody is up and crossing the circle. He takes Wayne by the collar of his jacket and lifts him out of his seat.

"I ought to fucking kill you," he says.

Mr. Hurley gets a hand on Cody's forearm.

"I think that's enough until next week. Thank you all very much."

■

Eddie makes breakfast for the family. It's something he does well. Breakfast is his specialty. He fries potatoes and sausage and eggs any way you want them. If the kids want cereal, he pours it out into their bowls, milk for Little Eddie, none for Eileen. He makes pancakes too, and waffles. Sometimes he just makes muffins or corn bread and serves it up with a big plate of fruit and yogurt. It's become their main meal of the day on Sunday.

Mary tells him he should get a cooking show on public television. No one specializes in just breakfasts.

"Right," he says. "The mortician chef. Don't bury it, recycle it. Curried colon, stuffed body cavity, arterial noodles, viscera casserole."

"Great big gobs of greasy grimy gopher guts," Eileen says. "Yuck!"

Little Eddie makes a sound for every word she's said. Some of the sounds approximate syllables. He sits on the edge of speech, poised to leap off into the language community. His mother is excited at the prospect. His father is a little sad because he knows that soon the acts of affection will be replaced by the words of affection. Acts and words will be the same. For Eileen, it's no big deal. She's been having conversations with her brother for over a year now. She's been translating the world to him and passing on his wants and needs to Mary and Eddie.

"No, no, no," Mary says. "A cooking show dedicated to breakfast only. Breakfast at Eddie Ryan's."

"Great. But I think I saw the movie with Audrey Heartburn and George Paprika. How about calling it *A Man for All Seasonings*?" Eddie says.

"You could have celebrity chefs like Basil Rathbone, Curry Grant, James Garnish, Jack Lemon, Ursula Endive."

"Nut Meg."

"Jane Fondue."

"Hey, Cody," Eileen says.

Cody is standing in the doorway. The kids look forward to seeing him because his pockets are always full of Hershey bars, Snickers or Milky Ways.

"The Lion in Winter."

"Good morning," Cody says. "What are we doing?"

"Talking."

■

"I have PMS," Valentine Gordon says. "Before I menstruate I become depressed and anxious. I retain water in my hands and my feet to the point where I can't wear shoes. My joints swell. My colon goes on the fritz. I have throat problems that slur my speech. I lose my memory and say my sentences backwards. I get cold sores, migraines and boils. Rum and Coke helps. It helps a lot so I drink it a lot and will continue to do so. I just won't drive anymore. I'll work around it."

"Perhaps you could see a doctor," Mr. Nims says. "A doctor could prescribe something for your condition."

"She doesn't need a doctor," the Blond Bomber says. "She needs counseling. Maybe some flower essences and yoga. She's ashamed of her body. She needs to knit or spin wool."

"Miss Bomber, maybe that's a bit much, a bit too fast."

The Blond Bomber takes out a pen and piece of paper. She writes a number down for Valentine.

"Here, honey. The PMS hotline. 1-800-222-4PMS."

"Maybe I'll try it," she says. "It's worth a shot. We don't have any health insurance. I guess I've got to do something."

■

"You never talk about your classes, Cody. The people in them. Who are they?"

"People from Keene and other towns. No one you'd know."

Eddie wants to say he might know them, but realizes how he usually gets to know people and feels uncomfortable to know so many only through death. He decides to let it drop.

PART TWO

7

On March 20, Mrs. Huguenot dies after a long and debilitating illness. She was a lifetime member of the D.A.R. and the Ladies Auxiliary. She belonged to the P.T.A. and on more than one occasion held state office in that association. Mrs. Huguenot held a weekly tea and hosted a book talk the first Monday of each month in the fellowship room of the Universalist Church. Though she did not attend services on a regular basis, Paul was her favorite apostle and *The Dartmouth Bible* her favorite text. Every Fourth, she gave a rousing exhortation to all who assembled on the common, inciting them to accept the modern-day challenge with grace and dignity, because God knows it isn't going to get any better.

She organized the first strawberry social twenty years ago and remained a strong influence in the event throughout her life. One year she forced its cancellation because the strawberries didn't come out and she couldn't truck the notion of frozen or foreign berries.

In her secret life, she had a room filled with doohickeys, knickknacks, thingamajigs and bric-a-brac. She knew an abortionist in Troy, New York, and sometimes made the arrangements for girls too young to be in the family way. Isabel Huguenot was a very prominent member of the community, tipping the scales at five hundred pounds.

Eddie Ryan has been waiting for Mrs. Huguenot to die for almost a year. When it comes, he and his family are eating spaghetti. They always eat spaghetti on Thursday nights. When the phone rings, Eddie's passing out garlic bread. He sends the pieces like flying saucers, landing them on top of the kids' plates. He and Mary look at each other wanting one to say, Let it go. Don't answer. They'll call back. But it never gets said.

Mary picks up the phone. She holds a hand over the mouthpiece and says, "It's Rose Kennedy."

Eddie knows Mrs. Huguenot is dead when he takes the phone from Mary. He listens for a while, then hangs up.

"It's Mrs. Huguenot," he says. "She's down for the count."

"Eddie, don't forget who you are," Mary says.

"Eddie, don't forget who you are," Eileen says.

The problem is, Eddie knows who he is. He's the one who has to lay her out. He's been anticipating the task of preparing Mrs. Huguenot for her final rest. It's haunted him. Over and over in his mind he's created plan after plan and now that the time has come, he isn't quite sure how to go about his business.

His first thought is to spring Cody from his drunk school class, have him come home immediately to mastermind the project. His intimate knowledge of the simple machines—lever, pulley, inclined plane, screw and wheel—would be invaluable. His next thought is to write an article for *Dodge* magazine on how he accomplished the feat of laying out a five-hundred-pound woman, but before he does that he knows he'll have to actually do it first.

"Little Eddie, stop slurping your spaghetti," Mary says.

He looks at his mother as if she has just crawled out of the floor. He puts his fork in his mouth and his arms to his sides. He moves back in his chair, making his body quake and shiver.

"Stop being a jerk," Eileen says. "This is a time of grief. Poor Mrs. Huguenot is down for the count."

Eddie picks up the phone and calls the morgue. Little Eddie goes back to slurping his spaghetti and his sister makes faces at him.

"George, Eddie Ryan here. I'm calling about Mrs. Huguenot. Listen, George, I got one question for you. Just how debilitating was this illness?"

Eddie puts the phone down without saying good-bye.

"She debilitated about fifteen pounds, Mary. That brings her in at four hundred and eighty-five pounds. He said something about not worrying because all the weight was on the inside."

Eileen gets out of her chair and walks around the table to Little Eddie.

"Come with me," she says, and leads him off.

"Mary, four hundred and eighty-five pounds. He says we have to move her. They couldn't get her in the cooler. Maybe we could take her to Pittsburgh, cremate her in a blast furnace."

■

Raudabaugh is down at the sugarhouse when Rose Kennedy calls him. Dome, Mrs. Huguenot's husband, vested her with the responsibility of calling around. Rose is the new president of the D.A.R. She was Mrs. Huguenot's protégée. She weighs two hundred and is pushing for three. Whether Dome asked her to call round or not, she would have. She likes to talk on the phone.

Raudabaugh likes sugaring, though he doesn't go at it the way he used to when he was a younger man. He's too old to carry the yoke and buckets back into the woods. He taps a few trees along the road now, ones he can get to with his pickup truck. He's thought about switching to a pipeline but he thinks the plastic taints the sap and is convinced the squirrels would eat up his lines.

At his sugarhouse, Raudabaugh has a coffee maker, a stack of dirty magazines, a lawn chair and a telephone. He likes to fire up the boiler and cook the sap down to a grade B. It has more maple taste to it that way and fewer people want to buy it. He doesn't like people coming by.

Rose Kennedy tells him Mrs. Huguenot has died. He's saddened by the news because when he was a younger man he was sweet on her. He and Mrs. Huguenot used to go down to the sugarhouse and boil all night long. That was before the war, before Dome came along, and it was before she outgrew anything that a tentmaker could piece together.

Raudabaugh merely acknowledges the verity of Rose Kennedy's

message and hangs up the phone. He sits in his lawn chair and rests a boot on his stack of magazines. A quiet steam rises up from the pan and vents through the roof, some of it condensing on the rafters and coming back down like rain. He tries hard to see ghosts wavering in the steam's body. He tries hard to imagine it's more than just steam, but he can't. He thinks about the times when the two of them boiled late into the night. They roasted hot dogs in the flames that licked from the open door of the firebox and baked potatoes in the coals. Some nights they settled eggs into the pan to hard-boil and ate them with cider. She took up a good part of his life, the years when events get set in the mind like gold leaf. It's dull and dim now, resting dormant until some light from the present skips across in such a way as to blind out all other time.

"By Gawd," Raudabaugh says, "tonight I'm going to boil some sap like we used to."

He opens the petcock on his holding tank and floods the pan. He fishes back into the woodshed, finding pine splits so dry they *tonk* like bowling balls when clapped together. He cranks open the damper, flings back the door and rakes down the coals. The fire glows below his waist as he stirs the sap. He can feel the rivets on his overalls heat up as the steam billows to the rafters.

Raudabaugh steps outside. He pulls the flap back from his zipper and falls down in the snowbank. The steel teeth hiss when they hit the snow. Steam rises up around him. He laughs and goes back inside to throw more wood on the fire, to bring the sap to a real rolling boil for dead Isabel.

■

Thad Bushnoe pulls his cards close to his chest. He's just filled an inside straight and can't believe his luck. The other men at the table eye him. They know he has a good hand and are intent on screwing him. It's not that they don't like him, they just like putting one over on him better.

The Doody brothers look at each other and smile. They're no fun to beat at cards because they grin when they're lucky and scowl when they aren't. They run heavy equipment and it's something they're good at.

Joe Paquette rubs at his grease-blackened hands. He's a trucker and hates to lose. Whenever he does, he tells the winner he's going to kill him. He says, Goddamn you, I'm going to kill you. But he hasn't killed anyone yet.

Barkley Kennedy is the oldest one at the table. He looks at the other men, and not seeing the flicker of an idea in anyone's eye, feels it incumbent upon himself to change the rules. The question is whether to do it after everyone reveals his hand or before. Either way it doesn't matter. Thad's a young carpenter and has been so happy since they voted him fire chief, he takes pretty much whatever's dished out.

The red phone rings and Barkley snatches it off the hook. Answering the call should give him time to troll a little before he sets the hook because this is the phone the fire calls come in on.

The younger men watch Barkley. They look up to him. Since he retired from his law practice in Boston, he's settled permanently in Inverawe. He's been accepted as one of them, a distinction reserved mostly for newcomers who are at least six years dead, or so it seems.

Barkley now teaches a course in ethics at Bolton Community College and another one in fly-tying. There are rumors he takes photos of nude women, but no one ever says anything about it. They are just rumors purveyed by the small-minded, the mean-spirited and those of low birth.

"It's Mrs. Kennedy, boys. Raudabaugh's sugarhouse is on fire. She saw it from the conservatory with her telescope."

Barkley always refers to his wife as Mrs. Kennedy. Everyone jokes that he probably does it when they're alone too, and of course he does.

"Damnit," Thad says. "I knew it."

"Rotten luck, Thaddy," Joe Paquette says, flipping his cards in along with everyone else except Barkley, who holds back until last.

Thad looks at Barkley, who gently shakes his head and closes in the fan of cards he holds.

"I'm sorry, Thad," he says. "You know, I really think you had us this time."

Joe Paquette throws open the overhead door. A gust of wind blows the cards into Thad's lap. Dick Doody fires up the pumper while his brother Tom starts the Dodge Power Wagon. The other men pull on their bunker gear, pants, boots, helmets and coats.

Across the back of each one in Day-Glo green letters are the words
INVERAWE VOLUNTEERS.

Barkley passes Thad his white captain's helmet and shakes his
hand. He then hits the red button, activating the sirens on the roof,
setting them to braying in the night. The '76 1800 Loadstar International roars out the doors with Dick Doody at the wheel and up
to the common to wait for the others. Tom follows in the Power
Wagon and Thad comes behind him with the tanker. Barkley closes
the doors after them. He wants to dally because he knows Marie
Paquette will be along to man the phone and call mutual aid for
cover. He likes Marie. He thinks she has a nice unit in an artful sort
of way. But he doesn't wait long. He follows the trucks in his Volvo
with the beer. He knows the trucks will only wait a minute to warm
up, then they'll go off, the rest of the volunteers coming on their
own.

Eddie Ryan is in the embalming room when he hears the siren.
He's measuring door openings while Mary puts the finishing
touches on Clifford Manza, a farmhand for Louis Poissant who died
of a heart attack before or after he fell in the milk tank and
drowned. Either way, his death was a blessing, say people who knew
him, because he was lame, almost blind and given to forgetfulness
and kleptomania.

Mary's washing his hair and putting color in his face. Few people
will see him, but she likes to do the best she can because God knows
there isn't much you can do for people like Clifford when they're
still alive.

"I have to run," Eddie says.

"Be careful. You know I worry every time."

Eddie goes up the stairs. His gear is in the closet by the front
door. He steps into his boots and pulls up his bunker pants. He gets
his coat and helmet and goes out the door. The cold night air
strikes him more severely than if it was January, the warm days of
spring being only a deception played on you by the night.

Parked near the common, he can see the trucks, their drivers
looking at their watches, gunning the engines. Three other men
have already climbed aboard. Marie Paquette comes winging by in
the latest junker Joe has overhauled for her.

Eddie runs across the grass of the common, his boots clumping
on the ground that's frozen up again over the last few hours. He

jumps on the back of the Loadstar, cursing himself because he's forgotten his gloves.

■

Louis Poissant parks his Cadillac behind Bolton Hospital. He watches Dr. Pot from over Inverawe get into his Tercel and pull away. It was Dr. Pot who performed cardiac massage on Clifford. He insisted Louis leave the milk house, and ever since, Louis hasn't liked him for chasing him out of his own barn and not letting him back in until Clifford was stitched back together. Louis gets out, gently closes the door and lights a cigar. He pulls his wool coat tight to his neck and walks to the gray unlit steel doors. The air bites at the bare flesh between his shoe tops and the cuffs of his trousers. He's a squat man whose pant legs always seem to descend straight from his waist, moving only a shade at the knee with each stride.

Louis opens the doors and goes down the concrete steps. Beside him is a wide track with a conveyor belt. As he walks along, he's saying, *"Buffalo gals, won't you come out tonight, won't you come out tonight."*

At the foot of the stairs he opens another door. George is sitting at his desk filling out forms. Against the wall is a gurney. It's loaded down with what looks to be a mountain under a sheet.

"What the hell are you doing, bringing down six at a time?"

George lifts out of his chair, his neck disappearing into his shoulders.

"Jesus Christ, you scared me. No. That's Mrs. Huguenot. She died this afternoon."

"Good God. There's enough of her, isn't there?"

George nods his head and goes back to work. Louis walks about the room, puffing hard on his cigar to keep a good head of smoke between him and the smell of death. He says to himself, *"Won't you come out tonight, won't you come out tonight."*

Finally George drops his pen and sits back. He folds his hands and rests them on top of his belly. He's relieved to know he's done for the night unless there's an emergency. The newly dead of Inverawe, Bolton, Keene and all surrounding communities are duly logged in and waiting for a ride home.

"How long have I known you, Louis?"

"Oh, I don't know. Long enough, I guess."

"How long we been doing business?"

"Many, many years, I'd say, George. At least one."

"They've been good years too, haven't they? You're my best customer. Well sir, tonight ranks right up there with the best of them. I've got three pairs of rubber boots, two pairs of Timberlands, a pair Adidas sneakers, a pair of women's pumps and a pair of ten-and-a-half triple-D wing tips. All for you."

"Triple-D wing tips. Jesus Christ. What'd he have, webbed feet?"

"Accident last week over on the interstate. Massachusetts driver. A traveling salesman who ain't traveling no more."

"Figures," Louis says, reaching for his wallet.

"Don't it, though," George says, nodding his head.

■

The fire engine slows almost to a stop as it negotiates a hairpin turn leading up the mountain to Raudabaugh's sugarhouse. Eddie's hands have lost their feel for the stainless steel grab bar. He drops off the back and waves down the Volvo following close behind. Barkley reaches across and opens the door for him. Eddie squeezes his stiff body into the bucket seat.

"Good evening, Mr. Ryan," Barkley says.

"Good evening."

Barkley downshifts and drives in tight behind the engine. He enjoys driving the foreign car on the back roads. He likes working it through the gears, feeling it surge into the corners and flatten out on the straightaways.

"Mrs. Kennedy called to tell me about Mrs. Huguenot."

"She died?"

"Yes. You didn't know?"

"No. I have been down to the firehall all afternoon helping the boys plan a fund-raiser for a new truck. I know they were called out last week to assist in getting her to the ambulance. They had to remove the picture window and take her out with a forklift, bed and all. Real troopers, those fellows."

Eddie feels himself shrink inside his coat. For a year he's feared the job he must begin tomorrow.

"Mr. Ryan, in the back you'll find a little something to fortify you against the cold."

Eddie turns toward the back seat and when he does, his knee hits the stick and knocks the car out of gear.

"Nuts," Barkley says as the engine whines, and he gnashes gears trying to shift.

"Sorry."

"Quite all right. These cars are made to take it. Quite remarkable, they are."

Eddie pushes books and photo equipment aside and finds a six-pack. It's hard to turn in the small car. Once back around, he can see the glow in the sky from Raudabaugh's burning sugarhouse.

"You boys will have your work cut out for you tonight," Barkley says.

Eddie doesn't say anything. He watches the glow that caps the horizon. The Volvo shoots down a dip in the road and the fire all at once seems to be on top of them. Cresting the hill, they can see the pumper parked twenty feet from the stock pond. Pickups are pulling in from the top and the headlights of others are coming up behind them.

Barkley parks the Volvo behind the pumper and jumps out. Eddie reaches for the door handle but can't find it. Men are streaming past him toward the truck.

Dick Doody pushes in the clutch and slams the tranny into fifth, switching the drive from road to pump. He lets off the clutch and the pump starts turning. Joe Paquette and Thad bust ice and run the four-and-a-half-inch suction hose into the pond, the strainer floating at the end.

Eddie can see them from where he sits. He tries to crawl across the seats but he can't make it past the steering wheel. His knee knocks the car out of gear and it starts rolling backward. He thinks he's going to roll all the way down the hollow and just as that thought begins to take grip, the Volvo thuds into a truck parked behind him. It's Benware Smith's snowplow.

Benware comes up to the car and helps Eddie get out. When he sees who it is, he steps back. Eddie Ryan makes him nervous.

By now the Loadstar is turning at 1,500 RPMs. Dick Doody holds the hand throttle, looking for a sign from Thad. Joe Paquette and Tom Doody have the inch-and-three-quarter preconnect out of the hose bed and are running through the mud toward the fire. Eddie and two other men hook a three-inch line to the discharge gate while two others are running behind Joe and Tom with the nozzle end.

Inside the pump, the oil in the primer is going round and round.

Thad never watches the pressure gauges. He turns his ear to them, listening to tell the priming status. Finally a splash of discharge flushes out under the truck. Thad turns the gate slowly, waving a finger in the air, letting Dick know to wind her up another thousand RPMs.

The fire hose begins to swell out like a python sending a lamb to its tail. Joe Paquette pulls back on the nozzle lever and water shoots forth at 100 psi. The first blast busts in the windows on the north side, shoots through the sugarhouse, and busts out the windows on the south side. Seconds later Eddie and Tom Doody open up with the four-inch hose, caving in the wall. A tremendous hiss goes up from the evaporator before it topples, exposing the firebox and arch beneath it. They glow for a moment before they too are clouded in smoke and steam. Joe Paquette and Dick Doody take out the smokestack and blast the steam vent off the roof. The four-inch line takes out the opposite wall and the front corner. The roof begins to quake and sway until finally it eases itself around in a slow pirouette and then drops all at once in a great whoosh of sparks and steam.

The men shut down their lines. Dick Doody cuts back on the throttle. He turns the spotlight toward what's left of the operation. He spots the woodshed not more than ten feet away to the south of the smoldering heap.

"You saved the woodshed, Thaddy," he yells.

Thad nods his head and lights a smoke. The men around him do the same.

■

After work the nurses usually go down to the Holiday Inn in Bolton for happy hour. Mary Rooney, a nurse at Bolton Memorial, likes to meet her best friend, Mary Looney, a hairdresser and cosmetologist. They have been best friends ever since high school. In the fall they played field hockey together and in the winter they were basketball cheerleaders. Mary Rooney always changes before going down to the Holiday. She takes a shower at the hospital to clean away the smell of medicine and sickness. Today she takes an especially long one. The smell of a dead patient is on her. It's an old smell. It's all she can think of. Old, nothing else. The smell of death is singular. It has no connection in the world, no connection everyone else knows. The only word to describe it is the word *old,* as if it's a smell that comes about with age.

"So anyway, Mary, it's the Huguenot woman. There we were, her and me, all six hundred ten pounds of us, one hundred ten of which was yours truly."

"Oh, honey, you're doing so well. How much so far? It must be ten pounds now," Mary Looney says.

"Yeah, about ten. Another four and look out, Florida."

Mary Rooney and Mary Looney plan to go to Florida for Easter. They have new beach wear they bought at Jordan Marsh in Boston. They are both brunettes, but they also plan on dyeing their hair blond when they get there.

When they come back to New Hampshire, they'll tell everyone the sun bleached out their hair.

"The D.A.R. came by to see her. Whoever gets to do her up will be much pissed off."

"Why?"

"Well, as I said, the D.A.R. came through and we didn't have her teeth in, so by the time we got around to it, rigor mortis had set in. Her face was all drooped and they wouldn't fit. Whoever gets her will have to get those teeth in."

"I think that you have fascinating work," Mary Looney says. "To think that you must be aware of so many technical details. In my business, it's the look we create. The aura as they say. We attempt an illusion."

"So anyway, I get her hands and elbows and legs tied off. Next I have to get her on the cart and in a bag and I'm thinking no way in hell am I going to roll her over."

"Just like a mummy," Mary Looney says. "Handling the dead is such *old* work. It's like handling antiques."

Mary Rooney nods her head. She looks at Mary Looney.

"Is that a new hair color?"

"It's kind of coppery. What do you think?"

"I think we need some refills on these."

Mary Rooney takes the empty glasses up to the bar. She orders two more rum and Diet Cokes. Ronny Rounds, an orderly from the hospital, is at the bar.

"Hey, Mare," he says. "Who is your good-looking friend?"

"Mary Looney. We went to different schools together."

"Oh, yeah. How about introducing us?"

"You buy."

"You got a deal," Ronny says.

Mary leaves him at the bar and goes back to the table. She tells Mary Looney that Ronny Rounds is an outpatient from the eighth floor, where they keep the nut cases. She tells her he's in for marrying thirty women all over New England.

"Maybe he knows my ex. I hope they catch up with him and throw him in the nuthouse too."

Mary Looney was married for a short time to an auctioneer. He left for Connecticut after a number of people blamed him for bidding up his calls. He promised to send for her but never did. He left her with a barn full of junk that her father now uses for a garage.

"Hello, ladies," Ronny says, putting down the drinks.

"Hey, Ronny, I do want to thank you and the guys for helping me out with that whale. You should've seen it, Mary. I go get Ronny and the rest of his nutty buddies to help me with the Big One. We get her rolled up onto her side and she lets out this huge groan. What it was, was air evacuating from the lungs, but these guys all think it's her coming back so they jump away and over she goes, right on her head. Ronny here falls down and lands right on her dentures."

Mary Rooney laughs out loud, throwing her head back and grabbing her chest. Ronny looks down at his beer. His face goes red. He can feel the bruise on his rear end where the teeth got him.

"My God," Mary Looney says. "That's horrible. What did you do?"

"We got old Ronny here a tetanus shot, of course."

"No, with the woman."

"Oh, nothing more to tell. We got some more guys and loaded her on. The guys took her down to George and I had to go to emergency to help out with a guy who smashed up on the interstate. Not much we could do for him, though."

■

Louis Poissant can see the flames across the valley from the Hill Road as he makes his way home. He knows it's Raudabaugh's place, but he can't tell which building it is. Below him he can see other lights coursing the roads to Raudabaugh's. He doesn't want to go but he turns in that direction anyway. He takes a right and drops down into the valley. He pulls up at the crossroad and waits to hear the fire engine coming in his direction, but it takes too long to come so he pulls out and steps on the gas. Beside him the brook runs down to the river. The big car snakes and tails its way through the night. Louis slows, making a sharp turn onto the bridge. He clatters across, the rap of planks under his tires, and then begins the climb up the hill. Gravel kicks the skirts and spews out behind him as the Cadillac lunges over the ground like a boat on the river.

Louis crests the hill and then floats back into the hollow. The corona of flames is above him and to his left. The automatic drops a gear and powers out of the hollow. The hill is steep. He can see flames reflecting in the windows of the barn and house, quavering in each pane of glass like ferns, identical in a field.

He gets out of his car and stands there with the door open. He thinks about getting back in and leaving this place. The fire engine can now be heard in the hollow coming across the bridge. Inside the car the steering column is buzzing because he's left the key in the ignition. Down the road he can see the power lines take on the sheen of approaching lights, the lights spotting the sky. He thinks again about getting back in the Cadillac and leaving this place, until finally he starts to run toward the fire, his pant legs snapping at his shins.

■

Eddie Ryan shuts down the three-inch line. One of the men throws the nozzle over his shoulder and starts back up the knoll. The other man sits down on a rock and lights a cigarette. Eddie sees Thad coming so he waits for him. Together they walk down to what's left of the sugarhouse. They stand, looking into the black sodden mound of charred timbers. Steam starts falling back down as rain on their heads and shoulders. Bricks and steel hiss and smoke as the big drops land.

Behind them a sudden glow comes out the woodshed, swooping around their backs, laying down their shadows across the collapsed building and up against the billow of smoke. They turn, thinking there's been some flare-up, fire traveling under the ground, a hot spot come to life. Inside the shed is Raudabaugh, his face black, his clothes torn and his hair smoking. Barkley stands next to him, trimming the lantern from which the light comes. Raudabaugh is sitting on a chunk of wood, his huge hands clapped to his bony knees as if he's holding baseballs.

"Good job there, young Thaddy," he says to the fire chief. "I think you saved her from the fire."

His voice is more like the ocean than a voice. It's the sound of waves dragging themselves over sand and stone.

■

Mary Looney, Mary Rooney and Ronny Rounds are by now two sheets to the wind. Ronny Rounds is making faces. He pushes his nose up with his finger, then with the first two fingers on his other hand he pulls down on the bottoms of his eyelids. Because he's drunk he really pushes and really pulls.

"You're disgusting," Mary Rooney says. "You're already a pig without doing that shit."

Mary Looney says, "Listen to this," and then she tells a story about a man who came in for a perm.

"He was dressed to be a woman but we figured out he was a man right away because he was wearing his tits all wrong. It was just me and the Blond Bomber from the hippie radio station. She was in for a tone-up on that mop she calls hair. She says to him, 'You're a guy,' and he asks her how she knows. She says, 'Yeah, your tits are all wrong, too high on your chest.' So we have him get undressed and we show him how to wear them right. The Blond Bomber even pulls up her top to show him how she wears hers. She's got a tattoo on the left one. It was the most *bee-utiful* thing I ever saw, one of those horses with a horn. Me and the cross-dresser just stood there looking at it. I wouldn't talk this way unless I was drunk, but she let me touch it. It was so warm. It was blue and warm. I thought it would be cold for some reason but it wasn't. It was warm. I told her it looked like it hurt and she said she couldn't even feel it. I'm going to get one, I've decided, when me and Mare go to Florida. I want one I'll feel all the time, though."

When Mary Looney finishes her story, no one says anything. They look into their glasses, look at their hands. Finally Ronny Rounds speaks up.

"What about the guy dressed up like a woman?"

"Oh, he was a fake," Mary Looney says. "The Blond Bomber is standing there showing me her tattoo and we look over and this guy's getting a hard-on. I tell you, we couldn't figure out what the hell he was."

"I want to go dancing," Mary Rooney says.

The three of them carpool into town, Ronny Rounds at the wheel, Mary Looney in the middle and Mary Rooney on the outside. They go to the Flat Street Bar and by chance the Blond Bomber is playing records, playing hooky from drunk school. Her hair shoots forth from her head like a spiked wheel but more full, like a porcupine with twelve-inch quills. When she sees Mary Looney she screams into the microphone.

"Yo. Mary Looney. You white chick. Be all you is. Scar tissue is forever."

"She's so different," Mary Looney says to Mary Rooney. "Who talks like that?"

Ronny Rounds grabs Mary Looney and takes her onto the dance floor. Mary Rooney heads for the bar. She thinks, I can't take this life much longer. The words of the song go, *Dance a little closer, dance a little closer tonight.* She wraps her arms around her chest as if she's cold and stands there at the bar, turning slowly at the waist back and forth. She used to think the difference was men had lives while women had to make lives but now even that sounds like just a bunch of words in her head. She thinks again about killing herself but knows it's only something to do.

"I'm crazy over you," Ronny Rounds says into Mary Looney's hair.

"I'll bet you are," she says. "I'll just bet you are."

■

The men sit in Raudabaugh's woodshed waiting for Tom Doody to bring on the case of beer. Thad and a younger man are stowing equipment on the Loadstar.

Tom Doody yells for light and Thad hits the switch for the spot. The sudden flood of it seems to knock him down. He goes onto his back and slides the rest of the way down the knoll, the case of beer held aloft to keep it from shaking.

Raudabaugh is telling them how one minute he was bailing sap onto the flames and the next he was down for the count. He woke up in the woodshed and was able to watch the volunteers douse the conflagration.

"It's just one of those unexplained things," Dick Doody says.

"One of those paranormal events like a woman lifting a Buick to save her child."

This is sufficient explanation for the volunteers. They're tired, and for most of them their suppers sit cold on kitchen tables. They pass round the beer and Raudabaugh works up enough energy to find a jug of his best cider.

"Either way, Raudabaugh, you're in good hands. We always bring Mr. Ryan along as a kind of special service."

Everyone laughs at this, even Eddie, though he doesn't think it's funny. Being a funeral director is tough business.

"Dickie," Barkley Kennedy says to Dick Doody, "I believe there's another case of that good beer in the trunk. Be a good boy and fetch it up here."

"Yeah," Joe Paquette says, "be a good Dickie boy and fetch it up here."

■

From her darkened house, miles away, Rose Kennedy sits at the table in front of her picture window. She peers through her telescope into the star of light made by the lantern in Raudabaugh's woodshed. Without looking away she jots down the names of the volunteers in attendance. When she has them all she goes to the phone to call their wives. She wants to let them know it will be a long night.

■

Dome, Mrs. Huguenot's husband, pads about the house in his bare feet. He finds his way with a flashlight. The floor is cold but there's plenty of room to move in, the pieces of furniture being moved farther apart with the more weight, the more girth Mrs. Huguenot took on as the years went by. He sits in her chair and isn't able to rest his elbows on both chair arms at the same time. He thinks about his '42 Harley-Davidson shovelhead under wraps in the barn they use for a garage. One day soon he'll wheel it out through the big door, fill the tank from a can of gas he has, fire it up and ride off into the sun, seeking a bridge abutment with his name on it. He laughs at such a foolish thought, gets up and fills the watering can, then gives a tiny drink to each of the thirty bonsai.

When he's done he goes to his room, strips down to his undershorts, puts three hundred on the bench and starts doing reps. His skin is old and slack but underneath his muscles are like rawhide. The heavier Mrs. Huguenot got, the more weight he worked to power off his chest, the stronger he wanted to be to have the strength to love her the way she deserved to be loved, and now she's gone and died.

The bar comes down and he can't move it. He's been thinking all this stuff and forgot to watch his count, forgot to listen, forgot to feel for the one before the one where his muscles go to fatigue and now he's alone in the dark room with the bar on his chest and three hundred pounds of iron on the bar and he can't budge it.

Dome laughs and pants, straining at the weight, trying to remember the words If I don't laugh, I'll cry; but he can't get them straight. He rolls to the right, pushing the bar with his left hand, and tucking his right shoulder. He tips the weight until it flies from his grasp, flipping and embedding its far end in the floor boards.

He lies there, panting, his chest heaving and his sweat gone cold.

"Shade in the summer. Warmth in the winter. I can't live without that big woman," he says, but knows he will.

■

Louis Poissant watches the boys run milking machines back and forth to the pumping station. The girls spill feed out in front of the animals. The faster they work, the more often they speak Canuck French to each other or not at all. Louis stands in the middle of all this, but not in the way. He stinks like smoke. His shoes are blackened and his trousers muddy. His hands have been burned and now shine in the light, salved to yellow with bag balm.

He wants to light a cigar but no smoking in the barn is a rule even he obeys.

■

Mrs. Huguenot lies on the gurney, always moving. Her toes are tied and her hands are tied and her eyelids flutter against the tape that holds them shut. The tiny electrical conductions have shorted out, letting her brain begin to melt and run out her ears. She groans as air evacuates her body, strumming her throat, tickling her gums. There are stories of some sitting up, but not her. It's been years since she had a lap to go to. Lying down has lately been her thing.

Her mouth fixes, contorts and fixes again. Her teeth aren't in and they'll have to break her jaw before she lets them get back in. Her insides are on their way to slush and her blood goes the way of water, seeking its low point, seeking a way to run down her hills. She's coming out of herself wherever she can, generous with her giving before and after life.

Mrs. Huguenot lies on the gurney capacious with death while at this moment the people of Inverawe wait for morning to move them again.

8

Early in the morning Mary gets out of bed and goes to the window. Outside the world is gray wet. Banks of clouds came in the night with their load of rain and have been doling it out ever since. Behind her in the bed is her husband. He came home from the fire soaking cold, half drunk, stinking of smoke and horny. She wanted to be his lover but it was a pretty big bill to fill. She helped as much as she could but he finally fell asleep still smoky and soft in her hand.

Somewhere along the way she became filled with expectation so she went into the bathroom, turned on the radio and brought herself off listening to Roy Orbison sing "Pretty Woman."

Clifford Manza comes into her mind. Last night she washed his hair and put color into his slack and sunken face. She doesn't want his face in her head right now, but of late it's been a long list of dead men and drunk men. After Roy Orbison stopped singing, it was Clifford she thought of.

She crosses her arms and sighs. She wonders who she is and then smiles because it's such a dumb question. She knows who she is. She's a mother and a wife and a partner in this business. Odd, she thinks, how the list came to her in that order. It's his own fault he's second. If he'd been a little less drunk last night he could have starred out at number one, her number-one man. She's thirty and it's as if all she wants at times is his hands on her.

All she wants is his hands on her hind end, pulling her skirt up over it, or his hands sliding up her rib cage to the sides of her breasts, making her wet in the mouth, under her arms and between her legs.

Clifford Manza comes into her mind again and she knows she'll have to work harder to keep the dead in the basement, in the living room, in the church and in the ground. It's not Clifford at all. It's this ghostly season of winter into spring. She's on her third one in Inverawe and this is the first to tax her resolve.

She decides she'll be more of a woman. She'll fill herself with life so there won't be room for the dead faces. She's not sure how she'll go about it, but for now the idea of it is enough to sustain her.

She drops her nightgown there at the window, stands in her long johns feeling the cold of the room on her skin. It flirts with the blood in her veins, mottling her skin and making her nipples stand erect. She decides it's best the children always come first. It's the most human, most civilized notion a body can have. She catches herself on this. It's strange how what's come to be civilizing for humans is the sole reason to live for all other animals. Number one, she thinks, become less civilized and more instinctual.

She goes into the bathroom to pee, but doesn't. She only sits there, her long johns bunched at her ankles, and she thinks about her children and her husband. She feels herself rising, coming on like gangbusters in the life of this day.

When the babies got made, she and Eddie picked the days to do it. It's a secret she keeps because so many of her friends have had problems conceiving. But not her. She picked each day, told him tonight's the night and they made a party of it.

She kicks off her long johns and opens her legs a little. She touches herself again, the way she did last night. She imagines her fingers are a tongue. She watches herself in the mirrored tile on the bathroom walls. She likes what she sees and feels.

Downstairs the phone is ringing. She curses and steps into her long johns, skinning them up over her hips, and then goes for the phone. Cody is at the breakfast table eating cornflakes with the kids, but she doesn't see him in time. She lifts up the phone, says hello and gasps.

The kids laugh and Cody goes red as she ducks back into the hall to get out of their view.

"Mrs. Ryan. This is Dome. She wants to be buried with the goddamn squirrel."

"The squirrel?"

"Yeah. The goddamn squirrel that holds the ashtray."

"That will be fine, Mr. Huguenot."

"Name's not Mr. Huguenot. Name's Dome."

"That will be fine, Dome."

Mrs. Huguenot ran over a squirrel once. It had to have been retarded, people said, because she never drove more than thirty-five miles per hour her whole life. It was her way to lumber down the highway, piloting her wide-body Ford Crown Victoria over the frost heaves in winter and the muddy roads of springtime, rippled like corduroy, roads that turned hard as boiler plate in the summer and even harder in the fall when the frost began climbing into the ground. On the back of her car it said, I BRAKE FOR ANIMALS.

Hitting the squirrel was one of those moments that draws focus on the life in time. All people have such moments that bring about an abrupt end to what came before. All moments collide into that moment, freight cars turned to accordions. Time gets fixed and all else becomes known as either before the time or after the time.

"She pulled over beside the road and collected up the animal in her white handkerchief. She laid it on the seat beside her and headed straightway home. The next day she shipped it to a man in Georgia and a week later it came back holding an ashtray."

"That's fine, Dome. I'll tell my husband."

"We don't smoke in the house anymore. I told her to take out the ashtray and give it a bowl of nuts to hold. It'll look like a joke. It'll look like the little S.O.B. is stealing them."

"That's a sweet story, Dome. I'll tell my husband."

"She said to me, 'Harumpf, tonight you'll sleep on the divan.' 'Good,' I says, 'the little pisspot can feed me cashews.' "

"I'll tell my husband."

"Okay. I just wanted you to know."

Mary reaches around the corner to hang up the phone. As soon as she does it rings again. Joe Paquette can't get in with the Doodys' backhoe to dig Clifford Manza's grave. It's been raining too much.

"I go in there in this weather with the frost still in the ground, I'll skin up the sod everywhere I go."

"You've got to, Joe. That funeral is this afternoon. You've got to get in there now."

"No can do. Just have to keep him on ice."

Mary hangs up. She doesn't like talking to Joe Paquette when she's bare-chested. He gives her the creeps. She goes back upstairs and shakes Eddie awake.

"Come on, lover. You've had enough beauty sleep. You've got a full day ahead of you."

She gets Eddie into the shower and turns it on. The pipes bang and the water hisses, going from too cold to too hot to not so bad.

Mary sits on the toilet seat and tells him how he has to pick up Mrs. Huguenot, dig a grave for Clifford Manza because Joe Paquette can't, get Clifford to the cemetery, put him in the ground, embalm Mrs. Huguenot and get a grave dug for her. Probably two graves.

"And finish what you started last night. No special order. Just don't make me wait too long or I'll take my love to town."

"Cody," Eddie yells, causing Mary to jump and go for a robe.

While Mary gets Eileen off to school, Eddie and Cody sit with Clifford Manza.

"How was class last night? Didn't get caught driving, did you?"

"Fine," Cody says. "One of the guys brought in his recipe for home brew. The psychologist let him write it up on the blackboard and we all copied it down. Have you heard of this PMS stuff that women get? They get it right around their time of the month and sometimes it raises all kinds of hell with them."

"Yes. I've read about it. Why?"

"Awhile back one of the women said she drank because of her PMS."

Mary comes into the living room.

"Don't want to be telling you two your business, but you better shag ass." She smiles and goes back down the hall to the kitchen.

"Boy," Eddie says, "something's got her all cranked up today. Something's up. Something's gotten into her. She even looks different."

Cody shrugs, then says, "I heard you got tore up a little bit last night. You and the volunteers."

"Cody, it's a little desperate for the business right now, schedule-wise. I have to get a grave dug for this old fellow by noon today. I have to pick up Mrs. Huguenot and prepare her. Just a whole list. Can you help? I'll pay you extra from our cordwood deal."

"Pay me? Shit. I eat your food. Me and the machines and the horse sleep on your land. Sometimes you are really stupid. I'll get your grave dug. You be there in twenty minutes to show me where."

Cody gets up and leaves the house, slamming doors. Mary comes back in the living room.

"What did you say to him?"

"Why?"

"He took Little Eddie and left. He seemed pretty pissed off. Said he was going for a ride."

"Nothing. What are you wearing?"

Mary twirls in her denim mini-skirt and blue tights. She smooths down the front of her sweater, smiles and leaves the room. Eddie thinks how long twenty minutes is and how much two people can accomplish in that amount of time. He tells Clifford he'll be back in a little and heads for the kitchen.

"Come here," he says to her, "I've got something for you."

■

Eddie parks the hearse outside the walls of the cemetery. Cody and Little Eddie are already there, sitting in the cab of a backhoe, its yellow paint blistered and spattered with shit.

"Where'd you get this?"

"Just show me where and what."

Eddie goes back to the hearse and gets a tube of white carpenter's chalk and a shovel. He motions for Cody to follow and he does, driving slowly behind.

The cemetery is the oldest in town. The earliest marker is Erasmus Elbridge. He died September 2, 1732, the very second he got shot in the temple when his best dog went to step over his .50 caliber Brown Bess and touched it off, a hell of a way to go when you're taking a leak in the woods.

Erasmus missed the big war, the Revolution, but he shares the ground with twenty-eight who didn't.

Eddie goes west down the lane flanked on both sides by tall thick round top stones. Old cemeteries are some of his favorite places on earth, especially this one. When he has the time he comes to read the stones and imagine the lives. He can track the history of the country here, the wars of the nation, all of them. The diseases: influenza, typhoid, measles, polio. All the young women who died giving birth to the children of old men. The man who bet he could eat a pound of raisins and won the bet, but died of the consequences. The woman stabbed and scalped by the Saint Francis Indians, her hair bountied to the French. The Navy veteran of 1812 whose stone is now wrapped in the trunk of an elm. The ones who died from too much heart or not enough.

Eddie stops near the back wall where the land falls off through the trees, a thousand feet over a half mile to the river. He chalks out a rectangle from east to west, points out the side for the dirt and motions for Cody to follow on, leaving the spot where Clifford Manza will live out the rest of his death beside his wives.

They bear right and continue down the lane to a wide terrace. These are the Huguenot plots, two for her and one for him when he's ready. She'll have a beautiful three-state view. Eddie chalks out the two for her, then goes to the hoe.

"He be all right with you or do you want me to take him?"

"He's fine," Cody says, tickling the boy through his down jacket.

Little Eddie kees and bounces on Cody's lap.

"There's tarps in the shed for the dirt. Cut the sod out and stack it as best you can. I don't know why Paquette couldn't do this. This ground's okay. Go twelve feet on this one. We have to pour concrete. I couldn't get a vault big enough. I'll have Mary drop by with a Thermos and some sandwiches. She can take him home then. He'll probably be ready to go."

They nod at each other, their lips drawn tight, then Eddie turns and goes up the lane. He gets in the hearse and leaves.

Eddie finds the Doody brothers out at the Creamery. It's under new ownership and they've been contracted to build some kind of animal park out of what used to be the driving range. At the moment it's turned back into a swamp and there's nothing they can do.

Half their equipment is stuck and the other half is broken down, except for their backhoe sitting on the lowboy waiting for Joe Paquette.

Dick Doody gives Eddie a cup of coffee and explains how Joe got in a fight with Marie last night and that's the reason he didn't dig the grave, the reason he dusted. He tells Eddie they got left high and dry by him too.

"More like deep and wet," Tom says.

"Fuck it," Dick says. "I'll get right over and dig those graves for you."

Eddie explains how Cody is already doing it.

"Where'd he get a hoe?"

"I don't know, but it's under control."

"We want to talk to him about that Cat and his skidder," Tom Doody says. "We'd like to make him an offer. His lowboy too. We used to move him and Trimble's operation about every six months. What'd Trimble do anyways, sell out to him?"

Dick tells his brother to shut up. He tells him it isn't any of his business. Eddie's relieved. It's the first time he's been confronted with the need for an explanation.

"Can you guys lend me a hand?" he says, needing to change the conversation.

"You said something about it last night," Tom says. "Me and Dick been talking it over. No way in hell you're going to get her in your hearse. Don't worry, though. We've got it all figured out."

■

Eddie Ryan rides in the middle between Dick and Tom Doody as the ten-wheeler pounds over the asphalt toward his home, the funeral home. Dick makes wide turns to keep the lowboy that trails behind off the berm and on the highway.

For Dick, driving is a full-body activity. He double-clutches, hitting the gas and snapping in the two-speed axle. The mirror is never adjusted to his satisfaction and all the while a Styrofoam cup half full of coffee rides his hand.

Behind them is the lowboy and strapped to its bed is a box constructed from five sheets of three-quarter-inch plywood. Inside is Mrs. Huguenot, enjoying the ride of her death.

"We nailed it up last night," Tom says. "First we framed and spiked the sheet down to those ten-foot four-bys. Then we nailed up the top section so it fits like a lid with the sides attached. Dick got a new watch the other day, a Timex, and that's how the box was it came in. That's how we got the idea. She was a great lady. I'll tell you that. She gave us our start. It's the least we can do."

Dick pulls into Eddie's driveway. The rest of the volunteer firemen are there waiting to help—Thad, Barkley, Benware Smith, Raudabaugh and even Mr. Washburn, who owns the general store. Mary and Little Eddie are there too.

"People just started showing up," she says. "Thad brought the limousine back from the Creamery. Said he thought we'd need a hand. Then one by one they all showed up. Barkley is so sweet. A lech, but sweet."

It is a small town, Eddie thinks, as his heart fills his chest. At one time or another over the last three years, all of these men had assisted as bearers. They'd ridden with him to pick up the dead. They'd helped him get them down the narrow stairs to the embalming room and then back out again. He wishes Cody were here to see this and not off alone digging graves in the gray wet of the morning. He wishes Cody were here to see the town at work.

Already the Doodys have unstrapped the box and the men are taking positions on the four-by skids, each man needing to bear a hundred pounds of wood and woman. They march across the sloppy ground and skid her down the stairs and into the embalming room, where they set her on a casket truck alongside the table. Then they dismantle the box and get her onto the table still in her bag.

"If you could help me with Clifford Manza, I'd appreciate it," Eddie says.

The men carry Clifford to the limousine. They all agree to come back tomorrow to help move her upstairs and again the next day to get her to the funeral.

"Thank you," Eddie says. "You're all great friends."

They smile and wave him off. They tell him he'd do the same for them and then laugh as they think how silly an idea that is.

"Good-bye," they say, and leave, Dick and Tom back to the swamp, Mr. Washburn to his store, Thad to the house he's building, Benware to the state shed and Barkley back to Rose and retirement.

Not a soul had come by to see Clifford Manza. There was to be no funeral, just calling hours and a graveside service to be conducted by the family of the man he worked for, Louis Poissant. It would be in the rain.

But Eddie isn't sad. He slipped a little note into Clifford's pocket, a tanka of sorts. The second line was Osteomyelitis and the last line was Milk is good for you. When Eddie gets there, Cody is nowhere to be found. The graves are dug but Cody and the hoe are gone. Louis Poissant and his family are waiting in the Cadillac. Eddie pulls the hearse in and shuts down the engine. Kids, young people, come pouring out of Louis's car. They're the kind of kids who look like they've been rained on all their lives so Eddie doesn't mention the wet or worry about it with umbrellas, though he's brought a dozen.

There's a woman with the kids. She's kind of stepmother to them all, like Wendy was to the Lost Boys. Eddie figures it's one of those patched-together families, a raft of kids and a youngish sort of woman.

Many hands lift. Small and big feet shuffle over the wet ground and the pine casket is deposited over the lowering device. No one speaks. There's only the scuffing of boots, all kinds of boots, even different kinds on the same kid, and the sniffling of noses. Eddie introduces himself to the woman. He learns her name is Kay and that she'll be doing a reading.

"Should we wait for Mr. Poissant?"

"No way," one of the boys says. "He's still pissed about losing that tank of milk Clifford drowned in."

Kay steps up and reads from the Bible. She reads Ecclesiastes 3:1–9, John 11, and Luke 6:17–49. She then closes her Bible and tells them to say good-bye to Mr. Manza and they do.

"Okay, Mr. Ryan, you can lower away. Get your shovels, boys."

The boys go to the car and Louis pops the trunk. When they get back to the mound, the earth commences to fly.

"He wanted me to remind you that when you do up the bill, not to forget the rental of his hoe today."

Eddie nods his head as the boys lay in the sod and then head for the Cadillac with Kay behind them, herding them along.

■

Eddie sits in the embalming room with the five-hundred-pound naked woman. She's hanging over the edges of the table at least six inches on each side and her belly rises at least two feet toward the ceiling. The skin of her chest has slipped to cover her neck, chin and lips. Her face is more black than blue and her arms look more like flippers.

There's a knock at the door. It's Cody.

"No time like now to learn how to assist," Eddie says.

Cody doesn't say anything. He only shakes his head and whistles.

"What the fuck," he finally goes.

"First. Gloves, scrub suit, shoe covers, hats and masks and aprons."

Eddie hands out the necessary protective clothing to Cody. He explains how it's needed because of possible infectious diseases: herpes, hepatitis, measles, rubella, meningitis, the syph, clap, chlamydia, AIDS. Typhus from the *Pediculus humanus corporis,* more commonly known as body lice. "To name a few," Eddie says.

"Should I be here?"

"Consider yourself a member of the funeral staff. Cross your heart and hope to die."

"Sometimes I don't understand you."

Eddie looks at his friend. He's glad they're wearing masks, because right now he's not too steady. He wants to say, Be here with me, see what I do, tell me why I feel so fucked up when I should feel good.

"Get that hose. Make the water tepid. Too hot the blood will coagulate. We first must wash the body."

"That's two firsts."

"I got a flier the other day from the Memorial Star Registry. They match the name of a dead person with a previously unnamed visible star. It then gets recorded in the International Star Registry and the family receives a parchment certificate, two sky charts and the booklet 'Our Place in the Cosmos.'"

"My mother told me that before I was born I was just a star twinkling in the sky."

"My mother told me I was a twinkle in my father's eye."

"I think there's something to it," Cody says. "I like that idea. I think I'll have a star named for G.R."

"That would be nice, Cody."

It's been a long time since Cody has mentioned G.R.'s name. Eddie is happy. He thinks, What the hell, if the Star Registry will help, why not?

"Did I ever tell you I keep a journal?"

With the masks and caps, Cody thinks Eddie said urinal. It's the way it goes. Every time he gets a fix on his friend, he comes up with something out of left field.

"Why no, you didn't. Where do you keep it?"

"Upstairs in my room. You should consider it. It's a way of documenting your daily feelings, your moods and thoughts."

Cody finally connects with what Eddie is saying. He thinks about the brown-covered notebook Mr. Nims passed out in drunk school. He wrote some words in his he copied off the board, *alcohol is a drug, a powerful addictive drug.* The rest of the book is blank. He likes it that way, white and clear with thin blue lines.

When they finish washing Mrs. Huguenot, Eddie disinfects her nose and mouth.

"If she had any whiskers we'd have to shave them, but she doesn't so she's okay. Now watch carefully."

Without saying anything more, Eddie cracks her jaw so her dentures will fit. When they're in, he sutures her mouth shut. He swabs her eyes, applies Vaseline to them and gently closes them.

"Good night, old girl," he says, as if for him that's the final rest.

Eddie then coats her face with cream, while explaining to Cody how they must position the body for embalming and how important that is. They work silently blocking her shoulders, elbows, heels and buttocks. They elevate her head and tape her breasts in the proper position.

Eddie clamps the hose to the table and turns on the water. He next makes an incision in Mrs. Huguenot's neck, raising first her jugular vein and then her carotid artery. He inserts a cannula into the artery and a drain tube in the vein, clamping them in place, then starts up the embalming machine, pumping twelve gallons of one percent arterial solution of formaldehyde through her body while he and Cody massage and flex her. Her blood comes out still warm after all these hours of death.

When the injection is done Eddie removes the tubes, ligates the vessels and sutures the incision. He shows Cody how to clean the machine.

While Cody is doing that, Eddie stands on a chair and aspirates her body cavity. Then he injects two bottles of cavity fluid and buttons up the trocar incision.

"We have to disinfect and sterilize all of this. She has a hair-

dresser coming in the morning to do her hair and then Mary will
do the cosmetics. We have to casket her and get her upstairs,
something I can't face right now."

■

Eddie slips into bed behind Mary. He gets his arms around her and
his tongue in her ear. She's wearing something small, satiny and
black.

"I almost couldn't wait," she whispers.

"You have been insatiable lately."

"I know. Hurry up. I want you inside me now."

Later, when the room is full dark and the sweat has gone cold on
their bodies, Mary gets out of bed and puts on her flannel nightgown. She whispers to Eddie that all the arrangements have been
made for the next two days. He only has to be present and smile
sincerely.

"You know," she says, "it was the longest obituary I ever went
to call in. Seems as though her and the editor were old buddies. He
took over the phone and told me he and Mrs. Huguenot had already written it."

"Something strange is going on," Eddie says. "Every step of the
way, it's like she was there first, making the arrangements."

"I know."

Mary gets back in bed and he pulls her to him. She works her hind
end into his crotch, her back against his chest.

"Mary," he whispers, "do you know anything about this PMS
stuff?"

"Yes. I know all about it. I've got it a little bit. I'm convinced.
Now go to sleep."

■

Cody jounces over the dark roads riding the hoe. The one head-
light it has left is wired to its post, where it bobs and rattles, its
sound unheard under the knock of the diesel.

He passes the County Farm, goes out the River Road and follows
it along the mountain. He makes the turn onto Louis Poissant's
drive. It seems to go forever until he reaches the farm.

The house is dark but there's a light on inside the barn. Louis's
there standing at the veal pens, letting a calf suck at his fingers.

"What do I owe you for the use of your hoe?"

"I wouldn't worry about it. One hand washes the other."

"Fair enough."

Cody rests his elbows on a pen and lets his hands drape over. A calf takes his fingers into its mouth and sucks on them.

"Kay in the house?" he asks.

"I imagine so."

"She doing okay?"

"Doing fine since she moved over from Winchester. Says she likes it better where nobody knows her."

Cody turns and leaves. As he goes out the barn door he looks at the immense dark house where Louis Poissant's tribe is asleep in their beds. He tries to figure out which window is Kay's but it's only something to think about. He gets in his truck and leaves.

■

That night Eddie dreams he's a little boy and it's Saturday morning, time to get up and watch cartoons. His mother and father are still in bed so he goes down the stairs quietly. At the bottom he's in his own house and Mrs. Huguenot is there in her casket. It's a house trailer with the roof peeled back, rolled up on a key like a sardine can. Eileen is there. She's rouged Mrs. Huguenot's cheeks to a high gloss and spread lipstick around her mouth.

She's saying, "My, what big teeth you have."

Eddie comes out of his sleep and sits up. He tells himself the dream is God getting even with him for being a fuck-up. It's the only thing he can think of. He records the dream in his journal, goes downstairs and pours himself a shot to numb out. He sees the cellar door is open and the light is on. He goes down those stairs too, telling himself with each step it can't be his dream come true, but the coincidence doesn't escape him.

Cody is inside the embalming room. He's leaning against the wall looking at Mrs. Huguenot.

"Cody, you shouldn't be in here," he says.

"I was thinking how happy I was that I did what I did with G.R. I don't know why. I just can't imagine him being worked on this way."

"For some, it seems to help."

Eddie holds a hand to his nose and mouth. The odor of formaldehyde seems stronger than it should be.

"I'd rather you said it was just a job you do."

"How the hell am I supposed to know the right words all the time? Sometimes I think I'm just wandering through like the next guy."

Cody stands straight. He wants to say Kay's name. He takes one last look at Mrs. Huguenot and leaves the room, leaves the house, shutting off lights and closing doors as he goes. For Eddie it's a blackout brought on as if by shelling. No electricity, no light, only the smell of burning and cordite and the suffocating odor of form-aldehyde. He stays in the dark a few feet away from the fat woman on the table. He stays in the cold dark until he begins to sweat, begins to lose his balance.

The formaldehyde becomes all he can smell. He turns on the light to find cavity fluid pooled on the table, surrounding the fat woman's buttocks. It leaked through the intestinal wall and left her body. He shakes his head, says, "The hell with it," and gives up for the night.

9

Eddie comes out of bed like a bolt shot from a gun when he hears
Eileen fall down the stairs. Naked, he goes down, taking two and
three at a time. She's sitting on the floor rubbing her head, bawling
her eyes out.

He snatches her up and holds her. His first impulse is to rub her
head for her but he thinks how dumb that is. Instead, he holds her
to him and sways, telling her it's all right.

"Is she okay?"

It's Mary at the top of the stairs, afraid to come down at this
moment. She won't tell, but she's convinced it's her fault. When she
was six months pregnant with Eileen, she slipped and went down
on her behind, ticking off each tread with her tailbone until she hit
bottom. Eddie was painting a house in Syracuse at the time. She
called and made him come home. For a week after that, she couldn't
sit. Every morning and night he described the colors in the bruise
before he went off to paint, leaving her alone because they needed
the money. She hasn't been comfortable around stairs since.

Later she went into premature contractions and had to be in bed for the rest of her pregnancy. She blames herself now for every fall the girl takes, for every trip, even though she knows it's silly.

"Bring her up. Bring her up here."

Eddie carries his daughter up the stairs. Every time he holds her he can't get over how long she's getting, how her feet and hands have become thin and fine, how much she's gotten to be like her mother.

"I hit my head," she snuffles into his neck.

"You'll be okay. I'm worried about the stairs," he says, "I hope you didn't break them."

"Daddy, how could I break the stairs?"

He doesn't answer. As he makes the top step he goes to hand her over to her mother but the girl grips his neck. He carries her into the bedroom and puts her in the covers. Mary gets in with her while Eddie pulls on some long johns.

"Were you going to go pee?" Mary asks. "You should have used our bathroom."

"Your door was closed."

Eddie gets into bed with them. He tickles Eileen and then Mary. They both tell him to stop it.

"I think I was going to pee, but I might have been dreaming."

"It's hard being a kid," Mary says.

"I hit my head once when I was a kid," Eddie says. "My father had a wooden cabinet in the basement. He kept his home brew there. His home brew, his empty bottles, his caps and his capper. I was riding my bicycle around the stairs. I was going like hell too. Around and around. If you went off the track you were a goner. You'd hit the oil tank or the furnace or a jack post or something. So there I am, going faster and faster and bang, right into the corner of that cabinet. Blood all over. And you know what? I saw stars, real stars. They were blue and red and silver and gold. They twinkled. They were three-pointed and four-pointed and five-pointed. It was beautiful."

Eileen thinks about this for a while.

"You know what I saw?" she says.

"No, what?"

"I saw hot dogs with catsup."

"You did not."

"Yep. Hot dogs. Mom, do I have to go to school today?"

"Yes, I think you have to go to school today. Tonight during calling hours, you, me and your brother are going out to dinner and a movie. Then tomorrow you can stay home for Mrs. Huguenot's funeral."

"My class is going to the funeral."

"Who says?"

"Miss Germaine. She says the whole school is going."

"Jesus Christ," Eddie says. "Where's it end?"

Mary reaches over and touches her husband. She's smiling.

"I'm starting to like this," she says. "I think it's wonderful the way the whole town is being."

Little Eddie yells from his room. The second floor is awake and ready for the morning.

Mary Looney and Cody are in the kitchen drinking coffee when the Ryan family comes trooping in. Mary is here to do Mrs. Huguenot's hair. Cody and Little Eddie will go to Keene to pick up the casket. His driver's license came yesterday so now he's legal to drive a set course, what's known as to and from work. He has his last class next week and if he graduates he'll get his real license back, a license to travel.

Eddie is bound for Rose Kennedy's house. She'll fill Eddie in on the rest of the details for the funeral, tell him where he has to be and when. At the last minute they decide Eileen can play hooky and go with her father and of a sudden the house is quiet and it's only Mary Ryan and Mary Looney alone with their coffee cups.

"Have you done this before?"

"No, and I'm really kind of nervous."

"Don't worry, I'll be there with you the whole time. When you're ready we can go down and get started."

Mary Looney picks up her kit and the two women go down the stairs to the room where Mrs. Huguenot is staying. Mary anticipates Mary Looney's sharp intake of breath, her hesitancy, her faint movement back toward the door. She takes her by the hand and leads her to the body.

"There, now we're over that," she says, knowing it's not true but convinced it's the best way to go. She leads Mary to a cabinet and takes out blue meds for both of them. The women dress in the gowns and aprons, then go back to the body.

"She wanted her hair to be down and spread out. She wanted it white."

Mary unblocks Mrs. Huguenot's head and lets it rest down on the table, lower than the rest of her body. She then unknots the woman's hair and draws it back.

Mary Looney steps in with a comb. She begins at the end and works her way slowly up to the scalp.

She gains courage as she goes. It makes her careful and tender. She uses a blue rinse on the hair. She pours it into the hair, catches it in a pan and repours it. As she does this it becomes snowy white. When she's done she blows it dry, all the while combing and combing.

"What we have to do now," Mary says, "is replace her color, conceal discoloration, and I like to make them pretty. I like to do that most of all. Make them pretty and handsome. I used to go overboard."

"What the hell," Mary Looney says, "I think it's a nice thought. I'll tell you who can do makeup is Kay Poissant. Any girls who know the business, learned it from Kay. She went to beauty school."

Mary assembles what she'll need on a tray.

"In Greece this has always been the women's job," she says.

"Hey, you're telling me," Mary Looney says, "we always get the shit work. But you know, who else could do it?"

"It was the women's job to anoint the body with oils and perfumes and spices. It was a sacred duty. She's an easy one," Mary Ryan says. "Sometimes the blood infiltrates the underlying skin from, say, bruises. Sometimes the blood just pools."

Mary closes her eyes and touches Mrs. Huguenot's face. She feels the slack skin for muscle and bone. She does it again. This time with her eyes open.

"Usually I do cosmetics after we get the body up the stairs, but Eddie is going to need help and wants it done. He has this lift but he isn't sure it's strong enough."

"My God," Mary Looney says. "I just realized what you see."

The two women look at each other and lists go through their heads: gunshot, child abuse, head-on collision, laceration.

"Come now," Mary says. "Cheer up. Spit spat."

It's something she heard Mary Poppins say. It seems to say it all. From the tray Mary takes a bottle marked Suntan. She shakes it, then unscrews the cap and lets a drop onto her finger. She puts it on Mrs. Huguenot's skin and works it in with her other three fingers. She does her forehead, feathering the blended color up and down, letting it fade at the hairline and eyebrows. With a beige she highlights the plane of the cheek. She then reddens the ears, nose and chin. She rouges the cheeks and then the lips with a lipbrush.

The eyes are next. She shadows the lids, spreading the color with her finger, and then lines the lashes.

"We have to powder her now."

When Mary finishes, she shows Mary Looney how to do the final grooming. She gently swabs Mrs. Huguenot's hairline with cotton wrapped around the end of a hemostat. She uses an eyebrow pencil to remove traces of cosmetic from her brows and lashes. She lets Mary Looney try it, then hands her some white shoe polish and a toothbrush and tells her how to do the touch-up.

"Oh, Mary," she says. "Her hair is gorgeous. You really do have a talent."

"Thanks," Mary Looney says. She knows it's not all that special but she likes Mary for telling her it is.

■

Mrs. Huguenot lies in state, ready to receive visitors. Eddie is pleased the first floor of the house has this double function. Used to be everything took place in the home back in the used-to-be days. The undertaker traveled with a cooling board and his tool kit. Door badges were attached to the knocker to indicate death, a rosette and ribbon, black for the old, white for the children and black and white for the in-betweens.

It was in the days when death still played tricks on the living. Death was vague, often indifferent. It seemed to come and go for no good reason. Bodies needed wakes, long delays just in case it was only a sleeping death. And sometimes it was. Sometimes bodies shrugged off death; men, women and children would sit up, then stand and speak to those assembled. It's nice when this can happen at home.

". . . Yeah, the whole fuckin' state of New Hampshire," the Blond Bomber whispers.

"Well," Mary Looney says, "I told you she was one big goddamn woman."

"Can we go? I already told you I think her hair looks divine."

"Yes."

The volunteers come with their wives, but again no Joe Paquette. He's off on a ten-day run, ferrying hay from Canada to Maryland. It's a job he takes whenever he and Marie fight.

Dome sits in a straight-backed chair, his arms folded, his cuffs and collar starched to points. Marie Paquette dotes on him. She kept house for Mrs. Huguenot. Working out the kinks in her marriage to Joe was Mrs. Huguenot's last project, one she didn't get a chance to finish. Marie was like a daughter to her.

Freddy Clough from drunk school shows up. He's brought two gallons of hard cider, something he's never without. Cody is pleased to see him. They are two of only three in drunk school who have yet to tell their stories. Larry Fish is the third.

He and Cody sit on the back porch sipping. Freddy's known Mrs. Huguenot ever since she was a young woman summering on the lake.

"We had a rumrunner, the Diamond Reo. My grandfather ran it on Lake Ontario, then brought it back to New Hampshire. I'd take her out in it for a jaunt around the lake.

"She was a looker," Freddy says. "She had a set of gams that'd bring tears to your eyes and a rack of tits you could rest a beer on. Then she turned into a tub, a real whale. Boy, even then she was beautiful. I can still see her, though, stepping over the gunwale with that long right leg. Jesus Christ."

Freddy says this as if he's dreaming, amazed by the vision of that leg. He warns Cody he'd better come up with a good story to tell Nims and Hurley, something up close and personal as the saying goes, or they won't graduate him.

"I just come from Larry Fish's house. He's sitting there sucking on his bottle of Seagram's. He thinks it's all bullshit, but I told him he's got to play along or they'll send him to counseling. Once those fuckers get their hooks into your brainpan, you're dead fucking meat. The two young snots are headed down the river of no return. They'll get sprung, but they'll have a hard row to hoe."

"What are you going to do?"

"I want to tell about the only girl I ever loved but I'll probably tell a different lie."

Eddie is happy to have his house filled with the bereaved. The dead are where he lives. In a way it makes his house churchlike, the place of ritual and pageantry. The poet in him thinks of the irony inherent in all of this and his good feelings begin to diminish, to slip away into that old feeling of ambiguity and inertia, the nothingness of indecision.

Barkley Kennedy sidles up to him, a glass of punch in his hand.

"Mind if I ask, just what did the old girl weigh in at?"

"The same," Eddie says. "People die without any material weight reduction. Viscera are not removed. One fluid is exchanged for another."

"Forgive me, Mr. Ryan, but on such occasions I'm moved and right now I'm moved to say I think you are an asset to this community. You bring together the history of your profession from the Egyptian surgeon forward. It's more, though. You've taken a place in this life."

"I thank you. But I'm just doing my job."

Barkley's face goes red. He gets up close to Eddie.

"Well, at least you don't steal from the living or the dead," he hisses, then walks away.

For Eddie it's the final piece in the puzzle. The early retirement of his predecessor, the good terms on the loan he received to buy the business, Mrs. Huguenot acting as agent. The guy must have been stealing from these people.

He shakes his head and wishes Mary were here so he could tell her what he just figured out.

Barkley goes onto the back porch for a refill. He thinks Freddy Clough is a charming man.

Althea Hall and Miss Germaine show up, two teachers from the elementary school. Miss Germaine thinks Eddie is cute. She tells this to Althea Hall, who tells her to mind her manners.

Mary Rooney and Ronny Rounds come by. So does George from the morgue and Dr. Pot, the town's general practitioner. Rose Kennedy plays hostess, taking around the register. She's in love with the flowers, cut roses, azaleas, chrysanthemums, and clusters of evergreen, the delicate turnings of the smilax.

The first floor fills with people. Mary Looney and the Blond Bomber try to leave by way of the back door. They take a sip from Freddy's jug and decide to stay a moment longer.

Rose puts a tape in the stereo. It's one she made at Mrs. Huguenot's request. "Lead Kindly Light," "Abide with Me," "Thy Will Be Done," "Over the Stars There Is Rest." It's the singing of Willie Nelson, Merle Haggard and Patsy Cline. There's also Bill Morrissey singing about a woman named Molly and Richard Ward singing, "It's So Easy to Pretend with You."

"Miss Bomber," Barkley says, "have you ever considered modeling?"

■

That night after seeing *Bambi,* Eileen has the first hot fudge sundae of her life. She thinks she's died and gone to heaven. Mary drinks a Sanka while Little Eddie sleeps on the seat beside her. He made it through the movie, but now he's done for.

"What was your favorite part?" Mary says.

"My favorite part was when Flower said, 'Who is that and why is he staring at me?' And Flower's mother said, 'He is your father. He is very brave and wise.' "

"I don't remember that part."

"It wasn't in the movie, but it's in the book."

"Oh."

"Mom, sometimes I wish I had a sister instead of a brother."

"I think all women wish they had a sister and I think all men wish they had a brother."

"Sounds like a lot of wishing."

"It is."

■

In the morning the men arrive. They come in their pickups and cars. The Doody brothers roll up in their ten-wheeler with the lowboy trailing behind. It's covered with sod, grass that's lush and green, grass that came in on a truck intended to resod the new animal park, but they've borrowed it for this occasion.

Cody is back at the cemetery motioning a concrete truck closer to the edge, finally clenching his fist to indicate close enough.

The driver gets down. It's then that Cody recognizes him to be Milt Tease from drunk school.

Cody shakes his hand and says hello. It's the first time they've spoken to each other.

"When the dispatcher called up this one I just had to take it," he says. "The old girl was a friend of my mother's. She cosigned for my parents' mortgage. If she hadn't done that I'd have been born in a box in East Bumfuck. Who knows."

"Well, good," Cody says. "That's good."

Cody reaches out and shakes Milt's hand again. He's glad to see him. Milt was the one who'd been drinking since he was a little boy, driving around in a pickup too young to drive or drink but doing it anyways. He's the one who said, "I should be teaching this class, I know more about drinking than anyone here."

"Well, good, Milt. That's good. Now what we're gonna do here is pour a pad, say about two feet. Then we're going to let it set up and put down some block on it. That'll hold up the casket and a form. We'll set the cores of them block so we can pour in all around it and the 'crete will flow to give us a uniform pour. We figure about twenty-two yards."

"Fair enough," Milt says. "The rest of the trucks will be waiting. Stan Garneau is driving now too. I got him a job at the plant. Did you know he's got a pet monkey? He keeps it on a chain. That little son of a bitch goes running around on that chain. It jumps off the furniture into his arms. Says he takes it swimming and it rides on his back in the water. I don't believe it, though. I think the son of a bitch would drown you."

"I couldn't say, Milt. Why would he lie, though? Could be true."

"Yeah, I guess it could."

Cody and Milt hook up the chutes and in no time six yards of concrete have plummeted into the hole.

■

It's a glorious morning, full of the March season. Winter is over and spring is on the cusp. It's one of those days when the air allows short sleeves while all around are remnants of winter, snow on the east banks of the brooks and in the heart of the high-masted forest. The sap runs to overflow as the earth creaks and groans, casting out the frost, heaving with delight.

Ten men lift the casketed body onto the lowboy and then it's driven down the road to the church. The whole town has turned out. The crowd is too big for the church, so the mourners are assembling on the common. Dick Doody parks in front of Washburn's store as the people come with lawn chairs. From the schoolhouse come the children, two by two, an older child assigned to a younger one. They carry their desk chairs over their backs or tucked under their arms. The first- and second-graders' chairs are carried by their assigned big brothers and big sisters. Each student carries a flower to place on the lowboy. They file into a crescent at the front, tossing up their flowers and then putting down their chairs, their attentions rapt on the beautiful bronze casket.

Cody arrives wearing a suit Mary bought him, so he could help out. He finds Eddie standing at the back.

"Cody. Look at you. My God. You're a pretty good-looking guy."

Cody shrugs. He feels silly in the suit. His face is bearded, red, ravaged by cold winters, hot summers. The suit looks good, but he doesn't think it goes with his face.

Cody pulls up a sleeve of his jacket to show he's only wearing the cuffs of the white shirt.

"She had to cut the arms off and then cut it up the back. Does it show?"

Eddie laughs.

"No, you look good."

Mary comes down the road with Little Eddie in the stroller. She's in her black dress, black stockings and black heels. She's let her hair go different, more pizzazz, a trick Mary Looney showed her. She thinks she's pretty hot and so does Eddie.

Cody scans the crowd. He's never seen so many people on the common. Mary Looney, Mary Rooney and the Blond Bomber show up. They're wearing their hair spiked with the sides and backs of their heads shaved a little. Cody wants to point the Blond Bomber out to Eddie, tell him she's a friend, but he knows that isn't true. By the time he's done, he sees almost everyone from drunk school there, alone or with friends or with family. Loretta Pelletier comes with her husband. Cody has a strange urge to punch the shit out of him because he knows Loretta is abused. He's having the thought when both Mr. Nims and Mr. Hurley come up behind him.

They say hello and Cody turns and nods.

"So good to see you," Mr. Hurley says. "I didn't know this was your line of work."

"It isn't," Cody says, and that's when Eddie breaks in, introduces himself, but doesn't say anything about Cody.

"So good to see you," Mr. Nims says to Cody. "Next week's our last week. It'll be your turn to tell us your story."

"This is my story," Cody says, and then he walks away from them to meet Mary, who's slowly working her way through the crowd. They watch him bend down and pick up Little Eddie, get him perched on his shoulders. He takes his cuffs off and gives the boy the cuff links to play with.

"Is there some kind of problem?" Eddie asks. "If there is, I'd like to know. Cody's a part of our family."

Eddie thinks how he almost said, Cody's apart from our family. The man named Nims is halfway through his explanation before Eddie hears what he's saying.

"He has to be cooperative or we must refer him to counseling and further evaluation. Next week is graduation and he hasn't said a single word."

Eddie speaks to Mr. Nims as if he were bereaved. He tells him calmly what a great fellow Cody is, how he's godfather to the children, a hard worker, indispensable to the business. He tells him Cody has recently suffered the loss of a loved one and is now experiencing the grief process.

"I'm sure you're familiar with the work of Elisabeth Kübler-Ross?"

Mr. Nims and Mr. Hurley ignore the question but say how happy they are they spoke to Eddie and then they go. Mary comes over to get the story. She says, "Why didn't you just tell them to fuck off?"

Cody watches them talk from the church steps. He wishes Eddie would mind his own business. He wishes the world would mind its own business. Little Eddie drops a cuff link. Cody squats down to get it. When he stands he sees Kay and Louis Poissant walking to the common alongside a line of parked cars.

As a minister, a rabbi and a priest climb onto the lowboy and take chairs, Cody goes back to Mary and leaves Little Eddie with her, then leaves the common as the service starts.

It's then that Mrs. Huguenot leaves too. She had a long go of it and now it's time.

She thinks, she could never understand her good friend Kate Smith, her wanting to be buried in a pink granite mausoleum at Saint Agnes Catholic Church in Lake Placid, New York. When she was dying, she thought about her poor friend still stranded in the church basement, long after her death because the cemetery rules don't allow mausoleums. At the end she thought about Kate, her loving husband Dome and the good people of Inverawe. She spoke to God. She said, Take care of Dome in the desert, poor, poor Kate and God bless America. Then she died.

People stood around her. They said, It's comforting to know that even in death some people don't change. She felt light and airy, her insides empty.

When the people left, she spent the night in Eddie Ryan's living room. He's the son she never had. He's such a good-looking boy, well mannered, literate, a fan of her fountain idea. She wants him to prosper, to be on the school board, to row the boat when the others fail. The people of a town need a woman to bring them into the world and a man to help them leave the world and that's the way it should be. She'll always cherish the little note he slipped her. It was a haiku and all the syllables were in their proper places.

Overhead, God and Kate Smith wait to greet her. By now she knows there's no hell. It's just a device so people will try harder to be good.

"I'm coming," she whispers, because souls are by nature quiet, and then she's off, a mass of a woman floating through the bronze lid, through the ceiling of air, into the attic and out the roof of atmosphere to step across the threshold of heaven. She wants to get a good seat.

■

Parked at the far boundary of the cemetery are the three concrete trucks. Cody is with Stan and Milton while the other driver dozes in the cab. They drink coffee from a Thermos while they wait, coffee, then cans of ginger ale, then another coffee. They drink so much it bloats them and they have to piss. With their drink they have half-pound Hershey bars and Mr. Goodbars, the biggest you can buy. Each one is tempted to find words for what they're doing but is embarrassed to do so. Stan Garneau has brought along his monkey so they feed it cigarettes and watch it do backflips while they wait.

It's late by the time the last of the stragglers leave the cemetery, having stopped on their way out to find loved dead ones, prominent dead ones and just the dead ones.

Dome kisses Marie Paquette on the forehead and tells her to run along. He doesn't want to miss this part. The rabbi sticks around too. Mrs. Huguenot agreed to have this done with ropes as in the Orthodox ritual. The rabbi smiles because he now sees there's no other way to do it.

The volunteers grab the ropes. Dome gets hold of one too. They walk down along the sides of the grave, then slowly lower her down, hand over hand until she rests on the cement blocks. The Doody brothers bring on the plywood cover. They lower that too until it rests on the exposed lips of the cement blocks. From where they stand, it looks as if she's floating, suspended in the earth. It looks more like something they dug up than are about to bury.

Eddie hikes up the hill and waves his arm. The three concrete trucks rev up, then come trundling down the lane, their huge barrels swaying against the sky. Cody comes across plots and gets there before the first truck does. The men nod and say hello but he doesn't say anything. He only nods back, then goes to directing the first truck, helping the operator buckle in his chutes.

The Doody brothers take over from here. They're big shots when it comes to pouring concrete and rightfully so. In their lifetimes they've poured enough for a small city.

"Open her up," Dick says, and the concrete begins its descent down the steel half tube. Dick works the chute with skill, keeping it low and moving, not letting it knock the box and casket off its pedestal, making sure the concrete seeps in underneath, seeps through the cores.

"More water," he says. "More water. I need it to run in under there."

When the truck empties, the driver pulls out onto the road to hose out his rig. Next in is Milt Tease. "More water," Dick says. "We don't want to knock her off."

Milt's load brings the pour up to the top of the box. He pulls out too and then Stan pulls in while Dick holds the chute easily, letting the concrete spew out and back, covering the top of the box to within four feet of the cemetery lawn.

Mesmerized by the flow of concrete, the men don't see Stan Garneau's monkey hoist itself out the cab window and then jump to the drum, the chain clinking on the metal behind him as he scuttles along the top.

From the truck's highest point, the monkey lofts himself into the air and lands on Dick Doody's back, toppling him over and into the grave, where he disappears in a splash, showering the rest of them with the cold gray mud.

It's Cody who sees him going and goes right in after him. He comes back up with Dick in his arms, the monkey's chain wrapped around Dick's neck and the monkey going berserk, then giving up the ghost before their eyes. To get Dick out, Cody has to go under and push him up. The others crowd the edge, getting a hand on him wherever they can. As he starts to go, Cody grabs his belt and prays it doesn't break.

The two of them get lifted clean out of the hole. Stan Garneau brings on a bucket of water while they work to get their faces cleaned off.

Cody looks up at Stan.

"I'm sorry about your monkey," he says.

"Looked to me like it was his own fault," Stan says. "Sometimes I wondered who was chained to who."

More water is brought and Dick and Cody are rinsed off, but they don't talk, they don't say anything. Nobody does until Dome steps up.

"Spruce up, boys. The old girl would have loved it. She's probably somewhere right now enjoying the thrill."

And she is.

10

Dome finally gives up answering the door. He leaves it open with a sign tacked to it: *Come in if you want.* He sits in the kitchen in a ladder-back chair nursing a beer. He wants the business of death to be over with. He's tired of receiving condolences from across the country, around the world, International Red Cross, National P.T.A., National D.A.R., Oxfam, Amnesty International, Nancy Reagan, Lena Horne, Malcolm Forbes and Zydeco accordionist Biff Dupré.

He drinks alone, happy to be that way as he doesn't really have a choice. Leaning backward, he hooks the heels of his black steel-toed engineer boots in the bottom rung of the chair, something Mrs. Huguenot always forbade.

"Sorry, honey," he whispers, dwelling on the heady smell of the freshly oiled leather. "Sorry I forgot the fucking squirrel too."

Dome's got on his leathers. He's wearing jeans, fringed gauntlets, leather vest and chaps. He has on a new black T-shirt that says FUCK OFF in big white letters. His arms are bare, encircled with blue serpents, a griffin and dragons tattooed into his skin, forked tongues licking at his biceps, the finest black-and-gray work to be found outside a federal prison, work begun when he was a boy traveling with the carnivals.

"In here," he says, and a parade commences through the doorway. They've all come by last request, Dick and Marlene Doody, Tom and Jeri, Barkley and Rose Kennedy, Raudabaugh, Thad Bushnoe, Joe and Marie Paquette, Nancy Manza, Mary Rooney and Mary Looney and the Poissants and even Dr. Pot.

They come with cakes, pies, casseroles, lasagnas, stews, salads and Jell-O molds.

They've come to witness the bonsai Marie has told so much about, some real, some handmade with carved wooden trunks and silk foliage, replicas of replicas.

The women crouch down and study the details while the men fidget, stand uneasily with their hands clasped behind their backs. They feel clumsy in the face of such delicacy. It draws on them, though, and they can't help but look.

Bonsai fill the house. There are Japanese maples at three different heights, all in black porcelain rafts. There's bougainvillaea and a sixteen-inch braided Ming ficus. There are lilacs and azaleas, wisteria on the coffee table.

Barkley Kennedy gasps and silently claps his hands.

"A study in mauve, a symphony in mauve, mauve on mauve. I can't get enough."

Raudabaugh picks at the scabs on his face. In his mind he puts miniature sap buckets on the maples, builds a little sugarhouse and turns out maple syrup by the teaspoonful. He imagines them to be little carvings hewn down to scale. He decides his sap buckets should be made as the trees were made, produced of miniature rungs, staves and rounds. Little man, little spigot, little brace and bit.

"My God," Marlene says, "an apple tree with blossoms smaller than a fingernail. A lot smaller. Look, a whole orchard."

Mary Looney registers the color as one of her favorite fingernail paints, the color she's wearing, but then thinks the blossoms to be even more lovely. She's moved to put her hands in her pockets.

There are French roses too, with silk flowers, pink, yellow and dusty rose, and birches, an entire stand of birches, none more than twenty inches high. There's Australian brush cherry, parsley aralia, strawberry guava, dwarf black olive and buttonwood. There's cypress, juniper, white pine and trident maples, boxwood clinging to rocks, windswept larch, cascading serissa and slanting black pine.

Next to the wisteria on the coffee table are tiny rakes, hoes, brooms, spades and pruning shears.

Joe Paquette finds a dwarf hemlock still under wire. He figures it to be twelve- and fourteen-gauge heat-treated copper. He thinks about the guy wires that anchor his antenna, wires that run through his engines, through his house. He gets a look at the pot from all sides, sees a tag with his name on it and sets it down immediately, afraid he's been seen at the business of seeing his name.

"Some of her best pieces ain't even here," Dome says from the kitchen as if he's addressing the refrigerator. "They're on loan to the National Bonsai Collection at the National Arboretum."

Raudabaugh thinks he's heard the word *burrito* and his stomach lurches.

"There's a three-hundred-and-sixty-year-old Japanese white pine and a hundred-and-ninety-year-old red pine that was a gift from that bugger Hirohito. Only bonsai they ever let out of the palace. Most of her youngest trees are forty years old. Anybody want a beer? They're in the fridge."

Raudabaugh says he'll take one, then he digs a finger into his ear. He thinks he may have come up short in the hearing end of it from the fire. The only Jappo bugger he knows of is Tojo and that son of a bitch swung. He doesn't know why Dome would bring that up. He tells Dr. Pot he shouldn't take offense.

"No, no," Dr. Pot says. "I no take a fence."

"You'll see the name of one of you taped to the back of each pot," Dome says. "She wanted each of you to have one."

Dome takes a drink and squares his shoulders. He continues, "She wanted me to tell you these can live over a hundred years and are to be passed along from one generation to the next as a reminder of the people who cared for them over the centuries. Cuttings are to be taken and propagated. There are sheets of directions for each one and general booklets. Anyone can learn great love and a respect for nature and other universal, spiritual truths."

Dome's chair thuds onto its four legs and he comes into the living room. He goes to each pot. He doesn't know their names, but he knows them by what they do. He recites a piece on each one, pointing as he goes.

"Imagine a tree holding on to a rock in a gorge, two human families, aged deadwood, slanting with Jin, reaching to heaven, mountains, waterfall, great age, storm, dragons climbing into the sky, struck by lightning, male, female, parent, child, earth and heaven, man and divinity, husband and wife."

He drinks from his beer and the people listen to it go into his mouth and down his throat. They can tell he's tired and are ready to catch him if he falls. Then they hear Eileen whispering to Little Eddie.

"This is the church, this is the steeple. Open the door and see all the people."

She makes her fingers go like worms to tickle Little Eddie's face. He laughs and it's a sound they all recognize.

■

The men sit in the kitchen on chairs, counters and the floor. They hold their bonsai in their laps, each knowing why he received what he did. Thad Bushnoe sets his windswept fire thorn aside to pass out beers. He hands the cans one at a time and they make their way around until everyone has a cold one.

"So," Tom Doody says to Dome, "what've you got planned now?"

"Jesus Christ," his brother says, "you say the most stupid friggin' things sometimes."

"Boys," Barkley says, touching the petals of his silken lilacs.

"Do you mind if I smoke?" Thad asks.

"I don't give a fuck," Dome tells him. "Just don't burn up the place."

The men laugh and several of them repeat Dome's words, *Just don't burn up the place.*

Rose Kennedy comes in for paper plates, cups and bowls so she can begin to serve the food. The men stop talking. She smiles and nods at them.

When she leaves the kitchen, Dome tells them he's getting ready to take a trip. He has a few things to take care of. As soon as Eddie Ryan comes by with the bill, he'll fire up his bike and ride off into the great yonder. He has stops to make, Laconia, Unadilla, Sturgis, Daytona. There are the drags, bike christenings, rodeos, jamborees and wild-tit contests. If he can hit the Bluegrass Poker Run, he knows his old buddy Malcolm Forbes will be there and maybe Liz if they aren't on the skids by then. It's been forty years since he went down the blue highways and he's determined it won't be another forty.

Louis Poissant's boys keep an eye on the empties. As they get set down, the boys take them outside to the garbage cans, where they're draining them all into one, trying to work up enough for a single can.

Cody goes into the living room. He tells Mary he'll relieve her for a spell and takes Little Eddie in where the men are. He looks for Kay, but sees she didn't come.

"Forty years ago," Dome is saying to the ceiling when Cody gets back. "Forty years ago. Fifty years ago I was a Communist."

The men look up, amazed to hear this, as if Dome had just said, Fifty years ago I was a woman.

Barkley Kennedy covers his smile because fifty years ago he was a Communist too and can't imagine telling anyone.

"What's he say?" Raudabaugh asks, but nobody answers.

Dome looks at his watch.

"She left a little something for all of you. I suppose I could leave you with a little story."

Dome's story:

I was with the Lincoln Brigade in '37. We was some poor sons-a-bitches, I'll tell you. We took a lickin'. Stukas. Nazi dive bombers. *Guernica.*

After that I got picked up by the OSS. They shipped my ass to North Africa, kicked it out of an airplane in the middle of the night. There were stars below and the friggin' desert was like a griddle. North Africa, September 12, 1940. El Agheila, Tobruk, El Alamein, the Qattâra Depression, the badlands.

I tell you if them Stukas hadn't left for Stalingrad, old Dome wouldn't be here today to bury the little woman. They would've knocked the hell out of us. The Tigers and 88s was bad enough. They could pour it on. Matildas cracked open like walnuts. I'd get my nose down to the ground so tight I could smell a Chinaman's touchhole.

I'll take them Rajputs any day. Them boys go out at night and come back with ears.

It was North Africa I had my first Hog. I was a dispatch rider.

When they brought in the bikes, they were all Beemers and Trumpets, but I seen this one rare breed of a looking machine. It was an experimental XA, built for the Sahara. A one-of-a-kind and I said that's the baby for me. Forty-five cubic inches with a drive shaft, horizontally opposed two-cylinder engine, oil-bath air cleaner, no skirt, blackout lights, rifle rack, olive drab, hand and foot shift.

Seventy miles an hour, max. Except for old Dome's. I bored the cylinder a full eighth, put in oversized valves and flathead pistons. That got me up to eighty-five and then I got an extra fifteen from Dome's Best. It was a fuel mix I got from some of them flyboys. Twenty-three skidoo. That shit would boogie-woogie. Saved the ass of old Dome on many a late-night junket across the barren waste. Cheek to cheek.

Into the blue by the light of the moon, always keeping height so you can turn down when the soft patch comes. Butter-yellow ribbed sand was safe and shining purple meant liquid bog.

I'll tell you about that joy-juice, Dome's Best. The boys all made petrol fire to cook over. They'd mix up a concoction of sand, water and petrol in an old tin and then they'd make their little porridge from biscuits and bully beef. Or tea. The Brits had to have their tea. Never saw an army that had to piss so much. Tea always gave me the dripping pisses and a limp dink. Something that truly saddened the sultan's maidens. Truly saddened old Hekmet, the belly dancer at the Melody Club and the whores of Cairo.

Old Dome of the Sahara. Dome of the desert. Sandstorms, mud bogs and potholes that'd snap front forks and necks without discrimination. The flat glare of sand and the long shadows. Sand drifts blowing off the dune crests. I was all duded up in a burnoose, gas goggles and a respirator. You needed them too. They have a wind that blows across the Libyan desert, over the Qattâra Depression, the sand sea, Gebel el Akhdar. The wind is called Khamsin. It's a hot wind, one ten, forty miles an hour. The sand comes like bird shot, like hot rivets. Bedouin tribal law permits a man to kill his wife after five days of it. That wind can rip a phone pole out of the ground. It causes electrical disturbances, drives compasses crazy. They claim it was responsible for setting off an ammo dump explosion. In winter it can go below freezing.

Blinding squalls. One sandstorm so bad, the Argylls fought the Camerons.

By then I had the Harley tricked out with a rack of Tommy guns

across the handlebars. After a while they stopped giving me mes-
sages to deliver. They'd just say, "Dome, why don't you go out and
raise a little hell." They'd say it just like that. "Dome, why don't you
go out and raise a little hell."

I did too. Whenever the Greeks or the Gurkhas were on the
move, I'd tag along. Them boys practiced what they call today
psychological warfare. Only for them it was pure unmitigated joyful
spite. They loved the night and so did I. Still do. Your Greeks like
to collect Italian ears. Keep them on a loop of ropelike beads. Oh,
them boys were dogs. One day the Germans sent back a Gurkha boy
they'd made to shave. It's their greatest shame to do so and that
fellow killed himself. Those boys were hot, mister man. That night
every one of them slipped out of camp against orders and when
they got back and in the light they looked like they'd been swimming in blood. They were black with it, slick and shiny. I was there.
I saw what they did. It was jugular veins a-poppin'. Blood just
a-gushing.

Another of your pantywaist outfits was the L.R.D.G., the Long
Range Desert Group. They drove Chevys. Can you believe it? They
had all the navigation devices, theodolites, sun compasses, azimuth
cards, navigation books and chronometers. They'd go like hell until
they got lost, then they'd go like hell some more. I'd find them.
Bring them back.

Old Dome drove by the stars. The North Star was always one and
a half degrees from true north. That's all I needed.

The big push came late in the fall of '42, El Alamein, Algiers,
Oran, Casablanca. It's then I hear about Fred Sharby dying in the
Cocoanut Grove fire. It comes in a letter. Most men don't open
their letters, you know. They get them and hang on to 'em. Carry
'em around for days. They're afraid to open them up and at the
same time they're savoring them, anticipating them like thoughts
of a cold beer or a snake.

I grew up with him. Played ball with him. He went back in after
his family and never got out. People died there against the doors.
They died of the fumes, stacked up like cordwood, the strongest on
top, the weakest at the bottom. Just like life. The paint was clawed
off the doors. I seen 'em die in fire. Melded together like waxes or
steel. First there's smoke, then there's flame, then there's the explosion. . . .

Joe Paquette shifts where he stands. When he was a schoolboy,

not long ago, he won the Sharby Trophy for being the best football
player. Every year when it's given, Coach Bucky Malpezzi tells the
story of Fred Sharby. It's a story that makes people sad, makes them
try to be better people.

Dick and Tom Doody look at the floor. They know the story too.
They busted holes in the line for Joe to get through, his pigeon-
toed loping gait taking him to daylight to be bushwhacked by
scrawny safeties.

. . . By then I'd had a bellyful. I filled the tank, strapped on
another ten gallons of Dome's best and disappeared into the
blue . . .

"I was in the heart of that continent for two more years," Dome
says, "and that's a whole other story, but this is history, boys. This
is what it's all about. So don't piss me off.

"And so if you'll all take your leave now, I'm about ready to head
out again. Remember, short visits make for long welcomes."

■

By the time Eddie Ryan gets to Dome's house, night has come. The
lights inside are off but a faint glow seeps out from the barn floor.
Eddie goes there and finds Dome lying under his Harley, an original 1942 four-five shovelhead. The rearview is clipped off and its
fluids are puddled on the concrete. A squirrel holding an ashtray
is lashed to the handlebars. Dome's smoking a cigarette.

"Good evening," he says to Eddie, who only looks on at the
calmness of the situation. "Would you mind lifting this off me?"

Eddie comes forward and between the two of them they're able
to right the bike. Dome touches the jagged post where his mirror
broke. Then he limps about the garage, making his way like a bird
in water.

"Son of a bitch," he says. "When those babies go, it's slow
motion all the way. You lay it down and hope to God you're out
from under it. I could've kept it up except for my gear being that
little bit extra. The straw that broke the camel's back. You got my
bill?"

"It runs pretty high," Eddie says. "There were a lot of extras.
The casket alone was five thousand dollars."

"I don't give a shit. The old girl had it all planned. She wanted
the thirty-two-ounce solid swell-top bronze model with silk covering and all-around hardware."

"There's the enclosure too."

"She wanted the goddamn enclosure, Mr. Ryan. Just don't get your piss warm. You ain't paying for it."

Dome hobbles over to his acetylene torches. He opens the valves and regulates the mix. From over his workbench he takes down cans of chili and potatoes and a tin of Spam. He sets them on a steel plate, and punctures the lids with a spike. Then he sparks his blowtorch and begins heating them for dinner. Eddie hands over the itemized bill when Dome motions for it.

The cans begin to rattle on the plate; juices begin to gurgle from the punctures.

"Jesus Christ," he says. "I guess there *were* some extras. A friggin' forklift. I'll be damned. Why didn't you call me up? I'd like to have seen that."

"No, that's only a lift I had to rent, not a forklift. She was a large woman."

"You're telling me. Warmth in the winter and shade in the summer."

Dome keeps reading while the cans get to clattering. They look like they'll dance off onto the floor.

"Fair enough," Dome says, looking up and nodding as if to seal the deal. "You'll stay for supper."

Eddie knows he doesn't have a choice. He watches Dome hold each can with a pair of eighteen-inch channel locks while he peels off the lids with pliers.

"You start with the chili," Dome says, picking up the can of potatoes, "then pass it to me. We'll keep things going round that way."

"Are you still thinking of the pink granite mausoleum like Kate Smith wanted?"

"Not right now. I plan to swing by Lake Placid on my tour and get the lowdown. She empowered me to do so. Poor Kate. God bless America. Her death was an awful blow to Isabel."

Dome sets down the Spam and sighs deeply. Eddie knows what this is. He knows it's the first time Dome has said her name since she died. It's the naming that brings on the realization of death. He's seen it before.

"It's only natural," Eddie says quietly. "It's only natural to have glimpses of moments like that. The sadness lives on for six to nine months. Then it starts to decrease. It's like having a baby."

Dome looks up at him. It's a look Eddie has seen before. It's a look that asks, Are you speaking to *me*? Then it says, *Why* are you speaking to me?

"Sometimes mourning can go off course," Eddie says, and he knows he's not saying this to Dome anymore. He's saying it to himself. "Mourning can go off course. Maybe nightmares or night terrors. One man kept a camera in his wife's closet for fifteen years. It was set to go off if the door opened. Another had his wife disinterred and reburied under his bedroom window."

Eddie keeps going, his voice only a whisper.

"The mourning is never completed. Sometimes there's a need for regrief therapy. It's part of the grief syndrome, part of the therapy of mourning."

"Mr. Ryan. Now I don't want to be a hard case, but I don't understand a friggin' thing you're saying. I yam what I yam and that's all that I yam. Southern Popeye."

Eddie can't help but laugh. Dome laughs too until the FUCK YOU on his T-shirt begins to heave.

"Eat up," he says. "Then I got a favor to ask you."

The men finish eating, scraping clean the insides of the cans. Dome tells Eddie about the tour he has planned for the summer. He tells him how in '47 he came back to the States and hooked on with the circus. He rode in the sphere of death and the motordome and that's how he got his name, Dome. He rode the rollers too, at fifty miles an hour on an HD 45.

"When you're on the rollers," he says, "you're going like hell but you're not moving. You can lean that bike right over, touch your kneecap to the floor. I raced the board tracks too. No brakes, no clutch, throttle taped and only a kill switch. You jump-started them and held on for life. A big man was supposed to catch you at the end because by then your legs were jelly. Let me tell you, I took some splinters as long as a tenpenny nail and I took some gold too on them tracks around Savannah and Daytona.

"The sphere of death was the best, though. My partner was a Chippewa Indian named Paradise Lost. We rode Indian flat-track motorcycles. Round and round inside that sphere. You tended to get pretty fucking dizzy.

"In 'nineteen, Paradise rode cross-country on a Henderson four-cylinder, the finest bike of the time, and he beat the living caca out of it, seven cylinders, four pistons, six wrist pins, two complete sets of bearings, two rods and twenty-eight plugs. The front jug liked to seize, so one day out in East Bumfuck he locked up and then shattered the front piston. He dug around in the cases and got out the big pieces, then shaped an oak branch for a wrist pin. It kept the rod straight and he kept on stroking.

"He claimed the best driving was on the railroad tracks. At fifty you only hit the high spots. The last time I saw him, we was in the sphere doing loopdy loops, crisscrossing round and round. The door come open and then Paradise was really lost. An ambulance with a nurse come onto the scene and I'll be damned if it wasn't Isabel Huguenot at right around one eighty and pushing like hell for three hundred."

Dome finishes telling Eddie the story and then they are quiet. They sit at the workbench, touching the hand tools, holding them without thinking. Dome snaps a set of vise grips onto his thumb, but doesn't flinch. When he releases them, the jaws leave their marks.

"Come with me," Dome whispers, and Eddie follows.

They go through the house to the back porch. Dome hits a switch and small pockets of yellow light splash the ground, making a path down into the hollow, where another, larger glow comes from inside a building.

"This is her garden and that's her teahouse. There's a pond down there. She always wanted to have some carp in that pond. Do you think you could look into that for me?"

Dome is whispering, so Eddie whispers back.

"I'll do what I can."

"In a day or two, I'm going to load the bike onto my pickup and drive south with my gear. Get out from under this weather. You watch the house for me and see if you can grow some carp when the time is right. I'll pay you for all of this, of course. It's what the old girl wanted."

Dome sits down and motions for Eddie to do the same.

"It's her garden," he says. "Her secret garden."

Breezes are in the trees and there's the sound of running water. It trickles over rocks somewhere in the darkness. There's another sound too.

"What's that?" Eddie says. "That thumping sound."

"It's her deer scarer. A length of bamboo on a pivot that fills with enough water to tip it. Then it empties and thumps back onto the ground. She claims the bamboo sings with the water running through it, but I never hear it. I bet you can, though."

Eddie thinks he can but doesn't want to admit it.

"There are spirits in those rocks. She said so. The rocks. They grow."

Eddie wants to get home. He's sad the old woman has died, and even sadder because that isn't the end of it. Somehow he feels he's been roped into another life and right now there are just so many he can handle.

"Here," Dome says, handing Eddie a check. "Paid in full."

Eddie folds the check and slips it inside his pocket.

"Now, goddamn it. You didn't even look at it. I could have cheated you or given you the one for the phone company. Now look at it."

Eddie takes out the check. It's for the correct amount and it's made out to him.

"There, now wasn't that easy? Easy and discreet."

"Mary usually handles these things. It helps keep the money part impersonal. The way it should be."

"She's a good girl too. But I've seen her. She makes out tough but she's a pushover."

"Listen. This is my business."

"Yes, and you get stiffed. Take this too. It's your tip. Please note it's in cash."

Dome hands Eddie an envelope. Inside are thousand-dollar bills, ten of them. Eddie shakes his head, starts to protest.

"You'll take them," Dome tells him. "It's what she wanted. She knows you get stiffed a lot. Don't worry about the money. She left enough to endow two chairs at the college and she set up a fund so all the children in town will have toys at Christmas. And all that's a drop in the bucket."

"I really can't," Eddie says. "It's way too much."

"You need it. Take it. Before you came there was no one to get these people through this end of life. Old Bushway was a body snatcher. He and George had a sweetheart deal where they'd transfer the bodies before survivors could say one way or the other. Then he'd just about hold them for ransom. Isabel got wise to him and forced him out. She thinks he was stealing fillings and rings but couldn't prove it. If you remember, you came by your establishment mighty cheap."

"Damn. Why wasn't I told? This isn't the way things should be handled."

"Don't fret, Mr. Ryan. It's like having a baby."

They both laugh and then Dome is quiet. A cool air blows up from the hollow where under the trees the snow is still heavy. The runoff can be heard from the mountainside, water making the noise of a wind, the bamboo singing and thumping with water.

"I think that's enough for now," Dome whispers, and Eddie knows it's time to go home.

When Eddie gets home, a strange car is parked in the driveway. Inside the house, Nims and Hurley and Cody are sitting at the kitchen table and Mary is serving coffee. No one sees Eddie standing in the doorway.

Cody is saying, "So after my mother went to Washington and pleaded with President Roosevelt and the Secretary of the Navy about my being underage to enlist, they shipped me back from Vladivostok, where I'd been guarding the brig. By then my body was covered with tattoos and I'd drunk a pint of vodka for each one. So at sixteen you can see I had quite a habit."

Eddie backs out of the doorway, smiling, and goes down the hall to the living room. He sits where he can hear Cody's story.

". . . My father was a drinker too. He always drank pints—pints of Hiram Walker, pints of vodka. We drank together until February eleventh, when he got his hands on a fifth. He hiked into the woods and drank the whole thing. Somewhere in the cold night, all by himself, he went from being passed out to being dead. Now when I drink, I drink alone."

Eddie puts his arm across his face, his nose in the crook of his elbow. He grips his shoulder with his hand and squeezes gently as if someone else is doing it and each time he pumps more tears into his sleeve, into the folded cuff. As sad as it is, he thinks it's a lovely story, one worth telling again and again.

11

In the spring the air fills with the smell of cowshit, its rich odor bursting from mounds stockpiled over winter because the snow-fields were too deep for it to be spread, the drifts too high, but now it's being loaded out and spread on the corn ground. The smell comes dispersed on the cold air, transporting its warm vapor for miles.

There's the smell of fire too, burning brush, mountains of slash, the butt ends away from the wind so the flame folds over like a giant hand, twig to branch to limb to trunk. And rubbish in the burning barrels and leaves in piles and the timothy at the edges of lawns still bent and brown on the frozen ground harboring plates of ice, grains of snow.

When the alarm goes off at noon, Eddie and Cody are at the kitchen table playing an endless game of five hundred rummy, one where five hundred must be hit exactly and to go over would mean forfeit. For Cody it's a way to keep off the beer and stick with the chocolate. For Eddie it's a way to keep him on the straight and narrow. They've come to know each other's tricks.

Mary is chaperoning a field trip with Eileen's class and she's taken Little Eddie with her. They've gone to the new animal farm that's opened up on the highway. As Eileen says, first it wasn't there and now it is. It's run by the Pet Man, a childhood friend of Isabel Huguenot's. He cashed in on merger mania when his buckle factory was glommed by a corporation of window washers that served Dade County and went on to franchising across the nation.

It's been a bad year for fire. An arson is torching houses in Jefferson; and at an elementary school in Keene a vandal doused a mimeograph with copier fluid and flicked his Bic. It's also come to be the farmer's last resort, his way of getting even, his way of rural renewal, his way of getting just a little warmth.

The men lay their cards facedown. Cody unknots the straps of his overalls from his waist and pulls them over his shoulders and clips them. Eddie slips into his bunker pants and boots in one motion. As they go out the door a gust of wind sends the cards skidding across the table and ticking to the floor. When they get back from the fire they'll have to start all over again.

■

The Pet Man wears a pith helmet, jodhpurs, black riding boots and a safari jacket. He carries a riding crop and wears a toy pistol at his hip. He tried a monocle but the goddamn thing kept falling out.

He leads the children through the animal farm, a wheel of wooden animal houses, all under the same roof so no one can get wet while they stroll the grounds. As a service to the community he's giving free private tours before he officially opens in June. He's taking a class of school kids a day these two weeks. Then he'll take the senior citizens, the D.A.R., the P.T.A., the volunteer firemen, the men's club, the Koffee Klatch and the Ladies Auxiliary.

He doesn't realize that because the town is so small, this means most people will have to go two or three times.

Mary sits on the observation deck in the slant morning sun with Miss Germaine, Eileen's science and math teacher. They drink coffee from Styrofoam cups while the smell of the deep fry gusts over their heads from the blower fan.

Miss Germaine's cup is ringed with red lipstick. She's wearing heels, a skirt and a leather jacket. She makes Mary feel like a mother and housewife, a frump. She wants this day to be over. She's decided she's going to change her life a little bit more. Maybe have a talk with Mary Looney.

Miss Germaine is telling how she might go back to school and get an M.B.A. With her math skills it would be cinchy.

Mary thinks how she read in *Newsweek* that business is sexy. She thinks, If the shoe fits, wear it, and for a moment wants to punch this woman in the face. It makes her feel ugly.

"This is real hands-on experience for the students," Miss Germaine says. "This is how science should be taught. What a resource."

The Pet Man tells the children about the special quarters that are off limits. These are the places where animals breed, get repaired, or put to sleep if they need that too.

"That's where we get up close and personal with the animals," he says.

"That's where they have sex," a boy says, but the Pet Man ignores him.

Eileen follows the group, holding tight to Little Eddie's hand. She's been put in charge of him. She's his mother for these few hours, a job older sisters take on for life.

"The holding cells are wire mesh with concrete floors. That's where the animals mate and recuperate, two acts which seem to go together."

The Pet Man chuckles at his own joke, but the children only stare at him, adult humor being an acquired taste. The Pet Man talks to the children this way. He never condescends and they appreciate it. The Pet Man believes that if you treat children as adults they will act accordingly.

The Pet Man is proud of his animal farm. His real name is Walter Disney and he plans to call his animal farm Disneyland Animal Farm. He knows he'll get sued, but doesn't care. It'll be his chance to tell the world how miserable he's been, having such a name to carry through life. He just finished painting the new sign this morning. It will be unveiled at the grand opening. When he's sued he'll take it down. It'll be good publicity.

"This is the bleeding-heart pigeon," he says. "Legend has it that the bird got its breast marking from flying into the side of Christ as he hung dying on the cross. The bird has borne the stigmata ever since."

He moves slowly through the aviary, giving the children time to find the birds that watch them from hiding places in the trees.

"These are cassowaries, great flightless birds, and these are fire-tufted barbets."

The Pet Man especially likes the story about the bleeding-heart pigeon. It's one of the few stories he tells. Usually he only tells where the animals come from and what they eat.

"Ice cream," Little Eddie says, words in his growing vocabulary.

Eileen shushes him. He knows the animal farm used to be the Creamery, a snack bar, driving range and miniature golf course. When the Pet Man came up from Florida and bought it, he shut down the golfing and put in his eleven-acre wildlife park with seventy species of mammals, birds and reptiles. He plans to use the snack bar to sell tickets, souvenirs and snacks. He's kept it open throughout construction because so many truckers and salesmen depend on it for breakfast, lunch or supper.

"These parrots are some of my favorites," he says. "Those are blue-and-gold macaws. There are more than three hundred species distributed worldwide. These macaws are from the Amazon basin. I've had them ever since I was a young man."

The macaws repeat the Pet Man's words exactly. The children laugh because the parrots' voices sound just like his.

"What's this bird?"

"A peacock," Eileen says.

She gives all the answers. Her classmates expect it of her. She makes it easy for them and the teacher. It's a burden she bears, being the one depended upon. She doesn't mind doing it so much as she minds the long moments of silence that come when others don't speak. Eileen, she's a brain.

"See the eyes on the tail feathers. The peacock was the favorite pet of the goddess Hera. One day she got angry at her servant Argus because he tried to deceive her. To punish him she plucked out his eyes and scattered them on the tails of her peacocks. Argus had one hundred eyes."

The boy who said the word *sex* asks what Argus was doing with a hundred eyes.

■

"I can't wait for summer," Miss Germaine says. "My skin gets so dry in this weather. You have such beautiful hands."

"Actually what I use is Velvatone," Mary says, looking at her hands.

"Velvatone skin lotion. Is that Clinique or Estée Lauder? I think I've heard of it. Maybe Shiseido?"

"No. None of those. It's made by a small company in Massachusetts and you have to send away for it."

"Like Mary Kay."

"Kind of."

"I'd love some. Between the dry weather and the chalk dust, my hands are a wreck."

"I'll get you a bottle."

Mary wanted to tell her it was made by the Dodge Chemical Company along with Kalip Stay Cream, Germasidol, SnyCav, Metaflow, Permaglo, Introfiant arterial chemical and other products for flawless embalming, but there never seemed to be an opportunity. She wonders what effect the old Viscerock, the chemical sponge in the handy eight-ounce jar, would have on Miss Germaine's hands.

"It's so sad about Mrs. Huguenot dying. I'm told she was a very prominent member of the community."

"Yes, she was. I don't know of a person more loved."

Mary believes these words and that belief grows even as she says them. She feels guilty for her meanspiritedness toward Miss Germaine. She realizes how Mrs. Huguenot made them all a little bit better at being human. She thinks of her tree, the 260-year-old Japanese white pine. It was the oldest one in Mrs. Huguenot's collection, the most valuable, the most beautiful. She was embarrassed when she found out it was hers, embarrassed because everyone knew it was the most special one there.

"I think dead people always look so unnatural," Miss Germaine says. "They never look like themselves."

Mary squeezes her Styrofoam coffee cup, feeling the brown liquid rise and fall. Of a sudden she's in a panic, wondering where her children are, wondering where her husband is. She stands on her chair, letting her napkin fall on the deck boards. Off on the far boundary she can see them. They are looking at a herd of musk-ox, watching them toss sheaves of hay into the air, breaking it up so the stems are not so tightly packed. She can see her children, Eileen at the fence and Little Eddie leaning against her, back to back, his head on her rump for a pillow. Mary sits back down and looks at Miss Germaine.

"Did you ever think it's because they're dead?"

■

The trucks are rolling before Eddie and Cody make it to the fire-house. The brush truck, crash rescue truck, tanker and engine are on the move. Dick Doody clutches and misses the gear, giving Eddie and Cody time to jump on the back platform of the Loadstar.

Coonie is there too, holding onto the steel grab bar. He takes Eddie's coat and helps him slip into it. He says, "The zoo," and Eddie Ryan knows this will be the longest ride of his life, a rift in time he's stumbled across, a crack between instants where he's gotten caught and doesn't know from first to second to after that. It's the way it becomes when one life becomes two and two lives become four, the way it becomes for a man who finds himself with a family.

■

". . . And these are my Australian snakes. Australia has more poisonous snakes in its population than any other continent, seventy species. And the odd thing is, lizards and boar seem immune to snakebite. Wild boar seem to love a good snake snack. Who knows what a species is?"

Eileen waits. She wants to give one of her friends a chance, but none answers.

"People are a species," she says.

"That's right. What does species mean, though? That's what I wanted to know."

"Well, you didn't ask."

Mary and Miss Germaine crunch their cups and throw them in the rubbish barrel. They descend the cascading stairway to the concrete path, strolling out to meet the children and the Pet Man as the tour comes back around to them. Mary can see him and Eileen having a discussion while the other children scuff at peanut shells and pebbles with the toes of their sneakers. Little Eddie sits at Eileen's feet about to go into a snit.

Mary goes down on one knee behind him, her hands clasping the insides of her thighs. She's about to whisper his name when the untended Frialator in the snack bar explodes, taking out the back wall, spewing grease flames onto the adjacent buildings, onto the cook and waitress, who carry trays of food onto the deck for the children. The flames cut off the exits to the parking lot, then get down to the serious business of burning.

■

By the time the Inverawe volunteers arrive, the whole complex is feeling the lick of flame. Glass is bursting from its frames and the extrusions are melting. Hidden explosions are going off with muffled thumps and high-pitched whizzes; sawdust, hay, tanbark, roofing, wiring, scaffolding, fencing and landscaping all catch and carry the lick of flame. All that is man-made is turning to gas, some wafting as roofs fall and some sinking into collapsed floors.

Volunteer companies from adjacent towns converge on the fire. A volunteer straps into spurs and belt. He runs up the utility pole and cuts the power while others hook up to the hydrant.

The man on the pole yells down that people are inside, people are in the center.

Eddie and Cody are already on the hoof, crossing the lot to the board walls that wing the snack bar, Eddie with an ax, Cody with a chain saw. Thad Bushnoe yells something about safe procedure, breathing apparatus, and then he too grabs an ax and runs for the wall. The other Inverawe volunteers do the same. Dick Doody drops the preconnect and starts to run just as his brother turns the wrench, sending a throat of water gushing from the hydrant. Its force knocks Dick on his ass and sends him scuttling across the asphalt, but he gets up and keeps running while other companies take over the hydrant to pour on the first water.

Eddie rears back and chops at the wood. He rears back again and Cody steps up, the saw torquing in his hands. He grips the throttle and tears into the wood, spewing sawdust and sparks from the nails he clips. When he's done, a panel drops, big enough to drive a truck through, and the men pour in, tumbling down an embankment, then barging through a burning hedge to the walkways.

The men run the paths that are laid out like the spokes of a wheel to the center hub, where there's a concrete pond. Mary has gotten Miss Germaine and all the children into the cold water. She has the chef and waitress mostly submerged and she's on her knees cradling their heads. The children huddle around her, their small bodies waist-deep.

Smoke and ash drift around them, but the men stop for a second on the bank because they are something to behold in the placid water made blue by the painted concrete. They are surrounded by pink flamingos and white ibis, a blue heron, geese and swans and their cygnets. Amongst the children are puffins, pintails and wood ducks, swimming in the water and dipping their heads to cast drops on their feathers.

The men wade in and pick up a child in each arm, fathers with sons, fathers with daughters, men with the children of their friends. Word goes back to bring litters for the chef and the waitress and they're carried out to an ambulance. Joe Paquette scoops up Miss Germaine and tells her, "This is your lucky day."

Eileen holds on to her father's neck as he carries her down the walkways behind Mary and Cody, who has Little Eddie. She holds her father easily, relaxed in his arms.

"Look, Eddie," she says. "The sky is on fire."

Eddie moves more quickly, slogging over the concrete in his heavy boots. He knows what she sees, the smoke is igniting over the hot spots as flames from the fire lick their way up the black plume.

Thad Bushnoe is with Mary. The Phoenix shield on his white helmet is scarred where he ran it into a timber. He's decided to quit as fire chief after this one. He takes the fires personally. It's as if they start up to taunt him. He's worried about his men, his friends. A month ago he went as fire chief to Pennsylvania to the funeral of two volunteers who died when the 250-year-old stone wall of a barn collapsed on them. Before that it was Wisconsin when three volunteers died from flashover in a training exercise.

The built-up pine timbers burn with brilliance, flinging brands in all directions. Smoke bursts forth in dense black volumes.

Another pumper now sucks water from the concrete pond but it's not enough. The fire drums and snaps through the lace of buildings, pens and habitats. More fire companies arrive but it's too late. Already the structures are white-and-black X rays of themselves. The eleven acres are burning. Steamy and smoldering, the Everglades, the Cactus Community, the Sonora Desert, the Gentle Woodlands, the Big Sky Country, the North Woods—they all take flame and burn in their independent way on the eleven acres of earth in the great conflagration.

Scattered among the firefighters are the animals, dashing from their homes or cowering under flames, where their hides crisp and their lungs sear until their throats close.

The birds take wing for the forest—pink spoonbills, marabous, snowy owls, barn owls, macaws, falcons and pheasant.

An okapi bolts through a fence, its head low, and takes out Dick Doody at the kneecap.

A lynx snarfs a rabbit and heads for the forest, its mouth full.

Japanese snow monkeys make for the trees, where gibbons whoop and siamangs hoot and holler while they swing arm over arm from limb to limb.

Mr. Washburn gets his hands on a fire hose, but it's a rainbow python turning in his grip and about to muckle onto him when Joe Paquette lops its head off with a fire ax. More snakes boil up from the ashy waters, diamondbacks, sidewinders, an emerald tree boa. Joe Paquette does the hotfoot dance, getting as many as he can while the snake house collapses around him.

Explosions go off underneath them as twisting color-coded pipes erupt from their culverts. Pumps, wires, switches and tubing snap, bend, crack and rupture. The one million BTU gas boiler goes off like a bomb and the 50,000 BTU air conditioner melts into a pool of aluminum.

The men knead their eyes, shocked as geysers of flame fount toward the sky. Wolves, bear, deer, bison, bobcat, camels and addax all head back to the wild as the Pet Man scats across the eleven acres, opening doors, breaking windows and nipping padlocks with his bolt cutters.

But the musk-ox hold their ground, shoulder to shoulder in a tight ring, their heads and horns pointing out. All around them the world burns but they don't move. They keep their ranks closed with the calves clustered together inside.

All others run. The gazelles, impalas and bongos bound for the perimeter. A bison takes out after Tom Doody, chasing him into the pond and then ramming its head into the rescue truck until it falls to its knees.

By late that afternoon the fire is out. Everyone is accounted for except the Pet Man. The only dead animals to be found are the snakes chopped into little pieces. The others have disappeared into the forest and sky. The game warden is convinced they'll die within a few days from the elements, from shock, from semis, from the gun boys who can't afford an African safari but always wanted to bag something more exotic than a whitetail.

"Old Walter Disney probably beat feet for the state line," the warden says.

"Who's Walter Disney?" Thad asks.

"He owned this place. I don't know what laws he broke, but I'll bet there's a mess of them."

"I thought Walt Disney was dead," Thad says to Cody.

"He is, but you know these fucking game wardens. They all think they're the Canadian Mounted Police."

The men look at each other. They know Cody to be right. As the saying goes, the season's always open on game wardens.

The search for the Pet Man finally brings them to the musk-ox, their ranks still tight even though the fire came dangerously close.

Dick Doody goes for the Power Wagon. He drives it slowly toward the ring of musk-ox and is able to disperse them after they cave in the brush guard and sink a horn or two into the core of the radiator. The calves follow, blatting and stumbling twenty yards away, where they form up again.

Lying at the center of where they were is the Pet Man, a death adder clutching his ankle, its thin stem of a body crushed by the hooves. It will be Eddie Ryan's job to ship him back to Florida in a corrugated shipping container via Sweet Charity Wings, an aerial burial service based in Houston.

■

When the fall comes, the bird hunters will kick the hedgerows for ring-necked pheasant, cockbirds that beat the air to gain flight for their heavy bodies; and when they are shot and turning in the sun, their feathers will color like prisms, only more subtle, more beautiful.

But what they'll find busting from the cover are the brilliant golden pheasant, the blue-wattled Bulwers of the Bornean rain forest and the argus of the Himalayas.

"Motherfucker, did you see that bird?"

"No, and you didn't either."

12

When you're in business for yourself, there's always something special about that ring of the phone. If business is good, it's a joyful sound, ringing out promises of the next big job, the big order to fill, the world beating a path to your door. If business is bad, it's always a major creditor, an unhappy customer, the preying tax man. The ring goes off like gunfire close to your ears and you get that feeling that comes when you're doing sixty and hit an ice patch for only a second. Your stomach slips and checks and you think, This time I won't answer, but you do.

The phone at Eddie Ryan's house is in the kitchen. It rings in the news of engagements, confirmed appointments, solicitations, salutations, gossip, birth and the business of death. The business Eddie Ryan in his weaker moments feels himself to be a part of. When his spirits are that way he can tell, because he's always more blithe, more courageous, more comforting.

Two calls come that evening in May. Mary, Eddie, Eileen, Little Eddie and Cody are at the table making their way through bowls of beef stew and a loaf of bread. Midway through every meal Cody has a habit of turning whatever he's eating into a sandwich. It's as if he gives up and reverts to simpler notions: good food is food eaten with the hands, life fits between two slices of whole wheat more easily than spread across a piece of china for the world to see. Eileen and Little Eddie take their cues from him. They put chunks of beef, carrots, onion and potatoes on a slice of bread, cover it with another slice and then mash it together, compressing it with the heel of a hand until it oozes out the side.

At first Mary fought this but once it became apparent that Cody had another habit of eating whatever they fussed over, she gave up. At least there weren't any leftovers.

"Cody, I hope you don't take this the wrong way, but sometimes you're like having a dog around," Mary says, watching him scrape what's left in Eileen's bowl onto another piece of bread.

"Oh no, don't worry about offending me. Waste is what's offensive. Got no truck with waste."

He mashes the bread together, then two-hands it into his mouth, taking a double bite and chewing it down.

The first time the phone rings, Eddie goes cold and his mind doubles back on itself. There'd been a lull in the dying since the Pet Man and work was slow. He knows of only two ways to feel about this, good and bad. The prospect of his families' well-being diminishes when others live, and prospers when others die. He's between a rock and a hard place. His only hope is that an ancient meanspirited man with eight children and twenty-four grandchildren has kicked in his sleep. Those are the easiest to take. The veil of grief settles gently.

It's the school calling.

They want to know if Mary would be interested in a job, finishing out the school year as a teacher's aide in the resource room. The woman whose place she'd be taking has just had a baby. It's come a month early. She and the baby are fine, but she won't be able to come back until September.

The principal presents it to Mary as if he's been highly inconvenienced by this. Mary thinks for a moment to tell him in a nice way to go piss off, but she doesn't. She knows the resource teacher, Mrs. Hall. She knows the woman works hard and needs the help. She suspects if she turns it down the principal will go back to Mrs.

Hall and say he tried, but couldn't get anyone, and there's only four weeks of school left, anyhow. He'll ask if she can go it alone in a way that will let her know she doesn't have a choice. Mary says yes, she'd love to.

Eddie and Cody think it's a grand idea, even when she tells them they'll have to take charge of Little Eddie from seven-thirty to three every day for the rest of the school year.

"No sweat," Cody says. "There's one of him and two of us. That's about even."

"It'll be fine," Eddie says. "But you know you don't have to. We still have the Huguenot money."

"I need to get out," she says.

They both know things have been a little slow. He touches her hand and it's enough to send her off in her head, excited over the prospects. They're both thinking how interesting the possibility is. Maybe it will open up some doors, get her back on track to finish her degree. His touch tells her, Don't sweat it, in a small way, it's a grand idea.

Mary gets up and collects the plates and bowls that have accumulated in front of Cody. Already they've been cleaned of leftovers and will take only a quick rinse.

"You and me, tiger," Cody says, running his fingers over the little boy's ribs like the keys on a piano, making him laugh and kick.

"Leave him alone," Eileen says. "He'll wet his pants."

"He probably already has," Eddie says, looking at his watch. "It's about that time of day."

"Out," Mary says. "All of you. I have to clean up and make an appointment for a physical tomorrow. I have to get out a dress or two and get them ironed."

They troop out the door, headed for the sandbox and the wading pool. Eddie is the last to go. He grabs Mary by the haunch and kisses her on the neck.

"I think it's neat," he says.

"*Neat.* What kind of word is that?"

"It's a neat word," he says, giving her another squeeze and heading out the door.

The second time the phone rings, it's late in the evening. Mary and Eddie share the newspaper while Cody sleeps on the couch. He has a cushion humped over the arm for a pillow and the other two cushions slid down to carry his back and his hind end. For the effort he's taken to make it comfortable, he's still managed to find sleep rolled to his side, one arm under him, his other hand in his pants pocket, the high leg cast over the bottom one and his foot square on the floor. He looks to be falling though he doesn't move.

Eddie gets it on the third ring.

It's Lionel Bibeau.

He says, "This is Lionel Bibeau. My father is Arthur Bouchea."

Eddie knows this part. It's how Lionel enters a conversation. Arthur is old and now Eddie thinks he's died. He's sad for that because Arthur's a kind old man. The year he retired as foreman from the blanket mill, one of his mill hands, a Bibeau woman, got her long hair caught in a shaft and it was pulled from her head. Arthur took her home with him. He was a lifelong bachelor so when Lionel was born, he became a Bibeau and not a Bouchea and grew to be a man himself with a good family.

But between the loss of her hair and learning her son couldn't be baptized, his mother became not quite right; and today the people of Inverawe hold to the sadness of this story as if it were their own. They know she left awhile back for Quebec to stay. Or maybe, some say, it was Lowell, Massachusetts. Either way, it helps the story to be more of a story.

"My daughter has died down in Springfield and I need for you to pick her up. Is that the kind of thing you can do?"

Lionel's voice is faint and ghostly. Eddie knows the sound and no matter how often he's heard it, no matter how good he is at what he does, it always gets to him in the first moment. He always has to grip something, the receiver, or the rolled edge of the counter top, and then it passes and he's doing what he does best, making death a little easier.

"She's down there in the morgue. They've had her for quite a while. I'm just terrified of cities and personally I won't even go into one. If I have to go down to claim her, I don't know what I'll do."

"Yes, Lionel. I'll take care of everything. Is your wife there with you?"

"She's here and so's my father. We're okay."

"I'll stop by tomorrow night and then we can talk."

When Eddie goes back to the living room, Cody is explaining to Mary how he can sleep anywhere he has to anytime he has to.

"It's something you learn to do," he's saying. "Why, I've slept in trunks and trailers, on pickup seats, on pine boughs, in moving vehicles and in the bucket of a front-end loader. One time I slept in the snowbank. I had a quart of vodka in me, though. It probably saved my life."

Eddie recounts the phone call and Cody immediately goes into speculation as to the missing details. He says he won't be able to sleep until he gets to the bottom of it.

Mary doesn't say anything. She touches Eddie. This time on the side of the head. It's her way of letting him know she's there without intruding. Every time she finds a different spot to leave her imprint, so it's not mere habit, an arm, a shoulder, a finger, his chest. She wishes he could be more professional, more slick, and in the same moment she loves him because he isn't.

"Take Cody with you," she says. "Eileen will be in school and Little Eddie can go with me."

"Well, I'd better get to work on this sleep thing. It looks like tomorrow is going to be a mighty big day."

"Yes," Eddie says. "That will be fine."

That night, Eddie and Mary lie in bed, the sheets thrown back and a small oscillating fan sweeping the room, sweeping their bodies with cool breeze.

"It never gets easy, does it?"

Her voice is a whisper, making the words not so important as that there be some sound between them. She's had to work herself up to say this much. It's difficult to gauge how fine his sadness is and she doesn't want to be the one to send him back down if he's already on his way up. She thinks that maybe that's what she's just done.

"I was just thinking about tonight, before. Cody and Little Eddie were feeding the horse and Eileen was being quiet. I asked her what was up and she wanted to know if you were going to be a teacher in her school. I told her, kind of."

"Then what'd she say?" Mary asks.

"Nothing. I think she's trying to figure it out on her own. It'll be interesting to see what she comes up with."

"What's up with you?"

"I had this thought where it will be better if I die before you do, because you can live without me, but I can't live without you."

"You're wrong," she says. "Dead wrong."

■ ■

■

Mary stands on the porch with Little Eddie riding on her hip. They wave as Eddie and Cody back down the drive in the '72 Cadillac limousine. She thinks again how she can't wait to get ahead a little so they can have it painted, anything but powder blue.

Cody doesn't wave. She knows he's worried he'll rip a seam in his new white shirt or catch a button and pull it off. He's uncomfortable in his dark suit, any suit, and has made it known every time he puts it on. Eddie makes him button the sleeves and collar and wear his tie snug at the neck. He's told Mary it has a remarkably civilizing effect. Makes him talk less, keeps him still. Otherwise he'd be orchestrating his speech with his hands and he'd be rubbernecking at every car they passed, every town they went through. He's a great one for knocking coffee cups off the dash and dislodging the rearview mirror from its perch over the windshield.

She must now go for her physical. Dr. Pot is the school doctor and does the physicals for personnel and student athletes. You can go to your own physician, but then the school doesn't reimburse. She decides she'll ride the Schwinn. Little Eddie can ride in the kid seat.

■

Cody starts up with his chatter as soon as they've crossed the river into Brattleboro and turned up onto the interstate, I91 South. He insists on keeping the map folded in his lap and verifying it against their experience on the road. He complains about minor discrepancies in mileage between the map and his reckonings. Eddie refuses to give him readings off the odometer, but does tell him he's going a steady fifty miles an hour.

Eddie thinks this to be worse than traveling with the kids. Eileen says only two things, How much longer? and I have to pee; and Little Eddie thinks the inside of a car is to be wandered.

As they pass each exit, Cody has a story to tell. Somehow the sign for Bernardston reminds him of a sex tape he heard about an Irish gamekeeper and an English lady. It takes up a good bit of the drive all the way to Northampton, Cody performing both roles.

"The Russian used to play that on the way to work," he says. "I was only a kid and he picked me up every morning. We had to drive to White River Junction. Usually I'd fall asleep but somehow I'd wake up with a hard-on every time. You could hear him and her huffing and puffing on the eight-track for the whole ride."

"Why was he called the Russian?"

"We were building a six-story office for the telephone company. It's still there to see, right across from the funeral parlor. That guy would come out and watch us work. The superintendent hired him to dig up a piece of the street with his little backhoe. I was down in the hole when he busted out some wires. Nobody knew if they were live or not. He told me to touch them. If they were, he'd give me a discount. We thought that was real funny. If you ask me, I think he was tutti-fruity. You know it."

"Cody, how'd the Russian get his name?"

"I heard you. You think I'm deaf?"

Cody ruffles the map and goes into a long one-man discussion on pro basketball upon learning its Hall of Fame is in Springfield; then he talks about the state of timber rights in the Berkshires to the west and how easily the laws are circumvented if the need should arise.

"The Russian," Cody finally says, "ran away from home and joined the Navy when he was fourteen. His mother found out and went to Washington. The War Department tracked him down. He was on a ship in Vladivostok, serving as a guard in the brig. The prisoners had tattooed his arms and shoulders. When they got him back, his parents put him right into the eighth grade. When we were in White River Junction that winter, he was in the habit of parking his VW Bug in the church lot next to the funeral home. One day the snow came off the slate roof and crushed it. That was the last time I ever had to listen to that sex tape."

Eddie thinks to say, I've heard that story before, but he doesn't. He lets it go.

A few miles out of Springfield, Cody folds the map and puts it in the glove box. He straightens his tie and brushes off his suit with the backs of his fingers.

He says quietly, "How is it we have come to be doing this?"

Eddie explains how Lionel didn't want to come to the city and asked for him to handle everything.

"He said he was afraid."

"I can understand that," Cody says. "A lot of people have fears, the dark, heights, closed-in places. Slamming doors can scare you."

"Thunder," Eddie says, "and cars backfiring."

"Look," Cody says, "a sign for the Basketball Hall of Fame."

■

Mary and Little Eddie get into the shower together. He stays near the back of the tub, up where it begins to slope, his small toes digging the rubber shower mat for traction. He likes getting in the shower. He laughs and keeps reaching into the spray and wiping at the water running down his face.

He won't talk when he's in here. He saves his words for when they're not expected. Mary's been told it's that way with second children, especially boys. They can go a long time before they speak. With so many other people doing the talking they must think, Why bother, I have what I need.

Mary stands with her back to the shower, letting it prickle her shoulders and run down her body, making rivulets along the lay of her skin over the muscle and bone. She knows down low the water spreads and gets him in the face. She protects him from most of it, letting him reach around her, to be in it only as much as he wants to. She washes the front of her, then turns to rinse, holding out her hands as if the water were flowers to be caught. As she does this, she feels something nudging between her legs, and reaching down, she finds it's her son. He's holding a cup there, filling it with the water that's run the length of her body, channeled to between her legs and now draining through her hair.

"What are you doing?" she says, smiling and laughing.

Little Eddie pulls the cup back and tries to take a drink, but it slips from his hands and bounces on the mat, sending a splash of water fanning up the sides.

When she's done with washing herself, she moves back to where he is and sits on the tub wall, making sure the shower curtain isn't pulled too tightly. One time Little Eddie brought it down and took it on the head. Everyone came running when he cried, and before they got their wits back, the bathroom floor was a puddle.

She holds her son between her knees and soaps his body from his feet to his shoulders, working the soap into a lather that makes his soft, white skin slick and slippery. She washes between his toes and fingers and he's tickled. She does the Little Pigs rhyme and he laughs again. She reaches between his legs and washes his penis. That done, she has him close his eyes and soaps his face and head, whispering all the while for him to keep his eyes shut, it will only be a second, it will only be a second.

When he's finally washed, she coaxes him forward into the spray, cupping her hand over his eyes so the spray won't prickle his face. This is the part he doesn't like and he fights her. He squirms and starts to cry, but by then it's over and she's pulled him back from the water. They are both laughing.

Mary shuts down the shower and sweeps back the curtain. She hoists Little Eddie out onto the floor and then gets towels. She takes them into the living room and he follows her, the two of them leaving small puddles behind them as they go. She lays one on the rug and he gets down on it, letting her fold the bottom half over him. He lies there looking up at her, watching, as she takes the other towel and pats her body dry. By the time she's done, he's rolled himself free and in the process managed to get dry. He's up and headed straight for Eileen's tall basket of toys and games she's allowed to keep downstairs, but before he can tip it over and spill its contents across the rug, Mary has him and they're headed up the stairs.

After she dresses her son, they go into her and Eddie's room. She smiles as she pokes through her underwear drawer, looking at a pair of new white cotton underpants, laughing, remembering her mother telling her to always wear clean underpants in case she was in an accident.

Mary said, at the time, "What if I'm in an accident and I get killed? It won't make any difference then, will it?"

Her mother said, "It will to those around who are left to suffer the indignities of having a daughter die in dirty underwear."

Mary wonders when she'll tell Eileen the same thing, mother to daughter. She knows she'll just blurt it out one day without thinking. She wonders what her daughter will say. Hell, she thinks, it's trouble enough just to get her to wear clothes.

Mary slips into a pair of shorts and a T-shirt. She keeps moving quickly to keep tabs on her son. Back downstairs she matches up socks and sneakers for them and a hat for Little Eddie to keep the sun off his head. That done, they're out the door and off.

Pedaling down the road to Dr. Pot's house, she feels younger.

This will be the first job she's had in a long while. Not that the work she does in the mortuary isn't a job, because it is. She's very good with what she does, assisting with restorations and cosmetology, but it's a job she does with him at the house. This is different. It's in the public. The paycheck will have only her name on it.

At Dr. Pot's house, just down from the common, she parks the bike and takes Little Eddie onto her hip. She climbs the steps to the porch floor. The sign on the door says, COME RIGHT IN. It's the same kind of sign you buy at K Mart that might say, KEEP OUT, NO TRES-PASSING or YARD SALE.

Dr. Pot's sitting in his own waiting room reading the newspaper. He gets up when she opens the door, setting off small bells that tinkle in the air. He smiles and gives the hint of a bow. The waiting room is clean and well lit. It smells faintly of incense, saffron more so than antiseptic. Mary likes that.

This is the first time she's been here. The family doctors are in Keene, the pediatrician is in a group of doctors who have the ability to provide many services, including a female obstetrician who delivered Little Eddie. In fact the doctor was seven months pregnant with her first when she delivered him. A coincidence that's kept them in touch.

There are posters of Greece on the walls of Dr. Pot's office, the kind you see in pizza parlors. Mary thinks that's a nice touch too. Different.

"I'm Mary Ryan," she says. "I'm told you do the physicals for school employees."

"The school," he says. "Yes, yes, the school."

He then explains to Mary how there's a slight problem. His girl didn't come in today, He tells her it's his policy to have his female assistant present with female patients and in the case of a child to have a parent. He tells her the girl who assists him went into labor on Sunday morning and delivered last night.

"With these physicals there is no need to disrobe, it's just a more comfortable situation."

Mary explains how she's just been offered this job at the school because a baby was born and he nods and smiles.

"I don't mind," she says. "I'd rather get it done with."

"That will be fine if you don't mind."

While they are talking, Mary puts Little Eddie down and he

wanders to the magazine rack. It now comes thumping to the floor and the magazines strew over the rug like wet fish. Dr. Pot laughs.

"I have just the thing," he says. "Please come."

Mary follows him down the hall, leading Little Eddie by the hand. They go into an examination room where Dr. Pot has opened a base cabinet full of toys.

"He can play with these and I also have something else."

He leaves the room and comes back with a glass jar of lollipops. "Okay?"

"Yes," she says. "He's learned to lick them and not eat them."

"Very good."

Dr. Pot sits at a desk after giving Little Eddie a lollipop. He motions for Mary to sit too.

"First I need information," he says, taking out a white form. "If you don't mind. Age? Height? Weight?"

Mary answers the questions for him as he asks them. He questions her on her medical history, childhood illnesses, immunizations, whether there's been cancer, TB, mental illnesses, brain disorders, blood disorders, nerve disorders, drug or alcohol abuse, heart medications, surgery. He asks about her deliveries, whether they were problem-free. He asks if her menstrual periods are regular and if she experiences any discomfort.

"Yes, they are," she says, "and no, I don't. But when I was thirteen they were excruciating so I went on the pill and was on it right up until I wanted to get pregnant and that seemed to happen right away. We went for natural childbirth, but believe me, I was rehearsing the names of the drugs right up to the last minute."

"No problem," Dr. Pot says. "No need to note that."

Little Eddie lies quietly on his back, holding a block up over his face, turning it in his hands. When he's seen all sides, he rolls over and picks up another one.

"If you don't mind, I'll need a urine sample."

He hands her a small jar and directs her down the hall. Mary goes into the bathroom. She realizes he's given her a rinsed-out mustard jar. She smiles and thinks, What the hell. She pees in it and screws down the top tightly.

Back in the examination room, Dr. Pot is passing blocks to Little Eddie. He takes them and drops them on the floor. Mary hands him the sample and he says thank you, wrapping a label around it and securing it with a rubber band.

"I now need your blood pressure."

Mary sits down and he puts the cuff on her arm, pumping it up and reading the gauge.

"Very good," he says. "You have good blood pressure. Now ears, eyes, nose and throat."

He takes a flashlight from his pocket and peers inside her.

"Very good," he says, "very good. Now hearing and seeing."

Dr. Pot puts the flashlight back in his pocket and goes out the door. He closes it behind him and then Mary hears him whisper.

"Can you hear me?"

"Yes, I can," she whispers back.

"Very good," he whispers.

He comes back in and closes the door. He has a chart of E's he's made with a Magic Marker. He asks her to start at the top and indicate the direction they are pointing.

Mary works her way through the chart.

"Very good," he says. "Now look straight ahead, spread your arms and touch the tip of your nose with your index finger. Right, now left."

When she's accomplished this he has her walk around the room on her tiptoes and then on the balls of her feet. He tells her she's done well.

"Now please sit down," he says. "Sit straight and breathe evenly."

Dr. Pot goes around behind her. He isn't touching her but his small hands are close to her body. He tells her, Deep breath, and then he says, Very good. He moves over her lower back, spine and shoulders.

He comes around to her front and she can see he has his eyes closed. He moves his hands over her shoulders, breasts, sides and stomach, his hands not touching her, his eyes closed, telling her to breathe deeply, then saying, Very good, each time she does. She watches his blank tan face and can now see that his upper and lower eyelids are traced with white scar tissue that meets where they close together.

Finally he opens his eyes and smiles.

"You've passed," he says. "I'm sorry these tests are so foolish but they are what is required."

"Your eyes," she says, now embarrassed for having asked.

Dr. Pot doesn't say anything right away. He goes to his desk and finishes the paper work. When he's done he looks at her for a long time. He then looks down at the floor and begins to speak.

"I was a professor at the Hue University," he says. "In January 1968 the NVA attacked the city. They fire the one-twenty-two-millimeter rockets and take over the Imperial Citadel on the north back of the River of Perfume. My wife and I had a house on Te loi Street. It's a street where the students walked and the tennis players met for drinks at the Cercle Sportif. It was cold and drizzly and misty. The rockets came all the time. There were dead women in their gardens, children crushed under roofs and rats eating at the bodies.

"The first of February they came with bullhorns calling us out into the street. They had my name. They knew I was a doctor so they took me away with them. They had tattoos that said, 'Born in the North, Died in the South.' To keep me from escaping they sewed my eyes shut."

Mary's hand goes to her throat. She fights the urge to show her horror, not wanting him to think it's directed toward him. But Dr. Pot isn't looking her way. He's looking at Little Eddie, now asleep on the floor.

"Later I heard there were forty thousand troops in the attack. Three thousand people were executed. It is said that it was done by the Black teams and American CIA.

"On twenty-fourth March 1975, they let me go because I'd served them well. They brought me south and let me back into the city before the siege to find my wife. The next day the shelling started. I found her in the Cathedral. We escaped east to Tan My and sailed for Da Nang on a Navy ship. Da Nang was swollen with families and missing children. The NVA followed. We went to the docks to get on a freighter. The barges were full. Women were throwing their babies to Australian girls and American girls who were leaving the city. Every time the barges were pulled away, the people grabbed the lines and tied them up again and the barges would be drawn back. My wife was caught in the ropes and was dragged into the water. The barge crushed her against the pilings when the people pulled it in. I watched it happen. There was nothing to do. So I went back into the city. There was peace after the capture. From there I went back to Hue. It's an old city. The pine trees in the mountains are beautiful, peaceful. The geckos cling fast to the white walls. The dead were everywhere, their skin was like tallow."

"How did you finally get out?" Mary asks.

"We were a very small group of trusted friends. We were twenty altogether. During five years we were able to put twenty million piasters together, enough to buy a ferryboat, food, water and weapons. We were only men."

Dr. Pot looks down at the floor as if he's now trying to find something he's lost and then he looks back up. Mary can tell he's there, thousands of miles away, the look on his face at once empty and searching, a look she's seen on her husband's face.

"We met on Cam Ranh Bay, the night of twenty-first June 1980. We came there from all over the country. There was a pearly fog over everything. We made it into the China Sea. There were pirates, but we fought them off. After twenty-five days we were picked up by the British and later went to France. The others stayed there, and I came to America. I have never heard from them, but they are still missing to me, *ils me manquent.*"

Mary sits quietly in the silence left behind after the story of Dr. Pot's life. She feels to be outside of herself, transported into other lives, Dr. Pot's, his wife's and in an odd way into her husband's, into those years he speaks about so seldom. She thinks about the small hints of a life lived outside this one, Eddie's preference for buttons because they don't make the sound zippers make, his choice of any color but black when it comes to garbage bags. She's sad for him and Dr. Pot, for all of them because they are now left to make their stands in only so many small ways and yet they don't complain, it doesn't control them. They just seem to have made adjustments.

"Hey," Dr. Pot says. "I tell you joke I see last night on *Hee Haw.* Man walks into doctor's office and says, 'My arm hurt every time I do this.' Doctor says, 'Well, don't do that. Fifteen bucks!' Get it? 'Well, don't do that.' It cracks me up."

Mary laughs at the joke. She's heard it before, but Dr. Pot's pleasure easily becomes her own.

Still laughing, he gets up and goes to his glass cabinets. From plastic bags he takes dried leaves, stems, root matter and seeds. These he puts into a large pestle and works them with the mortar until they are finely ground. He dumps them into a bag and hands them to her.

"If ever those cramps come to bother, drink this in a tea. Take these too, for him." He hands her a small fistful of lollipops.

"Thank you," Mary says. "He's been wonderful. This time of day he usually runs roughshod over me."

"I don't tell everyone this," Dr. Pot whispers, "but I melt a very mild sedative into the candy. It really makes a difference."

■

Eddie and Cody find out the Bibeau girl came in as a Jane Doe and in the shuffle was overlooked. She's been here for six months.

"There's no reliable exchange of information," they're told, by the man holding her file, an *Unknown* label marking its tab. "She was found partially submerged in a brook, wearing a watch and arrow-shaped earrings. She wore a necklace with a silver horn and a silver heart on it. She'd been killed by a shotgun blast. We found the man who did it, but he didn't know who she was either. There's no reliable exchange of information. It was just one of those human things."

The man tells him it's a problem that's only getting worse, runaways, young girls coming to the city, falling in with the wrong crowd and meeting such ends. Eddie knows it's true. He stops listening.

Back in the car, the Bibeau girl secured, they head for the interstate.

"That motherfucker didn't pursue shit," Cody says.

Eddie has never seen him this angry before. He looks for a convenience store and spots a 7-Eleven. He thinks they both could use a cold soda. Eddie tells Cody he's going in for snacks and to watch the car. He tells him he can take off his coat and tie, maybe roll up his sleeves and unbutton his shirt a little bit. Cool down, he says.

Eddie doesn't like the situation any better than Cody does, but he doesn't have the luxury of rage. He'll have to help the Bibeaus and Arthur Bouchea when he gets back and the last thing they'll need is commiseration. He must be prepared to offer a little more than just sharing in their misery. He must offer them some strength.

"You just calm down. I thought the guy was sincere. He didn't like the situation any better than you."

Eddie walks away, the sound of Cody huffing his disgust burning at his ears. Someone has spray-painted graffiti on the store windows. It says, "Nuke the homeless and steal their shopping carts." Inside, Eddie picks up a rack of Pepsi and a box of Ding Dongs. He gets a jar of jam too, knowing Cody likes to smear it on the small chocolate cakes. He gets a newspaper and then notices there are cameras watching him and the guy at the cash register is following his movements on a television monitor.

Eddie goes to the counter and takes out his wallet.

"So what's this, the last supper or what?" the guy asks, a stupid grin on his face.

Eddie hands him the cash, at the same time leaning toward him.

"Why don't you go fuck yourself," he whispers.

They make the interstate and within a few miles have left the city behind. They're moving north, into the mountains and stands of pine. Cody is finishing off his second Ding Dong, taking bites, then filling the space with jam he laves on with his pocketknife. Already his shirt is stained red and brown but at least he's calmed himself down.

Cody finishes his sweet concoction, then drains the last half of his Pepsi in one go, his throat working to take the liquid, burning with the carbonation. He smacks his gums, then sucks at his teeth.

"Don't think I'm done being pissed," he says. "I can't be bought off with a few sweets."

"No. It was nothing like that. We just needed a small diversion and I've thought eating to always be a pretty good one."

Cody belches, then holds his hand to his chest.

"Tickles the old heart," he says, and belches again. "Boy, I feel like I could puke."

Eddie doesn't worry. He's heard this before after one of Cody's binges.

They drive on, not speaking. Eddie still doing fifty, the old engine solidly humming along, Cody reading the newspaper next to him. Cars and trucks pass. People gape at them and Eddie returns their looks with a blank stare he's perfected for such encounters. They pass back through the same towns, Northampton, Deerfield and Greenfield, catching only glimpses of the Connecticut River meandering through the valley, low meadows running to its banks. They pass by cornfields, orchards, potato fields, onion fields and tobacco fields. From the highway can be seen the sheds used for drying the leaves. Their boards have weathered to silver and shrunk to make the gaps left for air even wider.

Eddie remembers an economics professor he had his first year at college. The man wrote his dissertation on tobacco farming in the Connecticut River valley. It's one of two places in the country where they grow cigar-wrapper leaf. The professor was from North Carolina. It gave him and Eddie something to talk about.

He thinks about the Bibeau girl and how she's now dead and there ain't no two ways to cut it. She'll never have the chance to learn about the tobacco from a college professor. There will be no more of those small moments of discovery when alls you can say is, Isn't it a small world. There will be a nice service and he'll hear again the words grace, God, love, rest, reward, final, peace, tears and heart.

But the dumb truth is she's dead and there's no good reason for it. He's thinking of his own daughter and clamps his hand over his suit coat pocket, measuring out the pressure, until he thinks he can feel pressed against his breast the watch, the arrow-shaped earrings, and the chain running through the horn and heart made of silver. At that moment he's afraid he's losing his nerve.

"The sons-a-bitches," Cody says. "This is the day for mother-fuckers and ever shall be. Listen to this."

Cody reads a story about how in Paraguay police have rescued seven Brazilian babies from a gang of kidnappers planning to kill them and sell their vital organs in the USA. The babies were three to six months old and destined to be killed at American organ banks for fifteen thousand dollars apiece. The authorities said, "We began to get suspicious when prospective adoptive parents wanted any baby, even deformed ones."

Eddie can feel his eyes burning and his stomach churn. He puts on his sunglasses and whenever Cody starts to speak, waves him off with a hand.

■

The children have gone to bed. Mary and Eddie are at the kitchen table. They share the facts of their day without knowing the other is holding back, without knowing the other is lost in remembering the day.

Cody comes in from the trailer with a blue brochure.

"I need two witnesses," he says. "I've decided to become an organ donor."

"Where did you get that?" Eddie asks.

"In Springfield at the morgue. At the time I thought it was a little late."

Mary takes the brochure and reads it over. She's familiar with most of the conditions from working with Eddie.

"Why don't we have these cards?" she asks him.

"I don't know. Just haven't gotten around to it. It doesn't matter anyway. Next of kin can authorize donation."

"Well, what if we go together?"

"Then one of the kids can do it for Christ sakes. Do we have to talk about this now?" he says, getting up and leaving to go outside, but he doesn't go far, he sits on the porch. Inside he can hear Cody saying he didn't think things went too badly today, though it sure as hell does seem like something is bothering Eddie.

"We'll leave him alone," she says. "Sometimes he just wants to be alone. Now look here, you've checked two boxes, any needed organs or tissues and only the ones specified below, and you checked all of those—eyes, kidneys, skin, liver, heart, pancreas and ear bones. You also checked that your body can be used for anatomical study."

"Guess I fucked up. The doctor will think he's reading a Chinese menu."

"You have to do the medical history on the emergency health part. Do you have allergies, diabetes, heart problems or epilepsy?"

"I would know if I did, wouldn't I?"

"Yes, you would."

"Here, I'll sign it and you get Eddie to sign it. He's probably on the porch. When the time comes, the doctors can figure it out, or better yet do this, decide on how much you want them to have, then cross out the rest."

"One part's got me hanging. It says here if you donate your entire body, your remains are cremated and the ashes interred in special graves by the Humanity Gifts Registry."

"You'll just have to think that one over. Meanwhile get Eddie to witness and then you can cross out, okay? I think he's out on the porch. He's probably cooled off a little."

But Eddie isn't on the porch, he's hiking down the road to Washburn's store, where there's a pay phone. He's put off calling Lionel Bibeau for too long and now he must. He knows it will be okay. He'll make his call, then put money in the soda machine and wrench free a Pepsi. He'll sit on the common and drink it, imagining Mrs. Huguenot's fountain to be there, trickling cold water over granite slabs. When it's late he'll walk home to his sleeping family—Mary, Eileen, Little Eddie, Cody and now the Bibeau girl.

13

Mary gets to school early. Eileen wouldn't ride with her. She insisted on taking the bus. Like usual, she said. Mary must go to the business office, then meet with the principal. She wishes so many things hadn't come together at once, the Bibeau girl, Dr. Pot's stupid trick with the lollipops and Eddie's disappearing. She was in bed, awake with the lights off, by the time he got home. He crawled in behind her, slung an arm over her and kissed her shoulder. He reached inside her nightshirt and held her breast, that's all, just held it and after a while his breathing evened out and she thinks he slept, at least a little more than she did.

In the principal's office, she's nervous. Too many years of schooling, where it's impressed upon you that the principal's office is the last place you want to be. She remembers how when she was in high school, streaking was all the rage. She and two other girls burst out the door at the back of the gym one day in body stockings and made it around the track and back inside before they got caught. The word went out, though, and before the day was over they were in the principal's office. He told them how appalled he was because the three of them came from such good families. But he let them off, wanting to avoid scandal. They came to think much less of him for doing that.

Mary finds occasion to smile as she remembers these events, her only scrape with public school authority. She reminds herself she's an adult, the mother of two, a married woman, a good citizen. Screw it, she thinks. It's just a job, persevere.

The principal hasn't come in yet. He's outside in the hall greeting students, joking with teachers. She can hear his voice. He sounds like a nice man. She only knows him to say hello, although she's seen him every time she's come up to the school for science fairs, story hours, bicycle rodeos and all of the ball games, the sporting events she and Eddie try to take in.

It's a small school and she has to admire his efforts. All twelve grades are in the same complex of three small separate buildings. The kids of Inverawe grow up together that way. The buildings are called towns—Bigtown, Middletown and Littletown—and the rooms are homes. Mary likes this.

Finally he comes in. He's wearing white, his shoes, pants, belt, tie, shirt and jacket all white. She doesn't feel so much anymore like she overdressed. On his desk is a gray cast-iron howitzer. He slips his pen into its barrel and sits down.

"Mrs. Ryan," he says, "so good for you to help us out on such short notice. All set at the business office?"

"Yes," Mary says, "everything went fine."

"Your physical. I hope it went well. Dr. Pot is a nice man. When the Methodist Church sponsored him, part of the deal was the school would use him instead of the students and faculty having to go to Keene. He's been wonderful. He attends our games as physician and actually saves the town quite a bit of money."

"Fine," Mary says, "it went well. He seems to be a sincere man."

"Good," the principal says. "That's it on this end. Mrs. Hall's home is in Littletown. The secretary can direct you. Maybe we can chat at the end of the day."

He stands and Mary stands. They shake hands and she leaves. She knows where Littletown is. It's where Eileen spends most of her day.

Mrs. Hall's in her home when Mary gets there. She's kind, but brusque in manner. Mary likes her immediately.

"This is Poissant day," she says. "It's the way the schedule goes.

We have Poissants on Tuesday and Thursday and then the rest come on Monday, Wednesday and Friday. You're Eileen's mother, aren't you?"

"Yes, I am."

"She's a crackerjack. One in a million. Remember now, don't be too ambitious. These kids don't need a busybody. This room is a safe harbor and whatever more we do is frosting on the cake. You'll be a helper, reading directions, monitoring tests, going over work sheets, that kind of stuff. You'll do fine."

And that's when Mrs. Hall shakes her hand and finally smiles.

On Mary's first day of school, she's put in charge of two Poissant boys, Maple and Micah, both ten.

They're dirty boys, yellow-skinned and yellow-eyed with redness seeping at the lids. There's a smell about them too, a smell of urine and sweat.

She can see already that these boys don't need to take a math test, they need a bath and some oatmeal, some fruits and vegetables. She decides then and there that at the appropriate time she's going to say to the principal, as harebrained as this sounds, I want you to figure out a way I can get these kids a bath and some oatmeal. Every day. And I'll do it. I'll even buy the soap and the cereal.

It's her job to help them get through a math test. Because they're resource students, they're allowed to take their tests in the resource room, something that pisses off the math department in no uncertain terms.

Mary reads the directions to them. One sits on either side of her. The only other sound in the small room is the hum of the fluorescent bulbs overhead.

She asks them if they understand but they don't say anything. They sit quietly staring at her face. She thinks of them as kit foxes, sitting on their haunches at the edge of a mowing, their lazy yellow eyes seeming to be close to sleep.

She gives them their papers and sits back. It's simple addition and subtraction. They do it on their fingers and with jot marks on a scrap sheet. Sometimes they combine both methods, sometimes they just put down a number. She looks over their shoulders and is confused by their answers. There will be three or four correct ones in a row, then one that makes no sense at all, then three or four more that are correct. She feels sorry for them and then for herself. It's going to be a long day.

Mary escorts Maple and Micah to the lunchroom, then goes into the teachers' lounge. It's two rooms, one meant for eating and one for working, but the way it's used is the men work and eat in one while the women work and eat in the other.

Mrs. Hall is already there. She has carrot sticks, celery, crackers and cheese spread out before her. Mary gets her lunch from the refrigerator and sits down too.

"How'd they do?" Mrs. Hall asks.

Mary explains how the boys did on their tests. Mrs. Hall smiles. She tells Mary how pleased she is the boys were able to get so many right answers. Mary realizes how she's been seeing things a little bit backward.

"Don't worry," Mrs. Hall says, patting Mary's arm. "They did a fine job. I'm sure they worked hard to please you. I think they're great kids. The stories they tell."

"I don't know how to say this, but is there any way we could get them a bath?"

Mrs. Hall smiles again and Mary can see how pretty she is. Her eyes get like sparks and her red lips pinch forward.

"Something strange is going on," she says. "That family I've known all my life. They have a history of intermarriage, deformities, mental illness, lupus, cancer, blindness, unexplained childhood death and women dying in childbirth. And I've known them all, the ones who lived, that is. In the old days I took them right to the washroom first thing every morning. We'd brush teeth, wash faces. We'd have a sponge bath and a shampoo if needed. You know most of them came right from the barn. Then the principal told me I couldn't do it anymore. It had to do with laws and regulations. Good laws, needed laws, but the old son of a bitch was using those laws against the special kids. I've been teaching these kids long before there was ever anything known as special education. Long before any public law. The problem is, good people made the law for bad people to carry out."

Mrs. Hall looks down at her food. For a second Mary thinks she's praying because she's so quiet. Without looking up she begins to speak again, her voice soft and muffled.

"I'm just getting too old. It wasn't any better back then than it is now, I guess. I'm just getting tired of the new. I probably should retire. I'm old enough."

Juanita Poissant comes into resource for the afternoon. Mary's first thought is to be as professional as she can, to look up the girl's file, but she doesn't. She sits down with her and talks.

She says, "Juanita, what a pretty name. How did you get that name?"

The girl takes a red plastic billfold from her pocket, opens it and takes out a card.

"My father was in love with Rita Hayworth," she says, glancing at the brown and creased paper. "They were born on the same day, October seventeen, 1918. Her real name was Margarita Cansino. Do you like my coat?"

"Yes, I do. It's lovely."

"It's made of chicken-feet leather. It's really quite rare. My father says the cow is the most tranquil animal. In World War Two, they lay quietly in the pastures while the war raged on about them. Did you ever hear of the India baby?"

■

Owen Poissant comes down from the high school to work with Mrs. Hall every day from two-thirty until three. He's assigned a resource teacher in Bigtown, but refuses to work with him. The teacher's only interest is in sports and he seems to think it's a cure for what ails his students. He and Owen just don't get along.

Mary works her way around the small room. She's anxious to hear the conversation, wanting to learn as much as she can. She has to cover her mouth to keep from laughing.

"Owen, honey, I know that's what it's called, but in this essay you can't call it a shit spreader," Mrs. Hall is saying.

"But, Mrs. Hall, that's not what it's called, that's what it is."

"This has gone on too long. Will you trust me? Just use the word *manure* for shit every time you possibly can. It's a French word. Say it. *Manure*."

Owen says the word and then she makes him say it again and again until his lips protrude and his cheeks are drawn in each time he does.

"There. Doesn't that feel good in your mouth? There aren't many American words that do. There are a lot of French ones, though. They have a lot of words for things we can't say. Americans are awkward about that stuff so we use the French. That way we can say it without having a mouthful."

She pats his hand and points at the clock. He collects his papers and books. Mary thinks how at this point in the session, each one of them moved a little bit slower. She realizes it's because they like it in Mrs. Hall's room. They don't want to leave. It's the end of her first day and she's sad.

When Owen is gone, Mrs. Hall closes the door and shuts off the lights. She rummages through her pocketbook, coming out with matches and a small thin cigar. She motions for Mary to come sit with her behind the partition near the windows. From there they can see the ball fields. School teams are at practice and pickup games are in progress. Mrs. Hall lights her cigar, kicks off her shoes and puts her feet up on the sill. Holding the cigar between two fingers and touching the tip to her lips, she takes long puffs, becoming relaxed, giving in to the exhaustion.

"He has to go home and shovel shit," she says.

Both women laugh as if drunk on the sound of the word.

■

On Friday, schedules are thrown for a loop. The principal announces an assembly for twelve-thirty. It will last an hour. The ladies in the lunchroom are pissed off and talk about throwing the little shit in the vegetable soup pot. The teachers know they'll be left with the students after the assembly until the buses come, not a happy thought; and for others, there are final exams that will have to be canceled.

What's happened is, a National Guard buddy of the principal's pulled some strings and they're going to have a Marine Corps band perform.

The teachers' room now appears to be closer to the front lines than the musicians have ever been. Lunches are being scarfed down and then teachers head for the hall. News of the concert was to be top secret, but like all military endeavors, it was leaked from administration to a stage crew member. The travel of a rumor in the public school could teach a prairie fire a thing or two.

"Hey, listen to this," a biology teacher says. "The promo sheet says these guys are a cross between Earth Wind and Fire and Blood, Sweat and Tears."

The earth science teacher and health teacher joke about using the concert as a basis for an interdisciplinary unit.

Mary keeps to the back of the auditorium. While the band plays, she tries to pick out as many of the Poissants as she can. She feels responsible for them and will be mortified if they get in trouble. From the back, though, all kids look to be the same. She hasn't learned them well enough to spot them, whereas other teachers seem to have the uncanny ability to ferret out the antsy kids, the spitballers, talkers and troublemakers from the long dark rows.

As they're taken out one by one over the first fifteen minutes, she sees none of them are resource kids. After that things settle. She still stays to the back of the huge room for fear of tripping in the dark and tumbling down to the foot of the stage, her dress flying up around her neck. Someone starts talking to her. The phys. ed. teacher.

"Did you ever notice," he says, "how poor people tend to tell you their whole life story if they get the opportunity?"

She turns and smiles. She confesses she must agree.

"The other day," he whispers, "I was in the post office in Keene and this lady was trying to complete a change of address. That's all, but by the time she got done, she'd told about her daughter who had a baby and lives next door. The baby is a girl and all three of them have the same name. I think the mother of this woman did too. It was a family name. Welfare was somehow in on it too. The line just kept growing so finally I got out of it and went to the cigar shop next door for *The Sporting News*. And this time there's a fat lady in front of me. She's got her shoes kicked off and her elbows up on the Lotto machine. She's thinking up numbers like it makes a difference and alls I can think is, there you go. It's like déjà vu all over again."

Mary can't help but laugh. She doesn't know if he's serious or not. Either way, it's funny. The band goes into a medley of Three Dog Night songs and for some reason the students respond with enthusiasm.

"How do these kids know this stuff?" she says, sensing him to still be standing nearby.

"Don't ask me, I'm tone-deaf."

The keyboardist takes over the next song. He sounds remarkably like Lionel Ritchie.

"He's really good," Mary says.

"Well, if nothing else, these kids won't go to their graves without seeing a black man in the flesh."

He goes on to explain how he went to Springfield for his phys. ed. degree. He was a football player and a lot of the team was black. He really got to like them.

Mary takes his words to be sincere. She looks at her watch, the digits glowing faintly in the dark. The end of the concert is coming near and she decides to get back to the resource room. If the exit of students is anything like their entrance she's afraid she'll be trampled. She knows she must also get to the grocery store.

"Hey, wait a minute," the phys. ed. teacher says, "I was wondering if you're stopping after work."

At first she doesn't understand what he's asking her. She thinks to say, yes, she needs to get groceries because Mrs. Hall is coming to supper. Then she realizes it's not what he means.

"After school every Friday," he says, "a bunch of us stop for beers."

"No. I can't. We have company tonight and I have to get groceries."

"Next week," he says.

"Yes, maybe next week."

Mary steps into the main corridor. She squints in the fluorescent glare. She's not sure, but she thinks he made a pass at her, then she feels foolish because it wasn't that at all. No matter, she says to herself, it sure has been a long week. The band goes into the "Marine Corps Hymn." A guidance counselor calls to her when she passes by. She stops and he comes out in the hall to meet her.

"They'll be lined up at the recruiter on Monday," he says.

She laughs.

"No. I'm serious," he says. "The Naval Academy now sends out recruitment letters to prospective students that begin, 'We're told you are an academic Top Gun.' "

Down the hall, the "Marine Corps Hymn" turns into "The Star-Spangled Banner."

"So how's it going?"

"Fine," she says.

The principal comes from his office. He still looks fresh, still a vision in white.

"Mrs. Ryan, may I see you a moment? Mary, I mean, you don't mind if I call you Mary?"

She says no, and follows him into his office. She's impressed again by how neat and orderly it is, except for the pencil protruding from the muzzle of the howitzer. Mary sits down. She's tired of smiling. Her mouth hurts from smiling so much. She's tired of doing it after a week and saying, fine, fine, but she doesn't know what else to do. She wishes she had no plans for supper. She wants just Eddie, the kids and a pizza. She hopes this one will be short.

"Mrs. Ryan, glad we have a chance to chat. I'm so pleased when members of the community come into the school. How's it going in Mrs. Hall's room?"

"Fine," Mary says. "She's doing a wonderful job."

"So often people are critical of what we do without understanding the job at hand. It's a monumental task."

"I can see that."

"How *is* the resource room running?"

"They are great kids. They give it their all. You seem concerned about something?"

"I have wonderful news for you. Your daughter, Irene, has been recommended for the gifted and talented program. It's really quite an honor."

Mary is surprised by this. She wasn't aware there was such a program. She's frightened too. It's the first time Eileen's name has come up in such a way. All at once she sees the future, her daughter grown and in the world. She wants to put the brakes on life, slow things down a little bit. She hopes he really meant Irene and he's mistaken her for someone else.

"Oh," she says. "You mean Eileen."

"Mrs. Hall has been here a very long time. She's near retirement, you know. Three or four years."

Mary thinks she now understands what he's up to. He's preparing to encourage her to return to school, finish her degree work and take over for Mrs. Hall after she retires. Mary's flattered by the gesture.

"Let me be frank, Mrs. Ryan."

Mary smiles. Whenever this gets said at home, the response is immediate: But you're Eddie, or Cody or Mary, not Frank.

"The school district has an opportunity to apply for a grant which would bring in software at little expense. One stipulation is that certain entitled programs be a part of the package. Mrs. Hall will not cooperate and I need her to."

"I really don't know anything about this," Mary says, surprised and disappointed at this turn in the conversation. "I really don't think I'm in a position to say anything one way or the other."

The principal sits back in his chair, the springs creaking and the cushions giving out with air. He stares at the ceiling tiles, the tips of his fingers making a point under his chin, and then he turns and comes forward, hands flat out on the desk.

"Mrs. Ryan, I've been told she smokes cigars in her room."

■

Mrs. Hall comes to supper right on time. Mary has the table set and the food is ready. Eddie has changed into khakis and blue Oxford shirt. Mary is proud of him. She thinks him to be so handsome. Eileen has put on a dress and Little Eddie has on clean sweat pants. Mary is proud of them all.

She pours some wine.

"A little bit of civilization," Mrs. Hall says, taking a sip. "Promise me we won't talk about how important it is to get a good seal on a Mason jar. It seems so many conversations hereabouts go that way and besides, I already know."

"No," Mary says. "Nothing like that."

Cody comes in the door next. He has on a clean shirt and a string tie cinched up to his neck, a piece of turquoise prominent where his collar meets.

"Cody," she says. "It's you, the Cordwood King."

Cody ducks his head and blushes. Mrs. Hall was his eighth-grade teacher, something he hasn't told Eddie and Mary.

"He was my first *special* student," she tells them, then gives him a peck on the cheek.

"This is wonderful," Mary says. "Cody didn't say a word."

"I'm not surprised."

Mary is pleased. She's survived the week and now it's come to rest on this coincidence. She feels beautiful in her dress and she's even more proud as she thinks herself to be at the center of these events.

"You look so elegant," she says to Mrs. Hall, admiring her red dress and pearls. She's wearing heels too and has her face made up.

"Not many opportunities for an old bird like me to put on the dog. I figured what the hell. We all look so handsome, don't we. We should be in the pictures."

Mary shows her around the house while Eddie sets out cheese and crackers and Cody opens another bottle of wine. Eileen and Little Eddie go back upstairs where Mary has snacks for them and their father set up the VCR with *The Last Unicorn* and two tapes of Disney cartoons. Eileen has been empowered as babysitter and they are to have a slumber party. Mary and Eddie have their fingers crossed.

For supper Mary has fixed a casserole with angel hair pasta, artichoke hearts and three kinds of cheese. She loves the names of the cheeses: Gouda, Romano and especially the third, Bel Paese. She's made a green salad with vinaigrette and picked up a loaf of Italian bread.

"It's all so beautiful," Mrs. Hall says. "You've gone to so much trouble. It's just beautiful."

Mary gets everyone seated and then goes upstairs to check on the kids. Little Eddie is curled up asleep on the rug and Eileen is watching the part in the movie where the magician sets free the unicorn from the witch's menagerie. She doesn't say anything. She goes back down the stairs.

Mrs. Hall is saying, "I'd just graduated from Radcliffe and was at the home of my best girl friend when the most beautiful man I had ever seen came walking into the drawing room. It was her brother, Walter. He was a geologist for Standard. At the end of the summer he was leaving for Venezuela. By August we were honeymooning in Nova Scotia and bound for Caracas by steamer. It was 1947. I was twenty-one years old.

"We had a villa in the city, but during the week Walter spent his time in Maracaibo or off in the jungle. I had a beautiful house of white plaster and varnished work. I had two servant girls, *zambos* they were called, an intermingling of Indian and Negro. On the weekend we had lavish parties. There were Socialists, Communists and anarchists. Rómulo Gallegos was a regular. He was a brooding and sensual man, quite impressed I'd read his books. When Walter was away for the week, Rómulo came by and we discussed literature and poetry.

"In February he was elected president. It was an exciting time. By November of the next year, though, the coup took place and he was forced into hiding. I was heartbroken. He was the most civilized man I had ever known. The night before he left he came to the villa and asked me to go with him. He gave me these pearls. I told him I could not and he said then that Walter and I should leave the country as soon as possible. At midnight he left the house. He said he would be near the great falls if ever I changed my mind. I was twenty-two years old. What did I know?

"It took awhile but I finally convinced Walter to leave the country. He was sent back a number of years later for a consultation, in and out they said. Well, he went in, but never came out, and that was that. I was alone with two young sons."

The candles sputter and flicker. Cody reaches out with his butter knife and irrigates them, cutting small channels in the soft wax. They all watch as it runs down the sides, hardening into white tears.

"And you must have come here shortly after," Mary says.

"How is he to work for?" Eddie asks. "Is he a good principal?"

"I'll tell you a story," Mrs. Hall says, "though I'm not one to pass gossip. Right, Cody?"

She pats his hand and he blushes again. He's been silent most of the night in the presence of his former teacher. Mary thinks it's sweet. They act like lovers or a mother and her son. Mary takes Eddie's hand under the table and holds it in her lap.

"Last year, there were rumors that the seniors were going to have a big beer party on Butterfield Hill. They go up there in their pickup trucks. All of them are of course underage and have been for a long time."

"Since the war," Eddie says. "In a few years they'll probably raise the voting age too."

"They may as well, Mr. Ryan. Most of this generation doesn't exercise their right at the ballot box anyways and when they do, they vote for baboons."

Eddie squeezes Mary's hand. It's the first time Mrs. Hall's teacher voice has made it into the conversation. He looks across the table and can see Cody grinning at him.

"So the principal heard about it, and that night of the party he got himself garbed up in his camouflage outfit and painted his face. He got his hands on a night scope and roped in the state police. Well, of course the kids were wise to what he'd planned and when he and the police burst in on them, they were eating potato chips and drinking soda. One student told me they came in with their guns drawn."

"My God," Mary says. "How could he do that?"

"That's pretty tough to swallow," Eddie says. "If it's true, it's about the most stupid thing I ever heard."

"Now, Mr. Ryan, you think about it. It is true and let me carry this thought. There isn't another person connected with that school who spends more time at it as he does. Seven days a week. I hate to admit it, but who works any harder?"

Eddie shakes his head. He wants to explain how hard he works so they can be seen one last time.

Thankfully, the phone rings and Mary goes to get it. It's difficult to hear who's on the other end. There's the noise of a crowd and loud music.

"Mary, this is David."

It's the phys. ed. teacher. She thinks he must be drunk.

"Mary, this is David."

"Oh, hello," she says.

"You ought to come out. Everybody's here. The place is really jumping."

"I have company," she says, coming to realize how strange this is, this young man asking her out. She thinks this is wrong, but then again she can't be sure.

"I have to go," she says. "I'll see you on Monday."

She hangs up and goes to the bathroom. The lights flicker and go on. She sees in the mirror the way she's made up her eyes to be more open, with eyeliner riding her lower lids and mascara on her lower lashes, making them long, and spidery, her face against death. She's taken time with her eyes, matching their brown, making them more dark, more bottomless. She pats her neck with water and bites her lips, watching them go from white to red, the blood rising inside them.

Back at the table, she isn't asked about the phone. People are smiling again. Eddie and Cody are listening to Mrs. Hall tell stories about Nova Scotia. She still owns the place in Tatamagouche where she and Walter honeymooned. Years later when they had the money, they went back and bought it. Mary's relieved. She doesn't know what she would've said.

When the laughter stops they look at Mary as if only now noticing she's back, but they don't say anything, so she leans forward, picks up her wineglass and says, "Have any of you ever heard of the India baby?"

■

Mrs. Hall sits on the porch, Cody on the steps at her feet. Mary and Eddie clean up the kitchen and wash the dishes. They move carefully, quietly so they can listen to the conversation.

"Call me Althea," Mrs. Hall says.

"Fine, Althea."

"You were one of those boys who wouldn't learn," she's saying to him. "You always had to do things the hard way. You fought me every step and if the truth be known, I loved you for it."

"Well, I'll tell you. There are things I wish I'd learned. Maybe I'd be a little better off."

"Oh, you foolish man. Don't you realize what you've got? You are the life most people are destined to only read about. They lack the courage and the spirit you have. Walter and I had two sons. One's a lawyer now and the other's a doctor. Both are in Boston and miserable. They are good boys but they are such godawful wimps. They think something's to be gained from life, but I'll tell you, for them life's the show and they're the audience. They just have better seats than most."

Cody reaches down to the step his foot is on. He grabs at something but comes up empty-handed. He looks at her and smiles, his hand open and palm up.

"I thought it was a piece of paper," he says, "but it was only light."

■

It's two weeks until the last day of school. Mary drives the River Road to Louis Poissant's farm, Owen sitting on the seat beside her. His shirt is ripped and his eyes are black and swollen. She makes the turn onto the long drive.

"This is so beautiful," she says, but Owen doesn't say anything. "I have never been down this way before."

Louis is walking to the barn when they pull in. He's a corpulent man, his chest sagging in his overalls like an old woman's breasts. A strap dangles behind him and his black boots are spattered with shit.

Mary gets out and walks up to him while Owen stands back by the car.

"Owen was in a fight at school," she says. "Some boys were

fooling around in gym class and it got out of hand. The principal
asked me to drive him home. There will be no disciplinary action.
Everyone shook hands and apologized. The principal said to tell
you at the end of the school year emotions run high and all things
being equal, he'd rather this be forgotten and everyone get a fresh
start in September."

Louis Poissant pulls at his chin. His eyes are red and watery, his
hair thin to gone. He looks at Owen, sees the boy's face, bruised
and rubbery. Mary watches them and she's certain for an instant she
sees a remarkable veiled love that passes between the old man and
the boy. She thinks the water in the old man's eyes to be tears.

"Just as well," Louis says. "He's had enough school for one
lifetime. He can be here with me from now on."

Mary doesn't say anything. She gets in her car, backs around and
goes up the long drive. In her heart she knows the boy will never
set foot in a classroom again and she can't help but think that isn't
so bad.

When she gets back she tells Mrs. Hall what was said. She asks
Mary to take the class for a little while. She says she wants to be
alone again.

14

Eddie and Eileen put the grocery bags in the back seat and then they get in the front and head for home. They pass Keene High School and go out the Hurricane Road. She tells her father she used to be a unicorn and rubs her knees. She's been riding in the shopping cart, her legs buried under things to eat.

"So when were you a unicorn?"

Eileen doesn't answer. She starts playing her kazoo instead. "Yankee Doodle."

"Hey. You weren't a unicorn."

"Yes, I was. Two hundred thousand forty million years ago."

Her voice is something he'd love to save for keeps. It has a sureness and clarity he's afraid will be lost as she grows older, becomes more speculative and watchful.

"And you and your unicorn friends traveled all around the world?"

"Yeah."

"What'd you see?"

She puts down the kazoo and looks out the window. He knows she's looking for something to see.

"We saw different kinds of animals."

"Tell me more about your unicorn friends."

"Well, first when we went we came up that road, came down here and one by one unicorns dropped off and when I saw this house I decided to go inside to see if I could find anything out. I'd been all around the world and came back to find where unicorns dropped off and found homes and turned into people."

"How do I know that's true?"

"Well. I'm afraid I'll have to turn back into one, but I want to tell you something. My power is only for good."

■

"Daddy. I want a cookie."

"What kind?" Eddie says without looking up from the paper.

"An Oreo."

"Okay," he says, getting up and going to the canister where the package is to keep it from the ants.

"No. I want an ice cream sandwich."

"You said Oreo and that's what you're getting."

Sometimes he gets impatient with her. She always seems to speak her first thought as a way of knowing it. Then she decides and speaks her second thought, becoming adamant in her decision.

Eileen calls to her mother and tells how her father won't give her an ice cream sandwich.

"I've had it," Mary says. "I'm tired of you running to me when you have an argument with him. You handle it."

"I can't run."

Eddie collects his newspapers and goes out the door to the porch. He sits there trying to get interested in a story on the elections in France. After surprising gains, the far rightist party has suffered a loss. He turns the page and it's the only story amid the advertisements, Oriental rugs, Dime Bank, Continental. He turns the page again and it's a story about a four-year-old girl getting killed by a bull alligator. It's the sixth fatality since 1948. When they found the alligator five hours later, it had the little girl in its jaws. A mother's quoted as saying, "People will be a lot more cautious."

"Great," Eddie says, and then he thinks, Fuckin' great.

Things quiet down in the house so he wanders back inside. It's been going on for a while now, Eileen at odds with the world. She claims each afternoon around four-thirty, This isn't my day. Then she'll cry a little.

Mary thinks it's because she's growing so fast. She tells Eddie about when she was a little girl and how the growing pains would rack her body. She claims she could actually feel it, as foolish as that sounds.

Eddie falls asleep on the couch. It's an uneasy sleep, though, because his son has discovered picture books. He likes the routine of having the same four books read to him over and over again. He gets impatient with having all the words read so he begins turning the pages himself. His way of letting on he wants to start up a round is by pushing the book at you, maybe dropping it on your face. The corner of a Dr. Seuss hardback jammed in your eye or raked across your lips. Eddie rolls to face the back of the couch, leaving only an ear exposed. He throws his arm over his ear and lets his hand dangle. Having kids is a form of insomnia.

When he wakes up it's dark. Mary has the kids down for the night and she's in the kitchen ironing. His supper sits like a rock in his stomach. His mouth is dry and he feels weakness, feels sticky from having slept in his clothes. Dozing off when it's light and waking to darkness doesn't seem to be the way it should go. Light to light or night to light or even night to night is the way of things. But this is like skipping a day, or perhaps even worse, it's being made to live out two days for every one there is. He must break this habit because now his sleep will be restless and there's even a chance that tonight he won't sleep at all. He'll pass the night in front of the T.V. or with a book, might even jot down some stuff in his journal. If that happens, the clock in his head will be out of whack for days. He's worried people will take note if they see his lights on at night too often.

Cody's been talking about going to Nova Scotia, salmon fishing on Cape Breton. Eddie goes into the kitchen to float it by Mary. Since they bought the business and came to New Hampshire they've never been apart.

"It says here in this magazine that each of us has to become more to become more to each other. That seems to make sense, doesn't it?"

"Sure, Eddie, makes sense," she says, dodging the nose of the iron in and around the buttons of the blouse she's pressing. "If you and Cody want to go fishing for a few days on Cape Breton, it's fine with me."

"How'd you know?"

"Cody's been pestering me ever since Mrs. Hall offered him her cottage in Nova Scotia."

"Why don't we all go?"

"Because when I go with you, I want to go alone. Besides, your son is starting swimming lessons."

"Well, do you think it's a good idea?"

"Cody says it's a good warm-up for other trips. He didn't tell you what they'd be, did he?"

"I feel a little strange going on his dime," Eddie says.

"You know you want to go and he wants a buddy. Take the opportunity. It's only three or four days. We've got extra money now."

So Cody drives and Eddie rides. They go east from Inverawe, leaving after supper a few days later to drive all night so to be in at six or seven in the morning. They are on the salmon run, fish that by nature are anadromous. They mature in salt water and return to freshwater, where they were born to spawn.

Ten o'clock that night they're in Freeport at L. L. Bean, where they drop a wad on fly rods, reels, waders, line, backing and tippets. They buy flies too: Butterfly, Cosseboom, Orange Blossom Special, Silver Doctor, White Hackle, Yellow Hackle, MacIntosh and Pink Lady. They pick up the *Nova Scotia Guide Book* and at a drugstore the September *Playboy,* entertainment for men. They want to see Jessica Hahn's new nose, teeth and tits, but it lies on the seat between them, unopened, forgotten underneath leader wallets and fly boxes.

By eleven they're back on the highway, the tires thrumming over the blacktop of Maine 195, busting through fog ghosts and wet stretches that make the fifteen-inch tires sing like ripped paper. From Bangor they take Route 9 to Calais and run headlong into a three-hour bank of fog for ninety miles over two-lane blacktop with uneven surfaces, off camber turns and random slick patches from rainwater runoff. It just about breaks their backs and at four in the morning when the border guard asks if they have any firearms,

Cody says no and it's a good thing because he would have shot the motherfucker in Bangor who sent them this way.

Between St. John and Moncton the sun rises on low spiky pines, brush and blueberry. The road banks are orange and gravelly and the water in the streams and lakes like caramel.

"She looks like she's been punched in the mouth," Cody says.

Eddie hears this in his sleep. He wakes and sees that Cody is talking about Jessica staring up from the seat between them.

"Novocaine," he says. "It looks like she's just had a tooth pulled."

Eddie stretches his legs and looks out on the roll of the low ground that runs before them. He's sweaty and chilled in the damp morning air. He'd been dreaming and now remembers it as if it really happened. He and Eileen were in the shower and she gave him a head butt in the crotch. His eyes went black as the pain shot off through his head. When he regained his composure, he felt compelled to explain the difference between men and women, so he asked her if she knew the difference between boys and girls. Eileen looked at him, her wet hair plastered to her head, one hand up, a foot lifted, and only the toes touching the rubber mat.

"You have big furs and I have little furs," she said.

Eileen then turns into Mary. It's late at night and the kids are asleep. He asks her how long it's appropriate for him to take showers with his daughter, to see her without clothes on. Mary laughs at him and calls him silly. He tells her he really wants to know.

"Don't worry," she says. "Those things take care of themselves."

Later on they get dressed, wake the children and drive to Mac-Kenzie's for a late-night snack, a three-scoop ice cream cone for him and a vanilla frappe for Mary. Eileen and Little Eddie have gone to sleep again in the back seat and they don't wake them.

On the way home they go by Green Acres, a trailer park, and see two trailers on fire, sheets of flames licking the sky, sending lit ash and black smoke into the air as the hulls twist and melt. Eileen wakes and starts to whimper. Eddie tries to get to her but the fire's now a magnet drawing on the car. The brakes are weak and the steering turns but the car doesn't change directions. That's when Cody spoke up and Eddie came back from sleep.

"It's probably that lip thing where they give you injections to puff them up."

The scrubby forests, stripped for pulp and left to fend, give way to expanses of farmland, red-roofed white barns, and wide mowings that furl to distant mountains, water or trunk roads. Eddie's dream comes back to him, the two of them in the shower, the pain that went from his crotch to his toes and his shoulders, emanating like that, hot and tumbling.

He now knows he shouldn't have gotten into it. It was a dumb question to ask about the difference between men and women because women hurt down there just as much as men do, if not more.

He knows it really wasn't all a dream because the reason he forbade her having that ice cream the few nights before leaving was because it was the last ice cream sandwich and he wanted it for himself.

He wants to go home and tell her he's sorry, 'fess up to what he didn't know then and has only now come to admit. He misses his family and thinks the word *sorely*. He rolls it in his mind. He sorely misses them and there aren't two ways about it. He wonders now, twelve hours and five hundred miles from home, if this roving is all Cody's made it out to be.

"Amherst, Nova Scotia," Cody says. "Time for breakfast."

They have eggs and sausage and fried potatoes. Cody doesn't talk when he eats, he only eats and he does it faster than any man alive. Eddie's still spreading jelly on his toast and Cody's done. He says something about the small eggs and checking on the exchange rate. He gets up and leaves. Eddie eats alone, thinking about how he got here, riding a bad dream.

The girl brings more coffee and asks if everything's all right. He knows it's not what she really means so he only smiles and says yes.

Cody comes back as Eddie is finishing his meal. He has three newspapers, an Atlantic Canada map and a stack of brochures.

"I filled the tank, checked the water and oil. Gas almost come to fifty dollars. Can you believe it? Guy says it's because they sell it by the liter. Fifty cents a spit. What'd you think of those eggs—small, huh? And that sausage? Those casings were about hollow. You ready? Bill's paid," he says, sliding the keys across to Eddie. "It'll keep you awake."

Eddie thinks Cody wants to catch some sleep, but he doesn't; he plows through newspapers and brochures, reading aloud when he finds something that sparks his interest.

"In Rangoon they're cutting the heads off policemen. Hundreds of people are dead. Soldiers, informers and police are being kidnapped and killed. It's an exercise in democracy." Then he says half to himself, "Maybe we could learn something from the sons-a-bitches."

Eddie winds through the streets of Amherst, pulls onto Route 6 and heads east into the face of the coming day. Somewhere in the night around Calais they lost an hour off their lives as they made the pass from Eastern time to Atlantic time. They won't get it back for three days. Eddie keeps driving, determined not to change the hands on his watch. He'll make the calculation in his head. The first time he started turning his watch back he ended up in Saigon. It was time he lost and never recovered.

Cody reads out loud, " 'Tatamagouche is on the north coast, the Brule Shore looking onto Northumberland Strait. In 1755 it's the place where deportations of the Acadian French began. The British fell upon them, seizing them and scattering them from Maine to the West Indies. The men were sent first, families riven, farmhouses burned and the land abandoned to waste.' "

The name Tatamagouche is Micmac for the meeting of rivers and Brule means burnt land. It's here where Eddie and Cody come to stay while the salmon run up the rivers a few hours away as they've done for thousands of years.

They keep driving east, and some miles past town Eddie pulls onto a dirt road and follows a web of lanes back to the water until they reach a cabin facing the Strait. On the porch are firewood and lobster traps, their wood dry, silver and brittle.

Cody marches along the outside wall, pacing off his steps and counting to himself. Twenty-four by thirty, he thinks. A good size. He could throw one of these up for nothing. What a great idea. He'll find some land and build a cabin of his own.

"See that sticker on the door? This place is patrolled by the Royal Canadian Mounted Police. That's what RCMP stands for."

Eddie unlocks the door and they go inside. In the front room is a bay window and shelves to the rafters. There are shells and driftwood, a collection of ships in bottles and cards indicating the builders, all from Cape Breton. There's a dart board, a set of rose-print china and decoys, blue- and green-winged teal, pintail, merganser, whistlers, black and wood duck.

There's a couch draped with a bedspread and a rocker with

frayed cushions on the seat and back, and nearby it a heavy lounger, dented as if two people have just left, copies of *The Saturday Evening Post* from the fifties stacked between them. There's a wood stove, a woodbox and an ax.

Eddie goes down a short hall. There's a bathroom with new plumbing, a room with a made-up bed, nightstand and lamp, beach towels heaped on a shelf. It's apparent the other bedroom is Mrs. Hall's.

There's a dresser in it with black-and-white photos in gilt-edged frames, a humidor between them. He figures they're of Walter and the novelist president. Stacked in a bookcase are geological surveys and annual reports of Standard Oil that stop at 1950. There are copies of *Doña Bárbara, Cantaclaro* and *Canaima* alongside *Ivanhoe, Evangeline, The Great Gatsby, Tender Is the Night, Light in August* and a collection of Tennyson. On the bottom shelf are oversized ledger books, their spines marked for years. He makes himself look away.

Brass ship's lanterns are over the bed and on the wall paintings and portraits diverse enough to make him think she picked them up at rummage sales. There's a portrait of John Kennedy and an old photo of a family standing around a hay rake. There's a framed newspaper clipping and playbill for Anna Swan, "The Giantess of Nova Scotia." Someone has penned the words *poor Anna we love you* in one of the corners. The ink is faded and Eddie wonders who wrote it.

On another wall are bouquets of dried flowers fastened to the logs with large copper staples. They're so frail a sneeze or the brush of a hand would scatter them into thin air. Eddie looks at the bed last, a five-point Hudson Bay blanket folded neatly at the foot of it. He sits on the edge and strokes the thick wall, looking at the bed's center, sagging to where two bodies would meet, rolling in toward each other in sleep. He gets up and backs out the door, closing it as he leaves. He decides he'll sleep on the couch and Cody can sleep in the first bedroom. He knows Cody'll understand.

∎

That first night after showers and supper in town, they sit up late listening to the radio, FM 96 from Charlottetown, Prince Edward Island. Eddie's tired, having had only a few hours sleep, and he's certain Cody must feel the same because he missed a whole night's sleep; but if he is tired, he gives no indication.

He sits on the floor loading each reel with a hundred yards of backing, thirty yards of line and twelve-foot nylon leaders. It was Cody who snooped out a hidden closet with the fuse box inside and tools on the floor. This gave him the idea the porch needed reroofing and that's how they spent their day. It was only three square of shingles and it *did* need a new roof, but it took up the afternoon and now their hands are black and Eddie's are sore.

From where they sit, they can stare out the window and watch the glow of lights across the Strait where the radio station is.

Tonight is the story of Prince Valiant. It's the story of Hugh the Fox becoming Hugh the Scout. Douglas Fairbanks narrates and Jeff Chandler is the voice of Hugh . . . *a strange group indeed that reached Camelot . . . Yeoman, seize that cutthroat rascal . . . brave men have but one recourse, to escape into the forest and live as outlaws.*

"Nineteen forty," Cody says, "that's when they did this show."

"How do you know?"

"The guy just said it."

"Oh, I must have dozed."

"I read in Mary's *Cosmopolitan,* it says Doug Fairbanks was a hard-drinking womanizer, a Nazi collaborator and a queer who still had a thing for young girls. He beat a dozen charges of rape."

"That was Errol Flynn."

"I thought it was Doug Fairbanks. Boy, that's a relief. Did you catch the one about Fatty Arbuckle and the guy who hung himself from the shower rod, handcuffed, wearing woman's underwear, and dirty words in lipstick all over him?"

"Yes," Eddie says.

"Jesus, I don't know how you read that magazine. All those perfume pages give me a headache."

■

By five o'clock the next morning Cody has them up and in the truck, drinks, coffee and lunches packed. They're off to the St. Mary's River, two hours away. The weather is high that day, blanketing the sky between them and the sun.

At the river they get their gear on and leave the road, wading through great masses of blue-violet lupines and trailing arbutus to work the pools farthest from the mouth—Harrison, Oak Tree, Tower Eddy, Crow's Nest and Graveyard, almost thirty miles north of where the fish begin their runs.

Eddie fishes in the way he imagines his father did, slow and deliberate, setting his fly down with barely a ripple, the leader descending and disappearing like a strand of hair blown in to barely dent the surface.

Eddie still has a black leather fly wallet his father gave him, the flies inside exotic and colorful, designed to tempt western fish, Alaskan fish that strike like hammers, fish that go after what you give them because they're just so damn ornery.

Eddie's father gave him the wallet when he was just a kid.

It was a Saturday and Eddie was out behind the house rifling baseballs into a sheet of plywood, trying to see the glimmer of a curve before they whacked into the strike zone he'd outlined with black paint. He had ten balls. They were brown and hard, ones he'd collected in the woods beyond where the American Legion practiced and played.

His father was in the front yard mowing the grass. Eddie worked through his moves, pick off first, pick off second, pick off third, full windup overhand, sidearm submarine. The lawn mower shut down and then a few minutes later his father came around, his hand wrapped in his T-shirt, the blood evident inside the cloth, red and dense.

"Go get me the first-aid kit from the trunk of the car," his father told him. "If your mother sees this she'll give me hell."

Eddie dropped his glove and went for the garage. He fished an extra key from inside the core of a concrete block where it was kept hidden and unlocked the trunk. The first-aid kit was inside the well where the spare was kept. There was a bottle of Hiram Walker too. Eddie took the kit and the bottle and went back around the house. His father was kneeling at the foundation rinsing his hand at the outside faucet, the cold artesian water running clear to his wrist, then turning red to the ground. The fat part of his thumb was gone.

Eddie's father picked up his T-shirt, dried the thumb and then held up his hand. It looked like a flower, a violet or an iris.

"Put disinfectant on that, a compress and then gauze, then wrap it with tape." His father's breath was sweet and his face pale.

Eddie handed him the bottle first, then went to work. He did a good job. He wanted to please his father. When he was done, his father looked at the job and nodded his head. He asked for another wrap of tape around his wrist to anchor the bandage, then got up and walked away. Eddie followed him to the corner of the house and watched him drop his T-shirt in the burning barrel.

Later in the day his father came to where he was on the back step, oiling his glove, and handed him the black wallet. Inside, the flies were vibrant, red, gold and amber. They seemed capable of unclipping themselves, of lifting off the cotton, capable of taking flight. His father nodded, letting Eddie know it was a gift.

He said, "Your folks fell in love and love's a very deep hole." Now the flies are frail like ash or flecks of wasp nest.

Eddie keeps casting, fancying himself to be shooting holes in the breeze, going after something perfect; and then all hell breaks loose. His fly is smashed by a large salmon. It takes him on long runs into the backing. It shines silver and gold against the dark shoreline, its upward-hooked jaw busting the water time and time again.

Stripping back line, he wades up to his chest, careless about his footing, just wanting to land that fish, and he does. Holding his pole high in the air, he gets it near and nets it, then lets it go.

■

Eddie goes for a walk on the beach when they get back to the cabin. He leaves the porch and passes down a lane banked on the sides with sweet red clover, Queen Anne's lace, goldenrod and blue vetch. To his left the ground begins to fall away to salt marsh, the reeds straight and green in long sharp files, skirting the edge and into the brackish water. Horns of cattails rise in the air, perches for small birds he can't identify.

He goes west when he hits the sand, passing under the high walls of the Brule Shore. Two boys are down there with scoops and forks loading seaweed into barrels. When he asks what they're doing, the boys tell him it's Irish moss the sea tosses up. They collect it, dry it and sell to the plant in Toney River.

"What do they do with it?"

"It goes into ice cream," they say, surprised at his question. "We have the best Irish moss in the world."

"That's good," Eddie says, and keeps walking until he reaches a point of land he can't get around. He stops for a smoke and then starts back, the waves raking at the stony beach.

The boys have quite a pile by the time he gets back. They work slowly under the cliffs. Eddie stops and suggests they be careful. The clay banks are weak and a falling stone from the top of the wall could kill them. Even a small one.

They look at him oddly.

"His uncle got killed that way," one of them says. "His cousin got a brand-new four-wheeler with the insurance money."

"That's nice," Eddie says, deciding he'll go back to the cabin and take his chances with Cody.

After supper Eddie sits on the front porch staring out across the Northumberland Strait. It's summer, but he wears a sweater and a jacket. Temperatures come in Celsius so he thinks he really doesn't know if it's cold or not. He thinks this and laughs.

Cody comes out and sits next to him. They watch the whitecaps, the flow that moves to the west. Prince Edward Island is a thin line of cobalt blue to the north under the powdery sky.

"There's a man on the radio who's formed the Lobster Party. He wants to stop the senseless slaughter of octopus. He claims their sucker cups are being used for the little plungers on the bottoms of bath mats.

"I tell you," Cody says, "some things I just don't get."

"Cody," Eddie says, "what is it about that water? I could watch it forever. It's the first thing I look at in the morning and the last thing I look at before I go to bed. Even in my sleep I know it's out there."

"I know what you mean."

"It's like you're always on the edge of something important. The edge of the earth. It seems bigger than the earth itself and it draws on you. That beach is like a zipper and it's coming apart all over the place."

That night the CBC interviews a correspondent over the phone who just got out of Rangoon. He's talking about years of unrest when he says, "Wait a minute, someone wants me. Okay, good night, honey. Daddy loves you too," he whispers.

Eddie is moved by this. He thinks how wonderful it is this man can do his job and love his family the way he does. He thinks it to be a rare and wonderful moment, one worth the drive.

Late in the afternoon of the next day they come back through Pictou. Cody wants to buy a Russell-Grohmann belt knife. Cormorants nest on the pilings along the causeway. They stand two, three feet high. Later Eddie finds a postcard of the cormorants. It says they're used in the Orient with collars around their necks to catch fish. He wonders if in Eileen's storybook, Ping isn't about a duck at all, but a cormorant. He thinks how the truth so often gets changed for the benefit of children.

Cody says he wants a bag of ice and a jug of Pepsi. He doesn't say so, but Eddie knows he'll pick a bar of chocolate too. He's eaten a bar of chocolate every night since drunk school.

This evening Eddie hikes east on the beach and comes across three young men with a Massey-Ferguson tractor. They're trying to rearrange the rocks that tumble down from the sixty-foot clay banks upon which sits an empty cottage tucked back in the pines. If he had to count the people he's seen since he got here, these would be numbers ten, eleven and twelve. He stops to talk with them because they don't seem too busy at the moment.

"What are you doing?" Eddie asks.

The oldest one speaks. He says, "This fool in Halifax seems to think the meeting of the earth and ocean can be prevented. They want to get together and he's not about to let them. He's hired us to come out here so that's where we are."

Eddie nods. He wants to stay and talk but tells them he has to get going.

They say, "Have a good un," and he leaves.

Fifty yards down from the men the beach gives way to a point of stone. It paves the shore and towers over his head, by reckoning sixty or eighty feet. He makes his way around this, stepping on the slick red surfaces, careful not to slip and go scuttling into the ocean.

The other side opens onto a crescent of clean sandy beach with no other access, as the far point is closed off with boulders the size of trucks. He steps out onto it and when he's there, he can't see where he's come from. Behind him, the clay walls run straight up to a brow of pines on the crest. They're tipped and canted, some by wind and others by erosion.

He keeps walking until he's in the center of the arc. He looks back and forth and can see no one, no access to where he is because of the poor angle he now has on the points of land. He considers this to be a find and has fancy notions about being the first man to set foot here, even though just the other day he saw a man and woman come from around the point he just passed. He wracks his brain trying to remember another moment in his life when he was the only sign of life. He can't and all at once his spirits soar and diminish as he's first heartened and then frightened by such imaginings.

He sits down here, his mind in pursuit of aloneness, but the more he works at it, the more other thoughts get in the way. It becomes 1947. Europe lies in devastation. China and Greece are engaged in civil war. It's probably the two-year anniversary to the date when Hiroshima and Nagasaki were vaporized. Israel is about to become a state and Gandhi is about to die. And here on this spot, he imagines a young Althea Hall, tall and slender, her body strong and brown, lying on this beach with her geologist-oilman husband. So many years ago, two lovers finding a moment, surrounded by a world on the edge of damnation. What times those must have been. What could they have been thinking as he coaxed the bathing suit off her bare white shoulders, revealing them to the hot sun? He helps her out of her suit, slides it off her legs, and then he steps out of his own trunks. She's lying there before him, her uncovered whiteness more so than the sand, and this thing of making love is still new to her, maybe even painful, but they both know it's a way out of the world, a way to be so unlike any other.

He's about to have them make love when a trickle of stone comes off the wall behind him. He jumps up and turns, an arm raised, afraid he's about to be crushed by a few spare tons of earth. He sees it's only a few stones, and smiles. Mrs. Hall and her husband fade from his mind and he's sad because he can see them go and in their place they leave behind fear where once, for a moment, there was courage. He wonders if the tide is coming in or going out. He wonders if at any moment he could be trapped on this crescent of beach, his back pressed against the clay banks as the waves lick at the toes of his shoes.

He thinks of Mary and wishes she were here. In his foolishness, he's longing for them to be young and about to make love in the sand and they would be so young they wouldn't care about the way of the tide. They would want and need each other, over and over again.

At the same time he's glad he's come to this place alone. He tells himself that it's being alone that lets you know why you are together. He begins his hike out of this place, not sure if he'll come back again.

When he gets to the cabin, Cody is awake and pacing the floor.

"Jesus Christ," he says, "where did you go? I almost called out the Mounties."

"I went for a walk."

"I tell you. I thought it was the end. Don't ever do that again. We're in a foreign land and there's no telling what can happen."

Later, when it's dark and Cody is dozing, Eddie goes into Mrs. Hall's bedroom. He turns on the switch and the bath of soft yellow light is enough to shake his resolve, but he keeps going. He sits on the floor by the bed and draws *1947* from the shelf, one of the few to contain a single year. It isn't a ledger book at all, but a journal. He finds this date in August and reads:

> *You are still asleep and I am outside. I know you've been here. There's still the ashtray. Your cigar is on the rim and there's a pile of ashes in it. The air is cold and fresh. It's bracing. The water is three colors, red, brown and blue. Red near the shore, brown in the middle and blue further out.*
>
> *I think about how much I love you. A gull just flew by. When I got here I saw everything was perfect, just enough room for two people. So much has happened and it has so quickly. I am afraid at the thought of going to Venezuela. I do not know if I can keep up. Already I am out of breath and feel as if I have been since I first saw you. I can see a boat on the horizon. It must be a lobster boat. It is the end of the season. I do not know even what season it is in Venezuela. You snore in your sleep. I tried cotton in my ears because I felt I should be with you afterwards. It didn't work so I went to sleep on the couch under our coats. The real truth is it was not like being in bed with you. It was like sleeping with a wall, if it wasn't another person. I should try to be better about this to be a good wife.*
>
> *I knew I loved you when you showed such compassion for Anna Swan and your happiness that she and her captain found happiness.*
> *You became so angry with her father. I hear you moving.*
> *Poor Anna, we love you.*

Eddie slides the volume back into its place. He finds the Anna Swan playbill and clipping. He takes them from the wall and reads about the life of Anna Swan. When she was four she was four feet six inches and by nine she was taller than her mother. She toured with P. T. Barnum, finally growing to be seven feet eleven inches and weighing 413 pounds. On June 17, 1871, she married Capt. Van Buren Bates, another giant. She gave birth to two huge baby girls, eighteen pounds at twenty inches long, and twenty-three pounds at thirty inches long. One died at birth and the other lived twelve hours. Anna died August 5, 1888.

Eddie sits back on the bed and tries to think about these things, but his mind gets all balled up. He reads again the line that says, "When Anna was five years of age her father took her to Halifax to place her on exhibition." He can't understand why the man would do that. He begins in his gut to work up a hatred for Anna's father.

"You son of a bitch," he whispers, "isn't life hard enough? Isn't life hard enough?"

Why'd he even have her? Eddie wonders, and then he knows how foolish he's being. It's just some quirk of the brain where coincidence seems like fate, the compulsion to make sense where there isn't any. He decides to be more content, to enjoy what he can. Maybe he'll talk to God, dump it in his fat lap.

"Hey," Cody yells from the other room, "no Holly Bridges tonight on the old CBC. She's gone to her sister's wedding. Not to fret though, the *Audible Ark* is set for nine."

In the morning they leave for Inverawe. They want to tell each other about the fish they caught and released, but they don't for fear of not being believed.

PART
THREE

15

The Poissants live alongside the world on hallowed ground, where more generations than can be counted lie buried on a break of hill, receiving the sweep of sun from morning till night, when it extinguishes in blue Vermont Mountains across the river. And always, the face of the moon, whether it's disappeared in daylight or full in the night, dark as inside your belly.

These newer graves, the ones less than three hundred years old, were dug by hand by Poissants. When they hit stone they used pry bars and levers. When they hit rock they used black powder and when dynamite came along, all the better. The ground humped, the granite fissured and the grave was made.

The graves are there to be seen in the winter, stones standing against the wind and blasts of snow, letting it pile high to their fronts and scoot round their backs like blown salt. In the spring it's the first spot where the grass turns green, its transparent blades like skin to light, and then the hot summer days come, indolent and torpid, hardening the grass growing over the bones that are being contorted, disassembled by passing boulders, and the groaning earth. Finally in autumn the red and yellow leaves fall to the sunken mounds. They go russet and dead brown while the hunters get out their orange vests, the birds begin eating their weight in seed or hightail it out of town over the heads of the people of Inverawe, who are stooped and tacking poly over low clapboards.

"Was that a flock of geese I heard?" a woman asks her husband.

"Fucked if I know," he says, his mouth full of nails. Then he stands to fart again.

Louis Poissant lives there now, between Canoe Meadow and Pow-Wow Rock with a parcel of children and Kay, his niece.

As Kay is marked as a mother, the children have their marks too, missing little fingers where drawbars humped and snapped them off. Or with lopsided heads, where they claim a tailgate dropped on them.

Eating is a way of life with them. They go to the barn and do chores, then come back and cook up dozens of eggs for something to do. They all eat from bowls with spoons and like a lot of salt.

The children are from young to old, some capable of a day's work so that's what they do. It's the most Louis asks of them. They've come to him from his brothers and sisters who've gone broke or daft or dead. On occasion he's sent some of his children to them or they went on their own. It's the way it is with big families, stopped by for the day to bale hay and stayed the season, stopped in for supper and stayed a year. They all live in the house when it's cold winter and sprawl onto the porches in summer. Some move to the summer house, an old yellow school bus, blocked up behind the barn.

Kay is here to stay. Her mother and father have died and her husband gone, except for the money he leaves and besides, she's a mother.

It was long ago when the Poissants first found themselves living alongside the world. It started to come to be on a night in 1649. Paul Champagne, at one time or another a freebooter, smuggler, Cavalier, Roundhead, royalist, Puritan, Protestant, Catholic and reader of poetry, was unfortunate enough to be nosing the prow of his cutter up the Boyne from Drogheda Bay on the Irish Sea, sailing the four miles to Drogheda, where he was bound without license for a load of the king's salmon, salted and sealed in barrels.

It was a cool night, quiet as the water lapped the hull, blocks creaked and sails went from slack to tight as he tacked against the breadth of the flow.

Nearing Drogheda, he could smell it burning, and then came the cries of the massacred. One by one his slim crew slipped over the gunwales and disappeared in the black water bound for the banks and the barren countryside. Cromwell and his Roundheads had gotten there first. They were in the midst of mopping up, heads on pikes, women raped and drowned, the dead lying about, the children with their heads caved in, dashed against foundations.

Paul Champagne came about, furled the sail single-handedly, and let out fifty feet of hawser. He skinned into the water himself and clung to the rope, praying the current that rose in Kildare in the Bay of Allen would drift him and his cutter back to sea, all the while cursing the likes of Milton, Donne, Suckling and Lovelace, poets, Cavaliers, Roundheads and all while he rode like a carp in the brackish water. What in hell kind of names were those for grown men anyway?

That night he sailed north to the Hebrides, where he took on provisions and hopscotched to Iceland, Greenland, Newfoundland, Nova Scotia and down the coast of America, places unnamed, water uncharted. He'd fancied himself to be a man of ill repute, but discovered he was infinitely outstripped in that regard by his betters to become shamefully a man of no repute. He had to rid himself of himself. He needed a new land, a better chance to start over.

In Newport, Rhode Island, he found himself employment in the thriving triangle trade, rum for slaves, slaves to make molasses, molasses to make rum. He jumped ship, stole back his cutter from the man he'd sold it to and sailed south to Old Saybrook and up the mouth of the Connecticut River, wanting to bury himself deep in the heart of the wilderness.

It was in the month the salmon run the Great Falls that Paul Champagne tacked north; schools of the fat, hook-jawed, silver-sided, red-patched fish knifed the water alongside the cutter, breaking the surface to leave wide hoops that held together while floating away behind them. At the Great Falls the Abnakis waited with weir nets and forked spears, having made the yearly journey from Quebec to catch the fish that tail-danced the white water, driven to spawn again. They thought Paul Champagne was a gift to them brought by the fish so when he told them he owned all of this land they smiled because they wanted him to have it. They thought ownership a novel idea.

They also smiled because on the deck of the cutter he had a milch cow he traded for in Deerfield. He held her by the neck when he spoke. It was a sight they'd never seen, Paul Champagne, the cutter, the milch cow and the salmon catapulting through the air.

To ice the deal, he gave them fishhooks they promptly worked through their earlobes and a box of cut nails come all the way from England that disappeared and which to this day has never been accounted for.

The Abnakis took him south to Canoe Meadow, a spot where they camped, smoking and planking their catch, hiding their canoes in a ravine channeled out long ago by the creeping ice. They hiked him and his cow to Pow-Wow Rock, a sacred boulder of immense proportion where meetings were held and the dead buried. It was here they declared he'd build his house and be custodian of the land and husband to the animals. They thought the milch cow was his wife but she was only a Holstein.

Over the years Paul Champagne prospered. He fancied himself to be the first white man to cultivate corn and discovered how to make maple syrup one spring while burning off the forest for more corn ground. Likewise he invented the birchbark canoe, deerskin moccasins, toboggans and snowshoes. Through rigorous programs of cross-pollination and aberrant seed stock, he separated pumpkins, squash, turnips and parsnips from the gourd family.

And he shared all of this with his friend the Abnakis, who took delight in rediscovering what they already knew. Paul Champagne became a shaman, renewing the spirit latent within their known lives.

For fifteen years life went on this way and then the cow died. Paul Champagne took an Abnaki bride in the spring, the daughter of a Catholicized chief who'd taken the name Poissant. He renamed her Goody and took Poissant for his surname. The celebration lasted until 1689, when King William's War broke out. It began a three-hundred-year lineage of declared neutrality in war by the men of the Poissant family as the world raged alongside them.

In this life, Louis Poissant, direct descendant of Paul Champagne Poissant, has been accused of being an arsonist, cattle rustler, land swindler, tax delinquent, animal abuser, water polluter, litterbug and scofflaw. Years ago he and his brothers ran the cows up the road to a pasture they rented in the next town. They'd do this the night before the tax assessor came by for a head count. In the morning he'd show and Louis'd take him through the barn, letting him tally the calves and three or four milkers too old to make the drive. The assessor had just traveled six miles leading to the Poissant farm, over roads splattered with cowshit to the town line, but he wouldn't say anything. He'd only let on where he was supposed to be next so the word could get passed along. He'd then have a coffee and tell Louis about the baskets of money to be made in kosher meats and all they'd have to do is get a pious Jew to make the skillful stroke. It'd mean a whole lot o' money. Easter lambs too, he'd say. Sell them out of the pasture but watch out for the Greeks, they'll slit a lamb's throat right before your eyes and then ask you how much you'll take for a dead lamb, the flies already congregating in the blood.

People claim Louis used to drive around the lake in the off season, pull up to summer houses and let the kids out. In a flash they'd be down through the cellar windows or in through a loose screen and back out the front door with whatever they could carry, with whatever wasn't bolted down.

But nothing ever seems to stick, only the reputation. Most people get along with Louis. The facts are, most people like him quite a bit even if he is always high on coffee and No Doz.

■

The Poissants are going to fix fence all week long. Tomorrow they'll be at Eddie Ryan's, reclaiming old pasture Louis has rented from him to run heifers, but today they'll spend on Rattlesnake Mountain, land Louis's father bought for a song during the war and people laughed at him because of the infestation of timber rattlesnakes thought to be there.

Within days the mountain was on fire, great billows of smoke darkening the day and flames that kept the night lit up. As soon as the volunteer firemen contained the blaze, it'd flare up again on another part of the mountain, seeming to course through the fissures in the earth, content to travel a half mile before geysering into the sky, seeking air.

The reports were rife of timber rattlers, yellow and tan, slithering from rock crevices, their flat heads and four-foot bodies darting between men's legs and across the roads and brooks surrounding the mountain.

The stories of rattlesnakes increased those first few years when the flames would start. The fires continued, always coming when the danger of forest fire was at its lowest, the source unknown, and their hot points seeming to be in five different places at once. People drove out to see them, slowly circling the mountain roads.

After ten years no more rattlesnakes were spotted and the fires stopped. Wild grasses grew lush in the high meadow, blueberry and blackberry climbed from the rocks on the southern face, foxglove and Indian paintbrush, their flowers hidden in the axils of scarlet-tipped fan-shaped leaf parts, blossomed from May to August; and all was kept trim and neat by the heifers Louis's father put out to pasture there.

Owen has already left on the Farmall with the brush hog. He'll drive the fire lanes, mowing the tough grasses and cutting brush so the young shoots can come, tender and green. His favorite thing to do is raise the three-point hitch, bringing the machine as high into the air as possible. Then he backs over trees four and five feet high or comes down on the tops of sprawling juniper, the stubby whirling blades pulverizing all they touch. Louis has mapped a path for him to clear, one they will follow with the pickup.

Rodman and Perley carry pointed cedar fence posts to the pickup, stacking them in the bed. Both are fourteen and they always compete to see who can carry the most. It'll be their job to rout a hole with a steel bar, set the post and drive it home with the thirty-pound maul.

Maple and Micah go for hammers, nails, staples, fencing pliers, wire-pullers and gloves.

Puss and Boots bring out a spool of four-barb Miracle Twist, a lead pipe thrust through the reel, each straining to hold an end. Puss is eleven and Boots is twelve.

Juanita and Kay bring out two grocery bags filled with sandwiches and two jugs of drink. They set the bags on the front seat. Kay asks Puss if she wants to stay home with the women but she says no, she wants to be with Bootsie.

Louis checks through the supplies as they come in. Micah has brought him a bucket full of nails gone to a rusty chunk.

"My new box," he says. "Have you seen my box of nails?"

"Staples are here and nails are here."

"Take those back. Find the nails. Go find them. Rodman, son, get a few plank. I want us to set some new corners. Perley, be a good boy and get some bare wire. It's always good to have. We want an ax too and that small chain saw."

Puss trips and falls but she still holds on to her end. The spool of barbwire slides down the pipe, hits her arm and rolls, gouging tracks across her forearm.

"Goddamn," she says, and Boots says the same thing.

Kay is there to pick her up. Boots sees the blood come in crimson lines, run to tears and go into her hand. Kay doesn't hesitate. She wraps the arm in her skirt to keep Boots from seeing any more of it.

"She's okay, honey," she says, patting Boots's head.

Louis comes over and has Kay unfold her skirt so he can look at the arm.

"Juanita, you go get a clean white T-shirt from my drawer. You'll be fine," he says to Puss. Then he tells Kay to wrap the arm and take Puss into Dr. Pot for a tetanus shot. "You go too," he says, touching Boots on the shoulder.

They wait until Kay pulls out in the Cadillac.

"Load up," Louis says. Maple, Micah and Perley jump in the back. Rodman drives today and Louis rides, already fishing through the bags for an egg salad sandwich.

The fence has wintered well, one deadfall needing to be cleared and two rotten posts to be replaced. They catch up with Owen by noon and all have lunch together. Owen doesn't say anything much while they eat. He thinks he's seen a chimpanzee skimming through the trees.

Louis tells them a story about how this is Rattlesnake Mountain and one night he and a hired man, young Clifford Manza, got lost up here chasing heifers.

The boys scoff at the thought of getting lost. They can't imagine how anyone could not find his way back to where he wants to be.

"Well, let me tell you, it was the first and last time I ever got lost and until it happens to you, you won't know what it's like. That's why we build good fence. I don't want to have to send any of you little pisspots onto this mountain some night because heifers get out."

"How'd you find your way out?" Micah says.

"I was stumbling through the woods, near panic when the earth dropped out from under me and I landed in a stream. Clifford came down on top of me. We followed it to where it came out on the Connecticut. Then we just headed upriver until we hit the highway. My uncle was there waiting for us, eating a hot dog. He told me he blew the horn but I didn't show so he went to get something to eat."

"Did he get you a hot dog too?" Maple asks.

"No, but I didn't care. I was glad to be in that truck."

"You see any snakes?" Rodman says.

"No, but I remember the days when there were fires. Those timber rattlers came boiling out of the ground between your legs. You'd see one or twenty. *Whoosh.*"

Louis shoots a stick forward, skittering it along the ground, causing the boys to jump.

Dr. Pot has been watching and listening, hidden in the cool, moist forest. He has been searching for eyebright, horse balm, motherwort, bergamot, self-heal, pennyroyal, purple trillium, ginseng and bloodroot, some illegal to gather. He'll dry them, seal them in bags and send them to Singapore. There they'll be sold to Orientals as cure for eye disease, as diuretics; for menstrual disorders, respiratory ailments, throat ailments; as abortives; to treat gangrene; as aphrodisiacs and insect repellents; but he always keeps a little of everything for himself.

He also comes to be alone in the forest, to take his shoes off and walk on bare wet ground. He likes to come in the morning when he can still find pockets of mist, cold white vapor he can get inside of. He's come to prefer these moments to the life he lives because he feels young again, filled with the prospect of meeting the woman he'll love, when all earthly things possess spirit.

He didn't know about the snakes. He decides it's a good time to go back to his car. He'd rather not speak to Louis Poissant. Some of the plants in his bag are rare and endangered and besides he's trespassing. Louis knows he's there. He's known all along. He nods and the boys look, surprised to see a figure disappearing in the forest.

"A deer," Louis says. "A little spike."

They finish lunch and go back to work, Owen leading the way through the trace of roads, Louis and the crew following, mending the fence, replacing posts, running new strands where needed.

Maple and Micah get into an argument over who their favorite teacher is after Mrs. Hall.

"Mrs. Ryan," Maple says, but Rodman tells them she isn't a real teacher, only a teacher's aide.

Perley fires up the chain saw to wing back some branches.

"She's married to an undertaker," Rodman tells the young boys.

"What's an undertaker?" Micah wants to know.

"When you die he takes you under."

Perley reaches overhead with the saw and presses the throttle. He's extended too far, though, and the engine torque sends the nose dancing round the limb and whipping past his thigh. The saw keeps going, ripping itself from his grasp and tumbling through the air until it hits the ground and stalls.

The boys stare at it only a few feet from them, its muffler steaming on the damp ground, the still chain sharp and gleaming.

"An undertaker," Louis says, "is what you'll need if you don't smarten the fuck up."

The boys stand there, each knowing in their hearts what it's like to learn something.

That night he sends them all to the barn to do the milking by themselves. They know why and even though it was Perley's accident, they don't complain. When Kay hands Louis Dr. Pot's bill for thirty dollars from the morning, he tucks it in his pocket. He decides it's one he'll just let slide.

16

While the Poissant tribe is building fence at Eddie Ryan's, Cody gets in his pickup truck and heads down the road into the sunlight that comes like slant wash hanging on a line to dry in the noonday sky, hanging down through white rumbles of clouds. It looks as if something big is going on up there, he thinks, some celestial rearrangement, a gathering of all the heavenly old-timers. It gives him a feeling of urgency, as if time were getting shorter.

Cody laughs. Given the scale of that world, it's probably just another day in the sky, diaphanous, streaming with color, a congregation of giant moths. He laughs again, wondering why he wasn't invited along to help out.

Going past the County Farm, he takes a left onto River Road, a route that can take you out of the town of Inverawe and into the next. Following it as it winds along the mountainside, he glimpses the river at times, white with light, shot black at the current and in the eddies, sometimes a half mile below the road. At other times the road is enclosed in a bower of trees, shutting out the time of day, making for the kind of darkness you can want to lose yourself in.

Eileen wants a dog so she can name it Luke and feed it rawhide bones. It's an idea she has in her head. Cody thinks as he drives along how it can't hurt, but her mother and father are against it. Something to do with the business. Cody wishes he could remember what exactly it was they said, but some ideas have no home in his head. A shade comes down in his mind that says, Don't bother, square peg, round hole. He gets that way, especially of late when the topic is ways to live better, ways to get with it. He admires Eddie because he straddles both worlds so well, the worlds of the quick and the dead. He's considerate of the way it was and the way it will be, his hands making up the cadavers like presents to be mailed and then the same hands giving comfort and aid.

Cody now feels a little embarrassed, a bit depleted for having thought outright so much, for letting his mind run to the poetic, the romantic. He knows it's not that, though. He knows it's because of where this road is taking him. He's set himself out on a great adventure and his mind has started juking around in his head. It's being giddy in its attempt to set the world right, be nice to all and come to peace with everything the way he thought to make a peace with the stars his last night on the mountain with G.R. He knows full well who he'll find at the end of this road, but has no idea what state she'll be in. He's wondering if he'll even recognize her or if she'll recognize him.

He turns off River Road and begins a descent to the river. At every bend he thinks the road may be opened up around on the other side, a chasm that leads to the underwater, hundreds of feet below, or maybe the mountain will shrug him off, ripple its back like a bull and send him and his truck tumbling in a cloud of leaves, a garland of grapevines. He sees himself hitting the brakes, but not soon enough, and then he's gone, skittering on the boiler plate of dirt road to the brink, where he hangs for a moment and then is gone forever. He laughs at himself, for having such thoughts, hoping he'd have at that final moment the wherewithal to thrust a finger into the air and yell, "Fuck you too, I'm a-coming."

At the last bend he can see only the river and is transfixed by its awful beauty. It seems to rest there, flat and so bright it could pass for chrome or stainless steel, all the while letting it be known that on the inside, it's a deep black moiler, fully capable of being home to giant ancient fish that'd swallow you up whole and shit you out as a dribble of brown scum.

His hands work the wheel while his eyes stare out on the water that takes his nerve, saps his resolve. He oversteers and it's the sound of the front bumper sweeping brush and the hump of the springs that jogs him back. He brings the wheel around and he's on a straight line to a farmhouse, small in the distance. It's at the end of this road that seems to have been gouged by a giant paw. He's got it in his sights.

Halfway there he clatters over a wooden bridge, to his left a waterfall, quivering and thin between the table of rock it drops from and the foamy pool it makes at the bottom before scuttling under him and falling, falling, falling to the river.

He pulls in beside a pickup and two cars that are either being taken apart or put back together. He can't tell which. A trail of parts, hoses and cables connect them. Maybe they're exchanging parts, a transfusion of metals. Maybe one's a donor car.

"Jesus," he whispers, "get a fucking grip."

The wind is now freshening west but he knows it came from the east, sweeping over the mountain, dropping to the river and coming back up this side. Off to his right he sees a woman in her garden. That deceptive wind, turned back on itself, frisks with the hem of her housedress, the green leaves at her ankles and calves, some of them to be eaten, some to be broken off, some to be left alone. In his heart he knows it's Kay even though he can't see her face.

She stands and stretches, her arms at her sides. She bends her wrists, letting her hands go out like fins, and she fans her fingers, moving them, letting the soil flick back to the ground. All in that motion she turns to see who has driven in, who he is. She shades her eyes from the sunlight and cranes her neck. Cody thinks he sees her smile, but then wonders if it's only something he wished.

She comes to the truck slowly, her walk almost a wander, and then there's a look of recognition and he's sure she's smiling, pleased to see him. She gets nearer, her walk more definite, striding through the mowed grass to the drive, stepping over the rainbows of gas that float on the mud puddles, and crossing in front of his truck.

"Cody," she says, putting both her hands on his forearm that rests in the open window. "It's you. I heard you were living in town and then I saw you at Mrs. Huguenot's funeral, but you disappeared and then I wasn't sure if it was you. Louis told me about your partner leaving. I was wondering if you were going to come see me."

Kay never had much truck with G. R. Trimble. She got into the habit of not saying his name long ago. Cody can't tell if even now she knows she's not saying it, but back then it was always, I'm your wife, but he's your partner.

"It was one of those things," he says, "the longer I stayed away, the harder it got to be to come see you."

"You shouldn't have let that stop you. You should've come anyway."

"It's just been the way it is between us. But now I was wondering and I had to. Lately I've been wondering about a lot of things. Trying to make peace with most."

She looks down through her arms at the ground, and with her bare foot she scratches at the calf of her other leg.

"What have you been wondering?" she says, her hair flanking both sides of her face.

"I have been wondering if we're still married."

Cody says each of the last three words as if they might be the final ones in his statement, his voice getting light, weakening in his throat.

"I don't know. I kind of took it we weren't."

"That makes sense."

She stands there, still holding on to his arm, her touch warm and heavy to him, more like something laid over his arm than a woman's hands.

"I saw your son today," he says. "He's over to Eddie Ryan's building fence with Louis and the rest of the tribe."

"You mean Owen. He's seventeen. He's a good boy. He loves his mother. He loves his uncle Louis."

The wind gives a gust, carrying up the rich smell of the river. It's the smell of whole sheets of earth sloughed off and mixed with water. It's pondlike, only rich with flotsam, rich with all that travels by water. It's the smell of sleep, birth and death. Kay grasps at the hem of her dress.

"There's nothing like the wind to touch everything," she says.

"I imagine it's different all the time."

"It depends on the season, but after a while it gets so there's nothing new. I know every sweep of air that comes to the banks of that river," she says.

She grasps his forearm again, letting the wind do with her dress what it will. She cocks her head and looks at him, speaking words as if just thought, just formed.

"You know," she says, "sometimes it feels like that whole river is running through my heart. It just takes my breath away."

They stare at each other as if they are strangers. He can feel her pulling on his arm, pulling hard, and then she pats it and strokes it.

"Stay awhile," she says. "Have a cold drink. Maybe some iced tea or lemonade."

She touches at her hair, tucking it behind her ears and patting it down.

"Yes, but not for long," he says.

She steps back, letting him open the door, and when he gets out, she hooks her arm inside his, her shoulder tight to his side.

They go to the house and inside it's cool and dark. Cody's eyes adjust. He can see how the kitchen isn't like Mary and Eddie's at all. There are no plants in the windows and the linoleum is worn out in places, scuffed through to reveal the floor boards and shiny nailheads. The base of one whole wall has been given over to boots and shoes and sneakers. They're piled there, a mountain of foot-wear you could fall into. There's a washroom too, hinge marks on the casing showing where there'd been a door at one time. Inside is a pile of wash so deep you'd have to walk on it to handle it, billows of wash.

But the kitchen is swept clean, the dishes put away and the coun-ters dry. The heady smell of yeast and creosote from the wood stove mingle in the air.

"Sit down," she says. "Take a load off and I'll get the drinks."

Glasses clink together as she brings them from the cupboard.

"Would you like some cake? It was my birthday last weekend. I turned thirty-eight. Most of it's gone, but I was saving a piece. I'd like for you to have it."

She doesn't wait for him to answer. She goes into the washroom and he can hear a freezer door yawn open. She comes out with the cake on a paper plate wrapped over with a piece of cellophane.

"It'll take a minute to thaw, but in this weather I don't know. One minute it's raining, the next it's hot, then it's cold and windy. About all we haven't had in the last forty-eight hours is snow. Maybe it'll snow."

She takes a pitcher from the refrigerator, water beading its sides as soon as it's brought into the room. The only sound becomes pouring lemonade and the *gluck* of ice cubes tumbling into the glasses.

"Here," she says, handing him a glass, then pulling out a chair and sitting down beside him, crossing her legs and pulling at the neck of her dress. "I get such headaches in this weather. I don't have one right now, but if I'm not careful I could."

She drinks from her glass, then holds it to her forehead. After a while she sets it down and fishes out an ice cube, holding it to her dusty neck. Brown water beads up under her hand and slips down her chest.

"You're wearing a ring," he says.

She looks at her hand as if she's surprised.

"Cody," she whispers, "could we slow down a little bit? We haven't seen each other in over ten years."

Her voice makes him think she's about to cry. It's fragile, the way old glass is, always ready and willing to crack, maybe shatter. Before, her words were cheerful, and now he knows they were a kind of lie.

"Tell me about yourself. Not ten years' worth, but the now of it. Your days. What do you do?"

"Well," he says, "I've got it in my head to travel, to see some of the world. Be kind of footloose."

"You're the wanderer," she says. "You were always the one to be roaming around and around. A real honky-tonk man."

"No, Kay, not me."

"I know," she says, patting his hand. "I think it's good. You always worked so hard."

Cody feels chastened by the past that she is to him. Their time together was short, but she had a way of understanding him like nobody else. Her ability to do that always amazed him, her ability to piece him together more by what he doesn't show or tell her than by what he does.

"Did you hate me much when I didn't come back?"

She doesn't say anything at first. He can tell she's working up the

courage the truth always needs when it's spoken. He knows it will
be the courage to make love or hate.

"I hated you more than any man who ever lived. But now I've
come to know how it is with men, so I don't hold it against you. I
know that the good ones like you will torment yourselves till the day
you die for being the way you are."

Cody wants to run from the room. He feels himself driven at that
very moment to draw back to the woods and fill his ears with the
sound of a chain saw. At any other time he would, but not now
because now seems to be a time to learn, a time to face up and pay
dues. The whole room seems to move out from under him and it's
only Kay's presence keeping him from rocketing through the roof,
through the blue and beyond to where it goes black and cold and
lifeless.

"I missed having your hands on me," she says, her voice coming
to him as if he were a little boy listening into a can to words
vibrating through a string drawn tight. Not much of a connection,
but one to cling to. "I remember how rough your hand felt in mine.
I had this fancy idea that when you touched me I was soft, so soft
you could feel it as pain. Isn't that crazy and you were always so
worried about running my stockings or hurting me. But I felt just
the opposite. Funny how things turn on you that way."

"The boy," Cody says.

"Not now. So much has happened. I'm kind of dead inside. It will
take a moment for me to come alive again."

Cody and Kay sit at the table drinking lemonade, its bitterness
passing between their lips and down their throats. Every time he
starts to speak she holds up a hand and whispers, Not now, not yet.
Her patience becomes his and he finds he's content to be there,
sitting in the kitchen where she spends most of her days.

Whole shadows pass over the house, sending it from light to dark
as the sunlight becomes buried in the tumbles of white clouds that
seem to like it so much along the banks of the river. The phone
rings, but she doesn't move to answer it. Neither of them is urgent
to find out who it is, neither of them has anyone else who shares
this life between them, spread as it is from more than ten years
back. Over that time they've happened to be lovers, husband and
wife, parents, separated, maybe divorced in fact, widowed in truth.
This moment has come to bear on them as a time of reckoning,

things tried but not accomplished, things they both still wonder about.

So it's here at the table, sharing lemonade, where in their privacy they let the years stack up, collide one after another. Cody thinks these things for himself and wishes them for her too. He looks into her face, wanting absolution for the past and some sign of all future, not necessarily a future together, but just that there'll be one for both of them, a sign that says, The burdens of the past aren't really all that heavy so as you can't carry them.

Kay stands up and takes his hand, tugging at it, but he feels dumb to stand. She tugs again, making him come to his feet. When he's finally standing too, she leads him down a hallway and then up the stairs. None of the rooms they pass has a door except for a bathroom and that has a shower curtain rigged across its entrance. At the top of the stairs is another room, this one with a door. She takes him inside and it's dark in there, but for the knives of light coming under the shades. She lets one up halfway and he can see her bureau and bed, a vase of white transparent leaves on the table next to it. In this light he sees the sheen of her nut-brown hair and for a moment it's all he can see. He's caught up in how beautiful her hair is and how he wants it tangled in his fingers, wrapped round his hands.

He then sees there are posters on the wall, posters of Marilyn Monroe lying on her back wearing black mesh pantyhose, Marilyn on the beach, Marilyn in bed, Marilyn perched on white high heels. She's looking over her bare shoulder.

"That one's from one of Bender's girlie magazines," she says, sitting down on the bed.

"Who's Bender?"

"He's a welder. He comes and goes. The first thing he does when he gets a new used truck is fill the tank and then put another five gallons in a can he carries strapped inside the box. He drives until he runs out of gas just to see how the fuel gauge is to be read. Ever since the oil embargo, he's lost his trust in fuel gauges."

"Sounds like a prudent man."

Cody wonders if she's brought him up here to make him feel pain by presenting him with the fact of this Bender fellow. If she has, he thinks, she's done a pretty good job of it.

"He paints his trucks primer. He likes the color and it always keeps its look. He used to drive around with a loose tire chain. You could hear him coming a mile off. *Boom boom boom.* That chain just a-beating hell out of the body."

"You know, I think I know this guy. I think I've seen him around. He carries torches and an arc welder in the bed of his truck."

"You must have passed him a few miles back."

"I didn't see anyone," Cody says, looking around the room, now wondering why she's brought him up here, wondering where the quick exits might be, then smiling because he never ran away from any man and then thinking that's not so funny.

"He's at the County Farm doing eight months. He was down to Keene, drunk, parked overnight when he shouldn't have been, so they put one of those steel boots on the wheel. He had a lot of tickets out. No inspection. No registration. So he comes out in the morning and when he saw what they did, he took out his torches and cut it off. They came for him last month. There was quite a fight. He put two in the hospital. That's his truck out there parked beside your own."

Cody looks out at the truck he parked next to. The steering wheel is all that shines. It's a log chain welded into a circle, but there's no equipment in the bed, only what looks to be dog-food bags with plants growing out of them where they'd gotten wet and gone to mold.

"What's happened to his equipment?"

"He didn't have any money to pay his lawyer. One day some men came and took it. The boys have been using the truck here on the farm."

"Do you love him?" Cody asks, the words coming more harshly than he wants.

"I don't know. It doesn't seem all that important anymore. What's love anyway? Fire and smoke. You can't eat it. It's just a good story."

She sighs and folds her hands.

"I'm sorry," she says. "I didn't mean to go on like that, but sometimes I can't keep it in."

Cody goes to where she's sitting on the bed, stands in front of her and puts his hands on her shoulders.

"When I stepped around and saw your face," she says, "I thought, There he is. He's come back to his senses. But I know that's a foolish thought."

Cody works his fingers into the flesh of her shoulders, kneads them, feels their strength. She lets her head forward against his belt and he touches the cords in the back of her neck. They feel so tight he's afraid they'll snap. He works at them tenderly. This news about a man named Bender isn't what he expected, but then again, he had no expectations. In fact the news of Bender makes sense to him.

"I go to the grocery store," she says, "and talk to men, stock boys, the butcher, bag boys and men who are grocery shopping. I make up questions to ask them. Sometimes I let a shoe slide off my foot. They always look. I think how much different I am from everyday people, but how I want to be one of them. I convince myself it's not too much to ask for, to be like everyday people."

She unbuckles his belt, undoes the button and then pulls down his fly.

"Come here," she says, looking up and smiling. "Lay down with me. I'll be easy for you."

Cody lies beside her, making sure to keep his boots off the end of the bed. She works her way up his body till she's on her back and he's on his side and she's cradling his head in her arms.

"You live at the undertaker's?"

"Yes."

"How is that?"

"He's come to be a good friend. His father died some years ago and he's all fucked up over it."

"Can't you straighten him out?"

"I'm only human."

"Oh, come on. Not you," she says in a way that makes him think she means what she says and is disappointed in his reply.

She works her thigh in between his legs, nudging him into life. He reaches for the hem of her housedress, trying to pull it up to her waist.

"It has buttons," she whispers, so he lets it go and undoes each tiny one until her housedress is open and he sees she isn't wearing anything underneath. He touches her and thinks how the feel of her skin is like something he's never touched before.

"I'm tanned all over," she says. "I sneak off into the pastures and lay there in the sun. I know I'm asking for skin cancer but I don't think it's so bad as long as I know I'm doing it to myself. You know what? One day I looked up and there were three woodchucks sneaking up on me."

They laugh, Cody keeping his hand on her soft round belly, the movement within coming up to meet his touch. He thinks about the Marilyn Monroe posters coming alive and how this is the way her skin must have felt.

"Your pants," she says, and he shucks them down to his ankles, where they bunch up around his boots. He then rolls up onto his hands and knees, looking at her, kissing her for the first time, and they both smile again because they know they taste like lemonade.

"Don't worry," she says, "it's my time of the month," and then she pulls at him. He arches his spine and he's in her and it's like his whole body going down through the surface of a pond, black with swirls of dust, and he can only think to stay there as long as he can and then come away with something of life, something alive. She too must be thinking the same because she holds him long after her fingers have marked the flesh of his back, long after her breathing has evened out and their skin shines with sweat, long after they've fallen asleep.

■

Cody pulls up to the boat ramp, shooting his high beams over the path of concrete and onto the ice. The brightness they cast makes him all but blind to the full light of the moon and dim stars coming in on the cold air. It's years ago and the Arabs have made him flush with greenbacks by shutting off the oil supply. Everyone and his brother want to buy cordwood and Cody has plenty of it.

He has a mountain range of it he's made by sending the chunks up a thirty-foot hay elevator and letting them drop off the end till the pile is so high they can't drop anymore. Then he pivots the base and sends them up again, from the woods to the splitter to the elevator to the mountain and the longer the Arabs hold out, the richer he gets.

Cody gets out of the car and leaves it behind, door open and engine running in the darkness under the hood. He runs before the headlights to a spot where their whiteness pools on the ice, and stands there feeling as if it's streaming in from the darkness to be at his feet.

Kay watches him, one hand on the cold steel of the shift and the other resting on her leg. She wishes he'd remembered to slam the door behind him because the air is rushing up her legs and under her skirt.

Back in the car, Cody unlatches the roof and powers it to a tuck behind the seat. It's a '66 Cougar, midnight blue with a white ragtop. He picked it up a month ago with the odometer showing only five thousand of the hundred and five thousand miles of highway and dirt road it'd been pounding over these past nine years. But it still has eight cylinders of big-block get-up-and-go with a full-blown double Holley carb, four on the floor, rubber in every gear, and it can still catch air on the humps or out of the dips.

Cody takes ahold the shift, wrapping his hand over Kay's. He slams it in first, guns the engine and pops the clutch. The Cougar lurches, then catches, whipsawing their bodies back and forth. It surges forward, setting them back in their seats, and just like that they've cleared the bare marbled aggregate of the boat ramp and they're hurtling across the sheen of frozen lake, doing all of fifty and still climbing.

Kay stares out in front of her, her arms now crossed over her chest, her hat blown off and her hair snapping out behind her in the swirl of wind. Her face prickles from the cold and then it's warm all over. From her ankles to her thighs she feels the pulse of blood throbbing warmth through her legs. She rocks her bottom to tuck her plaid skirt tighter, then reaches back up to hold the lapels of her coat close to her throat.

At sixty-five, Cody shuts off the headlights and it's as if they are stopped on the spot while now the whole world within the shell of the night ticks silently by, even though they've reached fourth and are doing seventy.

"Just like two dogs on holiday," Cody yells, his words clipping off in the wind, disappearing in the dark. "Duct tape," he yells for no reason, "the world's greatest invention."

When they get to the center of the lake he pulls hard on the wheel and they do three sixties, a dozen of them, like a skater gone down and spread-eagle at the end of a long whip. The studs in the tires cut a swirling line that tails snakelike behind them.

Cody and Kay laugh as their bodies slam together. He throws the Cougar into neutral, lets go the wheel and lays his head down in her lap. He stares up at her and the moon while they spin round and round together.

When the Cougar slows, he sits up again, working it through the gears and gaining speed. In the mirror he can see rooster tails pluming up from the studded tires, the icy billow hanging in the red of the taillights and the white of the moon.

Swinging by the shore, he and Kay tour the boathouses, docks, back porches, beaches and decks. As he drives, he prattles on about ice, its colors and what they mean. White is good, black is dangerous and ice has a grain like wood you can see and it can rot like wood and honeycomb like you know what. It's never flat or calm or of the same thickness. It makes noises too, whoops and cracks and booms.

Kay tells him she knows something about ice too and they both laugh because in the summer she works the takeout window at the Creamery and it's where they met in July. Cody was on his way home from the woods one night, loaded down with a jag of culls, red maple and beech. He stopped for a frappe and an ice cube. A branch had lashed him across his right eye late in the day and it was really starting to smart.

She could see him coming her way from the window. He wasn't more than seventeen but he walked like a man with a destination in mind, swinging his arms and rocking his hips. His clothes were mottled with gas and oil stains, his forearms thick and his hair filled with sawdust. His beard was thin and he'd shaved it into a chin strap. Under the smell of chain-saw mix was another, the smell of wood and sweat that comes out sharp and pungent.

Kay stood erect in her white cotton blouse and black skirt. When he got up to her, he didn't say anything, he stared at her chest and pulled at the hairs on his chin. Finally he grinned and looked up at her.

"I'll have some of that," he said, pointing at her right breast.

She looked down to where he was pointing and saw a chocolate stain. Next to it was a strawberry one and next to that vanilla. It was always this way. No matter how hard she tried, by the end of the day she wore most of the flavors on her chest where she bumped into cones or when she leaned over to scoop from the tubs. It was the kind of menu a boy likes to read, but it wasn't until now, seven months later, that he asked her to go riding in his brand-new used Cougar.

At the north end of the lake, Cody swings left and they ride at the shadow edge of the arrowy white pines rising up beside them in black profile, and underneath them on the bank are high blueberry bushes and, even closer, bent poplars and birches, their crowns bowed and encased in ice.

It's here where color seems to be cut into the air, gone to the dark side of blue and green. It's as if these bushes and trees and the sky itself have been erected to hold it in place, color so sharp it would cut them if they pulled over and tried to touch it.

"I have to say it's beautiful even though I'm freezing my ass off."

"Yes, it is," Cody says. "Sometimes when it rains on the ice and freezes over again, it's like there are spider webs and flowers held under glass. Sometimes you can see yourself standing on yourself when the sun hits it just right. It can stack up like that. Four or five reflections of you right there in the ice."

"That's nice, Cody. I am getting cold, though. Do you think we could put the top up and go to a movie or something?"

Cody lets go the steering wheel, turns around and hangs over the seat. When he comes back up he has a blanket for her.

"Wrap up in this. It'll be like a sleigh ride."

Cody swings left again, driving back to the center and parking the Cougar. He lets the engine idle, then shuts it down. They sit there, looking up at the stars.

"A long time ago, I got it in my head to learn the names of all those stars," he says.

"Sure. In your dreams," she tells him. "Do you realize how many there are?"

"No. I mean it. I have big plans."

"Yeah, Cordwood King of the world. I thought we were going out on a date. I put on a dress and heels."

"I said we were going fishing."

"I know," she says, "but I didn't think you meant we were really going fishing. This isn't my idea of a first date."

"It'll be fun," he says, then gets out of the Cougar and opens the trunk. He comes back to her side and hands her a pair of green wool pants, pac boots and a red-and-black plaid coat. He tells her to put them on so she doesn't freeze.

"Mr. Considerate," she says, but he's already turned and gone to the trunk again.

Kay kicks her shoes off and shimmies into the wool pants, pulling them up under her dress and buttoning them. She slides her feet into the pac boots and pulls the coat around her shoulders. The pant legs are straight like stovepipes and the touch of the wool comes like a hand on her skin. Already she begins to feel warmer inside his clothes.

She gets out of the Cougar and goes round to the back, shuffling her feet so the boots won't fall off. The night itself seems warmer, the light of the moon and stars not so distant, not so cold. Cody has his coat off and is taking out gear.

"Jesus," she says, "you really plan on fishing."

He picks up the auger, snapping the handle in place and turning down the thumbscrew. He goes ten steps out from the driver's door, sets the cutter blade to the ice and begins turning the handle. Five minutes later he's bored down eighteen inches to the black water. Of a sudden it boils back up the hole halfway, where it finally stops coming, rising and falling a few inches at a time, inside its column.

He does five more holes, all ten steps out from the Cougar, forming an arc that sweeps round the front end. Kay follows him.

"Why don't you do them all around the car and we'll play connect the dots."

"You're funny," Cody tells her.

"Why do men do that?"

"What?"

"What you just did. Men smell their armpits all the time."

"I wasn't smelling my armpit. I was wiping the sweat off my nose."

She can see the sweat on his forehead and where his hair has already frozen. Steam is floating up from his shirt collar and already the back of his shirt is a broad stiff stain at his shoulders running to a point at his belt.

"You're soaked right through from digging those holes. You'll freeze to death."

He goes back to the first hole, then one by one he cuffs aside the shavings, skims them and sets his tip-up baiting with cheese, the flags ready to spring.

"Please get in the car," she says. "You're being foolish."

"It's your fault. You got me mad."

"No," she says softly. "It's not like that at all. Get in the car, put the hood up and turn on the heater. We can stay warm and still see if we get a bite."

The first air to come from the vents is cold and it makes him shiver. Kay puts the blanket across his chest and then the warm air comes.

"There's a pint of blackberry brandy in the glove box," he tells her.

They sip from the bottle, the taste is warm in their mouths, and even more so in their throats until it hits their stomachs hot and fiery.

"That'll cut a chill," Cody says, letting the blanket fall from his chest. Kay slides the plaid coat off her shoulders and then undoes the black buttons of her own coat, opening it up. Taking out cigarettes and a matchbook, she tries to get a light but the heater fan keeps blowing the flame. Cody pushes in the lighter, but she doesn't wait and this time she holds the match too close to her. The flame seems to leap from her fingers to her sweater, catching the lint and sending tiny licks of flame shooting up her chest.

"That was the damnedest thing I ever saw," Cody says when they get the flames out. "Like little tongues of fire all over your body. It was pretty in a way."

"*Real* pretty," she says, "pretty scary if you ask me."

She plucks at the front of her sweater. Black threads of ash spring from it to blow away in the air of the heater fan. Then unmindful of his presence, she cups her hands over her breasts and gives off a long sigh, letting it catch in her throat.

"You don't know how scary," she says, staring out through the windshield. "I'll tell you, I remember how after my mother's surgery she was able to take her breasts off at night. She told me she kept them in a drawer by the bed because sometimes my father would wake up wanting to make love and she insisted on wearing them because she didn't like to make love without her breasts on."

Cody doesn't say anything. He looks at her, then out the windshield, trying to see what she sees.

"That's okay," she says, "you're a guy. You're supposed to be a little bit dumb. You probably better shut the engine off. There could be a leak in the exhaust and we could die from the fumes. It happens."

Cody shuts down the Cougar and they both watch the tip-ups, waiting for a flag to spring into the air. They pass the brandy back and forth, breathing in the air that's laden with wool and pine and warm, wet heat.

"So what are your big plans?" Kay says, looking away to the

points of light in the distance, to cottages that'd been winterized, to a car moving along the lake road, its headlights glimpsing through the trees.

"Wood," Cody says. "There's always money in wood and now that the oil's been shut down, the cordwood I stockpiled all spring and summer just keeps going up like money in the bank."

"That's good," Kay says.

She thinks about all the nights he stopped at the Creamery on his way home after working late. When he came in he brought the wood smell with him and chips of sawdust she'd have to sweep up after him.

He'd order the same thing every night—two cheeseburgers, fries, onion rings and from what she could see about a half bottle of catsup. When she finished cooking his order she'd shut down the grill and the deep fry, then the outside lights. When she was done cleaning up, she'd lean on the counter and talk to him while he ate. He got to asking her about the news on the radio, about what'd happened in the world while he was in the woods, so she'd listen hard and remember stuff for him, even writing it down on a napkin. Every night she'd give him the weather and the news, local, national and worldwide.

"That's good," she says again, "my mother always said you can love a rich man just as easily as you can love a poor man."

Outside the car, the ice booms, echoing like distant rumbling artillery. She starts in her seat so quickly it sends pains shooting into her neck and arms.

"Goddamn. I don't like the sound of that."

"It's just the ice," Cody says. "It does it when the temperature's changing, colder, or warmer. I meant what I said too. I have big plans."

"Are you sure they aren't just pipe dreams?" she says, working her aching shoulders and neck. "Boy, I almost jumped out of my skin."

The ice booms again. It sounds closer this time, its echo seeming to rise up underneath them, come inside the Cougar and live there for its life-span.

"Some people think this lake is bottomless," Cody says. "All the way to China. When I was a kid I used to come out here to fish all the time."

She wants to stop him and tell him he's still a kid but she knows it would only be mean, besides, she's one to talk at only twenty-three.

"Actually it wasn't all that long ago. I'd come out with an ax and a handline. One day I threw down that ax and it went skittering across the ice and, *plunk,* right down a hole I'd chopped. When I got down on my belly I could see it standing on its head, the helve upright and swaying back and forth as if there was motion in the water down there. Back and forth. So what I did was get a long pole and attach a slip noose to it, then I lowered it down, a line running along its length. It worked like a charm. I got my ax back. Ever since then I realized I had a knack for doing stuff. A way of getting myself out of jams."

Cody looks over at Kay to find her watching him. He says to her, "That was a sad story about your mother."

"She's a Jehovah's Witness now. Her and my father and other Jehovah's Witnesses ride around in a blue station wagon leaving off copies of *The Watchtower* and *Awake!* When people aren't home they set them inside the storm door. His name is Harold.

"This month's *Watchtower* is about childbearing among God's people, and Babylon, the third great world power. It's published in a hundred and three languages, some languages are monthly and some are semimonthly. The *Awake!* magazine is about the home-less, the universe and my favorite article is 'How Can I Fight the Habit of Masturbation?' "

"What does it say?"

"Read the Bible, think about God, avoid a diet rich in meats, spices and booze and pray like hell. I tell you, Cody, they're wearing me down."

"Well, I'm true blue," Cody says, hoisting the pint, "the real McCoy."

"I believe you."

The lake booms under them again, the sounds rising silently, twenty feet into the air, before hammering in the night like thunderclaps. When he helps her off with the wool pants and then her pantyhose he can't resist telling her they're a petroleum-based product and their cost will surely escalate. She shushes him to be quiet.

"Not now," she says, "tell me later. Just help."

Cody's rough hands leave them with runs and ladders, a small tear at the ankle, but she doesn't mind. She tells him when he grows up to be Cordwood King of the world he can buy her a new pair.

■

Cody pulls himself up onto his knees and sits back on his haunches. Kay has her hands over her face and she's breathing deeply. Her knees and the insides of her legs are stark white in the moonlight that comes softly through the windshield, the light itself the shadow while all around is darkness. The fine red line of a scar runs across her belly, low and close to where her hair starts.

He traces it with his finger and she starts to cry. It's his first time with a woman and each time she makes a sound he thinks of pain.

"I'm sorry," he says, not knowing what else to do.

"Don't be sorry. I wanted you to."

Her crying doesn't stop, though. She reaches down with one hand, feeling for her underpants, while still holding her other hand over her eyes. Cody helps her on with them and then with her pantyhose.

"You son of a bitch," she says. "Why did you wait so long to ask me out? Why did you wait? You never asked or called. Why'd you wait so long to come along?" She draws on every word of the last question as if it'd been locked in her head, frozen there, and is just now coming undone.

"I didn't know," he says, his words no more than a whisper.

"Is it because I have a son?"

"That's news to me."

He's smiling, happy for her that she has a boy. Something he'd like for himself.

"You are something," she says.

"A rock *and* a hard place."

"That's right and I'm caught right in the middle with my pants down."

"It'll be okay."

He helps her finish dressing and then he steps out onto the ice and buckles his trousers. He's certain he's fallen in love. He goes to each tip-up and sets off the flags. Kay watches him from the Cougar. He doesn't have his shirt on and he's too dumb to know the difference, she thinks, liking the thought of him being that way, liking the thought of him not knowing how to hurt. She watches him reel in the lines, white and silent under the moon, ghostlike in his movements.

He goes past her, she hears the trunk slam and then he's back in the Cougar sitting beside her.

"You forgot your shirt," she says, touching his shoulder. "Your skin is about froze."

"I know, but I don't even feel it."

Her hand goes down his arm and what she thought to be coldness is wetness. It's blood on his forearm, running shimmery to his hand. She holds it up for both of them to see.

"I guess I caught myself. I felt a tug after I shut the trunk. I must've hooked myself."

"You'll be all right," she tells him, daubing at it with a tissue. "Get a shirt on and let's get out of here."

But the Cougar won't start. Cody gets out and lifts the hood. He tells her to try it again and again until finally the battery goes dead. He comes back to her, his hands black with road grease and burned oil.

"Fuck it," he says. "We'll walk. It's a glorious evening."

And so they do, across the frozen lake and down the highway back to town. Cody's house comes first so they get his pickup and he drives her home. He asks her questions about her son, but none as to who the father is and she can't tell if he's being nice or it's more of his dumbness. Either way, she likes it.

At her door he kisses her, and then he's home and in his own bed, sleeping soundly, enjoying the gentle throb that comes to his forearm.

In the early morning he goes outside into a world of clouds and fog that lies heavy on the land. The air is thick like cotton, capable of being held, capable of touching back. He throws the stiff hitch tow bar into the back of his pickup, then drives the road he and Kay walked only hours before, the wipers swiping the moisture that forms on his windshield.

When he gets to the boat ramp he stops and gets out. He walks down to the edge and stands there, his hands on his hips, and one foot out in front of the other. For as far as he can see, there's only the bolt-gray chop of the water and even that disappears in the curl of fog and clouds the color of ash.

He looks down at the water lapping at the toes of his boots and begins to laugh, thinking it's all pretty funny when it gets right down to it.

■

"Did you ever try to remember me?" she says.

"One time I couldn't remember the color of your eyes and it made me want to cry."

And then he is crying, the way a man would, not very well. He's ashamed because he feels as if all of the Marilyn Monroes are looking at him.

"I try so hard," he says, "but I just can't get it all together. I don't know what's happening to me."

"You come back sometime in the night and I'll tell you. I know what it's all about."

"Tell me."

"Not now. You have to go. Just remember."

17

Mary stands at the kitchen sink filling a gallon jug to make up a batch of sun tea. Lemon wedges bob like sea otters in the plunge of water that goes tan inside the glass. With her hand she weighs down the tea-bag strings draped over the lip, letting the water run across her wrist, making the artery cool and more blue the length of her arm, numbing it with the cold artesian water spilling over her skin and into the mouth of the jug.

She considers herself to be beautiful this day, her stomach hard and flat, her full hips a bit more thin. She shifts her weight, feeling the sticky linoleum under her bare feet, and sighs, thinking she's put off too long again washing the floor. But not today because the kids and Cody have left early this morning to trek the mountain, gone off to where the high lines make their pass through the county, so this afternoon she'll roll up the cuffs of her shorts and knot her T-shirt till it's tight to her breasts. She'll lie out in the sun, and get tanned while she thumbs through magazines trying to find the ad she saw for a circle of hose you can run round your chaise and when the water's turned on, you're bathed in a fine mist that warms in the air before it settles to your skin. Seems like something enjoyable. Maybe she'll take the time to put on her two-piece.

Through the screen door rides the smell of dead flies. It comes from the fly terminator Louis Poissant gave them to keep the flies down. It's a gallon jug with an attractant mixture inside and a top the flies can get in through but not out. They fill the jug. It needs dumping.

The water goes down to a trickle. She shuts off the tap and unscrews the nozzle at the end of the faucet. The basket is filled with mineral. She takes a butter knife and scrapes it clean, listening to the chips fall wetly on the steel basin, pleasuring in these small contained acts, the movement, the sound, the feel of the knife and faucet parts. She decides it's because the house is so silent. Eddie is gone for the day, the children and Cody are off on a hike and the young man downstairs in the cooler surely isn't making any bones. He is a strange one, though, a body dumped beside the interstate. No shoes, no shirt, no identity. His face was gone. There have been a couple of these the last few years, up and down the interstate. People think they're contract killings committed in Hartford and disposed north. Makes sense.

She reassembles the faucet and opens up the tap again. Water runs full, plunging again to the floor of the jar and surging back up.

She thinks back to last night when she and Eddie made love, something that gets put on the back burner more and more often, supposedly an occupational hazard. She laughs.

They have a fan in the window and it made the dark room cool and airy. She doesn't remember how they got started. It's as if their sleeping selves willed it to be and it was more of them at that moment than who they are by day. But they were good at it, something learned when the love was young, learned well so it's long remembered. A little clumsy at first but it soon came back. Like riding a bicycle or matching up names and faces. Slow at first, but then the realization came quickly with a rush of familiarity.

Then, when he was full inside her, he'd soon go soft and they'd start again, until finally he said, "The bed. It keeps sounding like footsteps."

She told him to set the latch on the bedroom door and after he did that it was okay. But she'd heard them too and they didn't bother her and now she's wondering why she feels a little sad for him.

Her head is going back and forth, shaking, but only slightly. She shrugs and then sees from the kitchen window Cody busting through the hedge. Little Eddie's tucked under one arm and Eileen following behind, holding his hand, her steps coming in leaps to keep from falling.

Water fountains at the jug mouth so she shuts off the tap, the canting of her cold blue-tracked wrist sending dull pain into her arm. She hopes nothing's wrong and then thinks about how god-damn long it takes to fill a jug for tea.

■

At daybreak Cody skirts the hedge and wades the deep grass beyond, Eileen in his wake and Little Eddie riding in the carrier high on his back. At the edge of the meadow they go more lightly through the maidenhair fern and phlox and jack-in-the-pulpit and tiger lily. A small stream makes its pass here before disappearing into Mill Brook, and often the does come down to drink, stiff-legged on the wet cobblestones bulging out from the hummocks of moss and root.

Eileen stops and strokes the veins in the fluted leaves, thinking their color makes them skinlike for all the right reasons. The petals of the nodding flowers curve back to the stem. She cups them there and then draws her hand their length until they're closed.

"Look," she says, "it's like putting the peel back on a banana."

"Shush," Cody whispers. "The deer will never come."

Today they are hiking the mountain road. Yesterday they played with fire.

Like all boys, Little Eddie's favorite toys are his penis and gaso-line and matches, though never at the same time. If his father had only saved the hundreds of dollars that'd been laid out for Tonka Toys, Legos, checkers, jacks and sleds.

Ten gallons of gas and a box of Ohio Blue Tips couldn't cost more than fifteen bucks, even in the worst of times. Throw in a few plastic soldiers from any war, maybe some highly organized ants, red or black, and you're Uncle Cody and you've got some fun on your hands.

Eileen goes along with it. She likes to watch the heat from the fire

that becomes apparent only on the hottest of days. It hovers around
the flame like undulant sheets of glass, glass that can move like
snakes in a dance.

"Watch this," Cody'd said, lighting a thatch of dried grass clippings under a jar of red ants.

They watched the ants scurry about, then hiss and whistle, curl-
ing up into the hard shell of their abdomens.

"You're a sicko," Eileen said.

Cody went at the anthill with a Windex bottle he'd filled with
gasoline. He spritzed the hill and then torched it. Ant bodies
snapped in the summer heat. Some tried to get on a rock but the
heat was just too much.

"I liked it better when they were in the jar," Eileen said. "Those
little whistle sounds were their souls spinning off to heaven."

"Fuck it," Little Eddie said, a turn of phrase he picked up from
Cody.

"You're a sicko," Eileen told him. "You're a sicko Nazis."

Cody stopped what he was doing.

"What's a Nazis?" he said.

"You," Eileen said.

Cody took the gallon can and doused an outcropping of rock. He
then had the kids get back. He twisted long dried grass into a torch,
lit it and threw it. When the flame hit, the gas went off in the rock
crevices, went off like a cannon. Cody hadn't expected such an
explosion. The kids loved it, but it scared him just a bit. Good thing
the parents are away, he'd thought.

They wait until finally Cody says, "The hell with it," and slogs
through the stream, waiting on the other side for Eileen to pick her
way from rock to rock. She steps birdlike because on her back she
carries a knapsack filled with tuna fish sandwiches, chips, cookies
and a canteen. She doesn't want to get the food wet.

Just inside the woods they stop and lift back the trillium where
they have a secret garden of lady's slippers.

"Doing fine," Cody says, shifting Little Eddie a bit higher and
drawing the straps more snug. He doesn't like the lady's slippers.
They remind him of a science experiment he did in school. The
Cooperative Extension was letting out radiated corn seeds for the
kids to grow so they could see the effects radiation would have on
the seed stock. In each packet were seeds that'd been subjected to

an ever-increasing dosage, up into the tens of thousands of rads. The students germinated their seeds, planted them in Dixie cups and then watched them grow.

As the days went by the shoots with the highest dosages took on the colors of their paint boxes. The students agreed they were beautiful plants. It was like growing stained-glass windows inside the classroom. They'd draw the shades and shut off the lights, then circle the table, looking at plants that they swore glowed in the dark.

Within days of sprouting, though, they curled and shriveled, turned back into the soil and died. Cody remembers how sad they were, sad at the loss of beauty. The lady's slippers remind him of that time and they remind him, in all of their fleshy pinkness, of the first time he was with Kay, the only woman he'd ever been with. It frightened him because it looked as if an explosion had been set off between her legs. An explosion or a blossom. One or the other.

"Doing fine," he says. "You haven't told anyone, have you? You know it's against the law to pick them. You tell about them they'll be stolen and die."

He doesn't wait for her to respond. He sets out again, climbing higher on the trail now running parallel to the brook, traversing the mountain. Their destination is in the sky where the high lines hump over the mountain, where the right-of-way switchbacks under the spans of cable and the sun catches and glints in the dusty steel towers. They want to watch the boys on their dirt bikes, cobbled-up Hodakas, Huskies and Kawasakis, making their runs up the right-of-way between the stumps and boulders over pounded gravel while above their heads runs the high voltage that used to be nothing but tumbling water when it lived in Canada.

A dirt bike is something Cody thinks about getting. He likes the idea of flying through the air on two hundred pounds of machine capable of booming out sixty horsepower. Kind of like a chain saw with wings. Maybe he'll get good and ride the enduros—Baja, Unadilla, hell the trans-Sahara, Paris to Dakar. You never know. He wants Eileen along for her opinion. He wants to maybe talk one of the boys into letting him try out his bike.

The brook drops farther below as they continue their ascent. Its rush through places where the stone makes gorges becomes muffled, and in places where it spreads to pool it becomes silent in the breadth it gains. Slanted shafts and columns of light come through the crowns, catching a damp rock here and a tiny plantation of ivy there. Sometimes the light sparks in the flecks of mica, sending out beams in all directions, in all colors. Cody sees these and tries to convince himself again it's not coming from in the stone. Eileen sees these and knows for sure the light lives on the inside and isn't that wonderful.

Cody signals for a stop when they reach a deadfall laid across the trail. The wood is gray and hard and sounds like ringing stone when he raps it with his knuckles.

"Time for a snack," he says, "and a sip of water."

He lets the carrier down and lifts out Little Eddie, holding him in the air first so he can smell his diapers. He says, "No phone calls yet," and puts the boy on his feet, watching him stumble around a bit trying to find his legs.

They pass the canteen, Cody first and then Eileen. When she's done she holds it up to her brother's mouth, but he insists on doing it himself, managing to drench the front of his T-shirt. A present from Cody, it says, *"I'm the Only Hell My Mama Ever Raised."*

Eileen brushes at a bead of water as if wetness can full well be handled in such a fashion. Cody watches them move together. It's something he's seen before. They have a way they attend to each other, the way the boy looks up to her, almost in rapture, and the way she dotes on him, seemingly convinced he's her child too. He watches Eileen come to him with an apple, staring at it while she thrusts it toward him two or three times.

"What?"

"Cut it up the way you do."

Cody takes out his pocketknife and begins slicing sections and passing them out.

"I was just thinking about my great-uncle Ott," he says, cupping the apple and drawing the knife through its white flesh toward his wrist. "He was a miner in Nova Scotia. Springhill, Nova Scotia."

Cody has taken to versing himself this way since he found out Eileen is destined for the gifted and talented program when the school year commences in the fall. Much ado about computers, creative problem solving and the general all-round thinking of high-minded thoughts at an early age. "Create opportunities for them to discover" was one sentence that stuck in his head and in his craw, partly because when he first heard about it, he thought they wanted to stick her in with the retards.

"Tell me," he'd said to her father, "this creative problem solving. If they're to be all that goddamn creative how would they have problems to begin with?"

Eddie shrugged and said how maybe that right there could be the first question for them to answer.

"So," Cody says to her, "in the fall of 1956 an explosion down in the mine wiped out thirty of them. Down in the mine, three thousand feet. But he made it. Then in the fall of 1958, an earth disturbance, they call it a bump, killed seventy-six men. Nineteen were saved after a week of digging. Saved from the grave. He was one of the nineteen who made it to see the light of day."

Eileen swats at a deerfly with a switch of hemlock. It's dry and brittle and breaks off at her hand. Little Eddie picks up the broken stick and chews the bark off it, letting the chips wash from his mouth in saliva. His section of apple lies on the ground at the rounded toes of his sneakers.

"I saw Jim Rice do that with a baseball bat once," Cody says. "A check swing. He swung so hard it snapped off in his hands."

"What about your uncle Ott?"

"Yes," Cody says, slapping his thigh, "two years later, in 1960, he's run over by the milkman and killed deader than a fart. One minute he's standing there talking and the next he's fallen under the wheels and killed. What do you think of that, Miss Eileen?"

"It will forever be the fall of grief," she says, her head moving to watch the deerfly's path of flight. "Don't it getcha. Don't it getcha."

"How 'bout bombs?" Cody says. "Do you know how to make a bomb out of baking soda and vinegar?"

■

Little Eddie likes riding in the carrier on Cody's back. He gets his fingers into Cody's thatch of curly hair and then rests his chin on the top of his head. They move along in a slow ambling gait, rocking to the left and back to the right. Clinging to the head is like floating in the sea of his mother's belly.

He's nearing three, ready to push out into the world, ready to make his big move. Already he knows he can get his own clothes on, but why bother. He likes his mother to do it. She always smells so good and her skin is cool, even on the hottest days.

Branches come into view. He watches them come into his eyes and starts to cry, rubbing the backs of his fat hands into his sockets. His uncle Cody doesn't stop, but he does seem to take notice because now he ducks and dodges, swerving to account for the extra head on top of his own.

This toilet-training thing has him vexed. He thinks he may be ready, though. Now that the months have gone warm, his wet diapers work up an awful heat. It makes for unbearable rashes.

Awhile back he had a case of the shits. He never got to see much of it, but it came like water and his diapers were constantly sodden with the mess. It gave rise to a grand tirade on his mother's part when Cody slipped him a spoonful of chocolate ice cream.

"I saw that," she said. "Don't you understand he can't have chocolate?"

"Don't worry," Cody said. "Just a teaspoon. The little duffer can take it."

"Take it. Goddamn it, don't you get it? It goes right through him. I don't see you around when it's time to clean the bedding, or him. I don't see you there to watch the look on his face when he sits in the tub and those sores begin to sting."

He loves his mother. She drove Cody from the house and his father too when he tried to restore a little peace and quiet.

"You want quiet, you go outside because I'm ripping."

He loves his mother. Most times he doesn't know where she ends and he begins. He thinks about that and starts to cry.

"Cody, watch the branches," Eileen says. "You're hitting my brother."

"I haven't hit one yet. You just mind your own business or you can be the pack mule."

Little Eddie stops crying. He thinks about how far he's come along. Walking and weaning have been the biggies. The first was a trip and the second a bitch. It's not complete either. He still likes his bottle on occasion, especially when he wants some sleep. But he's given up the breast for good and that's something he'll always miss. He's heard that toilet training is on the way. Much talk between the big guys about bladder training, night dryness and learning to wipe one's own arse.

His head's getting heavy. He'll scrunch down in his seat, bury his face in Cody's neck, have a snooze under the green lights of the forest, a lullaby of monarchs overhead. And then he's asleep.

■

"Ain't nature grand," Cody says. "I want to just keep hiking, keep going north. Go to where the land leaves off and the ice begins. Stand where I can see the curve of the earth."

"I'm getting tired," Eileen says.

"Just a little farther, honey. We're almost there. Be of strong heart."

They come to a spot on the trail where a tunnel in the trees gives them a view of Vermont fifteen miles away. There's a brush fire over there. They can tell by the tower of smoke that rises from a hollow. Too broad to be a house. Emergency lights on vehicles coming down the interstate make small red and blue strokes in the sky and then disappear as they exit.

"I'm scared," she says.

"No need to be," he tells her, letting his hand drop to her shoulder and pulling her to his side.

"It could get us."

"No. It'd have to jump the river and then burn up miles of forest before it could get us."

"Little things can get to be big things."

Cody doesn't say anything, he only draws her in tighter. They watch the smoke and the lights for a while, Cody thinking about the girl's fear, wondering why the fire couldn't get big and jump the river, maybe even burn the river itself, send it skyward in a *whoosh* of steam. He knows fire can travel faster than a man can run.

"Come along," he says. "Not far now."

The forest thins and becomes strewn with boulders. They come to places where trees have been uprooted and shunted aside and then they hear the high engine whine of the dirt bikes, small tight two-stroke engines that can fit between the legs. They can hear them build their pitch, go almost silent at the clutch and then sky out again, squeezing all the RPMs they can.

"What a gorgeous sound," Cody says. "Two-wheeled chain saws. Ain't nature grand."

■

It's dark in the house, because everyone knows light is hot and dark is cool. Only the flickering light of the picture tube is there to make shadows. Little Eddie dozes on the floor, probably trying to figure out how he falls asleep where he is every night but wakes up each morning in his crib.

Eddie and Mary sit on the couch and Cody's stretched out in the recliner. They're watching the *National Geographic Special* on the Vikings, but they're listening to Eileen tell again the story about the children of Izieux. It's a story about forty-four children sent manacled to a deportation center and then Auschwitz, where they died. It's a story she knows by heart and has told for six nights running, ever since school let out for the summer, ever since the first day she heard it and dumped all the dried flowers out of her Bible, pining over their memory. Secretly she imagines she's one of them and often takes the name Liane or Renate. Sometimes both names and then she's two of them.

"And so," she concludes, "the Huns of Paraguay will not rest easy tonight."

"That's such a powerful story," Mary says, "but I do wish you'd leave off that last line. It's so melodramatic."

It's a line she picked up from the gym teacher who received Mary's wrath when she discovered he had the kids playing games called nigger boppers and death ball.

"Hey," he'd said, "lighten up. They're just names."

"You," she'd said, leveling him with her eyes, "are a fucking asshole."

"Melo-fucking-dramatic," Cody says, stomping out of the room, his heavy soles thumping on the rug and then turning to hollow thuds when he disappears into the kitchen. The screen door slaps shut and there's a moment of silence. Little Eddie starts to cry. Mary lifts him into her arms and they go up the stairs.

Eddie gets up too and turns down the volume on the T.V. set. He lets the room get quiet. Eileen stands alone, clutching at the hair on the right side of her head, her torso leaned to that side and her neck bent.

"Come here," her father says. "Come sit with me."

But she doesn't move. She keeps knotting her hair, twirling it round her fingers. Eddie goes and gets her, hoisting her into his arms. He thinks how tall she is, long fine bones, thin strong muscles. He carries her to the couch and sits back down cradling her in his lap, her knees to her chin.

"You have the longest legs I've ever seen," he whispers. "I don't know how you fit them under you. I don't know where you got them. Maybe from your grandpa Jim."

"I knew Grandpa Jim."

"Yes, you did know him. He was in the hospital when you first met him. You were one year old. You crawled around on his bed. He was smitten that very moment."

Eileen gets two fingers in her mouth and burrows down against her father's chest.

"Grandpa Jim had long legs," he says. "You must have gotten his legs. He was thin too. Thin as a rail."

She makes sucking noises but doesn't say anything. She only listens.

"I heard you had quite a day today with your Uncle Cody."

"You mean when Cody fell off the motorcycle."

"I didn't hear about that part. What happened?"

"Cody had one of the boys let him try out his motorcycle. Me and Little Eddie lay in the weeds and watched. They have the biggest bull thistles you ever saw in your life up there. They're purple. Big as trees. It was like being in the desert. Cody tried to go like the boys go, but he fell off, flat on his back. The motorcycle went *whoop* into the air and there was old Cody flatter than a pancake."

"I heard something else happened too."

"Well, when we were coming back, Cody said the mountain was so big it looked like it could fall on us. He started going faster and he took my hand and we were running. It seemed like the mountain really was going to fall on us. It was scary. But we made it."

Eddie holds her close, his fingers entwined at her rib cage. He likes to think he gave up long ago trying to figure out how stuff got inside her head, or how it got inside anybody's head as far as that goes. But he can't do it. He can't give up.

"You know your uncle Cody is afraid of being under the ground. It's one of the fears he has. Some people are afraid of high, high places and others are afraid of small, small places. Cody's afraid of being under the ground. These are called phobias. Here's one for you, agoraphobia. It's a fear of going outdoors, and zoophobia is a fear of animals, and terraphobia, I think, is a fear of the earth."

"Well, I don't like little places either."

"My point is, it must have seemed to Cody like he was going to end up underground."

Eileen doesn't say anything. He doesn't know if she buys it. He doesn't know if he does either. Mary comes down the stairs and stands over them.

"Time for teeth," she says. "Teeth and a story."

Eileen follows her mother to the bathroom, Eddie tagging along behind. He watches them inside the milky-white light of the bathroom, the tiles taking on a sheen from the glow. When Mary and Eileen are together, he's outside them. Their voices change and the rhythm of their words comes more slowly, more softly. The words themselves are a code they share, one that makes him feel more dumb with each word they speak.

He worries now about the kids being alone with Cody. It's a foolish thing, but he remembers when he was a boy and how he and his father took a trip to Fort Ticonderoga. It was the last time he ever got to go with his father alone. His mother forbade it after that because his father got them home way late and he'd been drinking.

Eddie has good memories of it, though, memories of being able to crank down the windows, being able to sit in front or back and to change places while the car was moving. He remembers sleeping too. Falling asleep at light and waking to dark. His father was happy. He let him carry his wallet and hand out the bills for a miniature cast-iron cannon. The dungeons scared him and then they saw a real prison in New York State, surrounded by meadows.

When he was almost a man, his mother told him how his father was drunk and he was angry at her for telling him.

Eddie goes out to the porch. Cody's sitting there having a smoke. Try as he might, though, he can only get a few drags before the paper's too wet from his fingers. He lights another one and in the flash of the match Eddie can see the sweat at his neck and brow, how it's gone to beading up and making tiny streams at his temples.

"Eileen told me about your day. Sounded pretty rough."

"Jesus, Eddie. I don't know. On *Twenty/Twenty* they said that a man what dies in a house comes to haunt that house. I swear to God that man haunts the mountains, the woods, the water. I swear to

God I could feel it moving. Any minute it was going to go, *harumpf*, then cascading mountain. A piece of the earth itself toppling over on us."

Cody works at his smoke until it falls away to his lap. He bats at the ash, sending it off on a short plummet. He's convinced he heard G.R.'s voice, but doesn't mention that. He tries to make conversation.

"Who'd you bring in today?"

"One of the Naked Men. He went right. His motorcycle went left and a Volvo finished him off."

"What the hell is a Naked Man?"

"Member of a biker gang."

Cody shakes his head. Eddie thinks to say something about how the man must have been an organ donor like Cody wants to be, but doesn't.

"You live and then you die," he says. "One takes longer than the other and right now I'm not sure which, and also right now I'm not sure which is the more enjoyable either."

"It's something to live through," Eddie says.

"Or die through," Cody tells him.

"Please don't be that way," Eddie says. "Please."

18

It's a summer of steam and goldenrod. Raudabaugh works in the cool cellar, in the furnace room adjacent to Eddie Ryan's mortuary. He dismantles the oil-fired steam-heating one-lunger, while outside the air is thick with moisture from the cuff of morning till the night chill, nuzzling moisture making steam banks up and down the river valley.

Little Eddie plays amongst the fourteen radiators his father and Cody lugged out the door. Half of them had to be brought from the upstairs rooms, quite a hike with 150 pounds of silver-painted cast iron. The last one stands in the kitchen, five foot tall and four foot wide. That one they'll need to break up or get an extra pair of hands, hands younger than Raudabaugh's.

The boy weaves his way through the field of radiators, leading a sprung golf ball on a string. At nearly three years old he's become a what-the-hell kind of kid, a quality his uncle Cody has rested on his shoulders. The boy makes word noises as he trudges bowlegged through the soggy grass, stopping on occasion to rake a stick across the chambers to make them sing.

Off the edge of the lawn, Eileen runs waist-deep through yellow flowers suspended in the air, running wild on slender stems. Whole valleys of undulant yellow flowers, growing abundant in the ditches, brimming the road banks and disappearing at the edges of the wet black forests. She runs after butterflies: monarchs, swallowtails and fritillaries. She likes to think they all had other lives. They all were something else in another time. Something human. Kicking her knees high to make it through the yellow thatch, she thinks she's a horse and her legs are green, but it's only the stain from pollen dust and water, a stain that stripes her legs.

It's a summer people will talk about in years to come, one noted for spawning molds, moist and blue like the touch of velvet, one noted for growing lush hay that just wouldn't dry, for being Raudabaugh's last, for having weather, as they say.

Raudabaugh sings while he works, not a song like in a book, but the song of what he's doing. His voice is thick in his throat, caught in his neck, still German. He chuffs out the words as he lets his sledgehammer come down on the cast-iron elbows, crushing them under its weight, letting lengths of pipe drop through the floors from above to his feet. And then he goes to coughing, his shoulders folding and releasing, folding and releasing. He works up green phlegm and spits it to the ground, where it lies, foamy and pink at the edges.

"Fuckin' cough," he says, fishing in his breast pocket for a smoke.

Eddie and Cody come down the cellar stairs and draw out the last of the pipes Raudabaugh has dismantled. The length of them is silver but their openings are brown and jagged, dripping rusty water out the low end.

Raudabaugh steps back, leaning a shoulder against the block wall of the mortuary. Eddie and Cody wait to clear away the new pile of wreckage Raudabaugh will make with his sledge when he gets his wind back.

"Jesus Christ," Cody says. "Just aching to get through to the other side, ain't cha."

Raudabaugh reaches up and takes his coffee cup down from the sill plate where he keeps it in a space between two joists. He gives it a swirl and looks into it. A skim of dust still rides the surface, making it mottled and gray. But he doesn't seem to mind. He sucks it all down and then drags on his smoke till it's an ember he doesn't feel touching his thumb and finger.

"The cost of a modern funeral, when done proper, can put a man under, so stuff that in your pipe, Mr. Cody, and smoke on it."

Eddie says he has to check on the kids and goes back up the stairs. He knows they're all right; he just needed a reason to leave the cellar. He doesn't think taking the new furnace in trade for Raudabaugh's funeral is right, yet he's the only one it seems to bother. Mary, Cody and especially Raudabaugh all think it's a good idea, something more people should consider doing.

Eddie stands at the top of the stairs in the wet, overcast light. He thinks about how they need a new set of cellar stairs, a new bulkhead, a bigger opening. Mary is down on one knee, tying Little Eddie's sneaker and talking to him. He can see the crease made in her leg where her shinbone and calf meet, the muscle taut as she now holds the boy. He can't hear what she's saying, but he sees her point to the road, then back at her son. She wags the finger in his face. She's teaching him something.

When one of the children is this close to her, Eddie tries to imagine again how they came from inside her and as they grow it becomes harder to do, even though he was there both times to bear witness. Eddie's bigger than his mother was and if Little Eddie keeps growing the way he is, he'll be bigger than his mother.

They look his way and he waves at them, then he goes down the stairs. Halfway he stops and steps back up, enough to see over the splayed-open wooden cellar door. Mary is sitting on a radiator with her legs stretched out in front and her arms stiff behind her, holding her up. She looks over her shoulder to the meadow where Eileen, stripped down to her underwear, prances in the goldenrod. Little Eddie picks up his golf ball and walks to his mother. He lays his head down in her lap. Without looking at him, she begins to stroke his back.

Eddie plucks at the front of his shirt where the sweat has it plastered to his body. He takes a last look at Mary and Little Eddie amongst the hulls of cast iron on the soggy ground and Eileen in the meadow now peeling her T-shirt off over her head. What he sees brings on tiredness. He wishes it were his back being stroked and he thinks the word *sadness,* but it can't really be. So he sighs and goes down the last four steps, into the coolness where the other men are.

Cody and Raudabaugh rest on their haunches, their backs against the block wall. They have fresh cups of coffee and smokes they just lit. Down low, where they rest, Eddie can see on the wall chalk murals done by the kids. There are stick people, houses and flowers. Off Raudabaugh's elbow is a tree and coming from Cody's shoulder is a spray of ferns. For a moment the two men look to be a part of the wall, something grown out of it, drawings that attain the third dimension.

"Tell the story," Cody says.

"What story?" Eddie asks.

"I don't think it'd be to your taste, Mr. Ryan."

"Oh, hell," Cody says. "He's been in war. There isn't much you could say that'd shock him. He's seen stuff that'd make lesser men cry in their sleep."

"Over Viet Nam?" Raudabaugh asks.

"That's right," Eddie says.

"Get pretty bad, I imagine."

"Pretty bad," Eddie says. "But that's okay. Go ahead and tell your story. I'd like to hear it."

Raudabaugh sets his coffee cup down and rubs his hands together. He motions for Cody and Eddie to come nearer. He clears his throat, letting a stream of saliva slip to the floor and puddle between his feet. Cody's gotten in the habit of looking to see what color it'll be, so he cranes his neck to see. It's white like paste.

"Last year the town clerk over in Ware is having trouble with her toilet not flushing. So she calls me up and has me come over. She's an old woman, ain't ever married. Got to be the town clerk right out of high school, probably fifty years ago. She's the one to get things done over that way. Makes them taxes go up and down. Gets your road plowed or not.

"So I go over and I run my forty-foot snake down there and nothin'. I mean, mister, it's blocked. I tell her we have to pump it and to call Ram Goerlitz. He's got the Honey Wagon, you know."

"I know him," Eddie says. "Big fat man. One of the Hinsdale volunteer firemen. Has the tank and cab painted to look like a bee."

"Ayah. That's him. He tells me he can come right over but I've got to find the tank and uncover it pronto. Either that or it'll be two days before he can get to her. I hold the phone and tell her, but that there ain't no way I'm digging up the septic. She says tell him to come on. She'll get Jan Weiner to round up his Boy Scout troop and bring them down to the job. She and Jan been sweet for years if you know what I mean."

Raudabaugh stops to take a drink of fresh coffee and to light another smoke. He draws deeply, chokes on the smoke and begins coughing it back up. Gusts of it blow in the men's faces. They look at each other and shrug. Eddie runs the number for emergency rescue through his brain while Cody claps the old man on the back.

"Jesus," Cody says, "I don't care if you die before the furnace is in, but at least finish the goddamn story."

"Don't do that, Cody. You don't clap someone on the back who's choking."

"I know that," Cody says, "but it's got to be better than nothing."

"I'm okay," Raudabaugh says. "Cut that out."

"We thought we'd lost you," Cody says, winking at Eddie, "good thing I was here."

"So, I shit you not, ol' Jan and the Boy Scout troop come marching in overland and I swear to God she hadn't even hung up the phone. Right there I say to Jan and them boys go to digging like gophers. The loam is just a-flying and it isn't before long they hit it. *Thud.* They get it cleaned off and then we sit for twenty minutes, drinking lemonade, waiting on the Honey Wagon and then here he comes, just a-jammin' gears."

"I know what you mean," Eddie says. "The men over there dread it if he's first one into the station. One time he dropped the transmission on the La France halfway to a fire."

"That's Ram," Raudabaugh says. "That's Ram all right. First words out of mouth is, 'Boy Scouts. Jesus Christ, Boy Scouts.' And he says it over and over again like they was somethin' he'd read about in a book and always wanted to see. 'Boy Scouts. Jesus Christ, Boy Scouts.' He says, 'Raudabaugh, Boy Scouts. Where'd ya get the Boy Scouts?'

"Well, Jan steps in and tells him all about it and Ram, he says, 'A Boy Scout leader. Jesus Christ, a Boy Scout leader.' It takes a while for Ram to get over saying it and he never does give up staring at them."

"What do you think it was?" Cody asks.

"I don't know. Maybe he'd just heard a joke about Boy Scouts and then there they were all of a sudden."

"Makes sense," Cody says, shrugging his shoulders.

"So Ram gets the boys back and him and Jan lift that steel cover and prop it with a two-by-four. Them Boy Scouts are about to heave their ration of lunch when the smell of those gasses come boiling up. Jan, he's white's a sheet and Ram's poking at the pipe and there comes a whoosh of water and Ram, he says, 'Now, ma'am, that's your whole problem. You shouldn't be flushing those rubbers down the john.' Me and her go over to look, and sure enough there's hundreds of safeties floating on the surface. Some of 'em are blowed up with gases and look like toadstools floating amongst the solids. The clerk, she's looking at Jan, and mister, I'm telling you she was shooting daggers. Jan, he turns on his heel, snaps them Boy Scouts in line and they do double time back through the woods, their flag just a-flappin'. I'll tell you, though, she was a good egg. Me, her and Ram got to laughing as hard as I ever have. It was her takin' it like that made me swear to myself to always keep it a secret and that's just what I've done. I haven't told a soul. Now you two fellas get out of here while I bust open that insulation jacket. It's asbestos tape and asbestos inside the tape and neither of you are used to it. I'll call when the dust settles."

Eddie and Cody go to the top of the stairs and wait. Below them they can hear Raudabaugh bashing into the jacket, tearing chunks of insulation from the shell of the boiler. Each handful he drops in a garbage bag and then wires it shut when it's full.

"This isn't right," Eddie says.

" 'Course it isn't right, but are you going to tell him? He'll laugh at you. He's old. He's like G.R. The old ones, they're different than you are."

Eddie starts for the front porch and Cody grabs his arm.

"Where are you going?"

"I'm going to call the Health Department. I never made the connection with the asbestos."

"No, you're not," Cody says, gripping his arm.

"Then I'm going to stop him."

"You're not going to do that either and you're not going to help him. The very old and the very young, they've got rights you don't have. If you stopped him, he'd hate you. Can't you see it's part of his dying? Sometimes you are the most stupid man I've ever met."

"Take your hand off me or we'll have it out right here," Eddie says.

Cody lets go Eddie's arm and backs up smiling. He doesn't want to fight his friend, but on the other hand he doesn't mind a fight.

"You get like him," Eddie says, staring at Cody. "At times you get just like he must have been. Can't you let him go? Can't you give him up?"

"I never give up anything. I carry it all around inside me from day one. I've never denied a day of it. It's like a long train coming. I love it. G.R. was my friend."

The two of them square off and wait, neither wanting to strike first, though at any other time Cody would have gone for a punch to the throat.

Eddie thinks how stupid this is to be standing out here about to fight Cody. It's the steam, he says to himself. It's the steam. He lets his hands fall to his sides, then he puts them in his pockets. He knows he's right and he knows Cody's right, maybe even a little more so. And right now he wants to rage about it. He wants a vision where life comes his way and he takes it with dignity and a little courage. Not to compromise. Not to endure.

"I'm sorry," Cody says.

But Eddie doesn't hear him. He's remembering the time when he was a boy and he ripped another boy's T-shirt. They were fooling around and he ripped the boy's T-shirt down the back. The boy didn't have many. He lived in a trailer with a lot of brothers and sisters. Eddie took off his own and gave it to the boy, made him take it. It was a pure moment for both of them and they were friends all that summer.

And now he thinks he's learning to be that boy, he's learning to be both himself and that boy with the ripped T-shirt and the new T-shirt offered up by the same person who ripped the old one. It's something he's just learned, or at least just begun to learn.

"I'm sorry," Cody says.

"No. Listen," Eddie says. "Hear that?"

No sound comes from the cellar. Both men go down the stairs to find Raudabaugh asleep against the block wall, chalk sketches of trees, ferns and flowers growing over him and a green garbage bag wired off and full of asbestos under his head for a pillow.

"Time for lunch," Cody whispers, and he and Eddie go up the stairs quietly.

They eat outside at the picnic table. There's tuna salad, pickles and chips. There's lemonade, ice tea and milk. Cody drinks ginger water: two quarts water, a half teaspoon of ginger, a cup of sugar and two-thirds cup of cider vinegar. He drinks it at room temperature, claiming it has properties even he hasn't come to know the extent of.

Little Eddie has learned to blow milk out his nose without it hurting. Cody gets a kick out of this, slapping his thighs every time. The sun has come out and turned the radiators hot. The picnic table is surrounded by them.

"You two are disgusting," Eileen says.

She sits in her underwear. She's green from pollen and sweat. She doesn't want to say anything about it so as not to draw attention. She hopes it will permanently stain into her skin.

They've been talking about going to the Rutland fair. Cody wants to see Boxcar Willy and the kids want to see the Milk Buds, a team of miniature ponies, and the dancing pig.

They're making plans. Eddie and Mary have never been. Cody finds this hard to believe. He tells them at the fair there's more. There's knockwurst, kielbasa, Belgian waffles, french fries, fried dough, fried cauliflower, guacamole, Yankee Boy hot dogs, shakes, beer and cotton candy.

"Sounds kind of international," Mary says. "Sounds more like a world's fair."

She looks at Eddie and smiles.

"There's the Hurricane Hell Drivers, the wonder knife, snowmobiles, *World Books,* tools, massage couches, siding, pet tags, hanging plants, shoes, the world's smallest horse, the biggest dead whale in captivity, the world's largest horse and Hitler's Mercedes automobile. I read it in the paper."

Little Eddie sends a stream of milk out his nose and over his lip.

"No, Little Eddie," Mary says. "You drink your milk and you, Miss Eileen, we don't enourage him."

"One time I was at the fair and we was in to see the gorilla woman. When we got in it was dark but they turned up all the lights and had us note the exits because it was going to be a terrifying spectacle. Then a gong sounds and a girl comes out in a bikini. She scrunches up her face and the lights go out. Just as quick they come back on and there's the gorilla woman in a cage. The guy, he says, don't worry because the bars are electrically charged. But then the cage busts open. Someone forgot to lock it. Lord help us, a woman screams. Screams and shouts, screams and shouts. Two men rush in wearing pith helmets but the gorilla slips between them.

"G.R. jumped up and punched it right in the chops. That gorilla went down like it'd been poleaxed."

"Sheesh," Eileen says. "I tell ya."

"Answer Man," Eddie says. "Time for the Answer Man."

"Go ahead, Answer Man. Fire away," Eileen says.

"Why did our pipes bang in the winter?"

"Because little people were banging on them with little hammers," Eileen says. "Sheesh, what a stupid question."

"It's the heat going into the cold pipe," Cody says.

"I agree with Cody," Mary says, "like when you put an ice cube tray under hot water. It cracks."

"That's right," Eddie says. "It cracks but it doesn't bang."

Little Eddie holds his pickle like a gun and yells, "Bang. Bang."

"We give up, Answer Man. Tell us." Eileen says.

"Okay. Steam builds and then shoots up the pipe. It picks up water that's returning and creates a wave. It pushes the wave into an elbow and it goes *bang.*"

"I'm really glad you asked," Eileen says.

"It's the truth. Raudabaugh told me."

"Speaking of Raudabaugh, do you think we should look in on him?" Mary asks.

"Nah," Cody says. "He's right where he wants to be."

Eddie plucks at his shirt. He can feel the mayonnaise from the tuna going sour in his stomach.

"We need a swimming pool," he says.

"Yeah," Eileen yells, "a swimming pool with a slide, but no one who's disgusting can go in it."

"How 'bout a pond?" Cody says. "On the land across the road. We could stock it with fish and have a diving board."

"We're not having a pond," Mary says, looking to Eddie, but he's already staring across the road.

"What do you think, Cody? Do you think it'd work?"

"Down to the left it's always been wet, ever since I can remember.

We'll put it right in the heart of those cattails. Two days' work. It's as good as done."

A clang comes from the cellar and then another one.

"He's risen from the dead," Cody says. "Time to get back at it."

The two men finish their lunches and head for the cellar. The light is dim so it takes time for their eyes to adjust. When they do, they see dozens of garbage bags, fat and wired off, but trailings of asbestos have burst free into the air and they still float in the yellow cast from the trouble light, riding high on the updraft made by a moving hand, or swirling round when a body turns.

Raudabaugh steps back when he sees Eddie and Cody. He finds the block wall to lean against and looks at them as if he's trying to recognize who they are.

"Good to see ya," Cody says. "I thought you were dead."

Raudabaugh stops him and stares into his face.

"Is that you, Cody? I thought *you* were dead. All this time I've been thinking *you* were dead."

"Not me," Cody says, shrugging off the old man's grasp.

"Must be G. R. Trimble then. Whatever happened to that old fuck?"

"He died and left the country."

"Ain't that a shame," Raudabaugh says, lighting up a smoke and then going into a thirty-second cough and hack.

"Couple years back he told me the damnedest condom story I ever heard," Raudabaugh says. "Seems he had this cousin, Mike, a Polak from Pennsylvania. He was a carpenter working on an office building. It was set up like a doctor's office, only the rooms were for one of them sex therapists. This fella, Mike, he tells this one boy who's doing the drywall just what them rooms are going to be used for. Sure as hell, that boy starts bringing in his used beetle skins and tacking them up on the studs and then Sheetrocking right over them. Isn't that the damnedest thing you ever heard?"

"Mr. Raudabaugh, you are so full of shit it's coming out your ears."

"You think so, Mr. Cody. You ask Mr. G. R. Trimble next time you see him. He told me the story just the other day and he says it's true. Now you take that sledgehammer and hit that furnace right where I tell you. She's all unbolted and she'll crack open just like an egg. That's the gospel."

"I will ask him," Cody says, taking up the sledgehammer.

"Right here," Raudabaugh yells, and Cody swings the sledge like a bat, striding into it, drawing on the muscles down into his legs, trying to hit Raudabaugh's hand before he can move it. The hammer makes contact with the furnace, riving the cast iron with one blow. A moment later there's a crash from over their heads that cracks the joists, making the men duck and dash off to the sides.

Mary is screaming. The sound fills the house, but like fools the men in their daze first look to the furnace. The sound seems to have broken forth from the most interior water chamber now revealed to them, section by section. The men look into the halves as if this is the best they can do when it comes to cause and effect. She screams again and it's this second one that smartens them up.

Eddie gets to the kitchen first. Mary's pulling at the radiator that's fallen across Eileen's green shins while the girl lies back and stares at the ceiling, her mouth open and silent, her eyes huge in their sockets and pure with fear.

"Get it off her," Mary's screaming. "Get it off her."

Eddie bends, sucks in and heaves. He gets it raised, straining so hard he hopes the arteries in his neck will burst through his skin, sending ropes of blood into the air, ropes that will hang him for being so stupid. Then Cody and Raudabaugh are there too and the radiator comes off the little girl's legs and thuds back against the wall.

■

When Eddie gets back from the hospital it's near midnight. He doesn't see Cody and Raudabaugh on the front porch until he makes the first step. All three act surprised but they don't say anything. Eddie sits with them. After a while they speak. They tell him they kept working and Little Eddie is upstairs asleep and now they are done and into their third quart of Cody's home brew, a recipe he got from Freddy Clough. In the morning they'll begin installation of the new furnace.

"It's a little heavy on the malt," Raudabaugh says, passing Eddie a tumblerful, "but it'll do in a pinch."

"Fuck you," Cody says. "It's maltier where there's none."

Cody's getting drunk, but right now Eddie doesn't care. He feels himself to be less of a father, less of a man. And it always happens this way. He takes blame for the slightest of indignities ever visited on his children, reproaching himself that they should have an ear infection, that they should feel the blush of shame, the loss of ignorance and innocence, and now to be nearly crushed to death. His heart is a fist in his chest and it's squeezing the life out of him.

"I never understood that one," Raudabaugh says. "In all my years I never caught on to how it's more so where there's none. Saltier where there's none. Drier where there's none. Fattier where there's none. Sweeter where there's none. I get the big idea, but I don't get how the words make it up."

Eddie drains his glass quickly and nearly sprawls across the men's laps trying to get to the bottle. Cody catches him and pushes him back up, knocking the glass out of his hand. The three men watch it hit the floor and then roll in a slow arc for the steps. What little light there is glows up from it and the thin liquid trail it leaves from off the lip shows like lacquer across the boards. The glass rolls to the edge, then bumps down the steps to the walkway, where it seems to pause before going to smash.

"Just like that," Cody says. "Here, take it."

Eddie takes the brown quart bottle in two hands and sits back down. The beer is warm and smells like bread rising. Drinking it gives him a small throb over his right eye. He holds a finger to it as if it were a pulse and empties the bottle.

"That's a blue moon," Cody says. "The second full moon of the month. It only happens every two or three years. Looks a little blue too."

"How do you know that?" Raudabaugh says.

"A woman told me about it once."

"It's the kind of thing a woman would know."

"She may have a limp," Eddie says, now feeling the alcohol. For reasons he can't figure out, he sees her on a runway in an evening dress and high heels walking toward an airplane. He wants to re- member to make himself write that down so he can think about it later. But for now she's out there and she's making her way to that airplane. Her legs flash from a slit in the dress and they're beautiful, but there's a hitch in their movement.

"Mary's staying over at the hospital with her," he says.

"Not to worry," Cody says. "She's young and strong. We'll have her doing a jig in no time."

"For the rest of her life," Eddie says. "She may have a limp for the rest of her life."

It gets quiet on the porch. The little bit of light has come to be enough to see all there is. It's even enough to make shadows on the grass and give off the colors of things. Shadows with colors. Raudabaugh coughs and the sound is like coarse sandpaper on coarse sandpaper. He keeps doing it until he hacks up phlegm and blows it into a handkerchief.

"Jesus," he says, daubing at the tears in his eyes, "sometimes that hurts like hell."

"I figured as much," Cody says.

Vesper bats swim the air in front of them, scooping at mosquitoes and moths, turning somersaults in the moonlight as they feed.

"Blind as a bat," Raudabaugh says.

Eddie holds the bottle by its neck. He holds it like a club and feels the dregs of beer washing across his wrist.

"No, you didn't," he says. "You couldn't have figured that. Doctors have abilities totally unknown to you. I can't believe I'm sitting here defending the medical profession while my daughter is in the hospital. Besides, she may not even have one, not if we work at it."

Raudabaugh daubs at his eyes again, then goes into another fit of coughing. It lifts his feet off the floor and makes his shoulders cave in.

"Mr. Ryan," he says, his voice no more than a strained whisper. "Mr. Ryan, I was wondering if I might see the room behind the block wall, the room where you work."

Eddie feels foolish for having gone at Cody again. He just wishes his friend weren't always so cocksure of everything or that maybe he were a little more sure himself. I'm thirty-eight years old, he thinks, and here I am railing against life, a thing I know less and less about every fucking day.

"Mr. Ryan," Raudabaugh says.

Eddie reaches to touch the old man and gets him by the elbow. He feels how thin and bony it is inside the shirt sleeve. He thinks to pull back but he doesn't. He lets his touch go even stronger.

"I really can't, Mr. Raudabaugh. Not tonight. Not after everything that's happened. It's really not a place I show people."

"We all have places like that," Raudabaugh says.

The old man's chest begins to heave gently with his crying. Eddie can see tears making tracks in the dust on his cheeks. Cody has his other arm and they hold on to him until his breathing slows to the point where it almost can't be heard. He stares ahead into the trees beyond. They're the color of gun barrels and the leaves are the color of things deep in a pond. The two younger men stare off, also trying to see what he sees.

"Now that I've gotten this far," Raudabaugh whispers, "I just want to see how it's going to end."

19

Mill Brook makes a long run through Inverawe before dropping to the Connecticut. It drains twenty square miles of rills and streams, rainfall, runoff and snowmelt, building five hundred feet of head, enough to have powered gristmills, fulling mills, linseed mills, a powder mill and sawmills; old-growth pine, hemlock, oak, maple and birch sawed into tens of thousands of board feet, turned into tipcarts, wheels, highbacks, shingles, tool handles, lath and box and pail stock, barns, houses and churches.

Up and down the brook can be found drill holes, but no more the rock-filled timber-crib dams, headrace canals, stone-lined tail-races, foundation walls and wheel pits. The harnessing of water to saw, grind, hammer and spin.

The brook runs parallel to the road, doglegs under the bridge just down from Eddie Ryan's house, then falls to the river, two miles away. It's just below this bridge where the men and machines will congregate. The day after the blue moon, the furnace went in, and the day after that, all the men of Inverawe who showed up to help will come back to commence the pond.

And it's here where two hundred years ago, on this same spot, young Shadrack Wheel, husband to Luna and son of Meshach and Zilpha, called the family from their sleep to the powder mill to witness his latest refinements in the intimate mixture of saltpeter, charcoal and brimstone. He'd been working late and was onto something big. But his refinements were lost that night and would go down in history as the achievement of the French chemist Antoine Laurent Lavoisier, director of the Royal Gunpowder Commission, and his assistant Éleuthère Irénée du Pont de Nemours, because Meshach had been into the rum and felt he needed a light to see better. The Wheel Powder Mill and the Wheel family were blown to kingdom come. Lavoisier went on to be guillotined and Éleuthère went into production on the Brandywine in his own powder mill, which was to be the kernel of the Du Pont enterprises, but that's another story.

It's only right that on this morning a distant relative, Ferris, should be sitting here now, astride a Case 880D crawler excavator ready to begin digging.

Cody stands in the strong bed of Mill Brook in his hip boots. The clear water sloshes over his ankles and laps at the boulder-strewn bank. He's smoking a cigar, a fat, rum-soaked Swisher Sweet. He rolls it in his fingers, uses it to point with, then clamps it in his mouth, the ash pointed skyward. Little Eddie rides behind him in the kid backpack. It's outfitted with stirrups so when he stands, he can ride with his chin on Cody's cap and that's what he'll do for most of the day.

Dome parks his Harley in the driveway and hikes down to Cody and Ferris. Cody meets him by the machine. He points out a map drawn in the gravel. Ferris doesn't pay much attention. He's the best hoe operator around. By eye he can dig a foundation to within inches of its necessary dimension. Because of this skill, he works only when he wants to.

"A two-headed monster," Dome yells, pretending to be frightened and ready to bolt, making Little Eddie jump in his stirrups and laugh.

"Two heads are better than one," Cody says. "I see you're back from the beyond."

"Right now I'd settle for just a little head," Dome says.

"She have false teeth, did she, Dome?" Ferris said.

"She did, Mr. Ferris. She surely did," Dome says, looking up into the cab.

Cody's been left in charge of Little Eddie while his father and mother are at the hospital. He thinks about the boy hearing such talk and decides to give himself up to it. What the hell, he's got to hear it sometime and besides he isn't going to grow up to be some Little Lord Fauntleroy. Not if his uncle Cody has anything to say about it.

"What glorious work," Dome says. "The digging of a pond for all the town's children to swim in. If I were a young man, you know what I'd do?"

Cody and Ferris don't ask.

"I'd get into the business of building playgrounds, those ones that are made of pressure-treated lumber. They're like little castles. Whole towns come together for their constructions. They're like habitats for gerbils and hamsters, only huge."

"That p.t. lumber will give you the cancer," Ferris says.

"Did that Malcolm Forbes fellow show up on his bike with Liz Taylor? Did you get to meet her?"

"Well, you tell me, what better way to get it can you think of?"

"Get what?"

From down the road come the combined sounds of half a dozen diesel engines. It grows enormous in the chill morning. It gets closer, becoming a calliope of horsepowers through double shift-ings, gearing down, stuck throttles, set idles and meshing gears. The rest are coming, a rubber-tired backhoe loader, an eighty-two-horse trascavator, a turbocharged D-6H Cat dozer and an HD-700 Kato excavator, a machine made by Mitsubishi, the fact of which reaps much shit from the owners of the American-made equip-ment. Cody wades into the brook and waves his arms the way men on aircraft carriers do. The operators turn onto an access road long before the bridge and come down through groves of poplar and clumps of juniper. Tracks and tires show wet from low marshy ground, but not enough to wait progress. Dandelions, black-eyed Susans, sweet peas, tickseed, milkweeds and thistles—all get trod under by machine after machine, but somehow look as alive and splendent lying down as they did standing up.

"Right cheers where the heart of it is," Cody yells. "We're gonna move five thousand cubic yards, dress it off and reseed by night-fall."

No one hears him. The machines are too loud. Track jobs fire up and swing down lowboys. The sound of over seven hundred horse-power fills the air. To a man, they think they'll be levitated from their seats. They idle down and jump from inside the machines to the ground below, secretly surprised at the shock they feel in their feet. Cody comes out of the water and meets them by his map near Ferris's hoe. They're all clapping Dome on the back, asking him about Liz Taylor.

"Five thousand cubic yards," Cody says.

"Five thousand cubic yards," Dome says.

The men laugh and start to bitch because it's Sunday.

"What the hell else are you going to be doing?" Dome says. "Botor moating?"

"Some of us like to be home with the wife and kids," Coonie says.

Coonie works for the town. He runs hounds with radio collars most nights in the fall. Makes cash money on coonskins. With the understanding that the pond will be used as a backup fire pond, he's taken it upon himself to bring the town's rubber-tired backhoe. He doesn't have a wife or any kids.

"Do a little barbecue," Dick Doody says, his brother Tom nodding his head in agreement, the sole proprietors of Doody Brothers Construction.

"Oh, come on, boys," Dome says. "What's it amount to when you're done? You've done all that staying at home doing nothing and gotten yourselves tired out for the rest of the day. You may as well come here and work. I can't think of anything more tiring than doing nothing."

The men nod their heads. They know Dome is right. It's the way their lives and the way they make their livings come together. Truck cabs get to be homes with two or three changes of clothes, book-work, a stashed bottle and a knife. Time on the road, time away from home makes the work a kind of house to live in.

"You men have to learn to recreate. This isn't work because you ain't getting paid. This is fun."

The men laugh at what Dome has said. They ask again if he met up with Liz Taylor.

When news of Eileen's accident spread through town, people started showing up. Installing the furnace and now building the pond are what these men can do. It's like bringing casseroles and cakes to the house. It's for them as much as anyone.

Over the sound of the idling machines, a ten-wheeler without a muffler can be heard coming on too fast. They know it to be Joe Paquette. He runs the dump, collects garbage, salvages junk cars and lifts weights. He's coming on with a load of bald tires that are going to be used to build the dam and the wings where the brook will flow in. The air brakes hiss and the truck slows. It's still rolling as Joe Paquette steps down to the ground. They move together until finally the truck stops behind him and he's coming over the guardrail down to where the men are. His face is drawn and white. He tells them he hasn't slept all night.

"She left me," he says. "She took the money and left. She said she saw someone in a movie do it once and that's just what she was going to do to me. It's like suicide."

The men stare down at their feet. Joe and his wife were the fighting kind, knockdown and drag out. Their fights were the stuff of their conversations with others. Marie would drop one shoe at the Lotto machine and stand there in front of a line telling Mr. Washburn how Joe had loosened her tooth. He'd stop for gas and tell everyone how she wanted to do more together so he bought her an exercise bike and parked it near his recliner in front of the T.V.

The young men don't want to hear this because they don't know if what he's saying is the true thing or not. They don't know whether to commit themselves to his heartbreak, while the older ones have long since grown impatient with Joe and Marie's bullshit.

"She dusted," he says. "She took the checkbook and juked. The house is like a coffin, only bigger."

"You can't leave a young woman out in the middle of nowhere," Dome says, throwing his arms in the air. "On one side of her is the dump, on the other side is junk cars and behind is a swamp."

Joe Paquette bristles. His muscles swell inside his T-shirt. He's about to speak when Raudabaugh comes picking his way through the machinery, touching each piece like a blind man. He starts right in telling his condom stories. The men have heard them before but they laugh anyway, even Joe Paquette. When they're done laughing, Cody steps into the center of them, Little Eddie jumping in his stirrups. He gives them the program and they all nod, telling him it sounds good.

"Let's get the show on the road then," he says, giving Joe Paquette a shot in the stomach and a wink. The men start to dig.

By lunchtime the flow of Mill Brook has ceased. The two hoes scoop out the gravel so fast the water only flashes in the hole trying to fill it up. The bulldozers work the banks, dressing off what the hoes drop, winging back and around to the dam, which is being made up with mats of tires. As fast as they can be laid, their hollows are filled with stone and gravel. A twenty-foot length of galvanized culvert ordered by the town for another job waits in the bushes to be put in for overflow when the proper height has been reached. Raudabaugh runs Cody's D-7H dozer. He's been acting a little touched since the night on the porch so Cody sets the gear and throttle and has him going back and forth over hard ground out of everybody's way.

People come by to watch. The men's wives and girl friends bring hibachi grills and start up charcoal fires. The older kids help with laying the tires. The hoe work gets to be competition between Ferris and the Kato, run by a new man in town named Diamond.

Cody and Dome go to the house to change Little Eddie's diaper. They make jokes about his tiny pecker. The boy laughs too as if he's wise to what they're saying but doesn't give a damn. What the hell, he must think, it *is* a tiny pecker.

"Look at that," Dome says. "The little feller hasn't been cropped yet. Make sure you peel that back and swab it off good."

"I know," Cody says. "I don't understand it. His parents are smart people. They should know about stuff like that. It's the sanitary thing to do."

"You're right there. My mother and father didn't know nothing about it and I had to have it done when I got into the service."

Max the cat jumps onto the changing table. His fur is knotted with burrs, matted with cobwebs. He treads lightly around the boy's head, making him laugh again.

"Get offa there, you old whoremaster," Cody says, swatting at his tail.

The cat rears up and swipes, then he jumps to the floor and scats out the doorway.

"In Africa they do their women too."

"The hell you say."

"Yes sir. They did me in the service. Piece of sand got under that skin. It's just like a wood chip under your eyelid. That is pain, mister. I had to walk around for a week, fighting the urge to get hard. You'd be surprised how often the tendency comes and not for no goddamn reason at all. There weren't no ice either in case of emergency. Willpower, boy. Willpower. Later on they handed out aerosol cans of freezing element. Stuff to freeze it. That's one great thing the war gave us, aerosol spray cans. Is his father cropped? Maybe that's why."

"I don't know. I've neither the urge nor the opportunity to find out. Seeing how I've come to be the boy's uncle, I should probably bring it up. It's in his best interest."

Cody and Dome finish with the change and Little Eddie gets hoisted back into the pack.

More people have arrived. Cody and Dome stand out on the porch. The smells of hamburgers and barbecued chicken come up their way. A Frisbee floats by and then a football. The machines look smaller from the house.

"It's quite the circus," Dome says. "About alls we're missing is the Hottentot Venus. She had lips that hung halfway to her thighs."

"Sure is. It's a wonderful thing to see."

The machines begin to shut down one by one. Men are jumping to the ground and coming up for their lunches. Joe Paquette can be heard coming on with another load of tires. The men run up the high side of the road bank, bending around sumac to get out of his way. They can see him laughing at them as they scatter. People on the lawn get to its edge to watch.

The air brakes whoosh and the truck shudders as the front end goes into the ditch. Joe Paquette jams the gears until he finds reverse. When he does, he begins backing and raising the dump body at the same time. Tires begin tumbling out the tailgate and over the back of it. He keeps going, trying to get them as close as possible to where they'll be needed.

Then, in a gentle sort of way, the truck's going over too, catching the guardrail cables, uprooting posts and easing on down. It seems as though the cables will reach a point where they'll snap back and sling him forward, up the mountain, maybe over it, maybe to the moon.

And coming up the bank is Raudabaugh on the D-7 Cat dozer, an avalanche of bald radials, punctured whitewalls and blown steel-belted all-terrains, pouring past the tracks and jouncing through the air. He stares into the back of the truck, watching the seas of black tires washing his way, until finally he gets his wits about him and stops at the same time Joe Paquette's truck stops its descent, the dozer blade and truck touching at once.

Silence comes after the diesels shut down, after the phantom engine noise has drifted from the air. It stays quiet like that and then a car comes from the same direction as Joe Paquette. Its fan belt squeals and it thumps dull and heavy with worn bearings. The car slows down until a brake line blows and it rolls under the front end of Joe Paquette's truck, which by now is pointing to the sky.

Marie Paquette gets out. She walks around to where Joe can see her and puts her hands on her hips and yells at him.

"Joe Paquette, you wear the brand of stupidity that all men wear. You are the dumbest son of a bitch that ever came down the pike."

■

Everyone is happy to hear Marie might be pregnant. Joe had been talking about taking a job out of town. Somehow he had it in his head he'd keep up all his other jobs too. But now with her maybe pregnant, everyone thinks it to be folly for him to do it. It's pretty much common knowledge that a man who takes a job out of state, leaving a pregnant woman behind, should be shot. Joe feels this too. A man like that should be shotgunned. If only he'd known. He's already hurt her, so many times.

Ferris and the man named Diamond sit quietly at the picnic table eating hamburgers, chips, and plates of potato salad. Other men sit with them, arguing the merits of the Kato and the Case. The Doody brothers and Coonie side up with Ferris while Joe Paquette sides with Diamond. Marie Paquette has Little Eddie in the house, rocking him into sleep, so Dome and Cody can watch the argument. As it goes, the Case delivers more horsepower, more displacement and more torque while the Kato has more reach.

"It all comes down to the man on the machine," Cody says. "Seems as though both operators are holding their own. Their machines too. Nothing against Mr. Diamond here, but I prefer American just on principle."

"It's the Mitsubishi boys and you know what they did at Pearl Harbor. They made all those planes. You've got to buy in. It's the future."

"Kamikazes. The divine wind," Raudabaugh says softly, his

throat a rattle. "Zeroes. Just tell me, Mr. Joe Paquette. Who won the fucking war?"

Raudabaugh's words put an end to the argument. They now all know that a day ago a lot more snapped than a little girl's legs.

Raudabaugh tells the men a story about a job he was on in Manchester. It was in the winter, a long time ago. The men were up five flights and it was quite a rigmarole to get down to the Porta Potti so they took to pissing down a vent pipe. Well, it kept freezing and freezing and day by day it worked its way up until finally that vent pipe turned into a fountain of piss.

"A fountain of piss," he says, slapping his thighs, tears of laughter rolling down his cheeks. The other men laugh too until Raudabaugh gets up and wanders back to the porch.

"He's just tired," Dome says. "The life, it expands; the living, it diminishes. That's the way it goes."

"You're right there," Dick Doody says. "You can't live no more. Not like you fellas used to. I wanted to get a carry permit and the woman told me they're tightening up on them. Said maybe for a twenty-two but not for a forty-four."

"I don't get that," his brother says. "Dirty Harry carried a forty-four and he was a cop."

"You know what I do," Joe Paquette says, "whenever Marie's mother comes around, that's when I clean my guns."

The men start laughing again and keep on until they see Cody and Raudabaugh headed back to the machines, their arms slung over each other's shoulders.

"Back to work," Dome says, staring off at them.

■

The machines are on the move again. Joe Paquette's ten-wheeler gets free and he and some high school kids ferry tires, while another crew lays cribs for the dam and winged-back walls at the pond's mouth. Diamond and Ferris work opposite sides, sixty feet apart, shoveling, swinging and dumping off behind them, while the other machines work the earth around to make the berm and the dam.

On Eddie Ryan's lawn the women have now gathered at the picnic table. They hover around Marlene Doody, Dick's wife, and Jeri, who's Tom's wife. It seems as though one of the brothers has had a vasectomy but they won't say which one. It's caused an awful row within the families.

"Let's just say for a second it was Dick," Marlene says. "I call up the garage and Tom says he's gone to the hospital, but won't tell me why. I'm sure he's had a heart attack."

"When it all comes out," Jeri says, "the other one says he doesn't even feel like he has a brother anymore. I said, 'What are you going to do? He's your brother. You've got to honor that.'"

Coonie blows the hydraulic pump in the town's loader backhoe. He limps it into the village shed and gets a ride back with Dr. Pot, who watches from the bridge. Joe Paquette waves up to him and he waves back, pats his stomach and shrugs. The men laugh and the more they do, the more he pats.

"Maybe he's the father," Dome yells, and Joe gives him the finger.

Dr. Pot laughs too and then drives off. Cody crosses back to the house to check on Little Eddie. He's fallen asleep but Marie still holds him, with maybe her own little baby sleeping in her belly. Cody backs out of the room and goes down to the bridge again. He stands, watching the work below. The machines all move together, only a few feet apart, huge iron, swinging, pushing, lifting, ripping and packing. He thinks to fetch G.R. so he too can come witness, but then realizes he's dead and is filled with sadness. He's happy, though, his memory played that trick on him, if only for a moment.

When he looks up, Louis Poissant's Cadillac is pulling over right behind him. Louis powers down the window and lets an arm hang out.

"Quite the public works project," he says.

Cody goes over and rests his hip against the door, his elbow on the roof.

"How's life at the animal farm?" Cody says.

"Goddamn kid had the rabbits in the house and they got into a bag of marijuana. They just went ape. They're back there now trying to catch them. Goddamn things are zinging all over the place. Zipping here. Zipping there."

Cody wants to ask about Kay, but he doesn't. The boy too, but he isn't really a boy anymore. His mind starts him down the road of could haves, should haves and maybes, but he stops it, hauls it back and just lives with it standing there leaning against Louis

Poissant's Cadillac. It's something he decides he'll always live alongside of, him and this feeling that's never further away than the tip of a finger on the hand of an outstretched arm. Never more than that. Never more than striking distance.

"How's the little girl?" Louis says.

"She's young."

"That she is."

Louis Poissant passes a cigar out to Cody. Then he strips the cellophane from another for himself. He strikes a match on the dashboard, lights his own and then cups his hands to keep the flame for Cody.

"That Ferris, he do some blasting?" Louis Poissant says.

"Seems as though he does."

Dome comes up the banking and climbs the guardrail. He sees who Cody's talking to and walks over.

"You got another one of them stogies for me there, Mr. Fat Louis?"

"What have you, taken up smoking again now that your wife's gone?"

Louis Poissant unwraps another cigar and passes it out the window, but he doesn't offer a light. Mrs. Huguenot used to give him awful tongue-lashings over the way he tended his animals.

Cody strikes a match off the roof and holds it out to Dome.

"How 'bout you," Louis says, "you know if that Ferris does any blasting?"

"No way," Dome says. "Get him the fuck away from here. He has a way of making me nervous."

"Well, I've got to be off," Louis Poissant says, starting the engine. "Over to Bolton to see a man about some cows. Good luck with your public works project. I hope the conservation people don't get after you. They're a bitch to deal with."

"You oughta know," Dome says, rapping his knuckles on the hood. "You run 'cross most everybody around."

"Yup."

Louis Poissant drives off slowly, his head always turning to see what's new and what's different, to see what's up.

Wives begin to pack up. Marie comes out to tell Cody that Little Eddie's asleep in his crib, will probably be out until suppertime, then she hooks a ride with Marlene Doody.

Down below, the men are angling the galvanized culvert into place. It hangs on chains from Diamond's bucket. They lower it into the trench, then the dozers complete the dam. As the trench fills with stone and gravel, more and more water flows into the pond. It will take some time before it fills to the opening, but the men don't wait. As their jobs finish, they load up equipment and wave good-bye until there's only Raudabaugh on Cody's D-7, passing back and forth over the top, making the grade flat and smooth.

Gray light steals down from the mountain. Cody and Dome watch him from the bridge, clear dark water passing under them.

"I'm getting old, must be," Dome says. "I'm afraid we've out-stripped ourselves. We've run out of bounds and don't know how to get back or whether we even want to or not."

"At least it's something," Cody says, letting his cigar drop into the water below and then waiting to hear its fire hiss and go out.

■

It's dark when Eddie leaves the hospital. He crosses the parking lot under the high banks of halogen lights. Clouds of sphinx moths are drawn to the glowing haloes where they tick and bat their wings. He stops and watches them high up, carrying the light on their scaly wings, and at his feet crunch variegated shells of the fallen on the pavement, still warm from the day's sun.

In the morning he'll come back to this place, only then he won't go home alone. They'll wheel Eileen into the elevator and out to the car. They'll slide her into the back seat and on the way they'll stop for soft ice cream, vanilla and chocolate swirl with sprinkles. Her legs are set and already on the mend and all the while will need watching. Therapy may be in order.

The air is still and cool on the ground, but there's a wind in the trees, moving the crowns darkly in the sky as the moon wanes. He has twelve miles to go and it doesn't matter if it's fifty. He likes to be in the car alone, feeling it move over the road.

Tonight he resists the urge to take stock of things. He'll enjoy the radio and the blow coming through the open window. He'll drive slowly, maybe take a left in East Granger Hollow and go home by way of the Hurricane Road. It's a road that runs out like a good roller coaster. There are dips, banked curves and quick humps. There are two plank bridges and if the moon is right, it will silhouette the fire tower on Highland Hill. It's a road he's traveled before.

But he doesn't go left and he doesn't take his time. He drives straight at what the speed limit allows. He's anxious to see that his son is safe in his sleep, still a boy who hasn't gotten much older, hasn't had a growth spurt. He'll quiz Cody on the day, want to know every minute of it while being fully aware of how thin it can draw him, living his life and the lives of his children at the same time.

A half mile from home the tires begin to pick up pebbles and stones, winging them against the underbody. The road gets rougher, like hardpan, so he slows down. Clods of earth and the muddy tracks of truck tires show in the headlights. There's another stretch of road, just before his driveway, that's been chewed up by the shoes of a track machine.

Cody's on the porch having a smoke and drinking store-bought beer. Only a can. Boxes filled with dirty paper plates, chip bags, soda cans and beer bottles lie at his feet. Eddie wonders about the rubbish. He hopes Cody isn't getting back into the beer.

"How is she?" Cody says.

"She's fine. She's tired," Eddie says, and then after taking a long breath he continues. "I'm tired. Mary's tired. But we're fine."

"The whole world's tired."

"Being tired helps."

"I know what you mean," Cody whispers as if he were talking to the son and not the father. "If I had my druthers, I'd feel tired all the time, after-work tired, that kind of tiredness."

"That's it. That's just what it is."

"Come with me," Cody says, popping out of the chair. "Come see what I've got."

Eddie follows, down the road to the bridge. They climb the guardrail and go down the banking, but instead of it being a quick descent, it's gradual and hard underfoot, no grasses, no goldenrod, no blackberry bushes spiking and dragging at your trousers. He follows Cody along a wide berm that tops the new banks of Mill Brook. Below him is dark, still water mirroring the night sky and in the distance the noise of the water dumping out the overflow.

"It's a pond," Eddie says.

"No shit, Sherlock," Cody says, and then he laughs.

"It's a pond."

"It's a pond all right and ain't it wonderful."

The two men stand there, shuffling in the gravel, hands in pockets. A stone gets kicked.

"Look there," Cody says. "The grass is already starting to grow."

20

Eddie helps Eileen into Mrs. Huguenot's baby carriage. It has tall sides, pneumatic tires and a frame hung on tight springs. The bonnet folds back like a convertible top and the front panel lays out flat on tiny links of chain.

Dome calls it her pram. He brought it over two days ago, then went to visit Raudabaugh to see his new reverse-osmosis machine, but found him dead in his new sugarhouse, sitting with his back to the wall and staring at the contraption that'd pump sap through membranes at five hundred pounds' pressure, sitting as if he'd only stopped to rest for a minute, to catch his breath. Now he's in the cooler at Eddie Ryan's house, resting quietly at 30 degrees Fahrenheit.

"When you hold me like that, our hearts are right next to each other."

"I know," Eddie says, easing her down on the pillows and then adjusting her legs so they won't rock.

"I want to go down to the pond and then to the soda machine."

Eddie wheels the pram down the driveway. Eileen lies back in the pillows, her legs straight out, encased in plaster. The left one will be fine but her right leg is still to be watched; there's trouble in her ankle. Friends have been coming by to see her. She assigns them colors from her box of water paints. They get to work on each cast. She tells them not to write their names but to make shapes of colors. Long parallels spiral the left leg and splotches make a ragged jigsaw of the right one. By now there's almost no room left but that's okay because most of her friends have had a chance.

"They are elegant, aren't they, Eddie."

Since the accident she's taken to calling her father by his first name.

"Yes, they are. What do you think elegant means?"

"It means colorful and cheery."

The tires on the pram are huge. They roll over the cracks and the bumps disappear in the springs, not like the stroller Eddie and Mary bought when she was a baby, four sets of double plastic wheels, a thing sold for its collapsibility with a foldout sheet of directions and warnings against pinched fingers. Eddie thinks how baby carriages have gone from being motor homes to sports cars.

Across the road is the new pond and this is where they stop. Eddie goes down on his knees beside the bridge abutment. He hands up stones to Eileen and she flings them, one after another, into the water below. She hits the surface every time, sending up geysers where the water claps together over the sinking stone.

"You throw like a boy."

"I know," she says. "I'm a good thrower."

"Most girls push instead of throw. You really whip your arm."

"When do you think our fish will come?"

"I don't know. Your uncle Cody is researching that. Maybe they come in barrels. He sent out a batch of mail last week and we should be getting some back soon. I don't know if it's such a good idea." Dome wants fish too. Maybe it will happen.

"At the Alamo they have giant goldfish. Mrs. Hall told us at school. The goldfish live in little canals."

Eddie gets up and dusts off his trousers. In the morning he hopes to be able to take care of Raudabaugh. He still doesn't know whether he's to be buried, cremated or entombed. He may even have to be transported out of state. Raudabaugh's nearest of kin is in Nova Scotia and they haven't been reached yet. Mary's been trying to get in touch with them for two days now. She even appealed to the VA, but they have no record of his rights to benefits or even of his service in the armed forces.

Now she's in Rutland, gone to the fair with Cody and Little Eddie. They went up in the late afternoon and won't be back until after dark. It's a ride of a couple hours. Eileen insisted they go and then she dictated a list of things to be brought back: cotton candy, a fat, soft pretzel, a candied apple and a prize Cody was to win, preferably a giant panda bear as big as a man.

Eddie turns onto the road again. The sun is going down and it's cooling off. Swallows inhabit the air, swift and graceful, dropping from rafters or eaves where they build their nests. They come down from the church steeple where they live under the cornice while the bats are higher up in the belfry. They will be out later.

The swallows flash before them as the sun sets in the west, looking like a bonfire on the horizon, whole stands of timber engulfed in flames.

That's what it would be if it wasn't just a sunset, Eddie thinks.

"Look at them go," she says.

"Swallows can cover as much as six hundred miles a day," Eddie says, "trying to find food to feed their little ones."

Eileen doesn't say anything and he wonders if she's heard him. She often gets that way, silently mulling over what she's heard.

These small facts of nature are what he has to pass along and their conveyance seems to do something for him also. It's as if he's telling himself these things too, telling them all over again. It comes in the stories he reads to her, stories read to him when he was a child, yet he'd forgotten most of them and only now are they remembered in the act of the reading.

The other night it was *Black Beauty*. They sat up until ten while he finished reading her the whole book. He wanted to see how the life of Beauty would turn out as much as she did.

"I feel so morbid, Eddie."

"Is it the children again?"

"Yes," she says, and sighs. "This time you tell how the story goes. I'm too tired."

"In 1944 there were forty-four children," he begins. "They lived in a stone house overlooking the snowy Alps. They were brought there to live because there was war in their country, but the war caught up with them. They were captured by the Nazis and sent to Auschwitz, where they died."

The story was in the news again, the children of Izieux. It got back in her brain and she's been pining away over their memory. She knows the names of two sisters. She's convinced she'll meet them in heaven and when she does she'll tell them how she's been looking forward to that very moment ever since she first heard their story.

"Why didn't they just run away?" Eileen says, after thinking about the story for a moment.

"Some of them probably tried to, but they got caught."

"I would have run away. I would have run away and hidden in a cave under the ground."

Eddie pushes the pram along the shoulder. Dead animal smell comes in on the air. It looks to be a woodchuck ahead of them, pounded flat in the middle of the road.

"I can see its teeth," she says.

"There's the paws too. He's a goner."

"How come there are so many dead critters on the road?"

"These animals have been traveling certain paths for hundreds and hundreds of years. In a way they really haven't caught on to the danger. They traveled their paths before the roads cut through and something inside them keeps them doing it. It's like the swallows. Some of those very birds we saw may spend the winter in Argentina. Rattlesnakes are that way. Some travel the same path for thirty years. Geese too. They fly south for the winter."

Eileen twirls a few strands of hair until they're knotted. She gets her elbows up on the sides of the carriage, raises her butt and settles back down. Eddie starts down the road again, going past the fence Louis Poissant built on his property to run heifers. Inside the barbwire, the young stock chews at the grass as it watches them go by.

"Well, whatever it was, it sure ripped the guts out of him."

"Yup, it sure did," he says.

As they near the common, they start passing white houses with black shutters. Lights are on in some of the rooms. The windows have many panes, four or six or eight. There are flower beds and wide lawns that come to the edge of the road. The backs of the houses are different. Some have sheds or falling-down barns. Some have new decks and blue aboveground swimming pools. All of the land behind the houses falls away to Mill Brook.

"I hope Juanita can come see me again. She knows the India baby."

"She's a nice girl."

"She has a coat made of chicken-feet leather."

The road widens as they get to the common. Eddie goes right, passing by the firehouse and the town hall to Washburn's store. It's closed now, but the soda machine still hums and flickers. Mr. Washburn's been talking about getting one of those machines that talks to you when you drop your money in.

"You know something," Eileen says. "Nobody and I mean nobody knows how old Juanita is. Not even the school."

"Somebody must know."

"Nope. Nobody."

Eileen has Eddie swing the carriage alongside the front of the soda machine so she can run the coins in herself, make her own selection.

"I'll do yours too," she says. "Give me your money."

"You pick for me too."

She hits the button and another can of orange rattles into the opening. They take their sodas and cross to the common. Eddie sets the wheel brakes and then sits down on the step that surrounds the monument. It's quiet and they can hear the humming of the one streetlight in front of the town hall.

"Are you still morbid?" Eddie says.

"Yes."

"About the forty-four children?"

"The India baby, too."

"Who's the India baby?"

"I can't tell you."

Eddie doesn't say anything. He tries to remember where he heard of the India baby. He's learned to let things like this go. The India baby could be something she made up that very moment and hasn't figured out yet what it is. He drinks his soda down and then crunches the can in the middle, folding it back and forth. She watches him and listens to the sound of the weakening aluminum and then another sound, a pickup truck traveling their way on River

Road. The tires slide in gravel and then squeal when they hit the tar.

Its headlights begin to open the night, growing more full. Eddie takes hold of the carriage, ready to move, but the truck makes the corner and brakes in front of the store. It's a blocked-up Ford with oversized tires. Four boys in baseball uniforms jump down from the back while another boy and two girls get out of the cab. They all push and shove each other, laughing and giggling, grabbing ass.

"Get some Cokes," one of the girls says, "and we'll have rum and Cokes."

She's a tall girl with blond hair, braided from the back of her head. She watches one of the boys work the machine. He has a way of punching buttons simultaneously or in quick repetition to out-smart it. Two and sometimes three cans rattle into the opening for the price of one.

The girl who wanted the Cokes shakes up a can and sprays the rest of them. Two of the boys get her back until it's running from her head and face, dripping from her T-shirt. Eddie watches them. He knows they're harmless, just kids having fun. They're probably twenty years younger than he is. Then he thinks he should say something. Mr. Washburn doesn't make all that much off the store. And Eileen is there too. He wonders if she's waiting for him to speak up, waiting for him to tell them to behave themselves as he would've told her.

The boy who's driving and the other girl now stand leaning against the side of the truck, away from their friends but where Eddie and Eileen can still see them. She leans back against the driver's door and he leans into her. They're kissing and he has his knee between her legs, working it up and down.

The blond girl comes round to their side holding three cans of soda gathered to her chest with her hand and forearm and a bottle of rum in her other hand.

"Take them," she says, "they're freezing my tits off."

"They don't feel that cold to me," the boy says, pinching her.

She kicks at him and he laughs, then he and the girl each take a can. They drink them down a bit and then fill them back up with rum.

"What are you two doing? Kissy. Kissy."

"Fuck off," the boy says, and they start to laugh again.

"Someone's over there watching us."

Eddie sees them all turn to look at him and Eileen. He wishes he'd said something now, rather than be discovered. He wants them to leave, to go away back to the town they're from.

"Some pervert," one of them says.

The girl with the rum tells them to shut up and that they should load up and get out of here before someone calls them in. They all climb into the truck, taking furtive looks at Eddie and Eileen. The driver turns the key but it won't start. The boys in back jump up and down, banging on the cab roof.

"I need a push," the driver yells, hanging his head out the window.

Two jump off and get the truck rolling down the road, then pile back in over the tailgate.

"A pervert," one of the pushers yells. "He likes them young."

The truck bucks; the engine catches and misses. The boys in the back are thrown forward and backward until finally it guns at full throttle and takes off down the road, empty cans being tossed over the sides.

In Eddie's hands the aluminum snaps and slides, cutting him across the heel of his palm.

■

Eddie and Eileen sit on the porch, on the new chaise lounge. It's long and wooden, lengthened out with a complete leg rest and packed with fat hard cushions. It's now full night and they've decided to sit here until Mary, Little Eddie and Cody get back from Rutland. They want to see what prizes have been taken and they want to hear about the fair, the dancing pig, Boxcar Willy.

Eddie rests against the cushions and Eileen sits between his legs, her head thrown back against his chest. They have a blanket draped over them, rising up to just under her chin. The air has changed. It's cooling and they speak out on how they hope it's a sign of things to come. Maybe the legs won't itch so much. Maybe she won't have to work the thin ruler down the insides of the casts so often to get at those spots.

"I'm afraid my legs will disappear if I can't see them," she says.

"It seems like that," he tells her. "But you can imagine them. Your brother, if he can't see something he doesn't know it's there.

He hasn't learned that just because you can't see it, doesn't mean it's not there. You can imagine it, though."

"I can imagine them not being there."

Down the Connecticut, in Ware, a storm has stalled out, chain lightning and thunder, rain and hailstones, rumors of yellow skies and tornadoes. From the gaps in the mountains, they can hear the music of Santa's Land in Vermont. It's one of those freakish sound things, like sound over water or the way sound is louder coming than going, but different. It's the way sound travels between and around mountains. The tinkle of sleigh bells fed into a speaker and sent hollow into the air over the miles to their house.

They've never been to Santa's Land. It's open in the summer, reindeer, goats and sheep. There are rides and movies, activities for the children. Santa shows up with a pack of elves and there's a gift shop. They talk about going sometime and they've driven by on their way to someplace else, but never stopped. It's come to seem farther away than it really is, farther away than the North Pole itself. Eddie thinks how the longer they wait, the more unlikely it'll be they ever go. And that will make it all the more strange, only the sound of a place coming to them faintly through the gaps. The sound of "Jingle Bells."

The night goes darker, an expanse of black ocean. Leaves begin to turn, gently tossing in noiseless wind. The sound from Santa's Land comes and goes, comes and goes. The storm stalled out over Ware may be making its way north.

"Look," she says. "Each star is a pool of water. Way up there is water."

Eddie feels unmoored and he knows she feels it too because she burrows into him, getting as close as she can, dragging her legs back, knocking them together under the blanket. It seems to be the house that's moving and the leaves at night to be still. The house has wrested itself from the earth and it's a ship on the sea, riding the flourish of wave, one moment vengeant, the next serene.

Eddie holds to this feeling. It makes him to be less in audience to the earth and more a part of it. Maybe hell is raging, he thinks, trying to make room for Raudabaugh, but he's laughing at them, calling them a bunch of assholes, little buggers. You think such stuff when you have kids. He'll write that one down.

"It's like *The Secret Garden*," she says. "Dickon and Mary get Colin

walking. They have crocuses, snowdrops, roses, irises and daf-
fydowndills."

She counts them off on her fingers, her voice a chanting song.

"Wick means alive," she says. "Colin was afraid of not living to
grow up. Daddy, say, 'Thou art as safe as a missel thrush.' "

Eddie says the words and then laughs. He tells her they're a fine
pair, his hand wrapped in a handkerchief and her legs wrapped in
plaster.

"We're a fine pair," she says.

The wind goes on, settling into a nice blow. It's out of its month,
something brought to them from a day in March, a nice present.
Raindrops come too. Huge as they are, they can almost be heard
whistling through the air. There aren't many, but the ones that do
come are fat and make splatting sounds, frogs in a pond. An upstairs bedroom door blows shut and the tin on a barn roof in the
village ripples and clatters. Then it's over.

"That was a close one," Eddie says.

She says it too and her body goes less rigid against his, then she's
asleep.

Eddie sits there wondering what to do. He wants a book or a
magazine or one of his journals, but he doesn't want to move and
wake her. This night was to be quiet, just the two of them, but it
got full with stuff: the pond, the critters, the kids at the soda machine, his hand and the storm. He wants to think on it, but he's tired
too, not in the body but brain-tired. He's all thought out and wishes
for sleep. Eileen rustles in his arms, speaks in her sleep.

"She looked like Mary."

"Mary? What do you mean?"

"Mary, your wife."

"Since when do you call your mother Mary?"

"Oh, Eddie, you know how it is."

"No. I don't know how it is."

"The girl with the soda in her hair. She looked like Mary."

Eddie doesn't say anything. He holds his hand closed to keep the
white handkerchief from unwrapping and thinks he heard, just
then, the music from Santa's Land again.

"Who's the India baby?" he says.

"A little baby girl with dark hair and skin. Black eyes. She lives
in a blanket."

An old memory comes into his head. He's a boy and he's lying on the braided rug in his mother and father's house. They had hot-water heat and it was always parched and dry in the winter. The T.V. is on, flickering in the dark room, black-and-white images that get to be blue out where he is. His father's asleep in the chair. All chairs face to the center of the room, but the T.V. is against the wall and to its right is the opening of the dark hallway to the bedrooms, and his mother sleeps in the one on the end.

She insists the chairs face the way they do so company won't think their lives center around the tube, as she calls it, only there's rarely any company and it makes it so those nearest the T.V. have to watch it over their shoulder.

There's only one channel and it has a commercial they run over and over. It's of a marionette, a puppet with strings attached to its jointed limbs. It clops on the empty stage, only no sounds come from its wooden feet. A hand in a black glove holding black scissors comes out from the side and snips a string. An arm falls and dangles but the dance continues. Then another string is cut and the other arm drops. Then each leg, one at a time, and the marionette hangs there. Vaccines against polio had recently been discovered and people were being made aware of them.

It was dark inside the house, black dark, the way it gets when a T.V. is on, the picture windows painted over with whatever's on the T.V. He lay there on the rug watching that commercial and his father was asleep in the chair, his head tipped over and resting on his shoulder, which had to be a painful way to sleep.

Later on, he remembers, he had to write an essay in junior high. Everyone picked a disease from a list the teacher passed around. His was poliomyelitis.

He wrote about the gray matter of the spinal cord, children in the summer and fall, fever, upset stomachs, stiff and painful necks, sudden chills and overfatigues, physical therapy preferable to the older practice of immobilization. Then he wrote about Warm Springs, Georgia, and how water springing from Pine Mountain benefited Franklin D. Roosevelt so he founded the Georgia Warm Springs Foundation to help others and had a cottage called the Little White House, where he died in 1945. The Indians knew about it long before the white men. The last sentence he wrote was "A cure is not available but much research is concerned with the problem."

The encyclopedia had been an old one and he didn't know it.

When the teacher pointed this out to him, he didn't know who to believe.

The year after, the assignment was dropped because so many kids had nightmares, because so many kids thought they had a case of the disease they studied.

"Oh, Eddie. America is so beautiful. The brooks and the mountains. This time I love you. This time I really do."

He thinks about polio and he's unfastened again, drifting in the air, calm and liking it there. He remembers standing in long lines of children with their mothers, lines that almost wrapped around a whole block at the head of the square. They walked forward, past the gas company, the bank, the church, the cobbler, the market and the barbershop. At the end was a doctor who passed out tiny cups of sugar water. He made sure you drank, then patted you on the head.

His father was across town in the factory. He was making screws and nuts and bolts out of huge coils of wire stock.

It was hot and when they got in the car, the insides of it were like an oven and he had to sit on the floor because the seats burned the backs of his bare legs.

That night when the marionette came on again, he kicked his father in the shoe to wake him up, but he wouldn't wake up and Eddie felt so all alone. Then he worried it'd happened to his father and kicked him again to make him move. This time he shifted in his sleep, and said, "What the hell's the matter with you?" and Eddie felt better.

It was years after when he learned about the connections between all of these things, the way words stand in for facts, the way the past lies over the present like laminate.

Mary is shaking him by his shoulder. He looks up and she's standing there. Cody is behind her smiling, holding Little Eddie in his arms. Eileen still sleeps, her head turned, her cheek against his shirt, and a wet spot where she's drooled.

"Did you have a good time?" he whispers.

"Yeah, me and the kids," she says, kissing him on the cheek. "Why don't you get the panda bear out of the car?"

PART FOUR

21

Late in August, Joe Paquette's hard-driving ways and poor maintenance finally bring him down. He's outward bound, hauling a double-tier possum belly, laden with first-calf heifers headed for Derby Line. He's high on No Doz, little white pills that peel your eyelids back and staple them to your forehead. Pills that shoot hell out of any idea you ever had about the twain of distance and time, pills that make your body and mind feel like a Slinky. On them pills, the lights they go on but it don't mean anybody is to home.

He dozes off and the big Diamond Reo hits the cables of the guardrail, ripping out posts like tent pegs, like a draft horse through a clothesline. It's airborne for a time and then it plunges into the mud flats of the Connecticut River, plowing a two-hundred-foot deadman furrow, and the water pours in after it, drowning Joe's dead body and whatever heifers are still left to die in the front of the trailer. His last thought: A big cat on the yellow line.

They bring in the heavy equipment, enough chain and cable to topple a building, more. Cody's D-7 Cat dozer and cable skidder are employed in the effort. The Doody brothers come on with their machinery and there's Ferris and Coonie and the town trucks. It's a night of red flares snapped to burn and spiked in the ground, trouble lights, beams and spots. The men are good at this. They have to be. They build the equipment, they run it, they maintain it and when machines go awry they have other machines to help mop up.

Rose Kennedy stays at the house while Mary goes for Marie.

It was bound to happen, is all she says, while they sit and wait.

Louis Poissant and Owen show up. They were Louis's heifers; now they're his beef. He doesn't say anything, but it's just as well Joe went off this side of the river because there were no blood tests on the heifers allowing them out of state.

Thad and Eddie and Dr. Pot are waiting in the mud when the cab emerges. All others have stayed clear. A sprung cable at such tensions can cut a man in half. They go to climb the running boards, but Dr. Pot misses and goes in up to his waist. He's about to slip down into the hole Joe's truck made and disappear when Eddie snatches him from the black water and passes him up to Thad, who lifts him to the busted window.

Dr. Pot climbs in and is back out in a minute.

"He's dead," he says.

Dr. Pot steps down and goes in up to his waist again, but Eddie drags him clear. The men coming down the cables hand him up the bank. The Doody brothers come on with the Amkus power unit. Ferris is with them. He's carrying the ram, the cutter and the spreader, the jaws of life. It's a hundred pounds of steel apparatus capable of exerting 120,000 pounds of force, force for ramming, cutting and spreading. Barkley follows with chains and Cody lords over the machinery atop, going from cable to cable, strumming each to make sure the pull is divided equally, listening to engines to make sure they're running smoothly with no cutout, no hidden beginnings of stall.

The men below get down to the job of opening up the cab and extracting Joe Paquette. Thad centers the three position valves on the power unit and jacks the throttle to its max. He anchors the base with his foot and grips the top of the roll cage. He pulls the start cord, quick and sharp, and the three and a half horses kick in, powering the four-cycle two-stage axial piston hydraulic pump, building it up to deliver ten thousand pounds of pressure per square fucking inch. It's a machine.

They run out sections of double steel-braided hydraulic hose and couple with the tools. Hydraulic fluid surges into the cylinders and they go to work, crushing the door downward, bursting out the hinges. They crib the floor and lift the steering column. Those close enough can hear the *eek* and crumple of the steel. They work slowly, no snapping or flying parts. They're careful of the power they hold in their hands, knowing a tool can slip out under force.

Other men have arrived. They stand on the highway forty feet up and far enough away to surmise that the truck traveled its length six times over on its way to the river. Louis Poissant and Owen come down the bank along a slack winch cable. Louis asks Thad if he could open a small hole in the possum belly so Owen can crawl in and shoot any heifers still alive, get what throats cut that he can.

Thad doesn't like the idea, but can't deny the common sense of it. He has Ferris go around to the back and cut open the jammed latch. From his coat Louis takes out a .22 revolver and hands it to the boy along with a box of shells. They swing open the door and the men on the bank watch him disappear into the black maw of the trailer, a penlight clenched in his teeth. They think they hear the faint snap of the pistol. It comes intermittently and sounds like caps or nothing at all. A state trooper comes over and asks what's going on. When the men tell him, he scuttles down the bank as fast as he can and grabs Louis by the arm.

The men on the bank can't hear what gets said, but they see Louis pull away and fall down in the mud. The lights are on them and Louis is talking. The men imagine he's telling the trooper to fuck off in a not-so-nice way. The trooper grabs him again and tries to put the cuffs on him, but he stops. They see the reason why. Owen has come out of the possum belly and he's holding the gun on the trooper. They wait for him to shoot.

Thad and Eddie see this too. They slog their way up to them and explain what's going on while Owen disappears again down into the trailer with a knife. The trooper confiscates the gun and goes back up the banking.

Ferris begins cutting roof posts and folding the roof back, crumpling fold upon fold. He then has to cut away the steering column, brake pedal, clutch and gear shifts. Dick Doody comes on with the ram and works at the seat and dash and stray pieces of steel from God knows where to get Joe free.

The men watch. They watch the other men at work. They watch them slog through the hip-deep mud, watch them fall into the river water and get fished back out. They make mention of stories they've heard about quicksand, whirlpools and carp so big they'd eat you alive. They tell of snapping turtles and eels. They tell about the winter and going through the ice while ice fishing. All the while, the brilliant lights cast down, making the surface bright and glowing, making it easy to see them do what they've volunteered to do, while underneath the water is black and cold.

The men down below take on the colors of the light and the colors shine with their wetness made slick by a sheen of clay and mud. They trample the sweet flag and trip on the sumac. They sweep back the rushes, the thick-stemmed reeds and cattails; while overhead and on the ground, back in the darkness, the night hunters, the barn owl, the bateleur eagle, the gray fox, the cougar, the rhesus monkey, the otter, snow leopard and Manchurian crane watch with heavy-lidded eyes.

When they finally get Joe out, they make no move to staunch the weak flow of blood as it drains from him. He bleeds out into the ground and water near the gouge he put into the earth's face. They go to zip him into a bag but it catches at his neck. They don't work it out. They strap him to a litter and Cody lets down a cable on his skidder. It passes from hand to hand down to the cab, where Thad and Eddie and the Doody brothers lift and hold. Ferris hooks the cable to the litter's frame and passes word back up the line. Cody winches them slowly as they hang onto the rails to keep it from dragging. As it rises, other men grab onto it and when there's no more room, they grab onto belts and coattails and Cody winches the train of men and equipment up the bank.

At the top they set the litter down. Barkley Kennedy sees Joe's Saint Christopher dangling by its chain, caught in the zipper. All others have backed away, not being able to look at the face death can make when it uses alloys, plastics, glass, steel, rubber, speed and force to do its bidding.

Barkley gets on his knees and palms the medal.

"We need a priest," he says, but he doesn't yell it. He says it softly to himself, his age apparent in his voice and the stoop of his shoulders.

No one comes forward. No one says anything and it becomes quiet. Barkley attends to Joe as if he's discovered a heartbeat or a pulse, or a breath of air, and declared it to be so to those who stand near, ringed as they are by heavy diesel equipment idling behind them, the whir of generators humming out the current that feeds the lights.

Barkley looks around the circle. He fixes on each man. He concentrates, looking at them intently. He looks to Cody atop the cable skidder enclosed in its roll-over cage and makes his decision. He goes to him, climbs the ladder and comes back off the machine with a can of motor oil. He dents a hole in it with his jackknife, then performs extreme unction, unzipping Joe to anoint what's left of his eyes, ears, nostrils, lips, hands, feet and loins.

He recites absolutions. He says, ". . . And the prayer of faith will save the sick man and the Lord will raise him up; and if he has committed sins, he will be forgiven. Load him up, boys. Time to break camp."

But no one moves. They're looking past Barkley toward where the river is. He turns from Joe to see Owen, covered with a red sheen of blood, rising into the lights from under the bank, the knife in his teeth and blood dripping from his fingertips, sparkly and red like tears of rubies.

"Jesus Christ," Eddie says, "I need a drink."

"Or six," Thad says.

Louis steps up with an armful of rags so Owen can wipe himself down. Eddie and Thad go forward and get Joe loaded into the rescue truck. Dr. Pot jumps in back with Joe and they slam the doors shut.

Louis and Cody are talking. Louis's asking Cody if he'll come back in the morning and help get the heifers out. Cody says he will.

"I'd do it now," Louis says, "but we have to go finish milking."

"Fair enough," Cody says, and walks him to the Cadillac, where Louis makes Owen ride in the trunk.

Cody goes back to the site and helps the men disassemble the equipment and pack it up. When there's enough room to pull out, Eddie gets in the rescue truck and drives away. He'll drop off Pot, and get permission from Marie to take Joe home with him.

The Doody brothers let Cody keep the ten-wheeler for tomorrow as they won't need it. They're the last of the volunteers to leave and then the trooper leaves and Cody's alone and it's quiet. He strikes up a conversation with G.R. He tells him how not more than a few hours ago it was just as quiet as it is now. In betweentimes the night got opened up with a fury of one man and a load of heifers dying, a fury of men working; all those souls headed for heaven must have made a helluva traffic jam. He tells G.R. how proud he is of the boy, Owen, for defending his blood and then he leaves to get some sleep.

■

Eddie hoses down Joe Paquette in the early morning that is still darkness with no light but for the stars and moon. He works his way around, figuring how much to do, trying to decide whether he'll have to cast a face or not. He finds old scars, old marks showing that when Joe had the chance, he lived this life and took his knocks.

There are new sutures too, just below his nipple, enough to close up a five-inch incision. The same incision Eddie saw on Clifford Manza, the result of open cardiac massage.

He works his way to Joe's left arm. He'll need to give Joe a new hand, a plaster one to replace the old one. His legs will need splints and maybe his face can be brought back, but it'll be a major job, a job for an artist.

He lays the arm back down and looks at the incision. This isn't right, he thinks. It didn't go this way. He rolls Joe into the cooler and shuts off the lights. Right now he wants nothing more than a stiff drink. Some Beam to settle him just a little so he can figure it out.

Outside in the dew, he thinks twice before knocking on the door to Cody's trailer. It's really a fine setup here under the moon. Cody's trailer stands in a copse of birch on the edge of the mountain road, the one Eddie hiked so many months ago to bring out his new best friend. The trailer stands as if it were gatehouse to the road.

Off in his stall, Buck snorts and thumps a knee against the wall. Eddie thinks of the horse as a sentient being, one made wise through the senses. He likes that thought. It makes Buck snort for him. Something more than clearing his nose.

Before Eddie can knock, Cody is out the door, closing it behind him. Eddie's never been inside since Cody moved it to their yard. He's never thought to ask.

"Sit awhile?" he says.

"Sure," Cody says, starting back to the house.

Eddie follows him through the track he leaves in the white glistening dew, a track he half-made on his way to the trailer, and now Cody is making the other half.

Eddie gets a ginger ale for Cody and the bottle of Jim Beam for himself. They sit in the living room next to Colleen Gunnip, a stiff that got brought over from the nursing home. Rose Kennedy signed for her.

"Who's this?" Cody asks.

"She came from The Manor. In a manner of speaking she's dead."

Cody laughs. "It's about time that place took a fucking fall," he says. "I trust you'll shoot me before you ever let me rot away in one of those places."

"No sweat," Eddie says, emptying his glass and refilling it from the bottle at his ankle. He plans on making the same pact with his son when he's old enough to understand the words, yet still young enough to be rash about life and death and giving his word.

Eddie wants to tell Cody about the incision.

"What's she doing here?"

"Rose was here with the kids. She let them leave her while we were out. Eileen told her it's how we do it. They were both quite proud."

Cody slaps his knee and this time Eddie laughs with him. He wants to feel he has all the time in the world to sit here and drink, gas with his buddy, Cody.

"Joe will be okay for a while," Eddie says. "He don't mind much. Were you down there when we brought him out?"

"Up top," Cody says. "How's everyone else doing?"

"Pretty well," Eddie says. "Pretty well. They're a little worried it all went like this. We have the fund raiser tomorrow night."

"You mean tonight."

"Yes, you're right. Seems I get that stuff mixed up. Seems lately I lose whole days at a time."

"No big thing," Cody says. "What really matters anyway?"

"You know something. People prefer death to be more humane. They like it to come quietly in the evening into hospital rooms, maybe some candles around. They like death to be explainable, to have facts, cause and effect, the why, the how. They like it clean too, as clean as possible. They'll say equipment failure or cancer and think something has been explained. Even doctors learn those to be explanations. They say, 'Cancer,' and heads nod. They don't have room for someone being crushed by a slab of concrete or a little kid at the school crossing being riddled by studs flying out of an overheated snow tire."

"That really happened?"

"Damn straight it happened."

"G.R. is proud of the way he died. I know he is."

"I believe you do," Eddie says.

Eddie wants to drink this whole bottle, wants to feel the bourbon coursing through his veins like tiny horses.

"Joe be much work? The reason I ask is because I told Louis I'd help him in the morning with those heifers."

"No," Eddie says. "I'll get it done. Right now I just wanted to sit awhile. And I wanted some company."

"At drunk school they said if you drank alone you got a problem."

"Did they say what the problem was?"

"Not really. They kind of insinuated."

"But they didn't say what it was."

"No."

The two men smile at each other. A sound comes from the bag Colleen Gunnip's zipped up in. Air leaving the body, like a snore.

"I hate them fucking bags," Eddie said. "Back before time. Back when Peggy Fleming was beautiful, we were doing a thousand bodies a month. I'd do six a day. We worked twelve-hour shifts, seven days a week. We'd clean them up as best we could. They were coming in with shrapnel, grenades, maggots. Anything you could think of. Grenades with the tops just hanging by a thread. Death certificate, thirteen copies. There was just so much you could do."

"I believe I'll have a little of that sweetener you've got, if you don't mind."

"No, no, have some. I wouldn't want to drink alone."

Eddie hands over the bottle and Cody pours about four fingers into his soda can, moving it in a pendulum to slosh around the drink.

"We marked them three ways. Non-viewable meant it was to be a sealed casket, no one was to look. There was viewable for ID purposes only, a family member could look but it wasn't advised. And then there was viewable for the public.

"The first two cases I got were a private and a corporal. The private was totally blown away from the chest down. He came in a poncho. The corporal didn't have a mark on him, not a single fucking mark. I learned something that first day. Dead is dead is dead."

Eddie sips at his glass until it's empty, but Cody doesn't drink. He keeps swirling it back and forth.

"At Khe Sanh there were rats. We lived in the ground. At night they'd bounce off your chest. We had to put the bodies on a rack because the rats ate through the bags at the high points—nose, toes, hands. We had a refrigerator unit we kept bodies in. One night we had six guys in the reefer and they hit us and the shrapnel went through the box. We had to take the bodies out and redo their charts. More wounds. The dead got killed all over again.

"It was good, though. It kept you busy. It was like the war had been going on a hundred years before you got there and would be going on a hundred years after you left. Then when I did get out it just got to be time to get on with life. I'll tell you what, though, where we were living in New York State, we couldn't get a property tax adjustment whereas a World War Two vet right next door could. It was the only time I got pissed off. I said fuck this and that's when we moved. Property tax or not, they killed them just as dead in both wars."

"What happened to the corporal?"

"What corporal?"

"The second one you did. The one who didn't have anything wrong with him."

"Internally he was all torn up inside. His intestines were mush, but to look at him you'd think he was only taking a nap."

"How'd it happen?"

"How does it happen? You tell me."

Cody doesn't say anything. He knows they're now talking about something different, something he's not sure of. He trusts his friend Eddie Ryan knows an answer, but he doesn't push him for fear of finding out that he just might not.

"It happens," Cody finally says.

"Yes, it happens."

■

When Eddie comes out of his drunken sleep, the darkness is just breaking up in the east. He finds himself to be covered with an afghan. He knows it's warm in the room but his sweat is cold, his mouth dry and cottony. He kneads his eyes with his fists, working up as much focus as he can.

Eileen and Little Eddie are sitting on the couch in their pajamas. Sitting between them is Colleen Gunnip in her nightgown.

The three of them are having a nice chat with Eileen doing most of the talking. They look over at him.

"I think he's awake," Eileen says, her hands folded in her lap, an afghan spread cross her mending legs.

Little Eddie crawls down off the couch and goes to Eddie. He knocks over the empty bottle as he gets up in his father's lap and snuggles in against his chest, lolling his head back and forth until he's made a comfortable spot for himself.

"Good morning," Colleen Gunnip says. "I brought the children down from upstairs. I hope it's okay. Your little girl was calling out for someone to come and get her."

"Good morning," Eddie says.

"I think there's been a little mix-up."

"I think I'd agree."

Mary comes into the living room. She's just getting home. She's been with Marie Paquette all night waiting for Marie's sister to arrive from Vergennes. She's tired and wants nothing more than a shower and some sleep, but she finds it in herself to greet Colleen as if she were pleased to make her acquaintance.

Colleen Gunnip says the children are hungry and asks if she can get their breakfast. Mary tells her where the cereal and T.V. trays are, and then she and Eddie go upstairs. He explains what he can, and when Mary goes to speak, he holds up his hand and shakes his head.

Mary makes a choice between laughing and crying. She decides to laugh.

"You stink," she says. "You need a shower."

And that's where they go and stay until the hot water runs out.

■

That night at the firehouse is the annual baked-bean supper and auction to raise money for new equipment. They have a long way to go. A used truck they bought in 1970 for thirty thousand dollars now costs three hundred thousand new.

The townspeople have been cleaning out their attics and barns. Donations have been solicited on the radio and fliers snagged under windshield wipers at the malls in Keene and Bolton.

The supper is four bucks for all the beans, franks, slaw, potato salad, kraut and brown bread you can eat. Afterward there'll be a dance.

The common is crowded with people come to get the news. Each carries a tray of food or a pot of beans or goods for the auction. Barkley stands at the monument telling them about Florian, the patron saint of the fire service, when the noise of the Doody brothers' ten-wheeler can be heard coming up the road.

The crowd turns to see who it is. They expect a truck, but what crests the knoll is Louis Poissant's Cadillac, the trunk open and full of kids covered with mud and blood. They ride comfortably, their arms slung over the sides and their heads back. They've sketched red stripes and arrows on their cheeks and wear crow feathers in their hair. They're having a high old time in the back of Louis's Caddy and now they're stopping for Brownie bars and Moxie.

Louis parks in the middle of the road. He'd planned to park in front of the store or swing over to the common, like he always does, but the road is lined with vans and cars. Behind him, the sound of the ten-wheeler grows from the other side of the knoll. It runs out and lugs down until the driver double-clutches it into a lower gear, then roars back up again. The sound is coming and Louis hears it. He knows what it is, but by the time he can get back on the gas, the ten-wheeler is over the knoll and bearing down.

Cody sees the Cadillac parked in the road, the passel of kids smiling and waving from the trunk. He hits the air brakes, putting the blocks to the wheels. He gets the ten-wheeler stopped at the point where Louis has pulled out, but the lowboy doesn't stop. It lurches on the hitch, snaps it off and drives forward, the bent and ragged steel of its front end gouging a two-foot trench into the road.

Cody pulls away down the road, leaving behind him sixty sides of beef, stacked like cordwood, their carcasses red and marbled, the bone glistening in the sunlight, and at the back end are thirty hides sprawled like rugs and thirty heads. The unmistakable smell of fresh raw meat comes up from the lowboy to take over the air. The quiet of the moment that follows becomes replaced with the trickle of blood running onto the tar.

■

After the auction they push back the chairs and fold up the tables. The people are fat with beans and beef and the Bill Starr Family Band is setting up to play square dance and round dance, and later, the kind of dance where the couples will get to do some sweating on each other.

The evening has been successful. They've had to throw open the overhead doors and let the night's festivities sprawl into the street and across to the common. Most freezers in town now have a side or quarter of beef. Antique dealers have come from Boston and Hartford to run up the price of the cast-off-goods—the crocks, quilts, iron toys, tricycles, wicker furniture and depression glass. Two weathervanes sell at a premium and the oak furniture goes at top dollar. Wooden tools, rusted tools, ruined tools all go for good money to hang on walls in dens and kitchens.

Swing 'em, boys, and do it right,
Swing those girls till the middle of the night,
All eight balance, all eight swing,
Now promenade around the ring.

Barkley is proud of himself. The auction was his baby, and as the items came in, he was wise to their value. He bid up every last one until it brought the big money. Now he's in the back with Rose and the children, keeping them at bay with stories so the young and old can spin about the floor doing squares and circles, two-steps and polkas. People have stayed on, people from Bolton and Keene and Walpole and Chesterfield; many of them firemen from those towns, all robust and hearty, no matter the effort. They wear their good clothes with their work boots and beepers. Already the warmth of the summer evening and the consumption of so many beans has made the night rich and heady. It will be a time to remember.

Duck for the oyster and on you go,
Four hands half around and don't be slow.
Duck for the oyster, duck!
Dig for the clam, dig!
Duck on through and home you go . . .

Barkley has Little Eddie on his knee and he's telling the children about a man named Christopher who one day was sitting on the bank of a river eating a ham sandwich when a little boy came by and wanted to cross over to the other side.

Rose sits close by. She stares at Colleen Gunnip across the way. She's convinced she knows the old woman, maybe from a convention, maybe from her younger days as a Boston deb. She wants to ask, but is aware of how embarrassing it could turn out.

"So Christopher picked up the lad in his arms, got him onto his shoulders and started across. As he went along he kept going deeper and deeper and the little boy became heavier and heavier."

Eileen sits in her pram, looking through the crowd to catch glimpses of Bill Starr's youngest on guitar. She knows she's in love with him. He's how Dickon looks in *The Secret Garden*. She's sure of it. She wishes he'd sign her casts and wheel her around the dance floor again and again.

"He told the boy he was going under and the boy said, 'No, you're not. Just keep going.' "

The song ends and Bill Starr takes the mike. He grins and stares at the back wall, the gray block and black windows.

"It's the new age," he says. "But I'll tell you, even if we *can* make electricity from shit, I still prefer hearts at Valentine's Day."

Everyone laughs, but Bill Starr doesn't take notice. He has that thousand-mile stare, the kind that holy men get, holy men, drunks and fools. The rest of the band listens intently. There's Bill Starr's youngest on guitar, the next youngest on bass, the oldest on drums and Bill Starr on fiddle. Bill Starr and his oldest son both look like they'd been dragged through the funnel of life while the two youngest are still sitting on the lip.

". . . And so as Christopher stepped out on the opposite bank, he looked down and the trees were below him, their crowns brushing at his knees and thighs, and he looked at his arms and they were like . . ."

But I'm giving up our dream house and roses by the door,
But that's all in the past, I don't live there anymore . . .

Barkley hunts for words to make his image.

"He-Man," one of the kids says.

"The Incredible Hulk," another says.

"Don't be stupe heads," Eileen says, patting her dress down over her knees, the hem to the edge of plaster.

"His arms were huge and filled with muscles, and you know what?"

"What?" they ask.

"The child was Jesus and he was heavy because he carried the world in his hands."

"The baby Jesus," Eileen says.

"The baby Jesus," they all say.

Then down the center you go once more
And promenade right off the floor . . .

■

One by one the children doze off and are either taken home or carted up to the town hall with sleeping bags and blankets. Colleen Gunnip is there watching over them. Her skin in the blue of night is white, almost transparent. She tends the children as they sleep, making sure they don't kick off their covers. When they do she gives them milk from a carton and tucks them in. Overhead the ceiling is high and vaulted. It's made of stamped tin painted white. The walls are robin's-egg blue and the windows are eight feet tall. Eileen sleeps in the path of the moon, her healing legs under a sheet.

"It's a full moon," she says to Colleen Gunnip.

"Yes, it is, dear."

"That means my real parents are coming tonight," she says, and then she falls back asleep.

Down at the firehouse it's past midnight but tomorrow is Sunday and not that many people burden the churches anymore. They'll sleep late, change the oil, pick up a game of hardball, barbecue some yardbird and let the lawn go for another week.

As the song ends, Bill Starr takes over the mike again. He tells them he has a little something special for them, something they've been working on for quite some time and wish to debut here in Inverawe. Bill's youngest steps up and takes over the mike from his father. They burst into a rendition of "Hound Dog," followed by "Teddy Bear." It brings everyone to the dance floor. They rock and roll, trying to make bodies built for work do gyrations heretofore reserved for youth or the bedroom. The boy squalls away while the volunteers and guests get all unseemly.

When they start pounding away at "Heartbreak Hotel," Eddie begs off to look for Cody.

"Oh, leave him alone," Mary says. "He's probably having some fun."

"Well, then I'll just get a beer."

"Get me one too if you can remember," she says. "I'm going to check the kids."

Eddie goes out to the pickups where the Doody brothers have a bar set up on the tailgate. Thad and Barkley are there too. Eddie asks about Cody, and they tell him he went off with the woman who came with Louis Poissant. They drove off in his pickup. Eddie asks who she is.

"Name's Kay. She lives down to Poissants'. Probably some relative of Louis's. She's a strange one."

"Who is she?" Eddie asks.

"I just told you," Dick says. "She moved over from Winchester a couple years ago. I think she worked at the Creamery, but Christ, that must've been fifteen, twenty years ago."

Eddie takes a beer from the cooler.

"I propose a toast," Barkley says.

"No toast, just tell us what the take was," Thad says.

They laugh because after a few Thad gets bossy.

"If it weren't for young Joey, it'd be some less," Coonie says sadly.

"I just can't figure it," Dick says.

"Could've been a hundred things," his brother tells him.

For a while the men try to figure out Joe's dying. They talk about hydraulics, metal fatigue, brake lines, tie rods, seize-ups, blowouts, bearings and drunkenness.

"You know, even if we figure this out, I still won't get it," Tom says. The others agree.

Eddie opens another beer and takes a drink.

"Why do you think they call them accidents?" he says.

The men look at him. They aren't sure, but they think truer words were never spoken.

"Jesus, you're right," Tom says. "That's it in a nutshell."

Eddie shrugs and goes back inside. He finds Mary and gets his arms around her from behind.

"You look pretty gorgeous tonight," he says into her ear.

She wants to shuck him off. He forgot her beer, which she didn't really want, and he didn't ask about the kids, who are fast asleep.

"I never asked you how it went with Marie."

"When was there time? What with your early-morning bender and old Mrs. Gunnip coming back from the dead. When was there time?"

"In the shower?"

"We were both distracted."

"So how was it?"

"She said, 'He was always shooting me down.' "

"That's it?"

"That's it."

Bill Starr's youngest starts into "Love Me Tender." Mary clasps Eddie's arms and leads him onto the floor. She turns in his arms and they begin to dance. She wants the music to lift her off this planet, lift her to where the air is cool and capable of purifying. She thinks she wants to take Eddie with her but isn't sure.

"How'd it go with you? You were down there a long time."

Eddie shakes his head. He doesn't want to talk about it, but try as he might, the acts of his day parade through his mind, the excision of mutilated tissue, suturing incisions, hypodermic tissue building, filling wounds, bleaching and masking. He even fixed Joe's buckteeth.

He thinks about Joe's teeth. It was Marie's one request that Joe's teeth not show. She'd looked at them long enough and he'd refused to get them fixed in life so she had Eddie do it.

Mary pulls him tighter. She remembers how much she loves to dance this way and how long it's been. She leaves off from her body, forgetting she has legs, and holds on to him as if her life depended on it. As they dance they're almost where she wants to be, and then next to them Eddie hears Tom saying to his wife, Jeri, "Why do you think they call them accidents?"

Eddie begins to laugh, quietly at first and then more loudly. He backs away from Mary and hunches his body with laughter. He leaves her there standing on the floor and goes out the overhead door and across the road. He tries for the darkness but can't make it and is left hovering over a garbage barrel, retching and heaving.

Mary stands alone amongst their friends and the strangers, and watches, ashamed, while Bill Starr's youngest sings, *"I'm so hurt."* All she can think is, Yeah, right, me too.

Someone in the back can be heard saying, "You know, I never would've thought that chicken plucker would've brought so much money."

■

At Joe's funeral mass on Monday, the priest tells how hope is like the sun bringing light to cast our burdens aside. He tells about the healing power of faith and recites the final commendation. Then Bill Starr and his youngest get up and start playing guitars. The priest comes down off the altar, his vestments snapping at his legs, making the candle flames bend after him. He makes a beeline for Eddie.

"What the hell is this?" he whispers. "What do they think they're doing?"

"Sounds like 'The Last Thing on My Mind' by Tom Paxton."

"I never let these goddamn guitars in my church. Jesus Christ, they never tell me anything."

That night at home Eddie writes in his journal. He writes:

> For all others it was a death made easy because of the engineering feat necessary to get Joe back into the ground in a more proper fashion. Marie took it well. I heard she had Joe insured to the hilt. Plus she got all that beef at a good price.

He looks at what he's written and thinks about driving the pen through his hand, but instead writes, *Somewhere Joe lost his heart.*

22

Some nights, Cody goes back to Kay's house. He stops at Washburn's store for half a sixer and a box of candy bars and then takes the mountain road. It's always dark, always close to the next day when he gets there and when he does, Kay's on the front porch waiting for him and the house is unlit except for the blue shadow of the television flickering over the length of a somebody gone to sleep in front of it.

She says to him, "Days get to be just memories I'll have, and it's only right the day should begin and end in darkness."

On those nights when he's with her, she has a way of being very much there and not there at all, coming and going as if in and out of dream.

■

"Three-thirty in the morning is the most beautiful time of day."

"I know," Cody says. "There's something about it."

"Did you ever notice how many photographs of sunsets you see, but hardly any of sunrises? That says something too. It says photographers are lazy people."

Cody thinks about the boy, always the boy. This will be the last time he brings it up, but he wants to know about her son, Owen. He was another man's child, but Cody married her. They got an apartment in Winchester, and after the first few years Cody began staying in the woods, cutting timber farther and farther away from home. He drifted from her life that way, so many years ago he can't even count them now.

He remembers her breast-feeding. Every time he was home, she held the baby boy to her breast, letting him suckle at her tit while they talked, while they ate their supper.

The last time they lived together, he woke in the night and she was sitting on the edge of the bed, her naked back white like milk, and her hair down around her face. He could hear the noises and when he rolled over, there was the boy standing between her legs, nursing at her breast. She was stroking his back and whispering into his ear.

In the morning they got into a fight. Cody told her three years was old enough to get off the tit. She cried and said that him drinking the breast milk was a way of returning her uterus back to itself after giving birth. The doctor'd told her.

Cody left and never went back again.

G.R. said she was just a tigress eating her young.

"Owen's a good boy," she says. "After my parents died, we moved up here. Uncle Louis has been like a father to him. He fell in amongst all the other strays."

"Did he pick up anything from me?"

"No, but when we still lived away from here, he used to have this thing for planes. Every day he'd pedal his bike to the landing strip and hang out. I got a call from him, asking if he could fly out to Albany, New York, in a jet. He put the pilot on and we talked. She was a woman and flew a Lear jet owned by an electronics company here in New Hampshire. So he flew to Albany. That's something. I myself have never been to Albany, New York."

They rock quietly in the glider. Kay's hands are folded in her lap; a beer rests on the wooden slats beside her leg, rocking with them. Cody has one too. He has it wrapped in a bandanna to keep it cold.

The river is off before them and they can see it, but they can't see it move.

Kay lights a citronella candle and sets it down between them on the glider. Its pungent smoke rises in the air as the light-yellowish oil cooks from the wax and hovers under the porch roof, making a cloud inhospitable to the mosquitoes. The two of them move closer to the candle, letting themselves be bathed in its smoke. It isn't long before the mosquitoes shy away and let Cody's and Kay's blood stay where it is, let them be the ones to say when and if it's to leave their bodies.

Louis Poissant always has thirty to forty veal calves on hand and the sound of them knocking in their tight stalls can be heard from the porch. One of them blats and then another one. The smell of ammonia rides the night breezes, makes its way to the porch. It's the gas made by the calves, chained so they can't turn around in their boxes. They're kept in a constant state of what amounts to scours, caused by the medicated formula they live off. Their whole effort goes into the making of pale meat that'll go white when it's cooked. He sells them fresh—the legs, loins, ribs and shoulders. The brains, livers, kidneys and tongues are the delicacies. They go for big money.

"I'm learning to hate this life," she says. "The living and dying comes too quickly. Last week we had a first-calf heifer go to calving. It was in the middle of the night. It wasn't much more than a yearling, but somehow the bull had gotten to her. She must have strained for an hour and then she didn't have any more left in her. She went down on her knees and that's when we got there. Louis beat her to get her up, but she was just too tired. She went spread-eagle on the floor. I could hear her pelvis cracking. Louis got his hand up inside her. He got hold of a foot and the uterus was wrapped around it, twisted on itself, trapping that poor baby inside. Louis tried to get it out. He tried to rotate the calf but he couldn't. At the time I felt sorry for all of them, even Louis. His head was broken out in sweat and he was working as hard as he could to save them. Then she died, right there on the concrete, died, right in front of us. The barn was quiet. I thought about that calf, wondered if it was alive or dead. I thought about it slowly drowning inside its mother's womb and how we couldn't do a thing about it.

"Louis started cutting. He opened her up and heaved that calf out right onto the floor, slick and shiny. Its tiny hooves were white and spongy. Its tongue was out, too swollen to fit in its mouth. Louis held up its front legs and cleaned out its nose. Then he beat the chest and when that didn't work, he gave it mouth-to-mouth. There he was, holding that calf in one arm and its mouth open with the other, his hand cupped over its nostril. Blowing and blowing forever and then he slowed down, his mouth staying on the calf's mouth a little longer each time. I sure wish I had a camera on me that time. He was getting tired. Finally he let it down in the sawdust and told me to go to the house. I wasn't needed, he said.

"The last thing I heard was the lock on his knife. I turned in the doorway, in its shadow, and there he was at the mother's neck, his arm sawing away, and then the sound of blood coming like a flushed toilet. Then it was quiet except for the trickle of blood. And then the flushing sound again as thick gouts that'd washed along the floor fell into the gutter. Louis didn't see me still there in the darkness. He went out the back door and drove in with the tractor. I couldn't take it anymore so I went inside, all the while thinking she hadn't really been dead after all, just laying there, not alive, but not dead either.

"The next day I went into the cooler for apples and there were the four quarters of the heifer and right beside it the carcass of that calf hung on the veal hook waiting for market. 'Bob' veal they call it, not fit to be eaten, but most people are too dumb to know once it's breaded, gravied, and garnished. That's what Louis says.

"I said to myself, God, Louis, how could you? How could you? But then I realized it wasn't the same for him. For him it's the way life is. It's the way life's got to be. How can that be, Cody? How can it be?"

Cody's gotten in the habit of not saying much when he's around her. He only listens. He wants to become good at listening to what she says.

The citronella and the beer are like a drug to him. He hasn't had much drink in a long time, and now it's going right to his head.

"One of my big problems is the mornings," she says. "I know the whole day of light is ahead of me. Days get to be just memories I'll have and I live them that way, like I'm living through memories I'll have."

"Kay," Cody says, passing his hand over the candle flame and resting it on her leg. "Kay, we could start up again. You and me and the boy."

She makes sounds in her throat and he can't tell whether she's laughing or crying. He clutches at the material of her dress, feeling the heat from the candle at his wrist, feeling it raise the temperature of the buckle on his watch strap, that metal burning into his wrist. He knows how foolish he must sound. He knows now he didn't mean what he said. It was something he wanted to say to unburden her, something from inside him, a chance for him to find the good in himself, a cruel and selfish act he's now ashamed of. He takes his hand back and cups his wrist, nursing it, feeling it pulse.

"You don't want to get messed up with me again," she finally says. "I'm as crazy as a loon. I always have been, only now I'm coming to realize it. I take antidepressants, sedatives, lithium. They have beautiful names—Elavil, Eskalith, Xanax, Halcion. They sound like the names of beautiful places, the kind you'd find around the Mediterranean or maybe in Africa. Lost cities sunk below the ocean where fish people live. But traveling gets me down. I get so weary. After a day here, I can't imagine having to plan an expedition. People should stay to home more. There are places I'd like to see, but people travel too much already and I don't want to be just another one of them."

"Where would you like to go if you could?"

"I'd like to go to Hawaii. They have white and black sand. They have snow skiing and free pineapples. Those people live under volcanoes and know it, as opposed to us who live under them and don't. I'd like to go there and meet Danno from *Hawaii Five-O.* He was Boy in the Tarzan movies, you know."

"I didn't," Cody says.

"I'd like to listen to Don Ho sing 'Tiny Bubbles.' I think he has about the sexiest voice I've ever heard."

"Yes, the man sure can sing."

"It's a song about champagne, you know."

They both look off to the river framed in the trees and backed up by black mountains on the Vermont side. It could be a lake the way it sits there, still, yet moving as it makes its way to the sea, carrying all of its secrets and not giving a good goddamn about them.

"I think," she says, "how it isn't far to paradise."

"Kay, I had a lot to learn, but I think I'm better now. Let me help you."

"You were just a boy," she says, "but you walked like a man, head up, chest out and cocksure. You were my ticket, but you left. You stuck around longer than most men would've."

Cody thinks back to Owen being the reason for his leaving. He's shamed again and hurts for the boy, who can't begin to know the way it is between men and women, why they do the things they do to each other. Cody thinks he should have been better than he was. He went in with both eyes open and yet in the end he couldn't be the man he wanted to be.

"I wish we could do it again. Start over," he says.

The screen door slaps shut and Louis is standing on the porch next to them in his bedroom slippers and overalls. He goes down the steps and trundles to the barn. Banks of lights go on inside and they see his shadow crossing the windows. Unlike him, his shadow moves evenly, quietly. You wouldn't know he's a broken-down seventy-year-old man who still carries a torch for Rita Hayworth, who hasn't gotten over the fact she married Aly Khan, a secret he keeps to himself.

"He does that every night to check the animals. Then he goes back to bed, but he doesn't sleep well. He lays there tossing and turning. I can hear him getting up and laying down, over and over again."

The lights go off and Louis's dark rounded hulk comes out the door. The smell of ammonia seeps out past him, leading his way to the porch. He crosses the yard, goes up the steps and passes them by without saying a word. The barn smells mix with the citronella, cowshit and ensilage, a combination that could make you retch.

"I'll bet he didn't even see us. He's such a good old guy and I really feel sorry for him. Me and Owen have been here since his wife died. Since then, it seems like he's only putting in his time. It's too bad she's gone. She was a pistol."

Kay insists she make Cody a coffee before he goes, at least an instant, and he says okay. They go into the house like thieves, treading softly over the threshold and letting the screen door go quietly back inside its jamb. In the rooms the children sleep. To them Kay is the mother and Louis is the father.

She turns on the water, letting it guzzle into the spout of the teapot. Cody watches her back, the planes of her shoulder blades bisected by the thin straps of her dress, the run of her spine until it disappears behind the gathered material.

"Kay, I know there are a bunch of people squirreled away in this house, but who wears all the shoes? There aren't that many of you."

"Louis picks them up in Bolton at the morgue. He has a man over there who keeps them in a box for him. Clothes too. They're the stuff people don't need anymore."

Cody looks to the pile. He feels his shoulders give off a quiver, but he doesn't say anything. He lets himself listen as intently as possible to the running water, trying not to think about the shoes of the dead that come into this house. He moves his feet, trying to get the feel of the floor through his soles. He tries listening to the water again, hoping that will do the trick but it doesn't, and so there before him he sees sneakers, penny loafers, boots, pumps, sandals, flats, high heels, wing tips and moccasins. Leather, plastic, canvas and rubber. Different colors. Different sizes. He looks at Kay's feet and is thankful she's barefoot.

"I guess it's not so strange," he says. Then the pot is full and running over, surging back up the spout and blossoming against the faucet. He doesn't say anything, though; instead, he gets up and goes to where she is, to see what she's looking at.

In the window is a reflection of the room, and it's as if there's a whole nother room outside in the dark. It's the same as this room. It has a table, chairs, a toaster, shoes, a bread box and flannel shirts and overalls hung on pegs along one wall. There are two doors, one into a room with flickering blue light and one that goes into the outdoors of that room, but it seems the only way in is through this window.

There's a pink moon in that room too. Cody moves his head to get a better look and there come to be endless moons. They get made in the mirror behind him and his moving has allowed them into the outside room.

"How did you do that?" she whispers.

"I don't know," he says, moving his head back.

"Now they're gone. We lost them. I can't find them in the darkness."

Cody moves again and the moons come back. A sound comes

from Kay's throat and she gets her body close to his, her hip nestled into his groin.

"There's something moving out there," she whispers, "where the brook falls into the river."

Cody listens and he can hear it too, the sound of an animal rustling in the bushes.

"It's a dog rolling in the garden crop. That son of a bitch. One day I'll shoot that dog. I've had enough of him."

She moves closer and he can feel her body urgent against his own.

"It's in our house outside the window. Go chase it off. Pitch a rock at it. Watch out for the river, though. It's a treacherous thing."

Cody goes out on the porch. His first thought is to get in his pickup and never come back, but he's done most of that once already. He lets it pass and thinks of her body next to his and how it was saying to hurry. He thinks about how she has a belly he can cover with his hand, the way the veins show in the backs of her legs, the red marks like tongues of flame at her waist and sides, her breasts starting to go slack on her chest, but still full and heavy. Her hands are red and when he's inside her she has a way of holding him as if life itself depended on it.

He passes in front of the kitchen window and stops, pretends to step around furniture and then trip over it. He makes swimming motions with his arms, then holds his nose and sinks to the ground. He can see her face close to the window. She's laughing and waving, her other hand held to her throat, her fingers lightly touching her skin.

He gets up and stumbles again and he knows she can see him passing through chairs and the table, a mountain of shoes and a wall of clothes to get to the back of the house where the garden is and the land pitches to the river. He picks up a stone and throws it at the noise. It goes quiet and then there's the sound of it scuttling off into the woods.

When he goes back into the house she's sitting on the table. He steps in between her legs and puts his arms around her. He can feel her lips at his neck and her hands fumbling with his trousers. He asks her if this is safe and she says, "I can't get pregnant because I already am."

He tries to back up but she won't let him stop.

She's still laughing and doesn't stop.

Afterward she insists they dance on the porch. She has him twirl her around, the hem of her dress flaring as Hank Williams sings on the radio.

"Sometimes I listen and dance with myself."

"I have to go," Cody tells her.

"I know."

"I love you," he says.

"I loved you yesterday, but maybe I dreamt it. I'm sorry. I didn't mean for it to come out that way. With you, when it's over, I never feel hollow. You're always still right there."

"You were going to tell me things about myself."

"We don't always have to be together from now on, but let's always be nearby."

"Yes. We should be."

■

Driving home in the truck, Cody thinks how he doesn't know if he's in love with Kay, but then again he's learned how love isn't what he thought it was. He knows she's shown him a way to be and though it's not what he wants, it will do for now.

He's passing the County Farm where the man Bender sleeps, and then he's on the road to Inverawe, to Eddie Ryan's house, where his new family lives—Mary, Eddie and the children in their beds and Buck standing stiff-legged in his stall, waiting for Cody to show, his big doe eyes filled with water, staring at the blank board wall as they turn to blue, as he slowly goes blind.

Cody drives on, thinking about the things she didn't tell him.

23

School starts after Labor Day. At the last minute Mary is hired back as a teacher's aide. The woman she replaced in the late spring has decided she doesn't want to come back right away, maybe never. It confirms in the principal's mind and some of the teachers' minds everything they thought about women having babies.

But for Mary it works out fine because Little Eddie is starting nursery school, half days, in the afternoon, this against the wishes of his uncle Cody, who truly thought the boy's education would be handed over to him. Eddie and Cody will have the boy in the morning, something that delights Cody while at the same time causing him to redouble his efforts in all that he has to teach him. They drop him off at one and Mary brings everyone home at three. Sometimes they run errands; sometimes Eileen has a doctor's appointment.

Eileen tells Eddie she isn't sure about the gifted and talented program. She's afraid she won't be with her friends. Word is, the gifted and talented kids are geeks like on the show *Head of the Class* on Wednesday nights. She likes those kids and is convinced she could offer them something, but in her book they're still geeks. Funny, but geeks. Besides, they make fun of Juanita and the rest of the Poissants.

"Do you know what a geek is?" Eddie asks her.

"A pencil-necked geek."

"No. It's someone in the sideshow who bites the heads off chickens, but not really. They're just actors."

"There you go," she says, holding her hands out, palms up, then doing a spin in her wheelchair.

Eddie knows she got him. He walked right into it. For a second he worries about the future.

Mary doesn't tell Eddie, but the main reason she takes the job is because she'd only be a wife if she didn't, a wife who paints the faces of dead people, does their hair and tallies their bills. She has this thought, then sends it out of her head and says she's taking the job for the money. Mary Looney will now come to take over her work with the dead.

"If it's the money," Eddie said, "we still have Mrs. Huguenot's tip."

"For a rainy day," she told him.

Eddie sometimes worries he'll put far more restrictions on the spending of that money than was ever intended. As of yet they haven't touched it.

So now evenings get regimented. The children want Mary at the end of the day so Eddie and Cody take over the kitchen. They make the supper each night and clean up. Mary chides them about two men doing the work of one woman. They're smart enough to agree with her, but it pisses them off.

Cody sets the table while Eddie finishes off the meal, spaghetti and meatballs. Cody fixes Eileen's tray. It's a wooden one he made for her. It sits across the arms of her chair. Never once has she complained. Never once has she lost her spirit.

"Come and get it," Eddie yells.

Mary and the kids come into the kitchen and take their places at the table.

"Any word on Althea?" Cody says to Mary.

"No. No one seems to know. They say she just up and retired."

Mary had expected to work with Althea Hall and was surprised to find her gone when she went in on her first day. The woman who replaced her was young and from New York State. Mary was fully prepared not to like her, but right off the bat she showed herself to be professional in every regard. Quite a relief to Mary. They even had mutual acquaintance with several places from the Syracuse days.

"It sounds fishy to me," Eddie says.

"What really galls me is how quickly she's forgotten. For the kids I suppose it's best, but I'll tell you, the rest of them just don't talk about it much. *C'est la vie.*"

"*C'est la vie,*" Little Eddie says, and they all laugh, then dig into their supper.

As they're finishing up, Mary Looney calls in to see if there's any work. She thinks that if enough people die, she'll be able to earn money to invest in a beauty-imaging system for her shop. She told Mary Ryan it was a new way of creating a visual statement.

Eddie tells her to come in the morning.

Her first job will be Colleen Gunnip, who's come back from The Manor. This time for good.

"Do you mind if I bring Iggy?"

"You really shouldn't bring anybody else along, Mary."

"He's not a person. He's my iguana. I picked him up in Florida. He gets lonesome. I take him into the shop with me all the time."

"Perhaps then you could keep him on the porch. I assume he's in a cage."

"Of course he is. Don't be silly."

"That will be fine then."

"Mr. Ryan, there's one other thing."

"What's that?"

"I've been thinking and I'd rather people didn't know I was doing this work. You know, my other job. I use my hands a lot and I'm afraid people would get squeamish if they knew where they'd been."

"No problem. No one needs to know."

"Good. I'll see you in the morning."

Eddie hangs up the phone. Earlier in the evening, he went down to the preparation room and slipped a note inside Colleen Gunnip's gown. It told her to have a nice time in heaven. It told her she was loved by all and that when this is over they'll see one another again sometime. He wrote her a haiku also, something about water, pine trees and nuthatches. He looks at Mary and Cody and shakes his head.

"Don't ask," he says. "You don't want to know."

After the dishes are done and put away, Eddie rinses the double sink, then fills one again with warm water. He waits until Little Eddie comes charging through. When he does, he snatches him up and stands him on the drainboard, stripping off his sneakers, socks, pants and shirt. He sets him down in the water, then stands him up and soaps him. He can't help but think this is how the boy must have been in the womb, slick and slippery, fishlike. He holds the boy close to him, afraid he'll snap out of his hands like a bar of soap or a tiddledywink.

He rinses him off, then lets him play in the water with a plastic cup, some measuring spoons and a sponge while Eddie sits on a stool, reading the paper. He sits so close, it gets splashed on and soon the pages are too wet to turn.

He takes the boy out, wraps him in a towel and sends him to the living room.

Eileen is next. She gets a big kick out of bathing this way. Cody has fashioned a frame that sits across the top of both sinks. She's able to lie out on the countertop suspended over the water from her thighs to her shoulders, and her castbound legs still high and dry.

"I'm ready to be bathed, my good man," she says, when she's finally in position.

"But I'm still hungry," he says. "I think I'll eat you."

"No, Daddy. No buzzles."

Eddie leans over, gets his mouth on the skin of her belly and blows hard.

Eileen laughs and pushes his head away.

"You know," she whispers, "that sounds just like a fart."

Mary comes out to get in on the high jinks. She suggests they all get forks and knives and have a bite.

"No, Mommy. Not funny."

"She's too skinny," Eddie says. "Nothing there to eat anyways. Skin and bone."

Eddie steps back and suggests Mary finish. He doesn't tell her he's uncomfortable washing his daughter. He'd rather let Mary think he's a little lazy than try to explain it.

"Where's Cody?"

"He and Little Eddie are looking for his organ donor card. He says he lost it a long time ago, but only now has come to realize it. He's worried about what the loss of it could mean. You know, if it got into the wrong hands."

They get Eileen in her pajamas and back in her chair. Mary stands behind her, combing out her hair. Eddie looks out the window and sees Cody and Little Eddie searching the ground around the barn. He goes to Mary and puts his hands on her hips. Mary and Eileen are talking about the gifted and talented kids. Eileen says they can be real smart sometimes, but they also cry a lot. A couple times she cried too because everyone else was so sad. They play great games, though, on the computer. They roll dice a lot too. She asks to go into the living room so she can watch T.V. When Mary comes back to the kitchen, she goes to drain the sink, but Eddie comes up behind her and slides a hand down the back of Mary's shorts. She laughs and elbows him to make him stop.

"Dice," she says, laughing some more. "They roll dice."

He holds her with the palm of his hand, moving it against the patch of material between her legs in a half beckon. He pulls his hand out and this time slides it inside her underpants, careful not to catch her hair.

"She said, 'Sometimes we pretend we're stupid things, like bacon or dirt.' "

Eddie unfolds her, feels her wetness beginning to seep.

"Dirt?" he says, his voice a little off.

"She said she wanted to be a horse, but the teacher wanted her to be wood."

Eddie keeps moving his hand, already beyond the point he ever intended. Mary sighs and when she does, comes an explosion and the sound of gravel clattering against the windows.

■

After supper and after he's had his bath, Cody takes Little Eddie out to the barn to get him dirty again. He thinks little boys should always be dirty, should always stink a bit.

Cody also needs help in finding his lost organ donor card. He's convinced it has the weight of a contract and possession is nine tenths of the law. He now wishes he'd never gotten it in the first place.

He stands at the door of Buck's stall, his right forearm a seat for Little Eddie's bottom.

"I'm much afeared the old boy is dying," Cody says.

Little Eddie tries to repeat what Cody has said. He does end up making a sound for each one of Cody's words.

Cody has kept the declining health of the horse from everyone but Little Eddie. The horse is old, too old to be propped up with drugs. Cody hopes that death will be kind, that it will come to Buck in his sleep and soon, otherwise Cody will have to put him down. He's all but convinced that Buck's gone totally blind.

Max comes out from behind a bale of hay. The back end of a critter hangs from his mouth. He sets it down and licks it. Cody can see the blunt head of a chipmunk, its rounded erect ears, the buffy stripes outlining each eye with a black strip running in between.

"You old whoremaster," Cody says. "What have you got there? Some dinner?"

Max watches Cody and Little Eddie. He's put down the chipmunk to see if they go for it, knowing full well he can snatch it up and be gone in no time flat.

Cody turns back to Buck. He makes clucking noises and taps on the stall. The old horse comes to him slowly. Cody reaches to touch his head and when he does the horse stops but not before he bumps the stall door with his knee, a gentle enough bump, but with enough force to make it clatter at the hinges.

"Good boy," Cody says.

"Good boy," Little Eddie says.

Cody tickles Little Eddie in the ribs until he laughs.

"More Cody. More."

"No, hey. You know what we have to do? We have to find that organ donor card. Christ knows what'll happen if it gets in the wrong hands."

He puts the boy down and then the two of them go to scuffing through the hay and chaff that mats the floor. Cody moves buckets and harnesses, grain bags and blankets.

They work their way out the door and around the perimeter of the barn. Cody follows the paths he's made from manure pile to garden, from grain bin to driveway. He and the boy move around the small corral behind the barn. They track along the stream and to the boulders where the corner of Louis Poissant's fence begins on Eddie Ryan's property.

Cody stops walking and the boy walks into the backs of his legs. Before them at the foot of the boulders is the back half of the biggest snake Cody ever saw, its front half disappearing into a woodchuck hole.

"Son of a bitch," Cody says.

He grabs up the boy and makes a run for the garage. He's convinced he's seen something not from this world, but something at the open point where two worlds meet, the world on top of the earth and the world underground.

He sets the boy on the riding lawn mower and tells him to stay. He takes up the five-gallon gas can and gets a road flare from behind the seat of his pickup. Back at the chuck hole, he can see the last of the tail disappearing, its girth at the tip still as big as a man's forearm.

Cody empties the gas can in after it, steps back and nicks the flare to life. He then lofts it through the air and even before it touches down, the earth rumbles, and he's knocked on his ass with the good feeling of accomplishment and that's where Eddie and Mary find him.

■

That night after the kids go to bed Cody allows himself to go drunk and Eddie goes along with him. They talk about digging up the ground to see what it was, but Cody gets scared. He makes Eddie promise never to open up the ground in that spot because he's convinced it's a place where the layer of earth is thin between this world and that world.

"You two take the cake," Mary says. "I'm going to bed."

"Stay with us," Eddie says.

"Yeah, right."

She gets up to go and Eddie says he'll be along soon.

"No hurry," she tells him, and goes up the stairs.

Mary looks in on the kids. Little Eddie is out cold and Eileen is reading by the glow of her night-light, her legs stretched out before her under the blanket. Mary steps back from the door. She feels as if her heart is getting weak. She doesn't want to be unhappy, so she hangs on to her tears and goes to her bedroom. There she undresses and then goes in to pee. Sitting on the toilet, she looks up and sees herself in the mirrored tiles. She tries to look away but can't. She's got herself fixed on the woman in the mirror and can't move. Watching her is a woman whose looks begin to look not like hers. The woman looks to be anticipating the answer to an unformed question and then she's breaking up, her sobs coming in heaves, her chest undulating, her shoulders caving in.

■

The air goes cold for a spell and then comes the odd discomfort of Indian summer, banks of warm dry air staying all day and into the night. It's the forerunner of the cold, that'll lock in the north states and the provinces of Canada until the next year is three months gone. It's the last chance to strap poly around the house from the windowsills to the ground and bank the foundations with straw.

Louis Poissant sells the heifers downcountry and Mary is glad because now they can be rid of the smell. She gives Cody the job of removing tiles from the bathroom wall. She tells him she's sick of watching herself go to the bathroom. He tells her it looks like a cathouse anyways.

In the county there's been a rash of brush fires. It's at the point where people are getting pretty suspicious. On Rattlesnake Mountain is the biggest. It's a good thing Louis Poissant has already moved his heifers out to another pasture. Eighty men are there now, working to contain the four hundred acres that burn, but it's rugged going. In some places the fire burns underground, melting the soles off the men's shoes. Mary predicted it.

One good thing about the fall, though, is it's a time when in the country people don't die as often because they have so many other things to do. They must button up houses, tack down roofing, clean the chimney, finish the harvest, finish the canning. For Eddie, it's time off to fight the fires.

Little Eddie has a persistent case of the shits again. They won't go away and his appetite is off too. Mary takes it out on herself because she isn't with him during the day to take care of him. She's tried everything—watered-down milk, apple juice, Gatorade and Jell-O. He's now on a diet of chicken and cheese. It's the same, though, one day he's good and the next morning he's filled his diaper, sopping through to his bed. She's convinced Cody and Eddie haven't been careful with the boy's diet. They don't understand the finickiness of the boy's intestines.

"No big thing," Cody says.

Mary hits the ceiling.

"No big thing," she repeats. "No big thing. That's what you said last time. You change that boy. You watch his face when you touch the cloth to his bottom. See the pain. Tell him it ain't no big thing."

"She's right," Eddie says. "Dehydration is a serious problem. Last year we had a woman go into the hospital for a hip replacement. She was an old woman, fell down through a central heating grate and lay there in the plenum for three days before anyone found her missing. She only broke her hip, but in the hospital they didn't keep her in fluids and she died of dehydration."

Mary looks at the two men. Her gaze at first seeks out their differences and then it withers as she determines they are just now both one and the same.

"You go to hell too," she says to Eddie, surprised she doesn't feel like crying anymore and letting Cody assume he's included.

The men go back to listening to the action on Rattlesnake Mountain as it comes in over the scanner.

It's Sunday night and they've spent most of two days on the fire line. They know they've fucked up, but they're tired just now, tired down into the bone.

When Mary finishes her tear around the house, she goes to the bathroom for a damp cloth. Eileen is in there sitting in her chair. She's unwrapped a box of tampons, skinned the sleeve of tissue paper off each one and pulled their strings. She's now trying to squeeze the cottons back into the cardboard sleeves. She knows she's done something wrong.

Mary shakes her head and tells her she should know better. Eileen agrees. Contrition is always the best policy.

"Please. You'll have to go to your room. Have your father take you up," Mary says.

When Eileen is alone she breast-feeds her doll, holding it close to her bare flat chest, stroking its headful of yarn. Max the cat usually watches from the floor, sprawled on his back, his eyes yellow slits in his head, but tonight he isn't around.

Eileen talks to him anyway as if he were there, as if he were her husband who pays her no mind. She pretends he's a prince turned into a cat by a wicked witch and one day soon he'll be conjured back into a man, someone she can marry. Downstairs she can hear the phone ringing. It's him, she figures, saying he'll be late for supper.

Mary hangs up the phone.

"I've had it with Max," she says. "You're going to have to take him and have him fixed. That was Craigs. He's been in their chicken house."

"God knows where he got it in his head he could fuck a chicken," Cody says, much amused by his own joke.

"He was after mice," Eddie says. "He's a great mouser."

"Mice or not, he's upset the hens and they won't lay. Last week it was Smithlers and he was down there having his way with their Persian. I just can't take it anymore. It's worse than having a six-teen-year-old son loose on the world with a driver's license. Mrs. Craig says that out in California you can get sued for what your cat does."

"You tell her this ain't California," Cody says.

Eddie's mother wanted the cat fixed too. She didn't like it when he brought his live prey into the house to play with. She considered it an aberration to bring nature inside, something that shouldn't be done. She was convinced the cat was killing her. She had swelling in the lymph glands and was convinced he'd given her cat scratch fever.

Eddie goes outside and sits alone in the darkness. Cody goes back to the fire. Inside the house Eddie can hear the scanner crackling. Thad is talking to another fire company, one located on the north boundary of the burn. The Red Cross is there too. They've brought roast beef sandwiches and urns of coffee.

For Eddie it's one of those nights that's come too often, too regularly to be discounted as the unusual. This Indian summer has come to be a time of reckoning. He's come to something and he doesn't know what.

Down the road in the darkness he sees the faintest of movement, an animal dodging back into the weeds alongside the road. He thinks it's Max on one of his night hunts. He figures he better get his hands on him before the Craigs and Smithlers form a posse.

Eddie gets down off the porch and hikes to where he saw the movement. As he gets to the spot he decides it's not the one; he decides it's a little farther away. He keeps going like this until he knows he's overshot the mark, gone way too far, because he can't see his house anymore.

"The hell with the cat," he says, "it's a nice enough night to take a walk."

Eddie keeps going down the road out of town.

It's quiet and before long he can't see any lights except those in the sky. Ahead of him he sees the movement again, the small figure ducking into the grass. It keeps ahead of him moving awkwardly, and away, as it scuttles along.

Eddie gets a fix on it and then there's nothing. He wonders how much of what he's seen he has invented and how much is really there.

Eddie whistles and calls out to Max. In response he hears a slight mew from off the road. Wading down through the timothy and plantain, he comes upon a scene where there's been a fight. Max sits on his haunches, one ear gone, an eye bloody and shut. At his feet is the biggest rat Eddie has ever seen. At least he thinks it's a rat. Its face is gone and its body is sodden with death.

Max is reluctant to leave. He fought hard to kill what is before him and doesn't want to go. He's proud of himself and wants Eddie to see what he's done, but he's in need of a veterinarian to sew him up and maybe save his eye.

As Eddie gets close, Max moves round his catch, always keeping it between him and Eddie.

Eddie gets down on all fours and works his way closer until finally he has Max in his hands. The cat doesn't like to be held, though. He scratches at Eddie, climbs his arms and bites him over the eyebrow.

Eddie takes off his shirt and wraps the cat in it. Max gives up the fight and rides quietly back up to the road, the warmth of his body coming through the shirt to Eddie's arm. Eddie pets his head and looks down. He sees the warmth is really blood and it's soaking through.

From ahead, Eddie can hear a car approaching. At the sound of it Max starts to struggle in his arms. Eddie's afraid it'll be someone he knows. They'll stop and he'll have to have a conversation with them, so he goes down into the grass by the road on his knees, then forward onto one hand, cradling the cat against his belly with the other.

The car rushes past, its tires a few feet to the right of his head. It slows down and stops, sits there for a moment. Eddie looks back over his shoulder and sees it's Louis Poissant's Cadillac. It sits there for a moment, its brake lights like red eyes in the night, and then it's off, disappearing along the windy road out of town.

Eddie decides he's just now come to like Louis for understanding he wanted to be alone, whether he knew it or not.

■

Monday turns cold and rainy. The fire on Rattlesnake Mountain goes out. There were no sightings of rattlesnakes from reliable sources, no carcasses to bear proof.

But for Cody and the Ryans it's a day of rejoicing. Mary's leaving school early with Eileen. The casts will be sawed off and thrown in the Dumpster. And there's mail, letters from Mary's cousin in Seattle and Mrs. Hall in Nova Scotia.

Eddie holds the letters, waiting for Mary and Eileen to get home. He's making a pizza for supper, Cody on vegetables, Little Eddie on his Big Wheel, tear-assing around the kitchen, ramming furniture and the legs of the grown-ups. He wears G. R. Trimble's hard hat and carries a wooden dagger his uncle Cody made him. Mary Looney's iguana escaped in the house last week and he's hot on the trail.

Max holes up on an old pillow. He lost his eye and the debate is whether or not to get him a glass one. His stitches are the kind that disappear of their own accord. He doesn't move much. He eats where he sleeps.

When Mary and Eileen get home, she insists on walking across the threshold. She's shy about her newfound ability to use her legs. She walks slowly, tenderly. Everyone stops what they're doing to watch her. Her father thinks he'll cry and has to make himself strong so he won't. He doesn't want to embarrass her by being the foolish one.

"You've got legs," he says.

Cody whistles and says, "Ohh, baby!"

"No big deal," she tells them, and they all repeat it again and again, even little Eddie. They repeat it and laugh as if it's the funniest thing they ever heard.

"No big deal," they say. "No big deal."

Cody gets her a chair to sit in. She gets into it as if it's her butt that hurts. Little Eddie goes for her with his Big Wheel, but Cody snags him and holds him.

"There's mail," Eddie yells, "real mail. Not just bills."

Mary comes into the kitchen. She's changed out of her school clothes. Eddie hands her the letter from Mrs. Hall and the one from her cousin in Seattle.

Inside Mrs. Hall's is a postcard. It's of the cormorants nesting on the pilings in Pictou Harbor. They're double-crested with hook-tipped bills. It says they are strong swimmers, propelling themselves with rear-set webbed feet while steering with a stiff wedge-shaped tail. They eat eels, cod and other slow-moving fish.

In the letter she apologizes for not saying good-bye. She decided on early retirement and has come back to her cottage in Nova Scotia to live forever. She tells them she thinks she saw the ghost ship in the Strait through the foggy gray vapors. She says to make sure Eileen is introduced to Longfellow's "Evangeline" while still at a young age. More importantly, make her aware of the story, she says. She thanks Eddie and Cody for fixing the roof. She says they are to come visit her in the spring. She gives her love to Cody and signs off with "We love you."

"I wonder who *we* is," Mary says.

"Maybe she's got herself a beau," Cody says. "Maybe a Mountie."

Eddie doesn't say anything because he thinks he knows but isn't sure. He thinks her man has come back and knows what a foolish thought that is, but can't shake it.

The second letter is from Mary's cousin. She and her husband have put down a deposit on a condo rental for a month this winter in Florida, but won't be able to go. He's been transferred to the West Coast. They don't care about the money as long as they can get the tax write-off. It'll be there, she says, please. Let me know soon. Bye, bye. P.S. We're talking divorce, nothing definite. Maybe just talk. You know how it is.

Mary tries to smile at their good fortune. At first Eddie says he can't go, but then he relents. He tells Mary to write back and they'll work out the details when the time comes. She goes to get stationery from the rolltop desk.

Hell, he thinks, we've earned a vacation. He wonders what the P.S. means, especially the last sentence. It's the kind of stupid thing people just write.

He takes up the mozzarella and begins to grate it. Eileen asks if

she can try but he tells her it'll be too hard for her to do. She
snitches cheese from the piles he makes.

"I love pizza cheese," she says. "I'm going to get married to it."

"Are you going to start swimming?"

"Mom said we might go next week to the Y in Keene," she says,
pausing and touching her head. "But I could've heard it in a dream
or something like that."

Eddie doesn't say anything. He works hard to keep from laughing.

"Speaking of getting married," she says, "I wish there was something besides boys to get married to."

"Why is that?"

" 'Cause of divorce."

"Is that why?"

" 'Cause they act so weird. Just as the women get ready to sit
down because they're tired, the men say, How about getting me a
cup of coffee. I'm gonna say, No way, buster."

"No way what," Mary says, coming back into the kitchen.

"No way, José."

"Did you know they shoot craps in that gifted program?" Cody
says. He's been thinking about the ghost ship. He thinks he saw it
too.

■

After supper, Eddie and Mary stay in the kitchen while Cody, Little
Eddie and Eileen go outside. They talk about the letters, Mrs. Hall's
closing and the talk of divorce. They don't know how to feel about
all this. They try to make sense out of the writings, so many good
things, so many fears lurking within.

From outside comes the snap of gunfire. Eddie shivers, moves so
abruptly he sends pains into his body. He hopes Mary didn't notice
but it seems to happen so often, a movement, a sound and he's
wrenching himself out of his body. It is only small caliber. Then
there's a louder one, the thunder of a .44.

Eddie and Mary go outside into the evening. Little Eddie and
Cody stand at the foot of the steps and Eileen is in the chaise. It's
still light, the sky roomy enough for stars and the moon and a slice
of the sun.

At thirty yards out are sawhorses and a board nailed across them.

The board has a shelf on it, and sitting on the shelf is a row of mirrored tiles.

Cody raises a .22 pistol and one by one the mirrors fracture, their jagged edges knifing the ground.

"I told them it's bad luck, but they wouldn't listen," Eileen says.

Cody goes out to set up another row of mirrors. When he comes back he smiles at Eddie and Mary, pleased with himself. He gets on his knees, his arms around the boy, and has Little Eddie hold the gun, his hands inside Cody's.

The gunshots snap in the air and the mirrors go down.

"Top that," Cody says to Eddie.

Mary wants to scold them, but can't even imagine where to start.

"Give me the damn thing," she says. "I'll show you how to shoot it."

Cody walks out to the shelf and sets up a new row. He then releases the clip and packs it again with shells while he walks back. He tells her it was G.R.'s gun and he could shoot the eye out of a gnat with it.

"Go for it, Mom," Eileen says.

"Show me how."

Cody shows Mary how to work the slide and the safety. He positions her erect, her knees flexed, both hands out and on the grips. She sights down the barrel and then looks at him and smiles. She fires, splitting one and nicking two.

"Your turn," she says, holding the pistol out for Eddie.

Eddie comes down off the porch and takes the gun. He loads it with a handful of shells Cody gives him. He takes stance and sights in the mirrors.

"You idiots," he says, coming out of his stance and pointing the gun at the ground.

Cody and Mary laugh. Little Eddie doesn't know why, but he joins in too.

"Give me the other gun," Eddie says.

"What other gun?" Cody says, shrugging.

"The other gun."

From under the steps, Cody takes out a .44 revolver and hands it over, telling Eddie it's already loaded and then saying, "Go ahead, but don't shoot yourself."

Eddie takes stance and sights down the barrel. He can see himself in the mirror aiming a gun at himself. He empties the cylinder, shattering all the mirrors that remain. The gunshots are loud and hurt their ears; his image goes to smash and flickers to the ground. Eddie hands the gun back over to Cody, goes inside and down to the preparation and stays there until he's sure they've all gone to bed for the night.

Later in the week, he writes in his journal.

> . . . *farmer breaks nozzle on tanker of molasses behind barn. Whole tanker empties down onto road. Cars collide. One man dies.*
> . . . *stone boat dragged over a boy's head. Bury ox yoke on small wooden casket.*
> . . . *student killed by studs flying out of a snow tire.*
> . . . *dog steps on shotgun and kills hunter while he's taking a piss.*
> . . . *man rolled up in leaves drunk, sent to landfill, buried alive.*
> . . . *man lays down in road to sleep one off, gets run over. Quite common in rural America.*
> . . . *debris inside lighter. Lighter doesn't shut off. Ruptures and explodes. Kills welder.*
> . . . *giant spool of wire comes off public service truck, rolls downhill, goes through shack like a buzz saw. Kills two people at their dinner table.*
> . . . *construction worker complains about unsafe bridgework so they make him lifeguard in rowboat. He tips over boat and drowns.*
> . . . *couple found froze in house. All furniture gone into wood stove. Ran out of furniture.*
> . . . *man mows lawn wearing headphones. Ground hornets attack. Lay there dying to what some people think was one of the better symphonies ever composed.*
> . . . *man dies at funeral on church steps. Relatives videotape it. Insist on aerial dispersal of cremains. Tape that too.*
> . . . *couple dies of hypothermia in water bed when electricity goes out. "They were so head over heels in love, even you won't be able to keep them under."*
> . . . *in one thunderstorm. Farmer dies when lightning strikes arms of spray rig, lightning down a tree root burns up pigs, dog on chain attached to steel rod dies when rod acts as lightning rod. Lightning travels ninety thousand miles per second. Only half the speed of light. If lightning can do that, imagine what light can do.*
> . . . *Eileen left for school this morning with her dress on backwards and no one thought to say anything. By the way, she has the casts off and is doing well.*
> . . . *Cody sat in the barn all night holding Buck's head in his lap. The horse was down on his side. They both fell asleep out there but in the morning only one of them woke up. Cody was thankful he didn't have*

to shoot the horse. Not that it would've bothered him, he says. If it had to be done, he'd have done it.

. . . Iggy peeked out over the lampshade. It gave us all quite a start. He opened his mouth and stuck out his tongue. Mary poked him with a newspaper. He skittered down the inside of the shade and even before he hit the floor, Max had him. We've made a pact not to tell Mary Looney. Eileen's idea. She said if I were dead she wouldn't want to know about it.

. . . called Mary Looney about needing her to do some work. Confessed she spent all her money at the dog races. Superfecta paid $3,448.80. Winners were Boston Deb, Estimated Income, My Mink Coat, Perfect Form, Hi Bio. She played Kinetic Energy, Hinsdale, Placid Red, Wilda's Bobbin and Poverty. She thinks it all means something.

. . . Marie called Mary to say she thinks Dome is going off his rocker. He insists she keep all the stoppers in the sinks and tubs. Claims djinns could escape from the drains and raise hell with the world. He told Marie she should never become emotionally involved with a djinn. She asked Mary what miscegenation meant. She told her he had a collection of little boxes made out of camel udders.

. . . Read about a little boy in Keene who dies in a sledding accident. Seems he went into the road and got run over. Can't help but think about my own son. My children. Why are the rituals of birth not of the same magnitude as the rituals of death?

. . . Did a house removal this morning. A young woman mixed up her drugs. I think on purpose. The mother was there and her sisters and her sisters' children were there too. They stayed close to the bedroom, kind of hovered. The mother told the children I was taking her back to the funeral home to make her look beautiful. Did my heart good. Pot called, insistent he sign certificate. Told him registered nurse already did it. Told him he wasn't needed. Told him to stay away.

. . . Went down to the preparation room this morning to see how Mary Looney was doing. She was sitting at the head of the woman, crying. I asked her what was the matter. She looked up at me. She said, "It's the tears. They keep falling onto her face and making the cosmetics run."

No, I said. I meant why are you crying. She told me, "It's because this is Mary Rooney, my best friend, and I didn't even know."

Kind of the straw that's breaking my back right now.

24

It's a half hour until daylight. Already the night is breaking up in the east, coming as a new horizon, one echoing the lay of the mountains enough to be a whole new range, higher and more distant, chalky under the gray furl arcing up and overhead and down again all the way to the west. It's the best light this day will muster.

Eddie remembers a day when Eileen couldn't sleep, her legs throbbing to the marrow, her initiation to the small pains that will come when the weather is so and be that way for the rest of her life. It was the same mantle of light, mottled and gray, the same coming of the day as if it were an afterthought, an idea not fully realized. He'd gotten out of bed to comfort her. They dressed and went out on the porch, then he wheeled her through the wet grass down to the sound of coons screeching in the corn. The water beaded on her casts as they struck through the grass, her heart solid and resolute, his dull in his chest, a little sunken, a few pieces missing.

She said she thought the coons sounded like children crying, or even being killed, and when she said it, they looked at each other, realizing just how true a thought it was.

Cody's a hundred yards away, astride the same ridge. He's found a warm high place to sit, a place with a good view, one from where he can see for miles, all ways in and all ways out, all the way down. It's on a cooling vent for a radio station's transmitter.

He doesn't know it, but every time he sits down, he cuts off the air circulation, causing the transmitter to overheat and shut down, thereby knocking the station off the air.

It's Pennsylvania in November, Centre County, the opening day of deer season.

■

Eddie and Cody drove into the Seven Mountains on Sunday, the day before. Opening the season in Pennsylvania is something Cody's always wanted to do.

"Pennsylvania puts enough hunters into the woods that day to make up the fourth-largest army in the world. A one-day army bigger'n hell."

"It says here you can't hunt in cemeteries or on the grounds of sanitoriums."

"It's a big state," Cody tells Eddie. "There will still be plenty of real estate, even without those places."

The tires on Cody's truck thrum over the highway, Route 45 out of Lewisburg, where they left I80. A painted sign on a front lawn warns of a speed trap within the next ten miles. Cody tells Eddie about his uncle who used to run a gas station. Every time the staties set up a speed trap on Route 12, he'd put out a sign to warn the motorists. It gave business a real shot in the arm. They tried to shut him down but the judge reckoned it to be like Paul Revere's ride. Almost the duty of any good citizen.

"That's a judge I'd like to run into," Eddie says.

"You could," Cody says. "He still sits on the bench in Keene. They say he's a good guy for a judge. Some of those guys in drunk school said so."

On the radio the Andrews Sisters are singing, *Don't sit under the apple tree with anyone else but me, anyone else but me,* Maxine, Patti and LaVerne, singing the words a man would, but back then nobody seemed to care.

" 'The Friendly Nursing Home,' " Cody reads as they pass it by. It's a habit he's taken up, reading every sign he sees. "If they have to tell you, it kind of makes you wonder just how friendly it is, doesn't it?"

The truck is laden with gear, fifty pounds per man, plus rifles and shells. When Cody learned the licenses alone would be eighty dollars apiece, he decided they'd rough it, camping out in the state forest, where already it's cold enough to begin snow making at Tussey Mountain Ski Area. The cost of the licenses also meant bringing food for the trip out and the trip back when they'd used up the four days they'd given over to the hunt.

" 'The Hamilton State School Hospital,' " Cody reads. "Well, I don't get it. Is it a school or a hospital? Is it state school, then hospital, or do you say, state then school hospital all like it's one word?"

"Jesus, I don't know. Sometimes you get fixated on the damnedest things. It's a teaching hospital. Trust me."

"Here's one," Cody says. " 'Clyde Peelings Reptile World.' Now there isn't much doubt about what that is."

"No. I guess not."

Eddie didn't want to make the trip. He hasn't held a rifle in years and swore the last time would *be* the last time. But Cody went ahead anyway, making plans; and with Mary's collusion, they arranged it so Eddie could go, whether he wanted to or not. Mary thought it'd be good for him. She also figured it'd guarantee the trip to Florida. He'd owe it to her and she wants it so badly. Maybe even them alone while the kids stay home with Cody.

"Did you pack enough fluorescent orange?" Eddie says. "According to the regulations you need at least two hundred and fifty square inches."

"All taken care of."

"They have safety zones too. It says you can't hunt, take, disturb or chase wildlife, or discharge a firearm, arrow or other deadly weapon within or through an area within one hundred fifty yards of a house, residence, camp or barn, stable or other building used in connection therewith without permission of the occupant."

"There's laws and there's the law," Cody says. "My grandfather told me, and of course it was before he died, that when he was a kid he used to do his best hunting while taking a shit. They had a privy with a grand view of the orchard, the sugar bush, the pond, and the edge of corn ground. A regular panorama of all nature's habitats from that two-holer. He had salt licks out there and every once in a while he'd bait with shell corn. He had a gun rest that'd drop down across the doorway and he'd be sitting there every morning by six for his daily constitutional. Mostly deer and turkey, beaded toms with three-inch spikes. Now the turkey's somewhat played out and you can't bait deer but I got to laugh, thinking about him sitting there with his trousers down, tapping off a shot at seventy-five yards and then just as cool as a cucumber wiping his cold red-ringed arse with a page from the Sears catalog, and packing home twenty pounds of old Mr. Tom Turkey. Look what I got, Ma."

"That's a good one, Cody. Is it true or did you make it up?"

"Doesn't really matter, does it?"

Both men laugh. Eddie has long since given up on keeping Cody accountable. He's come to expect Cody's flirtations with truth and appreciate them the way he appreciates his son's inability to distinguish beginnings and ends, what was and what might have been, a mind with no room for tomorrow or yesterday.

They ride in silence, passing through Vicksburg and Mifflinburg, Route 45 cutting a swath through the middle of each, their town centers a crossroad, maybe a stoplight. They pass Amishmen in black buggies and each time Cody slows down and gawks out the window. Each time he says they must be fascinating people or they must be curious people. By the time he passes the third one, he doesn't slow down, doesn't look.

"It isn't like they're on display," he says, anticipating a question Eddie isn't thinking. "It isn't like God gave us the right to look at what we want and to understand it all, and least of all, to think we understand it. Just now I'm a little ashamed of myself."

"You'll get over it."

"I probably will," Cody says. "Knowing me, I probably will."

Out of Hartleton they begin the climb between Thick Mountain and Buffalo Mountain. The road seems to corkscrew up and over the top. Eddie has to keep looking for the sun just to have a slim idea as to where he is.

"This is the range," Cody says. "We'll come in twenty-five miles southwest of here, the Rothrock State Forest. Tussey Mountain and Thickhead Mountain. A hundred and fifty square miles."

"I trust you've been here before," Eddie says.

"No, I haven't. That's the fun of it."

■

Eddie cradles his rifle in his lap and takes out the topo map. It's folded into a square, a square showing the lay of the land where he now sits. His stomach growls. Cody made breakfast: pancakes, bacon and what he called sheepherder's coffee. It was a volatile mix and now, an hour later, about ready to go off inside Eddie's stomach, maybe make the climb up his throat.

He takes out his pen and by cupping his hand and writing small, he's able to protect the words from the snow that's falling. He writes the words *azalea, lilac* and *deciduous.* Then he writes *cellar door, cellophane, celery* and *Ceylon.*

The word *whippoorwill* comes to mind. He writes that down too and thinks about it being a sentence, a command. His father used to wake him to hear its call, loud and rhythmic, over and over again in the night. The bird saying its name. His father called back, his father and the bird speaking to each other.

He writes: *One time a barn owl flew down the chimney and perched on a curtain rod. It was there in the morning when we got out of bed. Its face was white and shaped like half an apple and its eyes were black like seeds. My father said they eat rodents. They find them in rubbish dumps, waste lots, run-down farms and neglected cemeteries. My mother said it meant someone was going to die. My father said we all were someday. But he took a long time to say the word* someday, *or at least I remember it being a long time. We caught it in a net and let it go. My father wore leather gloves. He let the owl grab onto him and then he threw it into the sky, where it disappeared.*

■

Cody and Eddie packed into the Seven Mountains on Sunday afternoon. It took them three hours to hike the trail, to a spot where three counties meet on the map. From there they took a side trail, up through virgin white pine, stands of hemlock and thick growths of bare rhododendron. All the way Cody complained about the trail guide being in metric. It said, "Metrication is a patriotic measure designed to help end our cultural isolation and end our chronic balance of payment problems."

"Fuck that shit," Cody said. "A foot means something. A yard means something too. They are the words for things. Fathoms, what the fuck. Meters, what the hell do they have to do with? Kilometers. Shit, they ain't even as long as a mile. It takes more of them to go the same distance."

Eddie followed behind, the pack resting comfortably on his back, the straps more like arms draped over his shoulders.

"Laugh," Cody said. "That metric will fuck up all your sports, your sports records, all your carpenters and what about your Craftsmen tool sets? All your wrenches and your nuts and bolts?"

They crossed a pipeline clearing and then scrabbled hard up an embankment and came out on an old railroad grade, a large tulip tree growing in it. They followed the bed a ways and picked up a new trail that slabbed up the hillside and turned left up the ridge-line where the rock showed through with the polished sheen of a skull.

"It says in the guidebook that rattlesnakes are frequently heard under these rocks. Watch your step and check before sitting down."

"Too cold," Cody says, "and a good thing too. I've seen timber rattlers before. It ain't like the zoo."

They kept moving all afternoon, late into the day, and it wasn't until the moon became their only light that Cody found the high meadow he imagined he knew was there from studying the lines and intervals in the contour map.

"Here it is," Cody said. "Here's where we want to be."

They made base camp there, a hundred yards off the spine of a ridge that afforded a 270-degree view, somewhere in the Seven Mountains: Tussey, Thickhead, Front, First, Big Poe, Long and Strong, a place where whitetails offer themselves up to the pure of heart, a place where metrics can take a flying fuck, a place kept secret.

■

Cody's rifle cracks the air and Eddie has all he can do to keep from losing bowel control. The warm state he's put himself into goes ice cold with cramps and wet snow. A buck comes stumbling in his direction, then it's up and burning ground toward where he's propped himself against a tree. He drops his gun and scrambles to the other side, seeing only a flash as it nicks by, bounding for the thick cover of vine, hemlock and thorn.

Cody is close behind, running stiff-legged, his weight thrown back and his rifle across his chest. He picks up Eddie's gun and cleans it off.

"This will come in handy," he says, his face tight and drawn.

Eddie takes the gun and looks off where the buck disappeared. It's as if he can still see it, suspended in the air, holding steady, waiting only to touch down.

"The bolt froze on me and I couldn't get a second shot off," he hears Cody say. "I should be horsewhipped."

Eddie wants to say he himself was to blame, but right now he can't seem to work up the words. Instead he says, "Did you see a bear?"

"No, did you lose one?"

"I mean it. I think one came out of that laurel. It was like a shadow. The shadow of a man."

"Then it probably was a bear. He was probably just getting in for the night."

Eddie still holds the topo map. The ink from the words he wrote runs blue into the lines that track his palm and disappear under the cuff of his coat sleeve.

"Guess we'd better get up on it," Cody says.

They follow the blood trail along the ridge for the better part of an hour. Tracks, like narrow split hearts, imprint the snow and mud. A front leg drags a bit while the others dig deeper.

The blood comes more scarcely. They hope to find the buck, and at the same time hope the bullet passed through and already the wound is matted and closing, in case they don't find it.

The trail begins to descend the side opposite the one they hiked Sunday, traversing the mountain, dropping down through birch, maple and laurel. At every thicket Cody sweeps his arm out, motioning Eddie to stand while he goes in, taking the lash of thorns that come at his head, chest, arms and legs. After three of these forays, his clothes are torn and his face is bleeding. "I need a spell," Cody whispers, going down on his knees, holding his rifle across his thighs. "That's rough going through there."

Eddie thinks how he didn't want to come. He hasn't hunted deer since he was a kid and he was never very good at it.

■

Coreen Frangel drives through slush to the Eagle Ridge transmitter. On the side of the van it says, WRLT–FM, 24-HOUR CHRISTIAN-ORIENTED BROADCASTING. Her station went off the air at six forty-five, came back on and then went off again. It continued like that for two hours. The longest outage came during morning vespers.

At the cooling vent she finds footprints in the snow and a shiny brass cartridge case, with 30-60 SPRG stamped into the base. She pockets it and goes back to the van. Her station is coming in on the radio, loud and clear. Something about the church of the future. Something about that old black magic.

■

Cody is up again and on the move through thick cover. Wet snow lies across his shoulders like a mantle. Eddie follows him, working hard to keep oriented, noting each bench they cross and every hollow they drop into, pass through and come out of.

Cody stops and motions him forward. He points below, and when Eddie gets up to him, he can see a stand of oak, the leaves, red and yellow, still on the branches. All around them is grayness and air thick with wet snow, but here is a place where somehow autumn still holds on.

"Now watch he don't rise up right underneath you," Cody whispers, then he motions Eddie twenty yards to the right and they begin down the two sides of a draw. Eddie takes two steps and his feet go out from under him. He rides the rest of the way on his back, taking a roll at the bottom. Snow and mud have worked their way under his clothes and his face is smeared, but under the leafy trees it's dry and warm. A stream seeps from the ground, running through a swale of green grass, and there're signs the deer have been yarding here. Cody picks up the trail again without stopping and they leave the place.

A hundred yards farther and they break out into an orchard. They stop again under the apple trees, their black branches growing off in crooks and twists burdened with suckers shooting straight into the sky.

"I just don't get it," Cody says. "The goddamn things never run downhill. They always climb. Another thing I don't get is why some other one of these yahoos hasn't pocked it by now. There's hundreds of 'em within the sound of that shot.''

Eddie looks at his friend. He can barely recognize him. Frozen blood runs lie caked on his cheeks and forehead. His jacket is ripped. Puffs of down come out tears, ready to fall off and mat the ground. The backs of his hands are scratched raw and his hair and beard are full of twigs and thorns. Eddie begins to tighten from the fall he took. When they were tracking it wasn't bad, but now he's cold and stiff. He looks at Cody again, watches him intently until he walks off.

The two men go on. They pass through the orchard and down into a creek bottom where willow and poplar slow their progress. Cody motions for Eddie to come closer. He points to a mark made in blood the shape of a leg where the buck must've gone to rest. Over their heads they can see where it left the creek bottom and climbed the bank.

"He's over the top," Cody says. "He's up there waiting."

The bank is steep. They have to get down on their knees to make the climb, Cody first and Eddie close behind.

"What is it?" Eddie says, when Cody stops at the lip.

"I don't know."

Eddie works his way up to his friend's shoulders, gripping tufts of grass to keep from sliding back down.

Before them is a field of steel and aluminum and wooden shapes, all resting on concrete pedestals. Some are giant wings like on an airplane, only without body or fuselage. Others are upright, shooting into the heavy gray sky. There are aluminum boxes and columns and some shaped like doughnuts. The wooden ones have half circles cut out of them and stand, either opposed to each other or facing each other. They all come in pairs and look faintly human, man or woman, or even birdlike. The buck is amongst them, carefully picking his way from one to another as if he too has only wandered in and just now doesn't know where he is.

Eddie slaps Cody on the arm and points to the west. There's a white house on the edge of the field. In the falling snow it's hard to tell its true size. It's either huge and wall-like against the sky or it's a cottage, but nothing in between. Attached to the house there's a deck and standing on it are a man and a woman and two boys. They're watching the buck move in the field, his rack rising and falling as he stops at each shape.

"It's a sculpture field," Eddie whispers. "It belongs to them. You can't shoot that animal here."

"What in hell do you propose I do?"

"I don't know," Eddie says. "I just don't know."

Cody digs his elbows into the bank and gets his heel hooked inside a root. He reaches behind him and when his hand comes back around he's holding his hunting knife.

"Sometimes there are no good choices," he says, then he cuts the tuft of grass Eddie's holding to. Eddie pumps his legs, trying to stay where he is, but he can't. He slides down to the floor of the creek bottom on his belly and before he can sit up, the signature of Cody's ought-six marks the air.

25

Eddie and Cody leave the sculptor's house late in the evening with their deer in the truck bed. They leave on good terms, the kind of truce made when strangers are thrown together and only their discomfort can save them. The sculptor's boys liked to hold the guns and one of them dared to touch the hole in the deer's skull made by the bullet's entry. He stuck a finger in it the way Cody showed him, and when he pulled it out, it was tinged with red and pink, pieces of brain and bone.

Afterwards they all piled into the sculptor's Saab and drove to where the truck was parked. He and his boys hiked in, helped break camp and lug out gear. The boys fought over who'd get to carry Cody's duffel bag.

Eddie scribbled into his notebook lines from the sculptor's conversation whenever he got a chance. It went something like: *You know we started off the boys with no toy guns. It was the way we wanted to raise them, but now it's come down to no live ammo in the living room. The sculptor laughed at his own joke and Cody said, Oh, I can't agree with you more. The living room is no place for live ammo.*

In spring the sculptor will go out to his sculpture field with his Weed Eater and see for the first time the clean path of Cody's bullet from where it left the deer's head to where it went through the metal of two raised aluminum wings before flattening out against one made of steel, its velocity spent and waning. He'll look through the holes as if they were a glassless telescope and reinvent that day, that deer. He'll stand with his back to the steel and pretend it's incoming. He'll rest his temple to it and imagine how he'd drop. He'll remember Eddie as a man somewhat like himself and Cody as the man his boys still talk about.

■

It's a driving snow Eddie and Cody pass through, all the while cursing the lame-brained Pennsylvania motorists who don't have snow tires, let alone know how to drive in snow. They see them off the shoulders and stacked up at the foot of hills. Cody's pickup sashays round the corners, fishtails up the knobs, but still points straight.

"They don't send the plows until after it stops," Cody says. "They figure it saves trips, but what they haven't figured out yet is that by then it's turned to boiler plate."

Eddie doesn't say anything. It's late in the day and he's still cold and wet and tired. He drinks in the heat off the blower fan, feeling as if he could sleep for days and somehow be able to enjoy that sleep while he's at it. He thinks about the difference between a dead deer and a dead person and must confess to himself he's more reverent of the deer, less accepting of the fact of its death. At any moment it could get up from the bed and bound into the woods. He looks over his shoulder at it lying on its side. He sees a flash of orange as a hunter steps onto the road they've just covered. The deer wouldn't get as far the second time as it did the first.

"She's still there," Cody says, and Eddie thinks how strange that Cody would know what he's thinking, how strange that Cody called the buck a she and not a he.

"You said she. It's a he."

"I guess I did. Don't worry, *he's* still there."

Eddie hears a tenderness in Cody's voice, a tenderness he reserves for Mary, Eileen and Little Eddie and now dead animals.

"But you said she. Why'd you do that?"

Cody doesn't answer. He shrugs and opens the fly window. A

stream of cold air propels the heat over the dash, swirls it in the cab, and Eddie is wakened, brought back to the chill of his wet clothes, the pant legs stiffened with mud. Tufts of white down from Cody's vest surround them and in the dashboard lights his unwashed face is a mask of dirt and blood.

Farther into the valley, the snow has slackened and gone to rain, a drizzle that hangs in the air. Eddie doesn't know where they're going and he doesn't ask. He stays within himself, now liking the smell of wet wool, gun oil and cigarettes. Each smell has its own life in the air of the cab, wafting, swirling, rising up and settling down. And it's quiet in there too. The thick air muffles the engine sounds and the snowbound road silences the tires. Being this way makes so many things that seemed important not so important after all.

From a break in the trees they can see where the fog has blanketed the valley, a sea of it contained before them, and then after a few miles of switchbacks they're off the mountain and into it, the wipers whisking it aside in slow cadence. They're bathed in fog, rolling in it like breakers scuttling over the land. It boils up around them, swallowing them, the truck and the deer as they descend from the mountain.

Cody makes a turn and they're on a road where they'll have to pull over to let an oncomer get by. He makes another turn and they're on a one-lane track, the road becoming less and less of a road and more of a trail. Cody has to stop to move aside snow-laden branches that'd bent and snapped under the weight of the water they sponged. When he gets back in, he shifts to four-wheel drive.

Finally they come to a steel gate with a NO TRESPASSING sign bolted to it. Under it another sign says, SECURITY PROVIDED BY SMITH AND WESSON; and under that it says, BEWARE, OWNER ARMED AND DANGEROUS, and another, REMEMBER THE MIA-POW.

Cody pulls the pin in the hasp and lets the gate swing wide. They drive through and Eddie closes it behind them. They drive on, following no discernible trail, the fender sweeping back toppled boughs and branches that drag along the side, drop their loads and spring skyward.

The smell of woodsmoke mingles in the cab air, and a cabin comes into view, the mountain rising straight up behind it. The woodsmoke can be seen, a strata of it hovering above a pipe that comes out through a boarded window, and elbows into a length that runs up to be level with the peak. Both the fog and the smoke are gray but the smoke moves, making a seam in the other, making itself more gray in the air it commands, twelve feet off the ground.

Yellow light comes from the other windows, making the small cabin a place to stay, a home in this weather, more so than in any other.

Cody hammers on the door with his fist, yelling, "Mike, Mike. Open the goddamn door."

"Hold your fucking horses. Sam, get the goddamn door."

The door swings open and Eddie and Cody pass through. Eddie is struck by thoughts of warmth again, the warmth of fresh-baked bread, of laundry, the truck heater, wool and the wood stove in this cabin. Then he takes himself by surprise and he thinks the warmth of a woman, her touch, her breath, the between of her legs. He misses Mary and by now knows he'll miss her tonight as they sleep in separate beds miles apart.

At the back of the cabin is a cookstove, and on it a black iron skillet with an unusually long handle. The hiss of peppers and onions and sausage is loud in the cabin. Next to the cookstove is a bear of a man ensconced in a Barcalounger. He sits stiffly, a panel of plywood between his back and the cushion. Over his head is a square black nylon banner. There's a white-winged skull in the center and under it a stack of words: AIRBORNE DEATH FROM ABOVE. Within easy reach are a platter the size of a hubcap, two rifles, a pistol and a sixteen-ounce Blue Ribbon.

He spreads his arms wide and speaks in a naturally loud voice, a voice most men would have to strain to equal.

"Je-sus Chi-rist. I was just talking about you and that G. R. Trimble. Telling the Deer Drovers about the time the three of us went up to Zeno's one night and took on the entire Penn State football team and about fifteen faggot college boys. It was just like a John Wayne movie, bodies flying through the air, tables smashed to smithereens. That was almost four years ago. Where ya been?"

Eddie now sees there are three other men in the room, younger men, two of them wearing casts on their arms. They sit on broken-down furniture as if in attendance on the man in the Barcalounger.

"I knew you'd come. I knew at least one of you renegades from the north country, one of you Cow Hampshiremen would come down to get onto the big bucks again. I was just telling the Deer Drovers that very thing."

The man shifts in his chair to get a look at Eddie.

"Is that you, G.R.? No. By God it isn't. Who have you brought us, Cody? Who is that fella?"

"His name's Eddie Ryan. He's a good man."

"A Mick, by the Jesus. You've brought us a Mick. Your word's good enough for me. Come in. Come in. Nothing to worry about here. The Queen sucks."

Cody turns aside, letting Eddie pass into the room, and then he gives the door a shove to close it.

"This here's Mike the Polak. You'd better keep your boots on when you're around him because it can get pretty deep."

"Oh, the hell you say. Hear you talk."

"These here are Mike's Deer Drovers. That's Jim and that's Sam and that funny-looking one is Thomas."

Cody makes a move toward Thomas, who ducks his head and laughs.

"Everyone thinks Thomas here is simpleminded, but we *know* he is, don't we, Thomas."

"That's right, Cody," Thomas says. "We hear you. You tell it."

"Jesus, Mike," Cody says. "I don't see nothing hung up in them trees. That ain't tenderloin, is it? Smells more like farm-raised. Smells like hog to me. Smells like cabbage too. You got a crock of it somewhere?"

"Slow start, Cody. Slow start. But me and the Drovers come up from Pittsburgh and take the week. We don't see any sense in taking one before we have to. First day is amateur day anyways. We let them cull the herds and get the hell out of the woods. Then we get serious. We find them what's got our names on 'em. We hunt heads.

"We're a little banged up but we'll do it. We already got a couple bear. Sam scored at eighty feet with the three fifty-seven magnum rifle and Jimbo scored at two hundred feet with one shot."

Mike the Polak leans forward with great effort, grasps the skillet handle from where he sits and moves it rapidly back and forth, stirring the contents, causing them to flip up and over on themselves.

"So, Mr. Eddie Ryan, what's got you teamed up with this ridge runner and stump-jumper? He'll have you in the hoosegow before you know it."

"A little vacation," Eddie says. "A little hunting trip to Pennsylvania."

"Well, I want you to know, if you're going to hang out with him you're going to have a life of torment."

Mike the Polak and his Deer Drovers laugh.

"Alls I can say is, good luck. He'll drag you down, but he'll pull your fat out of the fire too, if that's what you need."

Mike works the iron skillet again, clattering it across the top of the stove.

"So, Cody boy. What's up with that renegade of a G. R. Trimble?"

"He's dead, Mike. He died last winter."

Mike looks up. He stares at Cody. Eddie sees the hurt in his face. It's as if he's been clubbed between the eyes with an ax handle. Not that it would hurt him. He just can't believe anyone would do it. The room goes quiet; the hiss of the skillet makes the only sound. The Deer Drovers look at Cody too, and then to the floor.

"Jesus Christ, I don't believe it. He was a great man. How'd it happen? Were you with him?" he says softly, now staring off with a look that's faraway, so far, a part of it will never find its way back.

"No, I wasn't, Mike. He was all by himself," Cody whispers.

"What's life anyways? We've all got life. The key is being bigger than life. Bigger than life itself," Mike says.

Mike stops talking and pulls at his chin. Then he says, "How'd he happen to be done?"

"Mike," Sam says, wanting to interrupt, "have some food. It's just about all ready."

"I thought it was strange to see you come this way alone."

"Oh, I've been traveling a lot lately. Nova Scotia and down here. This winter I got something big planned, but I don't know quite what. Maybe Africa."

"Africa! By the Jesus, wouldn't I love to get over there. I'd make 'em forget they ever knew Tarzan. Hey, though, seriously. I'll tell you what I'd like to do. I'd like to go north to where the earth ends and the ice begins. Hudson Bay. Anticosti Island. Hey, you want to ride shotgun? You wanna go with me? We'll leave right now?"

"What about the Deer Drovers?"

Mike looks at each one. He smiles at them and winks.

"Oh," he says, "we'll tell them all about it when we get back.

We'll take a video camera and record the whole trip. Look, there's Cody drunk. And look, there's Cody drunk."

"Don't touch it no more," Cody says. "I'm reformed."

"Did you reform before he died or after he died? Come on, Cody, have a little toddy with me and the Drovers."

Cody holds one hand inside the other and looks down at the floor.

"Mike," Jim says, "lay off him a little."

"Fuck you," Mike says, throwing an empty Blue Ribbon can at him, aiming for his head. He then struggles up out of the Barcalounger. The panel of plywood falls from behind him, clapping against one he'd been sitting on. He's an even bigger man than Eddie had surmised. Getting into Cody's face, he points a finger and is about to speak, but Eddie gets in between them and puts a hand on his chest. It's like touching a brick wall. Eddie thinks he must be armor-plated. Jim and Sam get beside Mike, ready to grab his arms.

"Mike," Eddie says, "it's a terrible loss for all of us. I don't know what's in your head, but Cody has no blame in the matter. He's conducted himself with courage and dignity. As far as the drinking goes, I can't see as though it was ever a problem. I handled the body and I know it wasn't anyone's fault."

"You handled the body?"

"I'm a funeral director. I handled G. R. Trimble."

Mike the Polak and his Deer Drovers make moves that wander them back from Eddie. He smiles at them and they smile back sheepishly.

"It's a job," Eddie says, "not a disease," and they laugh.

"I'm sorry, Cody. I shouldn't have sought blame. If it'd been you, I would've put him through the wringer too."

Cody doesn't say anything.

"Jesus," Mike yells, "there's a draft in here. What have you got, that door open? Close that goddamn pneumonia hole."

■

The men sit round a table they folded down from the wall. It's a full sheet of one-inch plywood hinged at the bottom and fixed with legs that swing down and clamp. It's Mike's invention and tonight will be a bed for two of the Drovers.

But for now it's strewn with the leftovers of supper: pierogie, kielbasa golompki, kiszka, baked potatoes, rye bread, roast beef, ham, bacon, cabbage, rice and boiled eggs. There's a noodle soup Mike calls oil soup, but, he says, he calls it that only when the women aren't around.

The men sit and pick at the food. Some have already lit up cigarettes, letting the ashes drop in their plates. They are fat and dumb with the eating. It's been a way to answer the news of G.R.'s death. It's made them lazy in their shock and grief, less bereaved, less sad.

Thomas says, "What the fuck," and makes himself a roast beef sandwich, thick enough to be most men's whole meal, not the last helping.

Mike has taken his supper in the Barcalounger, the Deer Drovers passing him what he calls for. The platter turned out to be his dinner plate, one he filled three time in the course of his meal. He belches and snaps open another Blue Ribbon.

Eddie feels good. His belly is full and he's allowing himself a cigarette. Cody has been quiet since Mike lashed out at him in his shock over G.R.'s dying. Eddie doesn't mind filling in.

"I know," Mike says. "What I say just sounds good, even if it is awful."

Mike makes a face and the Deer Drovers smile, but Eddie believes him when he says it's only talk. He believes Mike to be a good man who could get to like anyone if he met them.

"So you're an undertaker."

"It's a job," Eddie says. "Just like any other."

"I imagine it is."

Mike drinks his beer in long draughts. Sam passes out another round to everyone.

"You boys have had quite the event up there," Mike says. "Something about the police chief finding the skeleton of his wife's ex-husband buried in the front yard. Man by the name of some vegetable. Seems as though his own father told about it on his deathbed. We saw it all on *A Current Affair*. The show that Maury Povich does. Now there's a good Polak for you. He acts like one too, in most ways."

"Hey," one of the Deer Drovers says, "that guy's married to Connie Chung. Boy, there's just some things you can't figure out. She's a sweet one, she is."

"She's a sweet one all right. The Polaks, they get all the honeys."

Eddie looks to the two young men, with the broken arms, Jim and Sam, and asks them how they got that way.

"What'd you boys do," he says, "collide on your three-wheelers?"

"No," Sam says, as if it wasn't anything like that at all, though it could have been. "I was trying to replace a pane of glass in my bedroom window when I fell out of it backwards. On my way to the ground I caught my arm in the basketball hoop and ripped it right out of the backboard. It's probably what saved me. Then two days later, me and him are up to Buffalo Run to wet our lines. There we are, me and Jim standing in the creek waiting for the kingfisher. We see him hovering over the water, looking for a trout, maybe one of those bright-orange ones invented by our very own Pennsylvania Fish and Game. Palominos they call 'em."

Mike and the Drovers hoot and scream. Fish and Game is one of their more popular jokes.

"We knew it was his regular beat, up and down that stream," Sam says, once the laughter has died, "so there we are, standing stockstill, but he can still see us, of course. He don't let on, though. He don't give two shits about us. Oh, he was a beauty. A foot high, blue and gray. White below with a bushy crest on his head. He was up there rattling away and then he sees what he wants and drops like a dive bomber. Only problem is, he wants the same trout that's taken a fancy to Jimbo's Number Twenty Gray and Olive Midge Pupae. I says, Hold her, Jim. It's talons and wings against seven feet of high-modulus graphite, ultra three weight-forward floating buckskin and a point-zero-zero-three knotless tapered leader."

"Jesus, Mary and Joseph," Mike yells, setting the plates to chattering when he reaches over and slams his fist down on the table. "You fly fucking fishermen are so goddamn insufferable. Just tell the story, will ya."

"Well, there's Jimbo doing the gandy dance, fighting that kingfisher for the trout, when he loses his balance and goes ass over teakettle down on his stripping arm. He broke his rod too. It was a hell of a mess."

"Who won?" Cody asks.

"I got the trout," Jim says, "but they don't call him the kingfisher for nothing."

"They weren't going to put casts on our arms," Sam says. "It's something they try to avoid these days, but we says what the hell's the sense in having a broken arm if you can't get a cast?"

"I believe it," Mike says. "I believe that's just how it went. Cody, how is that Buck horse? You still got him?"

"He's a little blind, but no matter. I've retired him to stud."

Mike slams the table again. "That's the retirement for me."

"What you got in there, Mike? In your shirt?" Eddie says.

"Well, I'll tell you," Mike says, folding his hands across his chest. "My daughter brings home a poem and it's called 'Birches.' She says, 'Look, Dad. Look what these guys do, swinging from the birches. I'll bet you and the Drovers never did that.' 'Well, I says, you get your mother and sister and come outside and watch.' It was getting towards evening. Dan Bother and the *CBS Views* was just getting over. I think that night's news was Dan's sweater vest.

"Anyways, we all get out in the backyard, where I have a white birch, maybe forty feet high and a foot in diameter. The only one in the development. A leftover the landscaper had at the time. So I start to shimmy up it. By now the neighbors have come from off their decks and patios. The wife says, 'Mike, you get down from there this minute.' She talks to me like that, like I'm one of her kids."

"You are, aren't you, Mike?" Jim says, his mouth full of hot potato.

"Yes, I am," Mike says. "I'll tell you, though, my wife's a saint."

"But you didn't come down either."

"No sir, I didn't. I went shimmying up the trunk of that tree. I could've stopped anywhere along the way and swung it, but I didn't. I kept climbing and climbing. I wanted the length of that tree to go on forever."

The men can tell Mike's stopped telling the story to them and now he's telling it to himself, telling it to the far corners of the room and into the beyond.

"I kept climbing," he says, "and everyone on the ground kept getting smaller, and the smaller they got, the more I was running out of tree, until finally I had to decide to stop. It was too late, though. The top started to go and I wasn't ready yet to come down. So I pulled back and it went that way and before I knew it, I was swinging back and forth, trying not to let it fall, and then the fucking thing snaps off about six inches below my feet and I come plummeting to the ground."

Mike drains his beer can and shakes his head.

"So I'm laying there looking up into all these faces, my arms wrapped about the top of a birch tree. The neighbors stand there looking down at me. They're holding their barbecue forks and wearing their chef hats, aprons with lobsters on them. They've got drinks and tans.

"The wife says, 'Are you okay?'

"I say, 'I think I broke my back!'

"She says, 'Oh.' "

Mike goes silent. Jim tells Eddie and Cody that Mike's wearing a body cast under his shirt. He speaks as if Mike isn't in the room and when they look back at him, he does seem to be elsewhere, staring off at the lantern across the cabin, his face closed and dark, his chest laboring inside the cast barely enough to keep him alive.

"He and the wife are on hard times," Jim says quietly. "He's been living out here at the cabin."

"Some things you have to learn and there's some things you shouldn't," Mike says to no one.

"What do you mean? Shouldn't learn or shouldn't have to learn?" Eddie says, feeling desperate to know what he means.

"Both, I guess. Whiskey, boys. That's what we need. Whiskey eases misery."

"Whiskey eases memory," one of them says.

Sam breaks out the bottle of Jim Beam and some paper cups. He passes it around, each man taking a few fingers' worth.

"Hey, you know what I love?" Sam says.

"No, Sammy boy. What do you love?" Mike says.

"I love it in that movie where the deer hunter guy holds up a bullet and says, This is this. What a moment. I know some guys who made T-shirts of that."

"*The Deer Hunter,*" Mike says, shaking his head. "T-shirts."

"Mike," Cody says, "I have something for you. It's from G.R."

Cody stands and clears his throat. He takes from his breast pocket a wad of patching material. He unfolds it and turns out a small object he holds in the palm of his hand.

"G.R. would have wanted you to have this," he says. "There's a story to it. It goes like this. He who wears this talisman shall draw from it the strength to forever be worthy of the name Ie Shon Onta Ke. The Indian name given to Toussaint Charbonneau in recognition of his missionary work with Sioux maidens. It means, One whose man-part is never limp."

Cody opens his hand and the men come close to see what he holds. They stare intently into the palm of his hand at the tiny set of balls and cock made of silver that shines in the light of the lantern. Then they look to his face and think he's bleeding again as his tears track red on his cheeks.

■

That night, Eddie and Cody sleep on the floor of the cabin. The liquor is gone and both have had their share. Mike and the Drovers have passed to sleep and now the cabin smells of woodsmoke, stale beer and the remnants of supper.

Eddie lies awake, listening to Cody talk in his sleep, and thinks about going home.

He decides he hasn't been much of a man lately. The thought comes to him that way, quietly and sanely. He's come all this way and now he realizes it. Inside it gives a small place to rebuild, but not foolishly, not heady or too quickly, but slow and piece by piece.

"Things I know," he whispers. "I love Mary and the children. I will die or kill for them. I miss my father and always will. Things are not right in town. Someone is stealing and depending on me not to know."

Eddie touches his breast pocket, searching for a pen. He wants to write these words down just as he said them so he can have them forever, study them if his resolve weakens.

Cody speaks out again in sleep. Eddie reaches over to him and shakes him out of his dream.

"Eddie," Cody whispers, "is that you?"

"I'm here."

Cody rolls over to face him and Eddie can see how his face has gone to black with scrapes and scratches.

"I dreamt you were dead," Cody says.

"I'm here."

Cody presses a finger to his lips and makes a hush noise, then he tells Eddie all about Kay. He tells how he's been trying not to love her because of the man named Bender, but he can't help himself.

He tells Eddie he's always loved her because back then everything in the world was perfect only he didn't know it. It was before he went away into the woods and ruined his life with her. He tells Eddie that Kay is pregnant.

Eddie goes to speak again, but Cody hushes him and rolls away.

Eddie lies there in the darkness thinking about Cody's love for Kay and how a life can be thought of as perfect. Cody a father.

PART
FIVE

26

Cody gets nabbed again by the police. He's been to Freddy Clough's house. Leo Comeau was there with six GIQ's of home brew. Between Freddy's hard cider and Leo's brew, he'd gotten a pretty fair jag on. He'd been going like that ever since Pennsylvania.

The last thing he remembered was Leo telling him that after you reach a certain age the DT's won't kill you. A young man they'll kill but an older man will make it. Has to do with building up a tolerance.

When the police find Cody, he's still in Keene, parked beside a snowbank on Water Street, sleeping it off. He wakes when one of them raps the windshield with his nightstick. They've got him surrounded. He knows the jig is up, but what the fuck, he starts the engine, slams in the four-by and plows into the car in front of him, his high bumper crumpling back the hood, shearing off the top half of the radiator. The cop car lurches back as its doors pop open. He puts it in reverse and plows into the one behind him. The cops are yelling, going for their radios, going for their guns. Cody shifts again and swings out onto the street. His only thought is to cross the border into the land of Louis Poissant, land that was one time holy, land that at one time was outside of this world, and that's good enough for him. He knows it's where Kay is this very minute and it's where he's always wanted to be.

It isn't long before he's up on the highway making tracks for Inverawe. He thinks he's made it but even he can't outrun radio waves. In his rearview he sees them opening up the night with their lights and strobes, their Plymouths running hard over the boiler plate left by the snowplow.

"What a glorious night," he yells. He whoops and screams, beats the dash, wishes he had a gun because that's what outlaws have.

He makes the summit running hard under the moon, the blanket of stars, the Big and Little Dipper. He knows they're getting a kick out of this: Cody on the move, headed for a showdown. He makes gain on them, his oversized tires drumming the road, content as they are for any small purchase to keep them from skeeting into the puckerbrush.

He passes through East Inverawe and two more cars pick up the pursuit. He's been expecting them, expecting them to be troopers, the men in black boots, jodhpurs, round-brimmed hats and Sam Brown belts. He wouldn't mind so much getting nabbed by those guys. They're straight shooters.

He wings by and sees they aren't troopers. They're more of Keene's finest in hot pursuit. Cody keeps trucking. He can't let them catch him. He'll kill himself before he'll go to jail.

He makes a turn and begins hammering down a side road, making for the lacework of dirt lanes, one-track roads, farm roads, logging roads, roads never mapped.

He keeps going, stitching the snow with his tires, leaving tracks wherever he goes, and they follow, the policemen in their blues, babbling on their radios, fingering their shotguns that're racked toward the ceiling. They think they're God's patrol on the scent of the devil and they are good and pissed off by all those crumpled hoods and busted radiators left back in Keene.

Cody crests a hill. Another road and he'll be at Kay's. She'll tell him he's a big man, he's her hero. And Louis will come out with an eight-gauge, invoke the name of Paul Champagne and jack on both triggers, sending fountains of shot through the air. It'll be blue and red and yellow and light up the valley like fireworks in July. They'll all dance back to another time when life was good and clean, the good old days when you ate, drank, fucked and went to church on the Sabbath.

Cody begins to cry. The tears track the web of capillaries too close to his skin. His chest heaves and his body wracks with sobs as he realizes his foolishness while at the same time begging that he be allowed a dispensation, begging that he be whisked out of place and time and set free to stride the map, to rest the clock of time.

In front he can see the yellow beacon of a plow sweeping the black pine forest. It's the Doody brothers' ten-wheeler laden with salt, tons of it, tons of truck and plows and salt going ponderously down the road pushing a mouth of snow. He steps on the gas and watches that truck grow huge as he drives into the back of it.

■

Mary stands abruptly and then the scanner crackles with news of the accident. Eddie comes out of his chair and she gets between him and the kitchen.

"You're not going out there," she says. "You're going to stay here with us."

"I have to go."

"For God's sakes, can't you see what's happening to us?"

"You mean to me. You mean what's happening to me," Eddie says, slapping himself in the chest.

"You. Yes, you. You walk around like a dead man."

Eddie goes to speak, but he can't. The words that come into his head sound weak and stupid and then he says, "I was a son and now I'm a father."

"I know," Mary says. "You were a son and now you're a father."

"You don't know and I don't know and that's just about all of it."

Eddie leaves the room, gets his coat and goes out the door.

■

When Cody wakes, it's to the sound of his pickup being ripped apart by the jaws of life. He can see Eddie Ryan and Thad and the Doody brothers working to get him out. They're surrounded by the boys in blue still chomping at the bit to get their hands on him, hoping death hasn't deprived them. He figures it ain't heaven he's come to.

The hydraulic pump whirs as the spreader crushes the door.

Eddie pushes Thad aside and crawls in. He gets Cody's hand and they look at each other, then Eddie goes to speak and someone gets him by his feet and drags him out. A policeman takes his place, makes Cody take a Breathalyzer and reads him his rights.

"Jesus Christ," Eddie yells. "He could be dying in there. Get the fuck out of there."

He grabs the policeman's legs and then two more cops grab him and shuttle him aside. Thad and the Doody brothers step up.

"You let him go and let us work," Thad says, "or we'll throw down right here and have it out."

The cop squirrels his way out of the pickup and tells the others it's okay, he's got what he needs.

"Get the column, Dick," Thad says.

Dick Doody sets the spreader and raises the column. Eddie gets back inside and goes over Cody's body, touching limbs for feel, asking him questions about what day it is, what his name is.

"Just back out," Cody tells him, "and when I get out of here I'll tell you what day it is."

As soon as Cody is standing they surround him and cuff him.

"He goes in the rescue truck," Thad says.

"It's his choice."

"You know it's not his choice. He goes in the rescue truck."

Without another word they hustle him into a car and head out for Keene, leaving the volunteers standing by the road in the snow and salt, ripped steel and broken glass.

■

Eddie Ryan drives the rescue truck back to the firehouse while Thad and the Doody brothers chain up Cody's truck and haul it slowly back into town. Marie Paquette is at the firehouse. She's wearing an immense overcoat. It drags on the ground while the cuffs hang to her knees.

"Dome wants you to come to the house," she says to Eddie.

They go together, passing under the streetlights, their steps muffled by the new snow. Marie opens the front door and goes in.

She sheds the coat in the kitchen. Underneath she's in her robe. Eddie follows her to the weight room, where Dome is on the bench, pressing weights toward the ceiling, his bare chest blue with new tats and bristling with sweat. He brackets the weights and sits up. Marie towels him off.

"Go down and get him," Dome says. "I called in one of the old girl's markers. You better hurry because they'll work him over if they get the chance."

■

Eddie and the judge stand at the front desk waiting for Cody to be brought out. A policeman is telling the judge they were only trying to help when they saw him parked on Water Street. They thought he was dead.

"I understand," the judge says, and then he takes Eddie aside. "I suggest he leave the state for a while. He was carrying two licenses. His own and one for a G. R. Trimble, who the truck is registered to. He didn't steal it, did he?"

"No."

"I assume you know this G. R. Trimble?"

"Yes," Eddie says.

"This is a big pill to swallow," the judge says, "but then again, she was a pretty big woman. I think we'll be okay."

The sound of doors opening ends their conversation. Cody is brought up, flanked by two policemen. Eddie takes him by the arm and they leave together.

A sliver of light comes in the east as Eddie and Cody make the drive to Inverawe.

Mary wakes again and it's still dark. She looks at the clock and sees it's six. She wonders if Eddie will come home. She's afraid to look. She's afraid to move around for fear of waking the children, so she snaps on a light and begins making a list of things to take for their trip to Florida, but every time she goes to write, she stops and stares down at the page.

■

A man, a woman and two children sit in Fay's Country Kitchen in Carlisle, PA. They left New Hampshire at midnight on Friday and now they're breaking open blueberry muffins. The man has just left behind him most of a year of wreckage and he's got another month to go. The woman has left behind the echo of a day's fight with her husband, and to her it's the story of her life to come and right now she doesn't want to think about it, but the angry words are still in her head, still swarming in the air.

"Cody is going with you," he'd told her. "He needs to get away from here to Florida."

"Let him buy a bus ticket."

"I can't go anyways. I have to stay here and work."

"You're a traitor."

"There are things I can't explain."

"Well, don't ask us to wait around while you figure them out."

The man and woman nurse cups of coffee while the children drink milk, wanting nothing more than to be wrapped in blankets again, asleep in the back seat, lulled by the thrum of the tires on the highway, the engine noise white in their heads.

There are toys in Fay's Country Kitchen, antique toys, dolls and trucks and trains and strollers. They're the toys offered up by a time past. They're made of steel and iron, all heavy with sharp points and throat-size pieces that can break off, and their paint contains lead. It slowly poisoned the toy makers, as they were in the habit of touching the tips of their natural-hair paintbrushes to their tongues. It poisoned the children who peeled it off and ate it because lead paint is sweet like candy, and once it gets in you, it wants more of itself.

The place is filled with students from the college and townspeople, those able to enjoy Saturday-morning breakfast with friends. When they bother, they look at the man and woman, think how odd they look together, think how the two must be married and how she must lead a life of misery with a man like him who isn't even smart enough to wipe the egg yolk out of his beard.

They look at the man and woman and write their lives in their heads. They think, Maybe she's a social worker. No, they're married and they're traveling. He's a vet and fucked up and she's in love with him. Maybe he's really good in the sack. The kids would prove that. They're beautiful, but then again all kids are beautiful, beautiful and innocent, innocent and sad. Maybe he's a vet like an animal vet. No, he doesn't look the part.

They look road-weary, tired from their travels, yet somehow

passing through the shock of life. Maybe we should call the police. Maybe someone has been kidnapped. Maybe there's mind control involved. Whatever it is, we'd like to close the book on this one. They don't fit. They can't be read into our lives. They aren't real to me so they aren't real. I can't write them the way I want to read them.

"It's not you," she says. "It's me. I just don't know what I want anymore. Nothing, I guess. I guess I don't want anything at all."

"You've gotten a pretty full dose of life."

"I know and it isn't over yet. What will you do?"

"Get a license first. Then I'll get out of your hair."

Mary touches his hand. She wants to say no. It's not like that at all. But she can't say it. She wants him to get a license and drive away forever. When she left, she'd called Eddie a drunk and a coward on top of everything else and meant it. She said she wouldn't come back.

"Fuck," she says, "I'm sorry. Things will work out. I know they will." She pats his hand and smiles. "Hey, no rest for the wicked. Spruce up. This too shall pass."

Little Eddie has learned to pee in the pot. He tells his sister when he has to go and she takes him into the ladies' room. One day he'll want to marry her and be sad for a while when he learns he can't.

When they come out Eileen leads him past the tables. A girl says hello, and she stops to say, "This is my brother and we're going to Florida. My father couldn't come because he has to take care of dead people."

The girl and her friends laugh.

"What does he do with the dead people?" the girl asks.

"He's a funeral director. He embalms them."

"Oh," the girl says, and then they all laugh again because they think she's cute.

"That's Cody with my mom. He can walk on water."

The girls look over and Mary smiles at them. They think she is more beautiful than she thinks. Their faint hearts wish they could have a life as exotic as the one they've made up for her.

"We're from New Hampshire," Eileen says. "My daddy couldn't come. Cody's driving us. He's the best driver in the world. Do they let you play with these toys?"

"No, but it would be fun, wouldn't it?"

"We never have fun," Eileen says, putting on a face. "We get beaten if we try to have fun."

"No, you don't," a different girl says, but she's convinced they do. She's a psychology major.

Mary stands and calls the kids over. She helps them into their coats while Cody pays the bill. She ushers the kids out the door and when Cody turns he panics. He feels the eyes on him, eyes over coffee cups, eyes over shoulders, eyes from bowed heads, eyes from the dolls.

He doesn't know what else to do so he waves and some people wave back, the some who think he must be a nice enough guy or really dangerous. God knows he's got a good-looking woman with him and two beautiful kids.

■

Eddie thinks, Those few hours after someone leaves to go on a long trip are like death, real death, not easy like the final irrevocable kind. You stand at the depot or in the terminal or at the front door and it's as if you are the hub of a wheel and there are long spokes going out so you might never touch what is the wheel. It's how you're a wheel on a stagecoach and always moving forward, but on the record of film it looks like you're always moving backwards.

Eddie has taken to stopping and standing in one place, wherever he is, on the street, in the grocery or at the post office. When he does, he waits until the traffic of people adjusts to form easy continuous patterns around him. Carts to his right and left, pedestrians coming to his corner and going off in all directions. Then calmly, as if he were going for a pack of cigarettes or a ball-point pen, or maybe a gun, he reaches inside his down jacket and thumps at his heart, looks around and thumps it again with his fist, harder each time, until he feels it pounding back at him, knocking at the back of his breastbone. It's the size of a fist and it's good at what it does. His fist and the fist of his heart punch away at each other like children in the schoolyard.

He gets himself out on that edge a little further each time and then he walks again, wheeling his cart, making the crosswalk or sending out a letter.

These are letters he mails to himself every day. He also writes letters to Mary, Cody, Eileen and Little Eddie. He sends them postcards too. They are postcards of the Church Hill Meeting

House, the Town Hall, Steam Town, the Old Man in the Mountain, Mount Monadnock, the White Mountains. He finds postcards with snow, all with snow, and writes smart-ass things on them like Wish you were here, Having fun on the slopes and Look what you're missing.

Letters to Mary are love letters. He feels he has to win her back, court her. He writes sexy letters bordering on the pornographic. He tells her about her body and what he'll do to it when he gets his hands on her again. He tells her he hasn't had a drink since she left and won't ever have one again. He's gotten out his father's book, *Twenty-Four Hours a Day*, one of the only things his father left him. He writes, "I read it every day to stay sober each twenty-four hours because if I don't take that first drink today, I'll never take it because it's always today." He doesn't tell her this, but he also reads the twelve steps of AA each day. He gets through them all except No. 8. When he gets to 8 he reads, "make a list of all persons who harmed and make them willing to amend their ways." It's not the way it goes, but he can't read it any other way.

The letters he mails to himself are the longest. For him the postmarks are a copyright, a guarantee that his words will be his through this life and fifty years beyond. It's something he thinks he needs because right now all his best work is gone or buried and it never bothered him until now.

When Eddie gets home he unloads the groceries from the hearse. He sets the bags on the counter, letting them slump against each other to keep from tumbling over. Buying food is something he's always taken great pleasure in. He likes to buy nonperishables in bulk, those things he knows they'll use a lot of. He does this without system, without checking the prices. Today he's bought fifteen cans of tuna fish and fifty cans of cat food. He has eight jars of spaghetti sauce and ten boxes of instant chicken soup. He thinks of it as a hedge against inflation at the very least.

One of the bags is soggy. In the bottom is an empty jug of Step Saver floor cleaner. He realizes he's been leaving a trail of blue soap behind him, probably miles of it. His first inclination is to find the irony in this. He smiles and curses himself for having such an old sad habit, being drawn by the magnet of irony, the maggot of irony, a sugar-tit for the mind, the gauge and veil of life we now all mistake for life.

He gets the groceries put away and goes out to the mailbox. He forgets his sunglasses and again he's blinded by the hot glare coming off the ice and snow that are covering the land. Even the black asphalt of the highway is white and shining. Eddie opens the small door and squints in. The bundle of mail is held together by a rubber band. He pulls it out and tucks it under his arm, then goes back inside, all the while holding a hand up to shade his eyes.

Sitting at the rolltop desk, still wearing his down jacket, he waits and waits for his sight to come back. He props his elbows on the table and holds his head, opening and closing his eyes, wondering if maybe this time it's gone for good, wondering if he'll ever see again.

To kill time he thinks about death. It's either the third or the fiftieth time today. One or the other. The other or even more. He lets himself laugh at this one and then he begins the business of forgetting everything he's ever learned about it. He goes through the list of what he knows about it, deleting each topic along the way, and then finally he gets down to himself and begins the task of forgetting who he is because he realizes that alls he knows is a lot of stuff about death and it's all wrong.

"There is a difference," he says, his eyes still closed, "between activity and stillness. There is energy in the activity. Energy moves the activity and energy can be neither created nor destroyed. Yet it goes somewhere. So I guess the question is, Where the fuck does the energy go? To death's hideout."

Eddie thinks he hears a knock at the door, so he stops talking with himself and listens. It is a knock, steel on steel, the hinged horseshoe on his door against its plate. Eddie opens the door and it's Dick Doody's wife. She has two jars of pickled beets. Mason jars to go on the shelf with everything else.

"I'm sorry to disturb you, Eddie. I didn't know you had company. I just brought by a little something for you people."

"Thank you, Marlene. You shouldn't have, but thank you."

"Are you all right, Eddie? Your eyes are almost shut."

"Yes, don't mind me. I wasn't thinking and I was looking at the sun after I got the mail."

"You watch that," she says. "You can burn the retinas in your eyes. A friend of my cousin's had his contact lenses welded right to his eyeballs for doing just such a thing. Skin cancer too. He got skin cancer."

"Thank you, Marlene. Thank you."

"You take care of yourself," she says, reaching out to him and squeezing his elbow. "They'll come back soon and everything will be fine."

Eddie stares at her through the slits of his eyes. He watches her back away from him and then turn and go down the steps to her car. After she goes he holds his forehead with his left hand, pushing at it until his head is back and his eyes are drawn open. He stands there waiting to pass out because alls he can see is the bright shapeless sun coming at him head-on and before he knows it, it's there and it's shooting through him again and again, streaming past his eyeballs and going off in his head like big guns inside a canyon.

When Eddie wakes up, Max is lying on his chest. They are chin to chin and Max is purring so neatly Eddie thinks he must have a machine inside his throat. At first he thinks he still can't see but then he realizes it's nighttime and he's stretched out on the porch. He's cold and the door has closed behind, locking itself shut.

He sets Max to one side and stands up, working his legs stiffly like a bird. The house is black inside, blacker than the night he finds himself in. Outside the night is blue and the stars pulse in the sky, flickering on and off in the celestial winds. Then he knows they're flickering because the wind is up and on the move. It's carrying the snow into drifts and shapes.

For a moment he thinks he'll stay right where he is, spend the night outside curled up in the warm snow. He did it once before when he was a freshman in college. He'd fallen in love with a girl that first year and after her exams at Christmastime he put her on a plane to fly home. When he got back to the dorm, he took a fifth of Jim Beam and went for a walk.

In those first few hours after she left, he thought he'd die, he thought he'd like to die. It was such a funny notion. He knew he should've been studying for a chemistry test, but he was filled with nothingness and as he was already being torn between being a poet or a doctor, he decided to be a poet and do what poets do so he kept walking and sipping, every once in a while checking his pulse until finally he couldn't feel it anymore. He didn't know if it was because he'd lost it or because he'd lost the touch to find it.

He came to St. Catherine's, lost in a run-down part of town. There was a life-size crèche, Mary, Joseph and the Wise Men around the crib of Jesus in the stable at Bethlehem. He went up to Joseph, thinking it a poetical thing to do, and kissed him on his plywood face. They were about the same size. For Mary he had to bend over a little to kiss her and when he did he saw where the white of her robes had been painted over to hide the words FUCK YOU someone had spray-painted on her body, the black shadow of those words still faintly coming through. He began to cry softly and then without control, feeling sorry for himself because he thought the words were meant for him and she was forced to bear them, and then he chastised himself for again being such a fool, a condition he thought he might never escape.

Behind the manger were piles of straw. It's there where an old priest found him in the morning still stinking drunk from the night before and well preserved by it. The priest took him inside and made instant coffee on a hot plate. Eddie guzzled it down, scalding his mouth and throat so badly he couldn't speak for a long time and then when he did it came out in a squeak.

"I'm lost," he told the priest.

"You're at St. Catherine's," the priest told Eddie, touching his hand.

"I know," Eddie said, "but I'm lost."

"No, you're not," the priest said. "You're here with me."

It wasn't long afterward that he joined the Marines.

■

Eddie tramps through the snow, rounding the house to find an unlocked window, but he doesn't have any luck. The back door is locked too and the bulkhead is drifted in so he goes to the garage for a snow shovel. He'll unbury the bulkhead and try that.

The bulkhead is on the side of the house where the wind drives the snow. It's a new one made of steel. He works slowly in the light that comes from the moon and stars. He has to start digging a path from twenty feet out because the snow is drifted so high. Cutting square blocks whose sides are as big as the shovel, he stacks them to his right and left, making a path bigger than he'll need but wanting to do it right in case somebody dies and needs to get into the preparation room.

The closer to the house he gets, the higher the walls of snow become. They grow as high as he can reach, so he has to either throw the snow over the top or carry it back to where the walls are lower.

When he's almost to the house he drives his shovel into the snow to lift the block he's cut and strikes the steel bulkhead. He hears the *thunk* and at the same time feels the vibration of it quivering into his forearms. He works more carefully, scraping it clean and then resting.

It's only now that he's done, he decides he should've broken in through a storm window or at least tried to pick the lock or jimmy the back door. Max sits at the beginning of the snow corridor as if to confirm what Eddie is thinking.

"You asshole," Eddie says, throwing a snowball at him and missing.

Max watches it pass by his left and yawns. Then he gets up and wanders back over the drifts, leaving small paw prints on the surface and disappearing into the night.

Eddie tries the bulkhead, but it doesn't budge. He knows it's not locked because the latch is bent. He goes to the garage to get the propane torch, but he finds the cylinder is empty. His clothes are wet with sweat from the work he's done and the breeze that rustles in the trees ever so slightly is now chilling him through to the skin. He could hike down to Doody's house or go ahead and break a window, but he doesn't.

He goes to his workbench and empties out a coffee can that holds assorted nuts and bolts. Then taking the five-gallon container of gasoline, he goes back round to the bulkhead. The first thing he does is practice.

Eddie pours a little more gas into the coffee can each time, sending larger and larger balls of flame into the night sky. The *whoopf* of the explosion becomes louder and louder each time; the hole in the snow gets deeper and its sloped sides black with carbon.

When he's had enough of this, he takes a full can over to the bulkhead and lets some trickle down the seam where the two steel doors are joined. He works quickly because the gas evaporates into the air. He does around the edges and then splashes what left on the red steel faces.

While backing up he strikes a match and the first things to go are his gloves and then the snow around him lights up. Later he thinks if it wasn't for the explosion of the gas in the seam he could've burned to death.

He's thrown back down the corridor and into the snowbank, where his body makes the impression of a man with outstretched arms and legs spread.

Eddie starts to laugh. He knows he's okay. Down the corridor he can see the bulkhead yawning open, still on its hinges. The siding is scorched in some places and the first-floor window is shades of silver, gray and blue. He shakes himself off and goes down the stairs into the black cellar.

■

Eddie begins his death thoughts again. Death is the opposite of love, not life, he tells himself. It has to be looked at in just that way because love is something not everyone has, whereas life is. We can't think about losing life because it's something none of us have done, but we've all lost love before. So death is the opposite of love and yes, it could even work the other way around, love is the opposite of death.

Eddie sips at his coffee and then holds that warm hand to his forehead. It's the first time he notices his eyebrows are bent and crinkled and in some places ten or a dozen hairs are melted together in a knot.

He thinks about the girl he loved so much, the one whose leaving made him decide between being a poet or a doctor if only for a year or two. He thinks about how right now it would be nice to call her up and talk to her. Doing so would give her reason to maybe reconsider some of her own choices in life. At the least it would give her a story to tell her new friends, a story that would be good for a season of conversations. It would only take a few phone calls to track her down. He could call information, the alumni office. They have all that stuff on file. Eddie smiles and thinks, Wouldn't it be nice if information could provide all it claimed?

He sits down at the rolltop desk. The mail received and the letters to be sent sit side by side in front of him. He picks up both stacks and works them together, shuffles them facedown like a deck of cards. He writes on the back of the first one, *a gathering of poems about death by Eddie Ryan.* What a good title, he thinks. The poems will be like flowers or children on a playground, all coming together yet separate in their own way, separate and alone like wheat or seashells.

He turns the envelope over. It's one to be mailed. It's a letter he's written to Eileen. It's another page in a story he's writing to her about an island and a lost tribe that never wants to be found. They live off the fat of the land and say kind things to each other whenever possible. They seek out opportunities to say how much they love each other.

Eddie worries a little bit because he doesn't know how he'll finish the story. For certain she'll not be content with the tribe staying lost forever. She'll think they are like those stupes on *Gilligan's Island*. Everyone on Eddie's island is related and by now she knows enough about love and death to wonder how they will survive. He decides in his next letter to have them find the fountain of youth. No matter what, she'll ask him, if they are truly lost, how come he knows about them?

The next letter is to Mary, one he hasn't mailed yet. It's the seventh, and in this one he apologizes for killing himself. It was about all he had left to say. That one he sets aside. A letter to Cody turns up next. He can't remember what he's written. It's information either on late-nineteenth-century funeral practices or on wax reconstructions warranted by such things as lacerations, decapitations, mold, skin slip or gunshot. They seem to be the things Cody's interested in.

He goes through the letters looking for one *from* Mary. He gets to the last one and sees it's addressed to him and the return address is his also. He can't remember what he's written. He can't remember if he wrote it before he wrote Mary's letter. He works hard to figure it out. And then he starts to cry because he doesn't know if he wrote it before or after the seventh one. He doesn't know if right now he's alive or dead.

He walks through the dark house feeling his way as he goes. He starts at a dress hung on a door, thinking it's a person. He crawls in bed with his clothes on and lies there with the covers to his chin. Then comes a thunder sound. It's the sound of snow coming off the slate roof and he can see ghosts of it pass by the windows on the way to the ground.

He decides that in the morning he'll bring Cody's pistol into the house. He'll keep it on the dresser beside the bed.

27

One by one the women move their beach chairs down to the water's edge. They sit just inside the wet gray line before the waves' last tumble; where they break, then charge up and around the women's thighs, surging to foam at their backs.

"Look at them," Cody says. "They have their legs open. I'll bet they're getting the thrill of their lives."

It's the second time this year he's seen the ocean, the second time in his life. He's been here a week and has yet to go near it.

"Jesus, Cody," Mary says. "Of all the things to say. So what if they are?"

Eileen comes to the blanket. She's impressed with having her legs back. She walks as if her feet are flippers, letting them fold and drag at the sand with each step. She thinks she has never enjoyed walking so much. She puts her hands on her hips and looks at them, but they can't see her face because it's early and the sun is behind her, its light tangled in her hair.

"Is he going to sleep all day?"

She's talking about her brother. He's under the umbrella on the blanket beside Cody.

"He'll be up soon," Mary says.

"I was just thinking. I wonder how much the ocean weighs."

Mary thinks it's a good question and tells her so. She says to Eileen, "Well, how can we figure it out?"

Eileen plays at thinking about this. She's already come up with some ways to figure it out that she knows won't work, but she offers them up anyway.

"We could put it on a scale," she says, "like a bathroom."

"Wouldn't that be something," Cody says, letting a handful of sand run through his fingers. "A scale big enough to hold the ocean." He thinks more about the weight of the ocean.

"A clue," Eileen says, "give me a clue to help me."

"Gallon of water weighs eight pounds the world around."

Cody says this holding his hands out and cupped as if he has a gallon of water in them.

"It rhymes," Eileen says. "Pound and round. That's easy. You figure out how many gallons of water are in the ocean and then times it by eight."

"Good one," Mary says. "Now how do you figure out how many gallons of water there are in the ocean?"

She thinks some more and then says, "It's the same problem I started with. It's like trying to figure out how many pounds there are in the ocean. That's not a good clue."

"Sure it is," Cody says. "There's fifty gallons in a fifty-gallon drum, there's ten gallons in a washtub and five gallons in a five-gallon pail."

"So."

"Well, I happen to know how big those things are. Ten gallons is eighty pounds and fifty gallons is four hundred pounds. But you have to subtract for the weight of the container."

"So."

"We just have to figure it by barrels or tubs or pails and then we got her."

"You're a tub head, Cody."

"Cody, don't tease her," Mary says. "Eileen, don't talk to Cody like that."

"No, I get it now. If we can figure out how big it is, we can figure out how much it weighs."

"Right," Mary says.

"So how big is the ocean?"

"How should I know?" Cody says. "We could find out how big it is across the top, but the bottom isn't even. There are mountains, canyons and valleys."

Eileen makes a kid sound that means, No way. Then she says, "Tell me again, Cody, how you outraced the coppers."

■

Eddie sits at the rolltop desk. Cody and Mary and the kids have been gone for a week. He hasn't had a drink in all that time and knows he's okay for now whether he has a problem or not. He's come to believe in the Serenity Prayer. He recites it out loud. "God grant me the serenity to accept the things I cannot change, the courage to change the things I can and the wisdom to know the difference." Also he's okay because no one has died these past few days.

That done, he's ready for the mail, one letter at a time to see if there's one from Mary, but first the junk mail.

He reads each flier carefully, wanting to put off the end of his search as long as he can in case he's met with disappointment. He reads about the price of milk and canned vegetables, meat and bread. He reads about snowblowers, snow tires and space heaters. There's a brochure for a new hearse, a superior "Elite," built on Cadillac's Fleetwood 6C290 commercial chassis. It has thirty-eight inches of rear-door height and over forty inches of headroom.

Big deal, Eddie thinks, I use trailer trucks in my business.

The first envelope he gets contains a brochure on Fred Hunter's Historical Funeral Museum in Hollywood, Florida. Fred has an ice-chest coffin, antique hearses, and nineteenth-century family funeral wreaths woven of human hair. He has a 1932 Henney hearse, a side loader with blue interior. It was custom-built for the Kick and Nice Funeral Home in Philadelphia, opened in 1761, the nation's first.

There's a 1922 casket made of inch-thick glass. It weighs fifteen hundred pounds and flattened the wheels of nearly every hearse it rode in. It also tended to tip over when the lid was up. There are woven reed caskets and human hair jewelry, necklaces and brooches made of intricately plaited strands of hair. Eddie wonders if Mary and Cody will go there and tour the museum. It sounds interesting. He hopes they don't.

He holds the next envelope, touches the Bellefonte, PA postmark. He runs a finger in the seam and opens it. Inside is a greeting card. It's of the work that Cody put a bullet through, only now it's sitting in a plaza in Seattle. The sculptor has enclosed a review. The back of the card says something ecumenical, all the best for the holiday season, and it's signed. The review says the work is about freedom, flight and escape. It's about exposure and concealment. It seems impregnable, yet vulnerable and no conventional way of approaching is the answer . . . a real freedom in a new postminimal, almost reconstructive way.

As Eddie finishes reading the review, the phone rings and he jumps.

"Daddy, it's me."

"Hello, how are you?"

"When we were at the beach we tried to figure out how much the ocean weighed, but we couldn't. Do you know how to figure it out?"

Eddie wants to tell her everything he knows, everything he's ever learned in life, but he can only think that the saline content of human blood is the same as that of the ocean. Not a bad start.

"Cody says there are mountains and canyons."

"Well, he's right. You'd have to know trigonometry and topology and there's a new science for measuring shapes in nature. The important thing is not figuring it out, but knowing how to figure it out."

Eddie can hear Eileen yell to someone in the room. She says, "Daddy says there's a new science."

"The hell you say." It's Cody's voice. He sounds cheated. He doesn't like the idea of a new science.

"Is your mother there?"

"Yes, she's fine."

"I love you. I love you all."

"We love you too."

Good-bye, they say, and hang up.

■

Little Eddie is already down for the count by the time the television is shut off.

Eileen puts on one of her father's T-shirts. The collar is stretched enough to drop past her shoulders and off her body, but she insists on wearing it. She wears it slung close to her neck on one side, while letting the other hang. Its bottom rides at her ankles.

Mary tucks her in and reads to her until she falls asleep. Again they've forgotten to say their prayers together, something Eileen wanted to start doing, so Mary whispers them silently, breaking the words out into the air close to her daughter's face. Words get charged, she thinks, and gain a life of their own; sometimes between two people they get too charged and the life can be a bad one.

She goes down the hall to Cody's room. She knocks on the door, but he doesn't answer. She figures he must be asleep too, so she slips quietly out the front door and down to the beach. The sand is still warm and far out she can hear the water, its roar muted in the darkness and distance. She goes to it and wades in, letting it lap at her ankles as she walks the shoreline.

It doesn't seem to fit, the sound still coming from way out and the quiet feel at her ankles. She cuffs her pants legs high and lets herself go deeper until the water wets them too, but she doesn't care.

She allows herself to think about something Eileen said earlier, about how easy it would be if you let yourself, to just keep walking and go all the way to France or Africa. If she did that, she'd be dead in a matter of minutes and that's funny to her.

It would be a good time to cry, she decides, but right now she can't. She doesn't know if it's from baking in the sun all day and being too dry for tears. All day she sweat at her brow and under her arms and down her chest and she decides those were her tears, those were the tears she'd have back now if she could.

"It's nice they came the way they did," she says out loud. "They just left me, leaving through different places."

And she's thankful for this, no wracking chest, no ache in the arms and shoulders. That's okay for now.

She walks a half mile, turns around and makes her way back to the condos. When she hits the asphalt and crosses the drive, she looks up and sees Cody in the sky, above her head. She holds the back of her hand to her mouth and closes her eyes. She then opens them to see him float through the air and disappear into the night. The next thing she hears is the sound of him piercing the water of the swimming pool. She laughs and goes over to the aqua-blue water and looks down into its concrete basin. She sees him inside it, his arms awkwardly sweeping out in front of him. He's cupping water in his hands and shoving it aside to keep himself moving.

When he breaks the surface she's standing there laughing. In one smooth motion he rises up from the water and stands beside her. He cocks his head and stares at her and then without saying a word he picks her up and throws her in.

When she surfaces, he's disappeared, and she wonders for a moment if he'd even been there or if she'd thrown herself into the water, clothes and all.

She goes back to the condo and stands at the door. To the right of it the light comes through the curtains of Cody's room. Letting the water pool at her bare feet, she looks to make sure no one is there. She opens the door, looks around again, then shucks her jeans and pulls her sweater over her head. She balls them up, gives them a squeeze, then ducks inside. She drops the clothes in the tub and towels herself dry. Taking another towel, she fashions a turban around her wet head, goes to her room and dresses and grabs a pair of scissors.

Next door the lights are now off. She knocks softly, turning the doorknob as she does, and goes inside. He's lying on the bed in front of her. He's wearing pants and he's barefoot. The room is blue except for the glow from his cigarette.

"Did you throw me in the pool?" she asks.

"Of course I did. Who else would it have been?"

"Why did you leave?"

"I don't know," he says, laughing. "It just seemed like the thing to do."

"You know, Mr. Cody. You are a deceptive person."

"You mean I'm a liar?"

"I have been watching you these past few days and you are not the man you seem to be."

"Who is it you think I am?"

"First of all, you're a young man. Much younger than I imagined. When I first saw you I couldn't tell how old you were, twenty-five, thirty-five, forty-five. There's something else. Something strange about you I can't figure out. Come here."

Cody doesn't move at first but then he gets up from the bed and goes to her. She leads him into the bathroom and sits him down on the edge of the tub. When she flips on the lights they both go blind for a moment and then they can see.

"Move up here," she says, tapping the toilet seat.

Cody sits himself on the seat next to the sink. Mary takes a towel from the rack and wraps it around the front of his chest, making sure it's tucked under his chin. She takes his beard in her left hand and squeezes it, the end of it coming out the bottom of her fist. With her right hand she cuts it away close to his chin.

She holds that first handful of beard, not knowing what to do with it, and then she sets it down in the sink next to her hip. She cuts more, letting the clippings fall into his lap, letting them collect on the backs of her hands. When she's cut as close as she can with the scissors, she sets them down, turns on the water and makes a soapy lather with her hands. She then applies it to his face. She gets the razor he uses to keep his neck shaved and finishes the job.

When his skin is smooth, she steps back and looks at him. She opens her mouth as if to speak, but she doesn't say anything.

She takes his hand and tugs at it, letting him know she wants him to follow. At the bed she stops and goes to his closet for a shirt, making him put it on, and then she has him lie down, arranging him on his back with his hands on his chest. She then lies down beside him such that she can get an arm over the top of his head and her hand onto his shoulder.

"You look like me," she whispers.

Cody doesn't say anything. He can't tell the nature of this woman. He only knows he feels weak inside, soft at the joints. It's as if he's been felling big stands of timber all day, lugging his weight and the pounds of a heavy saw, and now the day is truly done and he's in the embrace of his own tiredness, his own warmth earned out after all that work.

"You're a young man," she says.

"Yes, I guess I am."

"Younger than me."

"I don't know. Maybe."

Mary pats him on the shoulder as if he were a child.

"Who is Kay?"

Cody doesn't hesitate. He tells the whole story as best he knows it. He says nobody who works with their hands wears wedding rings because they can get you killed in one way or another. He tells her, She was a woman and I was just a kid.

"That's a nice story," she says. "I'll tell you one."

Mary tells how after her father died, she was in the attic going through boxes. She came across a box of *Playboy* magazines. Some of them went all the way back to the fifties. As she thumbed through them she could see that her father had pulled all the centerfolds. At the bottom of the box was another box and that was where all the women were. He'd taken scissors and glue and carefully rearranged their bodies. He exchanged heads and legs and breasts and sometimes only a hand or hair. He'd cut out only a pair of shoes on one and put them on another.

"He must have used an X-Acto knife on some," she says. "It was really amazing. He must have taken a long time to do it. I never told my mother. I just sent them all to the dump. Sometimes I think it's funny. Sometimes I don't."

When she finishes telling the story, Cody wants to tell her it's no big deal what her father did.

"Men have secrets because . . ." and he can't finish the thought because he doesn't know why. He wants to think up some other truths, try his hand at it. He wants to tell her he never really learned to swim, just jumps in and takes his chances, but can't bring himself to do that either, so he pretends to be asleep because he knows that's what stories told at this time of night are supposed to do to you.

Mary falls for it. She kisses him on the forehead and leaves the room to look in on her children before she turns in for the night.

The next day on the beach, Cody watches the women. He thinks of them as the summer girls, whether they are six or sixty. He watches them do their ballerina walks to the surf. They pat their tummies, smooth down their backsides and pull up their tops.

Eileen comes by from her wanderings along the coast of Florida. She hasn't got anybody to play with. She tries to work on her mother. She's on the blanket with Little Eddie. They're having fun just taking turns at lying on top of each other.

"Come on, Ma. Let's go swimming."

"We've been swimming all morning and right now I'm just too pooped to pop."

"I'll go," Cody says, standing and taking off his flannel shirt.

Eileen and Mary whoop with joy. All week long they've been trying to coax him in but he hasn't budged.

"Get some lotion on," Mary says. "My God, look at that man. I'm blinded by the light. It's getting dark. All the sun is getting drawn into his skin."

She throws the bottle of suntan lotion his way and between the two of them, Eileen and Cody, they get his body greased with sunscreen, then Eileen bolts for the water with Cody behind, not sure if this is all that good an idea.

When he gets close enough, Eileen splashes him. He goes in after her, up to his waist and that's okay, because it's plenty deep enough for her.

"Throw me, Cody. Throw me in the air."

Cody picks her up under her arms and lets her back down again to her feet.

"No," she yells. "Throw me, really throw me."

He picks her up and does it again, tossing her toward the shore. She keeps yelling to him.

"More, more. Do it again, Cody. Do it again."

They're having fun. Each time Cody picks her up and tosses her with the waves, catching her as she's washed back to him. She's laughing and bobbing, her head going under, then bursting through the foamy water as it flows back to him.

Cody is laughing too. She looks like a mink or a beaver breaching the surface, her girl body long and thin, made to move through water. Each time she comes up it sheds from her skin in a clear wash. She rubs her eyes and slaps at her cheeks. He does the same, feeling the skin on his face.

Working a little deeper, he casts her forward, and as she comes back he misses her leg and her hand and goes to grab her bathing suit. He gets a shoulder strap. It breaks off in his hand and she goes scuttling past him in the undertow. He turns and flails the water, sweeping back handfuls of foam to find her, but he can't find her and he's in a panic because he's lost her. He pounds at the water as if it were fire and then she pops up, standing shoulder-deep and laughing.

"You missed me," she says, the words teasing, taunting.

He gets to her and lifts her up, high on his chest, and holds her tight. It's all he can do to keep from shaking.

"I ripped your suit," he says.

"That's okay," she tells him. "We can sew it."

They go up to the blanket, where Mary is setting out sandwiches.

"I'm going in for a while," Cody says. "Too much sun."

He leaves them on the beach and goes back to the condo. He picks up the phone and calls Eddie Ryan and gives him hell, tells him what an asshole he's been, what assholes they've both been, and how they have to start working harder at life, even though they already work harder at it than most.

He says, It's like a little foreign car needs a little maintenance once in a while but the heavy machinery needs it all the time.

Afterward, Eddie sits out on the porch in the cold and sun. Max the cat is on the floor at his feet. He's lying on his back licking his belly. Eddie knows he can do the things Cody said.

He told Eddie, You should love that woman enough to fit her in your mouth. Hold her there.

Max rolls over, corkscrewing his spine inside his body so his hind legs go one way and his face another, as if to defy Eddie's sense of what he can and can't do.

He told Eddie, If you don't feel that way toward the woman, then you can't be a man. Could you die for her? If she said, Die for me, could you do it? Could you just die? No gun, no rope, just die.

Eddie has a feeling he is just now better than himself, better than he really is. He knows he can die for her and that gives him joy.

I can do it, Cody said, I can just die. I can will it. I can will my own death. That's the thing about love.

Eddie thinks of the way she has of kissing his shirt when they dance, her soft lips pressing into him. Then she looks up at him, smiles and lets her face go against his chest again.

The phone inside starts ringing. He nudges Max with the toe of his boot, tells him to stop playing with himself and goes inside to answer it.

28

■

"Cody, it's Kay. They brought her in this morning. She went through the ice with some of the kids. They brought them in too. They were ice fishing."

■

"Bender? There's no Bender jailed here. Never has been. Must be some mistake. Never heard of nobody named Bender."
　"He's a welder from Keene."
　"No welder here."

29

Eddie sits by the phone. He's been here for hours, sitting in this same place. He has it unplugged and wonders what will happen. Already Cody and Mary and the children are making their way north, traveling the highway, the eastern seaboard. They've crossed the Mason-Dixon and come closer. It's starting to get dark and he can almost hear the engine, still hundreds of miles away, still climbing toward home.

Knowing now the body of death as he does, renews again his sense of human frailty, the small things, the snip of a cord here, the dulling of a nerve end there, a cell that's gone mad in its need to reproduce, the way lungs and water don't get on too well together. He grows ponderous with this knowledge, with the phantom pain that swells so many empty chests. He begins talking to himself.

"Sigmund Freud said, Why live when you can be buried for ten dollars?

"Well, I got news for you," Eddie says. "Times are hard all over. It doesn't come so cheap anymore."

Eddie plugs in the phone and moves closer. He leans forward, poised, as if it will go off at any moment with backed-up phone calls. He waits, but it doesn't go off, so he sits back.

"Fuck you, anyways," he says to Freud.

Max rubs up against his leg, setting off electricity between them. In the darkened room, Eddie thinks he can see the blue licks of shock snapping in the air by his leg. He picks up the cat and holds him in his lap. Max sets out his claws, gripping and releasing Eddie's pant leg and the skin underneath, as if to offer up a little pain as a gift.

When he was a younger man, Eileen just a toddler, there was a moment when he drove through a place where crossroads meet. Another car moved on the intersection at the same time and Eddie hit the brakes. He promised himself at the time he'd always remember that moment when he hit the brake pedal and braced his other foot against the fire wall, because without thinking or looking he reached out his right hand and snatched her from the air when she came rocketing forward. A backhand catch he couldn't perform with intent on his best day. Here was where time began for him. He knew he'd be a good father. He knew he'd use car seats from then on.

He thinks about that day as he waits. He wants his children home where he can protect them. He wants them here, where he can feel their small pains, let their hurts cut through him, and assuage their fears. And he wants Mary too. He wants a getting on with life for better or worse, in sickness and in health. The rest is cake.

Last night to the north the warming started and a melting began. It moved south and stalled out high in the air over Inverawe. The snow in the mountains fell to rills, to streams, to brooks, to rivers. The tiniest of feeders became wet and watery, slowly swelling in the high country. By morning came a freshet, a sudden rise in the water levels—some said by nine or ten inches; water over ice running hard to the river, and the river itself cresting below Bellows Falls. What was frozen the day before became sodden and weak, and that's how Kay and Owen and Maple and Micah drowned. And now three of them are in Eddie Ryan's house and Owen is still lost and may never be found.

Max digs deeper into Eddie's leg. He strokes the cat's back, working up a good charge of static. He hovers his hand just beyond the black fur, making it rise and slant to his movement.

For no good reason, he thinks about Colma, California, where they have a concrete honeycomb for a graveyard. It's a place where families will never see the sinking. In fact they just nabbed some people in California, the directors of the Good Shepherd Funeral Home. Seems they owned a ceramics plant and the police think they disposed of as many as sixteen thousand bodies illegally over two years. Supposedly they were stealing gold fillings and organs too.

In India they're promoting fuel-efficient cremations. In Delhi alone they do fifty thousand bodies a year and each cremation consumes enough wood to supply a family with six months' worth of cooking fuel. Many families can't afford the whole burn so they throw what's left of the body in the Ganges. The new electric units take half the fuel. Hell, he thinks, ship the Californians to India. They'd take care of business. It all fits.

"See that, Mr. Freud, it's a whole lot more expensive than you think."

Eddie knows why he thought of these things. He stands up, causing Max to jump to the floor, and heads for the door that'll take him down the stairs.

In the preparation room he stands beside Kay with his hands folded. She stares up at him, her look hollow and lonely. The whites of her eyes are tinted yellow, her skin clear and blue, her lips purple. The water was cold so the swelling was minimal. She's a woman he remembers seeing so many times before but never connected her with the name Kay. He stands at her side and waits. He wants for her to wake and is afraid she won't.

He closes his eyes and reaches out to touch her. His hand goes onto her breast and follows its sag to her rib cage. He finds the space between her fourth and fifth rib and follows it up until he finds an incision no more than four inches long. He turns away from her to look for a pair of scissors. In the drawer he finds the trimming shears for Mary's pine tree so he uses those to snip the sutures. With a scalpel he lengthens the opening to accommodate his own hand. Then he closes his eyes again.

When he reaches in, his heart begins to throb in his chest. He's not sure, but thinks he must be having a heart attack. He decides if he isn't, he wouldn't mind having one because they can't be all so bad as what he's feeling right now.

He pulls his hand out and goes back onto a stool. He waits for his blood pressure to regularize, for his brow to run dry. He makes up his mind to go see the doctor.

Max comes to the door. Eddie can hear him outside, yowling deep from within his throat. It's the sound he makes when he sets himself off into another state, one where he'll use all his wiles with which to kill. It's a place where he goes in his cat self to take on an even match, more for territory than for food or joy.

Eddie opens the door and the cat runs off, first behind Raudabaugh's new furnace, then up the stairs, his front legs tucked short and his hind legs up and out like spring-loaded jackknives. Eddie follows him and when he gets to the kitchen, he can hear it too, the clatter of garbage cans coming from Buck's horse barn.

Some animal has found its way inside, an animal that roams at night in the warm and gauzy air and which is large enough to topple garbage cans and strew their contents, make them clatter on the floor and against the walls of the box stalls.

It must be a dog, he thinks, a dog that'd chase deer if given the chance.

Eddie goes up to the bedroom and gets the .22 pistol. He checks the clip and sees again the hollow points. It's what Cody had, hyper-velocity Stingers. Isn't more than one use for them. He shakes his head and smiles and worries a little bit about the smile.

"Piss on it," he says, pocketing the box of shells, and then he heads down the stairs.

Max is waiting at the door. He's got his back arched in a tight comma and is moving more like a liquid than an animal. Eddie's idea of keeping the garbage secure never involved guns and hunter cats, but sometimes things get started that way and sometimes it's a good idea to go along, if for no other reason than to see how it'll end, to be in on the end.

They cross the backyard, treading through soggy snow under the eave of stars. The air is warm and close, so near to being rain he doesn't know why it just doesn't go ahead and do it. Maybe it can't rain because the air is already too full of what is on the rise.

From across the road comes the sound of the overflow pipe, full-throated with the roar of white water that drives from its outlet to pound on new boulders, to make a new pocket in the gravel bed, thirty feet beyond the old one.

When Eddie gets to the barn he doesn't wait. He casts open the door and hits the power switch. Frozen in the flood of yellow light is a tawny cat, its long tail tipped with black. It's a huge cat, almost three feet at the shoulders. It poises itself on all fours. First its back is up and then down low, close to the floor. Both Max and the big cat make their throats quiver to eke out curled screams and hisses. The big cat goes up again and then back down to a crouch, the muscle rippling inside its coat.

Eddie raises the gun and fires, but the big cat is already on the move. It goes straight up into the air and then left, cutting a neat right angle in the light. Eddie shoots again, but again only where the big cat was. It comes off the wall, crosses in front of him and runs over Max, leaving him on his back clawing at the air.

They chase around the barn and already it's disappeared up the mountain road, but Eddie fires anyway, emptying the clip, shooting the night full of holes.

He reloads and listens. No sound comes out of the black forest. He keeps listening until all he can hear is the snow melting, until it comes to be a roar in his head, the roar of the ocean and a great wind in the trees all put together.

"Jesus Christ," he says. "That was some cat, Maxie."

He says this and then realizes just how big the cat was.

He goes back toward the house but doesn't stop there.

He walks with his back erect, lifting his feet high as he cuts a new path to the road. He follows the fence line, strides across the ditch and gets on the blacktop. From there he turns in the direction of the common and walks briskly. Pot's house is a quarter mile off and that's where he's going.

As he walks he can hear the snowbanks settling and the caw and hoot of winter birds, fooled by a full moon. He thinks about the mess he's gotten his life into by ignoring what he can't know. He chastises himself for not heeding more closely those worlds parallel to his own, the world of his children, his wife, his friends. And the world of luck and happenstance and coincidence, worlds that break all rules, effects without cause, action without reaction, ups without downs, downs without ups. And the dumb worlds of nature versus nurture, Darwin's notions of adaptability and survival.

This world, it snaps out signs in code. It's everywhere, not to be known, just to be suspected.

"Hey, Mr. Darwin," Eddie says. "What is, is, baby."

He can tell it's Cody's talk and he likes it. He gives up to it and lets himself get full, get brimmed over to the edge, where he hovers on the lip, glued there, ready to jump.

Pot's house is dark. Eddie doesn't hesitate. He takes the stairs and raps on the door until he hears Dr. Pot's voice calling out from overhead.

"Dr. Pot. It's Eddie Ryan. I think I've had a heart attack."

■

Dr. Pot hooks into his stethoscope and listens to Eddie Ryan's bare chest. He tells him to breathe deeply, to cough. He asks about irregularities, shortness of breath, pains in the extremities.

"Did I tell you," he says, "about my friend who some years ago had a gorilla come into his emergency ward. He looked and saw a gorilla on the cart. It was only a man from the circus in a gorilla suit. My friend thought it was very funny. Your blood pressure is not good. You should be on medication. You should have some weight off. You are too heavy for your heart.

"Anyways. You did not have a heart attack. Maybe some bad gas. Some indigestion can make that feeling."

"The incisions," Eddie says, "what do you do with the hearts? The ones you take."

Dr. Pot looks up from Eddie's chest. His face is blank. There is no sign of surprise or relief or fear or calculation.

"The physical heart," he says, "is researched for mechanical functions as opposed to liver and kidney, which are researched for metabolic function. The cardiac tissue is researched for degenerative diseases specific to children for unknown etiology. Can't think of the name of the disease right at this time. They use the electron microscope to visualize cardiac tissue, muscle and cell."

Dr. Pot looks away and sighs.

"Once the heart is dead," he says, "it is very hard to recharge and reactivate the electrical conduction pattern. Theoretically it is inconceivable, but with the use of the computer, they research electrophysiological patterns. I freeze the heart in liquid nitrogen. Also with computer they determine the sequence of nucleic acids. Very important in the study of heart disease to be able to make a heart on paper."

Eddie thinks about what Dr. Pot has just told him . . . to be able to make a good heart on paper. He thinks, To be able to make a good heart in life.

"Good money in hearts?" he says.

"Good money in hearts. Even better in corneas. The Saudis pay six hundred and fifty dollar each."

"It's wrong," Eddie says. "Can't you see it's dead wrong?"

"I know it is wrong, but only good can come of it."

"It's still wrong. It's against the law and there are huge ethical considerations."

"You break the rules too, Mr. Ryan. Where is Mr. G. R. Trimble? On the mountain? People say he was killed by his friend and where is his friend? You are like me. We have been to the same places. You have the same fear of darkness, nightmares, slamming doors, thunder, cars backfiring. Nobody else thinks about it, but we do."

"I was there, but here it doesn't work like that. You've got to understand."

"They're just hearts."

Eddie says, "But you don't steal what these people give freely."

"The hearts were still young, still without plaque. The money I make goes to pay for the people who can't pay. It's how I keep this office open."

"Joe," Eddie says. "His heart wasn't young."

"Very strong, though. He has a strong heart."

"Clifford?"

"I didn't take his."

"Kay?"

"It wasn't young but it was a very nice heart. I think she died of a broken heart."

"For God's sake," Eddie says. "You just don't get it."

Pot's breathing becomes imperceptible. He makes no movement whatsoever, and then he says, "There was one more, Mrs. Huguenot. I used a technique perfected at Mount Sinai in the forties. Jewish law forbade autopsy so to cover organ removal you go through the anus. I thought you should know. She sponsored me to come to this country."

"Where is Kay's heart?"

"I have it here."

"And the children?"

"Here too."

Eddie rubs his face until it hurts. His chest tightens and his breathing comes harder. Finally he stands and puts his shirt back on and gets into his coat.

"I need to know one thing," he says quietly, "I need to know she and the children were dead. They weren't under that long. I need to know they couldn't have been brought back from the ice water. I need to know there was absolutely no way."

Dr. Pot doesn't answer. He looks away from Eddie to the floor at his feet. "As far as I know."

Eddie goes numb inside. His breath shortens and for an instant he believes he'll pass out. When he comes around, he takes the pistol from his pocket. He holds it flat in his hand, running his finger along the trigger guard.

"It's come to the point where there are no good choices. What you've done, you've done to us all," he says. "There are some who'd swallow this, let it slide. They should die too."

He holds out the gun and Dr. Pot takes it. He thanks Eddie, tells him it wasn't always like this. One time he was a man, but not anymore. He thanks him again.

"Here," he says, handing over to Eddie a fistful of lollipops. "Have only one. It will help you sleep. There's a mild sedative in them."

"You'll be all right?" Eddie asks.

"Yes. My finest hour."

"Good," Eddie says, and they shake hands.

■

Eddie doesn't stop at his house. He walks past it, wanting to see the pond where a few days ago kids were ice skating, where a few months ago kids were swimming. He's trying to get up his courage to go back to where he lives.

As he gets near, he listens for the roar of the pipe and the plunge of water, but can't hear it. Behind him a car is coming but he doesn't look to see who it is. He keeps walking in the lane the car will need unless the driver sees him in time and pulls into the other one. The lights are on his back. They're yellow to white and he thinks they must be warm. The car slows and follows behind, its low beams washing out around him, closing in front of him, lighting his way.

The car follows him the hundred yards to the bridge, where he steps off the road to the base of the abutment. The driver pulls up alongside him and powers down the passenger side window. Eddie turns toward it and sees Louis Poissant sitting inside, his face aglow from the dashboard lights and the match he holds to his cigar.

Eddie rests his crossed forearms in the opening and bends at the waist to look in, his knees locked and his back straight. Louis chugs on his cigar and then breathes, sending out a puff of smoke that clouds his face.

"Nice night for a walk," Louis says.

"Nice night for a drive."

Louis chugs some more, sending the smoke to clouds inside the Cadillac. Eddie looks down and sees a black-powder Colt Walker lying on the seat beside Louis's thigh. The brass trigger guard shines, but the barrel is dulled and matted. Eddie reaches in to the door handle with his left hand and thumbs the latch. The door opens slightly and the overhead light goes on. The barrel shows red stains and the loading lever carries strands of hair and a piece of scalp and on the floor he can see three pairs of boots, two for children and one for an adult.

Eddie leans into the door, forcing it shut and extinguishing the light. Louis takes out his cigar and looks at it. He licks the wrapper leaf, then puts it back in his mouth, rolling it against his tongue.

After a while he says, "George, over to Bolton, tried to sell me their shoes so I got my gun. He told me about the doctor and then I clubbed him. He'll be okay."

"Cody's gun," Eddie says, suddenly frightened. "I left Pot Cody's gun."

"I shan't worry about that. People borrow guns all the time. Besides, it's too late. I was just over there. He already took care of business."

Eddie doesn't say anything.

Louis works on his cigar some more, rolling it in his lips and making the ash bob and glow with each draw.

"Mr. Ryan, you got a bill for me?"

"No," Eddie says. "Don't worry about it."

"I'll be needing that pasture again in the spring. You talk it over with your wife. I can see she's the business head in the family."

"That's a good idea," Eddie says. "I'll talk it over with my wife."

"Well, I've got to get home to bed so as I can get up early in the morning and go find Dr. Pot on his office floor."

Louis nudges the power switch on his armrest, enough to give Eddie the message. Eddie stands and the window closes. He watches the Cadillac go around the bend. He stands there long after it's gone, listening to its sound disappear. When no sign of it is left, he's startled by the silence. No sound comes up from the brook to replace the noise of the engine. He looks over the abutment and can see the dam has been swept open like gates, gone as if it were never there. No telling of it is left, only the gray back of the water, carrying small islands of blue ice that go to white in the rips, bobbing silently to the river.

■

When Cody and Mary and the children get home, Cody doesn't say anything. He holds up his hand and cocks his head. He goes in the kitchen and to the cabinet where Eddie keeps his liquor. He gets a bottle and goes down to the preparation room, where he goes inside and closes the door behind.

Eddie and Mary carry the still-sleeping children up to their own beds. Eddie can see how tanned they are from their time in the sun. Then he and Mary unload the car. It's early morning, the sun is shining and the air is growing cold again. The wet snowfields are going solid, hard with a glaze of ice that mirrors all light.

Eddie opens his mouth to speak, but Mary doesn't want to talk. She holds her hand up the way Cody did. Eddie feels as if he has a big hole inside him and everything on its edge is caving into it and the edge just keeps getting wider and wider. He doesn't try to talk again and helps with the unpacking.

The last suitcases are her own, and she and Eddie climb the stairs together. Inside their room, she sits him down and steps back, telling him to watch.

When she undresses, she's tan and pretty. She looks to be the only girl he's ever known. She comes to where he sits on the bed and takes his clothes off too, then she gets on her knees between his legs, wanting to taste him. He strokes her head and back, runs his fingers along the edge where the white and tan meet. She stands up and sits on his lap and they're face to face, her legs wrapped round his back.

"Be the man," she whispers, licking his neck and biting him.

Eddie stands, holding her up in his hands, lifting her and letting her back down. She lets her head go back and stiffens her body. She does it again and sounds come from her throat. She keeps riding him, now her neck pressed at an angle across his.

"You're holding back," she says, sending the words down his spine.

"Your diaphragm."

"We'll take our chances," she says, and he goes off inside her as his legs slowly go soft, and they settle down onto the bed.

They lie there for a long time, Eddie on his back and Mary on top of him, falling asleep. He looks up at the ceiling and for a second thinks it's water, but it isn't. It's the light bounding off the snow and coming in through the windows. He rolls to his side, letting her down, and he pulls a quilt over them.

"Go help Cody," she says, half in a dream. "See if he's okay. Have a drink with him. He needs you."

Eddie get dressed and goes down to the preparation room.

"Johnnie Walker is my best friend," Cody says, holding up the still-full bottle.

"Mine too," Eddie says.

Cody uncaps the bottle and they both have a sip.

"You know," Cody says, "I think my heart's given in."

"No," Eddie tells him, "it's just a little soft right now."

"You think so?"

"Yes."

■

After the funerals, Mary and Eddie drive home while Cody stays on, alone, to fill in the four graves. The cemetery society was hesitant to have the graves dug. They wanted to put everyone away in the vault until springtime so the ground would not be chewed up.

Rose Kennedy persuaded the other members to agree to a winter burial after Eddie went up to her house and almost pounded down the door. All was forgiven and the funerals proceeded—Kay, Maple, Micah and Dr. Pot—with Owen left to the river that swallowed him up and froze over again.

■

"Tell me you love me," she says.

"She told Louis she was planning on getting married all over again to Cody and she told Cody she was engaged to a man named Bender who didn't exist."

"She wasn't anybody's fool."

"I love you," Eddie says.

"That's okay. You showed me the morning we got home. Sometimes you go off. Way off. Just keep coming back. I'll settle for that."

And then after a while she says, "It's sad about Dr. Pot," and she waits, but Eddie doesn't say anything.

By the time Cody gets home, Eddie and Mary have the trunk of the car loaded with food for Louis Poissant and the kids. Cody goes in to shower and when he comes out, Tom and Jeri and Dick and Marlene Doody are there. They have casseroles and want to come along too. They shake Cody's hand and treat him with the respect that grave loss always affords.

Mary goes in to get Eileen and Little Eddie. They all pile into cars and start toward the common, where Eddie pulls into Washburn's for soda and beer. He tells Washburn where he's going and Washburn says he'll be along shortly.

"As soon as I can close up," he says. "I'll bring some more drinks from the storeroom."

Eddie lugs out the two cases and can see another car pulled up beside his own. It's Rose and Barkley in their Volvo. Coonie has squeezed in with the Doodys. Thad is parked behind the Kennedys.

He waves to them all and gets in his car. He looks in the back seat but Cody is gone.

"It was too much for him," Mary says. "Just let it be."

Eddie pulls out and the other cars follow. They take the River Road to Louis's farm.

When they get there, he's in the barn with the kids doing chores. Dome and Ram Goerlitz are there too, arguing about the best way to milk a cow.

Other townspeople begin to show up and the women usher the children into the house, where they give them baths and set the table.

Louis won't go in. He keeps making up chores to do. The men help him with cleaning the barn and finishing the milking. When that's done, he sets them to cleaning calf pens. Plates of food go back and forth between the barn and the house.

Louis gets Eddie alone and tells him in the spring he's decided he wants to move Kay and Maple and Micah to the hillside here on the farm. He's been told he can't do it anymore and wants to know how it can be done. Eddie tells him they'll accomplish it somehow.

They go back to cleaning stables and sweeping the mangers. Mary Looney and the Blond Bomber show up. They come into the barn and the men work a little harder in their presence.

Finally it's near midnight and they move in twos and threes toward the well-lit house, leaving the barn behind. They tread the ground that's locked again with cold and frost. They pass under the spray of stars and the fat moon, ringed with a circle of light that's taken up residence some thousands of miles out from its cold hull.

Eddie and Louis are the last to go. They shut down the lights and close the door and make the walk to the house, watching the uneven ground as they go, not looking up.

But if they did look up and looked intently enough toward the river, they'd see the black speck of a man in the far distance walking on the ice edge along the current. He has an ax over his shoulder and he's dragging a long pole with a grappling hook trussed to one end, its points bouncing lightly at his chest. He's walking the bend in the river in the direction of South America.

PART
SIX

30

Eddie begins to doze in the cab of Cody's brand-new rebuilt pickup. He sits upright on the hard seat, his head full of the new-vehicle smell, something now bottled and marketed by assholes who prey on other assholes.

The sun bears in on his right shoulder. It cooks his neck and cheek, making his body slack and languorous.

Behind him is death and life all at once, Mary and the kids and the killing that was in Pot's office. She didn't want him to go on this trip. She thinks Cody has gone crazy. Eddie told her he didn't know and didn't care. Besides, Cody said this would be the last one.

"Hey, what the fuck," he mumbles. "Hey, what the fuck."

He goes into a tentative sleep that has the ability to rocket you into wakefulness at any moment. It's a sleep where a guardrail becomes a man, a stone becomes a semi, a leaf goes to deer. Each time he comes awake he sends the feelers of pain from his forehead down into his neck, where they seep to his shoulders. He keeps nodding off this way, leaving blanks in his mind, blanks in the radio, blanks in the terrain. It's as if Cody is piloting the truck through tunnels in the mountains and Eddie wants for him to find one that never ends.

Cody starts pounding the dashboard with his fist. For this Eddie wakes up and stays awake.

"Goddamn it," Cody yells. "Goddamn it."

"What's the matter?"

Cody tells him how on the radio it said a commuter train derailed, forcing hundreds of passengers out of a dark tunnel.

"For Christ sakes, Cody, what's gotten into you?"

Cody beats the dash with his fist. A cup of coffee tumbles, its lash of hot liquid sopping the seat between them before it leaks to the floor.

"I don't get it," he says, "I just don't get it. What the hell does it mean, forcing the passengers to walk out of a tunnel? Most people live their whole lives in a fucking dark tunnel and these bastards make out like it's a big deal these people have to walk out a dark tunnel. At least they got out. What a bunch of goddamn babies we've come to be. Where's the courage? Where's the pain? Nobody suffers anymore. If you're sad, you're abnormal. Fuck that. I like being sad."

Cody tromps on the gas and passes half a dozen cars. With each one he leans over across Eddie and gives them the finger. He seems to feel better after that.

Eddie shrugs and sighs. Things between him and Mary have changed. There are things they don't tell each other anymore. She has begun at Keene State to finish her degree, something they didn't talk over; she told him she was going to do it. He knows it's good. He decides he doesn't want to think about it. He'll sleep the rest of the way through New York State.

It was Christmas when Cody came back to them. His face was seared from the cold and he wore his clothes bound to his body with twines and ropes and ribbons. The material bulged where bindings crossed, full of puffs of down or feathers or newspaper or fiber-glass insulation or hemlock.

He wore the ax strapped across his back and carried the grappling pole over his shoulder, its length stretched out behind him, scratching over the road, and the hook still bouncing against his chest.

He came into the kitchen that way, the door banging half-shut against the pole that stretched behind him. He sat down and Eddie lifted it off his shoulder and slid it out the door. Mary made him a cup of coffee and set it down.

Eddie and Cody pull into T.K.'s, Exit 60, I81 South. Both of them are tired and hungry. They've been on the road for six hours, six hours on this latest run.

The waitress's name is Mim. It says so on the name tag pinned to her smock.

Eddie watches the truck drivers, the way they eat their meals, trying to make them be dinners. They scrape the soup bowls with the backs of their spoons and then arrange their plates and cups and glasses just so on their place mats.

Eddie writes down on his place mat what he sees. He avoids thoughts and sticks to things like stainless steel, Formica, wood-grain laminates, paper towels, water, air, light.

The men keep eating. They hunker down over plates of hash and pancakes and meat loaf with gravy. Eddie wants to go home, take the phone off the hook, build a fence around the house and hide out from life. He writes down wants on the place mat. When he's done, he takes a sip of water and then sets the glass back down, but somehow it stumbles in his hand and spills a slosh of water onto his place mat. He watches his words float away in a blue wash of ink. He stirs them with his finger and thinks how pretty they look as their shapes go to dye the paper.

■

Cody reads, " 'The Endless Caverns of West Virginia.' What the hell does that mean?"

His top lip is white with Maalox gone hard in the hair of his mustache.

"It must have an end. Everything has an end."

The moon rides on Cody's left shoulder. It sits there like a parrot and Eddie is certain he can see the eyes, ears, nose and mouth tonight. The man in the moon is fat and happy.

"Troutville," Cody says. "Now there's a place for me. A place to spend my years of decline. Troutville. Place with a name like that can't be all bad. I'll get myself a little camp with power, running water and septic. I'll buy a VCR and see all the movies ever made.

I've never been to the movies except maybe once. All the towns in
the world named after fish. The boy would've loved that one.
Wait'll I tell him."

Eddie sits up and turns in his seat. He wants to say the boy is dead
and gone but he holds back and it's because for the first time he
just isn't sure.

Between Roanoke and Wytheville they run through the mountains. Eddie's heart goes out to his friend as he hunches behind the
steering wheel, peeking left and right at the snow-covered humps
of mountains rising up along the road. In the moonlight the trees
look like black spikes. It could've been there was a fire and now all
that's left are the charred stakes of sapwood. Emmylou Harris sings
about two desperadoes named Poncho and Lefty. Cody sings along
for a while and when the song is over, he hits the seek button on
the radio and for miles they listen to five seconds of every station.
They pass a sign that says FALLING ROCKS.

"There," Cody says, "I told you these mountains were about to
topple over. They're all running right into each other. The tops are
sluffing off and before you know it the whole damn earth will be
flat."

"They have their own society, you know. The Flat Earth Society."

"I'm not surprised. It seems like they've got a goddamn society
for everything these days. Every disease has got its own society. I'll
tell you, Mr. Eddie, the disease I've got hasn't got no society. No
friends either. It's one of those renegade diseases."

■

"Fancy Gap," Cody yells. "I used to know a girl with one of those,
but that was in another life."

The headlights catch the dun-colored white-tailed deer grazing
at the edge of the highway. They stand poised ready for flight, or
with their front legs spread and their heads dropped, their mouths
nibbling at shards of bent grass, grass that carries the lick of salt
from the trucks that make the roads safe from ice.

In the headlights they look gray or even green as they stand
there, ready to take off into the traffic or into the woods. The choice
is theirs.

"They look like women," Cody says.

"What makes you think that?"

They stare out the windows into the small plot of darkness opened up by the headlights.

"I don't know. Maybe it's their eyes. People talk about their eyes holding fear, but I've never seen it. Only grace and beauty. They must like that shot of light, like it in their eyes, like it to freeze them where they stand. I can't help but think they look like women, women who've lost something."

"You really do?"

"No. I think they look like women who have become girls again."

Eddie looks at his friend. He can see his cheek and neck, a side of his nose, his temple and an eye, all dimly lit by the dashboard lights. He feels as if his heart will catch fire, as if it will begin to blaze with the knowing of something that he has just now apprehended. He can feel stones moving in his heart.

"Yes," he says quietly. "They are women. Let's just not talk about it anymore. It's not because I don't want to. It's just that I want to think about what you've said."

Cody gives the hint of a nod and Eddie sits back, waiting for them to show beside the road, wanting to see them again and again, and after a few miles they do and he feels his heart begin to kindle again at the sight of them. There are four together and their heads are aligned with the points of the compass. Then they disperse, turn back to the woods and are out of sight in less time than it takes for these thoughts to happen.

After a few more miles Eddie lets himself go back into sleep, a rocking gentle sleep aided by the warm dry air rising from the heater vents, air that seems to touch with its own fingers his face and his hands folded in his lap. In that sleep he conjures up a dream of Mary and he can't imagine he's ever loved her any more than he does right now. He thinks to himself that death not only kills but death offers new love.

When Eddie wakes up, it's still night. The truck is parked beside gas pumps with the engine running. Through the driver's window he can see inside the station. Cody is holding his hands out wide and talking. The men he's talking to are laughing. Eddie figures he's just told them a funny story. He watches them inside the station. They're sipping coffee and talking to each other, taking turns to keep up the conversation. He looks at his watch. It's getting close to morning. To the east he can see a crevice of blue, the forerunner of the day. He wonders what state he's in. He tries to stay awake to ask, but all he wants to do is sleep, so he does.

■

"Amen," Cody yells as they descend on the world of Georgia in his pickup, the tappets singing in the engine.

■

Between Lost Swamp and Ossabaw Sound the Ogeechee River hooks, bends and turns on itself, bulging with six-hour tides that flood the marshes and timber swamps. It's here the Georgia razor-backs live off grasses, tubers, frogs, the young of rabbit, cotton-mouths and an occasional fawn. Growing out of their jaws are sets of tusks and sharpeners that work like a knife and steel. Their hides are a thick shell of muscle and gristle and it's needed because the hogs' second most favorite thing to do is fight.

Dewey and Ron stand at the fire barrel, treading in place to keep warm, waiting for Payton and the two hunters from New Hamp-shire. In back are the hunting dogs, and all around the camp, swamp and yellow slash pine rise into the gray sky, some giving way to the ice, going off like rifle shots. It's south Georgia, January, wet, and 27 degrees.

Ron asks Dewey if he heard the joke about the boy who fell in love with a mule. Dewey says no, and Ron's disappointed, as if Dewey might've been the one who could tell him a joke he's heard about but hasn't heard.

Payton pulls up in his truck. He slides out the door and in the same motion ascends the sideboards and begins handing down chain saws, a battery, gas cans and two possum.

Dewey and Ron lift the dog box and slide it onto the bed.

"Them boys from New Hampshire ain't here yet," Ron yells.

"I can see that, Mr. Ron. I ain't blind and I sure ain't deaf. Get them dogs up here. Now."

Dewey and Ron go out behind the shed and come back with two dogs.

"This one right cheer is Rambo," Ron says, hoisting up a black-and-tan. "He's 'bout as ugly too, but he's a ground-burning sum-bitch and he's been known to find a boar hog or two."

Dewey brings on Snowball, a husky shepherd mix with one blue eye. They latch the doors, then swing the boat trailer onto the ball and cuff it down.

Payton looks down at Ron and then to Dewey. Dewey don't ever say nothin'. He's always black with soot from woodsmoke. He lives in a school bus, burns an open fire and wears other people's clothes. He doesn't care about life so much as Ron does. Ron was in the National Guard.

"Gas in there for that motor," Payton says, nodding his head toward the boat.

"She's full," Ron says, and then he tells Dewey to go back to the camp and get the lunches and thermos of coffee.

Payton and Ron get near the fire barrel. They hold their hands out over the mouth of it, not feeling the licks of flame that wash over their palms. Dewey comes back from the camp in his four-wheeler. He has box lunches and three Thermos jugs of coffee.

"Where them boys at?" Payton says.

"Word I got was they driving in this morning."

"Dewey, open up one of them Thermos and get out that coffee."

While they drink their coffee, they revolve slowly near the hull of the barrel, warming all sides of their bodies. Dewey feeds the barrel with split pine. It hisses, snaps and pops, each time bursting sprays of embers into the air.

Somewhere farther back in the icy swamp, a tree trunk goes off, ripping open the morning. Dewey and Ron duck their heads at the sound as if sound could hurt them. Payton smiles.

"Sumbitch," Ron says. "That one was close."

A truck can be heard turning into the lane a quarter mile away from off the macadam. The three men watch for it. They see it's from out of state.

When it pulls in behind the boat, Cody is the first one out. He stamps the ground to make his pants legs fall straight. He nods to Payton, Dewey and Ron. Only Payton nods back.

"Thought they's two of you," Payton says.

Cody jabs his thumb in the air toward the cab. Eddie is now sitting up straight and rubbing his eyes. He's never been to Georgia before and can't believe how cold it is.

"Follow me," Payton says, going for his truck and starting the engine.

Ron and Dewey hustle to get the lunch boxes and Thermos jugs into Payton's truck. He shakes his head as they stumble over each other, but they don't fall.

"You skin them possum."

He closes his door, goes round the circle and in his rearview sees Cody pulling around too; and behind Cody he sees Ron and Dewey hovering at the fire barrel again, beaver castors and spoonlike baculums hanging from the beams over their heads. Another tree goes off and they duck.

At the landing in Richmond Hill, Cody parks his truck while Payton backs the trailer into the water. Eddie and Cody stand in the cold morning air, skinning down to their long underwear and dressing again in boots and woolens. From under the seat Cody takes the .44 in a holster and hands it over to Eddie. He tells him to strap it on and tells him it's loaded.

Payton floats the boat off the trailer, motors to the dock and ties up. He then pulls his truck up to where Eddie and Cody stand. He sees that Eddie has the gun so he talks to him.

"You're the first hunter. Then you'll go," he says, pointing at Cody. "We go wherever them dogs go. Now when I say to shoot, you shoot. I'll tell you when to get ready. That's it. Let's get up on it."

■

The water's rough and the snow is now rain. They hunker down on their seats, the dogs between their legs amongst buckets, lines, muzzles and cushions as they make the run across the Ogeechee.

Eddie and Cody sit with their backs to the bow to cut the wind. Eddie's stomach burns from no food and too much coffee. If it were otherwise, he'd be leaning over the gunwale puking into the river. Cody jabbers on about what a beautiful day it is, the kind that separates the men from the boys.

"Man against the elements," he says, "man against the elements."

Eddie's stomach begins to contract under his belt. He grabs Rambo by an ear, buries his face in the dog's neck and inhales deeply. The smell of the wet fur settles him. He looks over his shoulder and sees a world of fog and mist ahead, the thin line of land between it and the sea.

It's fifteen minutes before the thudding chop against the hull diminishes and they leave the river for the Cut. Here begins a web of canals—Peachtree, Valambrosia, Elbow, Walker, Red Dock and New Hope. All dug by slaves to make rice paddies now grown over with marsh grass and cattails.

The rain has stopped but by now they're wet; a stiff wind blows and the sky is ash white. From the northwest comes the sound of thunder. Payton tells them it's Fort Stewart practicing artillery when it's raining to keep down the brush fires.

Payton cuts power to the engine. He rummages through the gear at the bottom of the boat for muzzles. Cody helps him get them over the dogs' noses and jaws and secured behind their ears.

"Now what are you boys looking for? We got red boar, blue boar and black boar. We got trophy boar and we just got boar."

"Nothing special," Cody says. "We're just out for some recreation on a beautiful day."

Payton laughs and this cheers Eddie. Cody's love of the day comes inside him and he forgets his stomach, his lack of sleep and the bone-chilling cold and wet. He's had enough of life for a while and thinks how fine it would be to ride on this gray water through the banks of mist.

"Bow, Rambo. Bow, Snowball," Payton yells. "Hunt 'em up bo. Hunt 'em up. Find a big boar hog."

The two dogs scuttle to the bow. They crowd its point, their noses sorting out what rides the wind.

Payton fires up the motor and they putt ahead into the Cut. Inside, it's a different world. Marsh grasses are bent and each one is encased in a cylinder of ice. Jagged plates of it have formed at the banks and pockets of mist rise up around them.

Rambo and Snowball hover at the bow, their backs a sheen of frozen spray. Even with the motor sputtering, everything is quiet and still. Eddie feels himself to be coming alive in this place of urgency. He's warmed by the feel of his own blood as it trails through his body.

They ride the canals all day, setting out the dogs and following them into the marsh a short ways. They're soaked to the bone and at times caught by the stiff wind. For every movement, there's the throb of dull pain echoing through their limbs to their guts. Each time they come back to the boat, the dogs huddle between their legs to keep warm. Payton gives them a spell, then sends them to the bow again.

Cody looks at Eddie and asks him if he's ready to pack it in. Eddie tells him no, tells him he's enjoying himself.

"Jesus Christ," Cody says, "you're thriving, aren't you? Never seen you so beamish."

Payton runs the boat aground. The dogs tumble off into the swamp. He tells Eddie and Cody it's time to do some real walking. One of them will have to stay with the boat, run it around to the other side. The other one will come with him across the marsh to the levee, a half mile away.

"I'll go," Eddie says, getting out of the boat first.

Payton gives Cody directions through the network of canals, then gets out with Eddie. Already the dogs have disappeared in the thick brown grasses that rise over the men's heads. They shove Cody back into the deeper water and plunge into the weedy wall in front of them.

Away from the canal, the land changes. In places it's flooded and there are holes you can't see where you can go in over your head. Payton slogs through, telling Eddie to walk where he walks, to drag his feet a little so the grasses will mat his way. They come to a clearing and Payton points out a mound, a nest a hog has built up to keep dry.

"They don't like to get wet," he says. "And they're awful swimmers."

He points out some fresh scat and a stunted pine the hogs have been scraping. He tells Eddie they do it to scratch, but what happens is the resin gets in their bristle and it makes a tough shield.

"We have cut the hide off a hog," Payton says, "and had double-ought buck come rolling out like marbles. What I'm telling you is, these motherfuckers are tough and when you're that tough, you tend to get mean."

As he finishes telling this to Eddie, the dogs bay up a hog a hundred yards away.

"Hear that kee. That's Rambo," Payton says, and he's off running.

Eddie follows close behind, finding strength he hasn't used for some time now, but the ground isn't safe. First it's hard and then it's mud and it happens that fast. Both men go down hard, sprawled out in the cold water. They get up again, though, and keep running. Ahead, Eddie can see an awful thrashing, great waves of marsh grass getting swept aside by the fight underneath.

Another fifty yards and he and Payton are on the levee of a canal. Cody can be seen at the far end of it, just entering, the throttle opened wide.

"Gawddamn," Payton yells, and jumps in, breaking through the skim ice and swimming to the other side. Eddie doesn't hesitate. He goes in too and scuttles up the bank. On the other side is another backwash. Payton has crossed it and Eddie goes too. He's up to his waist and churning to shore when the hog comes out where Payton went in. They look at each other for a moment and then the hog disappears.

"Don't shoot," Payton yells, "don't shoot. It's a sow."

Eddie stands in the water and it feels warm to him. He thinks he should like to stand there all day, panting and sweating in the cold air. When Payton comes out of the grass holding the dogs by their collars, Eddie is laughing and letting himself piss right through his long johns and wool pants. Payton starts to laugh too.

"You all right, Eddie," he says. "You all right."

Cody is on the levee when they get back. He has a tar bucket he's filled with sticks and driftwood. He has it lit and a fire comes from its opening. It's smoky but warm and the men get over it, letting the fumes bathe their chests, necks and faces.

"You both all right," Payton says. "Both you Yankees."

They stay there on the levee and eat their lunch. A redtail hawk scissors the air and Payton points out a palm tree where one summer a copperhead bit him. He tells about the night he was coon hunting on the river. The stick came off in his hand at full throttle and before he could shut down the motor he hit a submerged log and capsized. He dove in to cut his dogs free but got his hand between his knife and a collar by mistake and sliced himself up pretty good.

"I thought, Gawddamn, that's some tough leather, and kept sawing away. Finally I figured it was my own hand. Thirty-seven stitches."

He holds his hand up to show them. The scar is white and marbled as if he wore a string of pearls under his skin.

"Your dogs," Cody says.

"Lost two."

He tells them that a twenty-minute boat ride from here there's a POW camp. Him and his daddy built it for a movie company. They got the contract to build the camp and then they ferried the crew and movie actors back and forth all summer. It was a Viet Nam movie, one where the hero goes back years later to free his buddies. Ron and Dewey got parts as dead men.

"We ate steak that summer," Payton says.

They ride for another hour. Eddie is beginning to nod off. The calm has made him cold again. He looks at Cody and wonders how his friend can go so long without sleep. He glances back at Payton and realizes both he and Cody wear the same look as they slowly scan the grasses. Both men have shut down, holding their energy in abeyance. They've gone down inside themselves, where they'll stay until they need to be different. Eddie thinks about this and then does it himself, pleased with how easy it is.

They pass under an osprey nest. Rambo and Snowball leap from the bow into the water. They bay up a boar hog sleeping at the edge and the fight begins. Payton runs the boat aground and Eddie is the first one out following into the marsh grass. Payton is behind him and Cody pushes off to get around to the other side.

Payton soon overtakes Eddie as they crash through the mud trying to get in on the fight. But again, breaking out on the far side is another canal and by the time they get there, the hog is in the water and the dogs are on its head.

Payton jumps in, grabbing the boar by its ears and dragging it to shore. It goes under and he goes with it, but when he comes up he's alone. They collar the dogs and wait, but it's no use. The boar's sunk in the cold water and is drifting to the sea. Steam billows from them as the air takes out body heat. They stand waist-deep in near-frozen water, waiting for Cody.

He has the bucket fired up again and Eddie and Payton thank him. Their jaws are tight with cold. Their clothes crack with every move they make. They ride slowly, Cody at the throttle, swinging near the bank to collect more sticks of wood for the bucket. Payton lets the dogs get warm, then sends them to the bow. Away from the heat and smoke they get doglike again, dancing and skittering, craning their necks and sniffing the air.

"Hunt 'em bo," Payton yells, his voice hollow with cold. "Find me a big boar hog. Git that hog. Git 'em."

He looks to Cody and then Eddie.

"Almost kilt me one of them stunt-men boys," he says. "He was fuckin' with my girl friend. I caught up with him at a red light. I stopped right behind him, got out and walked up to his car. I told him don't be fuckin' with my woman and he told me to go to hell just like that. I told him I been to hell and started wailing on him. He had them automatic windows, though, and powered my arms up in it. The light changed and he took off. He dragged me all the way to the other light. Burned the shoes right offa my feet. I got my knife out and was gonna stick it in him, but he dropped me and left the state for Texas. No matter. We'll meet up one of these days."

Rambo kees and yips while Snowball stares forward, her good eye blue as slate and the other milky white. Payton jabs the air with his thumb and Cody swings the boat around. The dogs explode from the bow, beating the air for land. It's a two-hundred-pound black boar hog and he's madder than hell. He has no intention of drowning. He tries to break for it, but Rambo gets an ear and Snowball clamps onto his hind end. The three of them tumble to the ground.

The boar comes up fighting. As he gets one dog down, the other jumps him. More than anything he wants to sink a tusk into Snowball's soft belly and lay it open to her neck, but neither dog backs off. Sheets of marsh grass fall under them while mud and water fill the air.

Cody runs the boat up and the three of them follow behind, trying to get in tight, sometimes knee-deep in the rising tide. Payton grabs Rambo by the tail and drags him off. The dog has lost an ear and blood wells from its head. Eddie gets between Snowball and the boar, then raises the .44. The hog comes on and he fires, dropping it at his feet.

31

That night they lose the electricity to an ice storm. The crack of limbs and trunks explodes in the air. You know what it is, but every time one goes off you sit up a bit.

Eddie and Cody are waiting for Payton to come back, take them to a turkey shoot. They eat boar and venison, yams, black-eyed peas and biscuits. They live by candlelight while Lance, the camp manager, sips Evan Williams from a Styrofoam cup.

Lance says the only calibers worth a shit are the .22, .38 and .44. The rest can go to hell.

A truck can be heard negotiating the mud and ice of the lane to the camp. Headlights bob in the darkness, scan the windows. It's Payton. He doesn't come inside. He just sits out there and waits.

"Your ride," Lance says. "I'm going to my girl friend's trailer for the night. You're welcome to come when you finish your night's adventure. I have *The Sacketts* on video. She still has power over there."

Eddie and Cody thank Lance for supper. They get dry clothes

from by the stove and pull them on. While they dress, Lance tells them not to go out back to take a leak. He tells them Payton's daddy keeps his best boar dog out there.

"He's the High Low dog and he'll eat your balls if you stumble over him. That is if he doesn't do it anyways."

Outside it's colder, but the rain has let up. They stand on the slick steps feeling the close air nuzzle at their bodies. The coldness charges at them, barbed as it is with air that cuts and ice suspended.

The two friends hesitate there, each waiting for the other to go first. They haven't slept much in over thirty hours but at this moment are more alive than ever. They are more like one person standing there waiting for a half to move.

"Let's go," Cody says, and they pile into Payton's truck.

In the cab light they can see he wears the mark of four fingers on his cheek. His eyes are red and swollen.

"I see your girl friend is left-handed," Cody says.

Payton can't help but smile. He passes a rifle and a shotgun over to Cody to hold so he can work the shift. They go back out the lane, past the shed where Eddie's skinned boar hog hangs from a beam, snout to the ground.

They leave the county for one farther south. Payton doesn't offer the name. Eddie rides silently, feeling himself to have been stripped bare these past few days and only now to be dressing again, piece by piece. He thinks these things but doesn't dwell on them for fear of shattering the thought like too much weight on glass.

In this new county there are lights, few at first but then they become more common. They're the lights strung on trailers, the soft greens and yellows and reds of plastic Chinese lanterns on cords that swoop up to hooks and back down again. They're the lights high over a yard, splashing out whole pools of yellow that glaze the twists of grass, broken fences and parts of cars.

Payton begins to get off the roads, stabbing through the muddy fields to connect with a lane on the other side. The roads go from bad to worse and one time he drowns the points in a watery hole. Even then they don't talk. They sit quietly waiting for it to dry out under the hood and then they fire up the engine again.

Finally they come to a steel gate and from the wet blackness a man emerges. He sees the truck and swings back the gate. Eddie waves with the toss of his hand but the man doesn't wave back. He only stares.

Farther down the road the lights come on again. There's a shack and poles with spotlights aimed at a shooting range, blocks of wood thirty yards out from the open side of the building.

The other men are happy to see Payton because he's the best shot and not too happy for the same reason.

"Now," Payton says, "there's twelve stations and twelve shooters. A dollar buys you a shell. Then there's the side bet. That's another two dollars. Closest shot to the center wins meat and the side bet if he's in it."

After the first shoot, a man on a three-wheeler comes riding out from behind the shed. He's got an uncapped bourbon bottle in his coat pocket and the contents slosh out as he takes the bumps, staining the green material to black.

He drives by each post, taking off the paper targets. At times he snags the rear wheel and almost tips the rig.

"That old boy ain't right in the head," Payton says. "He's a Yankee too. He was a door gunner. The way I figure it is, some people the war made that way and some people were that way before the war. They're the ones that give war a bad name. Problem is, I can't figure out which one is which."

Eddie can only nod as he comes to realize he's in the midst of a people on hold. They live before the next war or after the last one. Payton points out the shrimper who shoots third. He tells Eddie the guy made three trips in the boat lift from Cuba and watched the women and children machine-gunned in the water when they broke the cordon and swam for the boats. Eddie thinks about Mike the Polak climbing spindly birches next to the barbecue pit and G. R. Trimble as he's come to know him. Eddie feels himself to be lifted, and to be set down again on air or water, close enough to land to know it's there but a ways off from it.

"Who's the guy over there who keeps staring at us?" Eddie asks.

"That's my daddy," Payton says.

The man is about Eddie's age, only life hasn't been too kind. He's dressed in green camo and his face is stitched with whiskey webs. They trace out from his eyes and lace his cheeks.

"He was in Viet Nam for six years. He was a Marine, wounded four times. I never seen him sleep. Whenever I touch the bedroom door he's always up, waiting on the other side in the dark."

At midnight they bring out the turkeys. In the lights their green and red and yellow-brown plumage goes metallic, oscillating to be color on color. They put the turkeys in boxes behind the posts. With conduit clamps they fasten the turkeys' necks to the wooden blocks, then bury their backsides in sand.

A bobbing head shot with a .22 at thirty yards. Payton shoots two and Cody one. The other two go to the shrimper.

Tonight is his birthday, Payton tells them as they drive back to the camp. A year ago he spent three days in jail for cutting up an ol' boy who stole his rifle. Awhile back, he and Leann lost a five-month-old baby boy. He says he doesn't like to talk about it. He says it was something inside that couldn't be fixed. And now tonight he's nineteen years old.

Eddie begins to cry silently in his seat by the door. Cody pats his knee and tells him he's getting to be an old man, an old softy. Eddie doesn't say anything but he smiles through his tears and places his hand over Cody's and they ride like that.

When they get there, Eddie hands Payton a fifty for being a good guide. He tells him to give the boar to Dewey or maybe to someone else, someone who needs the meat. Then he goes inside.

The camp is smoky and warm. Lance must have just left because there's a lantern going and a fresh log in the stove. Eddie swings couches around to face the fire, one for him and one for Cody. They'll sleep down here in the dry heat of the stove.

That night, by candlelight, Cody tells Eddie things that are in his head and in his heart. He tells a long story about a two-legged dog, the hind legs being lost to a mowing machine just like that, *snick, snick*. So at Cornell they made a set of mechanical legs and the dog went on talk shows, but the legs of wire and steel were only good for sitting on so the dog's appeal as a guest declined rapidly.

Finally, they let the dog alone and it learned to hike its rear end into the air and run around on its front feet, but of course it was never so fast as it was with legs. Then again, it couldn't have been that fast with four legs either.

"It just goes to show you."

"Show you what," Eddie says.

Cody tells him if he doesn't get it, he sure as hell can't explain.

"You're drunk, Cody. Go to sleep and in the morning we'll get a fresh start."

The wind picks up and from outside come the sounds of yellow

slash and swamp pine bursting at the trunk, slabbing off and going
to the ground, clipping limbs on the way in a shatter of sound. All
around them is the crunch and tear of trees falling in the night.

"I must talk," Cody says. "There are things I have to tell you."

"What's wrong now?"

"When I die, I hope all the nurses have big cleavages."

"Don't talk to me about death."

"I hope I'm on a motorcycle going about a hundred and two and
when I hit the bridge, the speedometer gets stuck there so everyone
will say, When he died he was going a hundred and two."

The two men sit, their bedrolls pulled up to their armpits. They
pass the bottle of bourbon between them, each feeling the warmth
at the opening left by the other's lips.

Cody tells Eddie he'll have to stay behind and help Mary and
Eileen and Little Eddie through life. He'll have to be his own father.

"All my earthly possessions I leave to you," he says. "I hope
you'll share them. Be generous, but at never more than fifty dollars
a whack. Have another kid or buy a nice dog, one that'll lay at your
feet and keep them warm when it's dark. A dog with big eyes that
are always full of tears."

"You're getting foolish," Eddie says, "which is okay because
sometimes that's how you are, but now it's just stupid."

Cody looks at him. Eddie can see in his eyes the amber of the
bourbon and then the yellow and green of the candle gone to
fluorescent. Eddie looks at him for as long as he can and then he
looks away, the liquor rising up into his own tired head and making
him weak and sad.

"The day is coming," Cody says, "I'll have to help Kay and the
children on their travels. Help them get to where G.R. is, and when
we get there, we'll build a house where one day, one at a time, we'll
all be together again. It'll be a warm tight house in the winter
with a glassed-in porch about the whole perimeter, a house to be
proud of.

"Maybe you killed Pot and God knows you hated doing it and
forgiveness has been passed around."

"I killed Pot," Eddie says, "and God knows it was something that
had to be done. Retribution will have its way."

"I bet he took it quite well. His people were never ones to be
impressed by death. In fact, he'll stop in and see us at the new

house. He could come back as a cricket, or if he's lucky, some kind of rodent."

"You go to sleep," Eddie says.

He wants to tell Cody about the hearts but he doesn't. He wants to tell him he didn't kill Pot, but realizes Cody won't have it any other way.

"You have a lot of work ahead of you in this life. You have to go back and straddle that line between life and death. You have to let the living know it'll be okay. It's not something to be afraid of and you have to send the dead off, fit and pretty."

Cody folds and unfolds his hands. He takes up a knife in one and a bottle in the other, content to be holding onto something. "Mary will be gone to school when you get back," he says. "You be there for her."

Eddie wants to speak, but Cody won't let him. He puts a hand over Eddie's mouth and only removes it from time to time to let him nurse off the bottle until finally Eddie falls asleep.

Cody pulls in next to him, body to body.

"Me and ol' Payton," he says, "we're headed off to Texas in the morning. When you wake up I'll be gone. I want you to know, I've had a change of heart about a lot of things. Not that I'll change my ways. I'll just think about them differently. We've both been carrying around our secrets and now that yours is out, mine's out too."

"Cody," Eddie says, raising his hand.

Cody takes Eddie's hand and puts it back down on Eddie's chest.

"Go back to sleep," he says. "Don't worry about me. *Adiós, mi amigo.*"

■

In the morning Cody is gone. The lodge is empty. The smoke of the stove has cooled. It's found its way into the beams and furniture, the bedrolls and the floors. It comes off on your hands with all that you touch.

Eddie sits up and gets his feet on the floor. He knows he's alone and isn't sure of how that feels. He dresses slowly, taking care that his socks are straight, that the heels of them are snug and not twisted round his ankle. He tucks in his shirt and belts his trousers, making sure they are even, not gathered to the front or back. He takes the time to lace his boots all the way up, and when he stands, he shakes his legs so the seams fall straight.

In the kitchen, he makes sheepherder's coffee, a handful of grounds thrown into a pot of water set to boil. He waits for it, sitting on a stool by the burner to keep warm. He starts to think about going home, but sets those thoughts aside. There will be time to do that later. Right now he's interested in thinking about nothing and doing the same. He tries hard to do this. It's not an easy thing. He's pleased when the pot starts to rumble. His coffee is ready.

Eddie takes his cup and wanders about the lodge. He hasn't seen it in daylight. He stops at the back window and looks out in the swamp. The air is so full he can't tell if it's raining or snowing. Out the window he sees a dog sitting on its doghouse. It's twice the size of Rambo and Snowball. It looks to be part mastiff and part St. Bernard. The dog stares back at Eddie and then Eddie realizes the dog has been staring at him all the time, through the window.

Cody's truck is still parked in front and someone is sitting in the cab. Eddie goes out to see who it is. He's startled by the clap of the screen door behind. It comes distinct in the heavy air. It's the only sound he's taken note of since he woke this morning. He crosses the lane and thinks how spongelike the earth is here. It invites his step, softens his stride.

In the cab is G. R. Trimble. He's been smoked down to a rail of a man, his face and hands brown, shellacked with pine resin. He sits at the steering wheel, ghostlike, with his legs bent and lashed to his chest, his hands clasped round his shins. His chin rests on his knees and he's smiling. Next to him on the seat is Cody's open duffel, the one he's carried with him on every trip.

Eddie takes G.R. up into his arms, holding the stiff wooden body against his chest. He's light to carry, like a pail of ash or a basket of laundry. Eddie takes him inside where it's warm and they both sit in front of the stove, Eddie drinking coffee and G.R. looking ready to come alive.

Eddie watches him, waiting for him to say something, to make a move. He can't imagine how anything so fragile can hold together. The punchline to a joke comes into his head: *it only hurts if you get your thumbs in the way.* He starts to laugh and the sound of it fills the lodge. He laughs so hard the tears run down his cheeks and he feels them tickling at his chin. G.R. bounces on the couch beside him as the laughter wracks at Eddie's chest.

Eddie opens the door to the wood stove. A billow of smoke comes out the opening and washes over him. It comes until he smartens up and opens the damper. He feeds in sticks of pine and then there's only warm radiant heat waltzing in Georgia. From his own duffel bag he takes out his stack of journals. There's twenty years' worth, all the same, all eight and a quarter by six and seven eighths, all narrow-ruled single-subject spirals. This is the baggage that holds his life, holds it hostage. Everything he thought he knew.

One by one he feeds them into the belly of the stove, watches them curl and go yellow to blue to brown. As each goes up in flame he feels the burden of one year after another of his past life lifted from his shoulders.

The flames quake and shiver as the pages in their burning give off more light and more light. He goes drunk on this discovery of fire, redeemed by light and heat.

When the last of the journals are gone, he lifts G. R. Trimble into his arms and cradles the shrunken body against his chest. He makes no sign, says no word, and feeds him like wood through the mouth of the stove with gentleness and compassion, heedless of the blisters that come to his hands. While G.R. takes torch, Eddie sucks at his burned fingers, tucks them under his armpits, then squats at the opening, letting the ghosts of heat wash his face and neck, letting them bathe his body with the scent of smoky pine.

Inside he sees the consuming flames, imagines them to snap out words dancing in code and imagines himself to be able to read the words. Inverawe, Tatamagouche, Bellefonte, Savannah. He sees the India baby, the children of Izieux, Evangeline, and his father waving. There are ducks and deer and planets and stars. Max the hunter cat. Animals painted on the walls of steel.

He'll go home now, he decides, pick up where he left off, be the man that he is.

EPILOGUE

In the late spring, on a day when in the ground there's a perfect balance between the reception and radiation of heat, Eddie Ryan and Louis Poissant climb to a high meadow overlooking the Connecticut River. They wade through the Indian paintbrush, buttercup, black-eyed Susan, red and white clover. Louis carries a long-handled shovel and uses it like an oar to help him make the climb. Eddie wears a knapsack, his thumbs tucked into the straps, and following behind, he catches whiffs of the barn drifting from Louis's trousers and coat.

The sun feels warm on Eddie's neck and he can feel the sweat cool at the small of his back and under his arms. He thinks how wonderful gravity is and how in a town like Inverawe its tug is a little stronger, a little more profound. He thinks about how it takes so many to fill in the center and hold it the way a fat woman did so many months ago.

When they reach the top, Louis stops and looks around. Eddie waits for him to decide on a spot.

"Here," he says, pointing with the shovel.

Eddie lets the pack slide off his shoulders and takes from inside it a sheet of poly. He unfolds it on the ground and then takes the shovel from Louis. He cuts into the sod, lifting it out in neat squares and placing them to the side. He keeps digging to where the soil is black and loamy, carefully dumping each shovelful on the poly. When he's past the frost line, he stops and goes to the knapsack again, coming out with three freezer containers, each filled with the hearts that Louis held back—Maple, Micah and Kay.

Eddie goes down on his knees to set the containers on the floor of the grave. They are cold in his hands and bulge with the contents that've expanded from freezing. From his breast pocket he takes out folded slips of paper, a note for each one of them. He looks up and Louis nods his head as if to say it's okay. Eddie slips them in amongst the containers.

When Eddie stands, he passes the shovel over to Louis. The old man takes it and leans on it for a moment. He catches Eddie's eye and nods toward the woods.

"Don't look," he says, quicklike and quiet. "You'll scare him off."

Eddie Ryan smiles as he realizes who it is. Old Louis begins to cry. He tells Eddie he's long since past the age of living but can't seem to find a way to die.

"What I'm trying to get at is it should've been me and not them." He cuffs at his cheeks where the tears are, not liking them on his face.

"He's out there," Eddie says.

"No, he tain't. It's the ghost of old Paul Champagne and Goody. It's their wedding anniversary. They come round every year 'bout this time, back to Canoe Meadow."

"That's nice," Eddie says, and then he goes down on his knees again and starts sifting the earth through his fingers, letting it fall into the hole.

Louis gets down on his knees too and they work together, taking smaller handfuls each time, letting the earth fall from their hands, pure and fine as dust or ash.

"That's enough," Louis says. "We'll let him finish."

Eddie stands and helps Louis to his feet. Louis works his right leg and says, "Charley horse." Eddie gets an arm around him and feels how most of him is coat and shirts. Eddie takes up the shovel and together the two of them walk off the mountain.

ABOUT THE AUTHOR

ROBERT OLMSTEAD was born in New Hampshire in 1954. His work has appeared in *Black Warrior Review, Granta, The Graywolf Annual 4, Story,* and *Louder Than Words.* He is currently writer-in-residence at Dickinson College in Carlisle, Pennsylvania. He is a 1989 recipient of the John Simon Guggenheim Fellowship and the Pennsylvania Fellowship for the Arts. His previous books are *River Dogs,* a collection of stories, and *Soft Water,* a novel.